TEMPTATION

Also by Douglas Kennedy

Fiction
State of the Union
A Special Relationship
The Pursuit of Happiness
The Job
The Big Picture
The Dead Heart

Non-fiction
Chasing Mammon
In God's Country
Beyond the Pyramids

Temptation

Douglas Kennedy

HUTCHINSON
LONDON

First published by Hutchinson in 2006

1 3 5 7 9 10 8 6 4 2

Copyright © Douglas Kennedy 2006

Douglas Kennedy has asserted his right under the Copyright, Designs
and Patents Act, 1988 to be identified as the author of this work

Hutchinson
The Random House Group Limited
20 Vauxhall Bridge Road, London SW1V 2SA

Random House Australia (Pty) Limited
20 Alfred Street, Milsons Point, Sydney
New South Wales 2061, Australia

Random House New Zealand Limited
18 Poland Road, Glenfield
Auckland 10, New Zealand

Random House Publishers India Private Limited
301 World Trade Tower, Hotel Intercontinental Grand Complex,
Barakhamba Lane, New Delhi 110 001, India

The Random House Group Limited Reg. No. 954009

www.randomhouse.co.uk

A CIP catalogue record for this book is available from the British Library

Papers used by Random House are natural, recyclable products made from
wood grown in sustainable forests. The manufacturing processes conform to
the environmental regulations of the country of origin

Typeset by Palimpsest Book Production Limited, Polmont, Stirlingshire
Printed and bound in Great Britain by Mackays of Chatham plc. Chatham, Kent

ISBN 9780091799649 (Hardback – from Jan 2007)
ISBN 0 09 179964 3 (Hardback)
ISBN 97800917969694 (Trade paperback – from Jan 2007)
ISBN 0 09 179969 4 (Trade paperback)

For Fred Haines

'It is not enough to succeed. Others must fail.'
Gore Vidal

Part One

One

I ALWAYS WANTED to be rich. I know that probably sounds crass, but it's the truth. A true confession.

Around a year ago, I got my wish. After a ten-year bad luck streak – a toxic accumulation of endless rejection slips, and 'we're going to pass on this', and the usual bevy of near-misses ('you know, we were really looking for this sort of thing last month'), and (of course) never getting my calls returned – the gods of happenstance finally decided I was worth a smile. And I received a phone call. Check that: I received the phone call which anyone who has ever scribbled for a living always dreams of receiving.

The call came from Alison Ellroy, my long-suffering agent.

'David, I sold it.'

My heart skipped five beats. I hadn't heard the words 'I sold it' for . . . well, to be honest about it, I'd never heard that sentence before.

'You sold what?' I asked, since five of my speculative scripts were currently doing the Flying Dutchman rounds of assorted studios and production companies.

'The pilot,' she said.

'The television pilot?'

'Yep. I sold *Selling You.*'

'To whom?'

'FRT.'

'What?'

'FRT – as in Front Row Television; as in the smartest, hottest producer of original programs on cable . . .'

My heart now needed defibrillation.

'I know who they are, Alison. FRT bought my pilot?'

'Yes, David. FRT just bought *Selling You.*'

Long pause.

'Are they paying?' I asked.

'Of course they're paying. This is a business, believe it or not.'

'Sorry, sorry . . . it's just, how much exactly?'

'Forty grand.'

'Right.'

'Don't sound so enthusiastic.'

'I am enthusiastic. It's just . . .'

'I know: it's not the million-dollar deal. But that kind of a slam-dunk for a first-timer is, at best, a twice-a-year event in this town. Forty grand is standard money for a TV pilot . . . especially for an unproduced writer. Anyway, what are they paying you at Book Soup these days?'

'Fifteen a year.'

'So look at it this way: you've just made almost three years' salary in one deal. And this is only the start. They're not just going to buy the pilot . . . they're also going to make it.'

'They told you that?'

'Yes, they did.'

'Do you believe them?'

'Honey, we're living in the Forked Tongue capital of the universe. Still, you might get lucky.'

My head was spinning. Good news, good news.

'I don't know what to say,' I said.

'You could try "Thank you".'

'Thank you.'

I didn't just thank Alison Ellroy. The day after I received that phone call, I drove down to the Beverly Center and dropped $375 on a Mont Blanc fountain pen for her. When I gave it to her later that afternoon, she seemed genuinely affected.

'Do you know this is the first time I've received a gift from a writer in . . . how long have I been in this business?'

'You tell me.'

'Try three decades. Well, I guess there's a first time for every-thing. So . . . thanks. But don't think you're going to borrow it to sign the contracts.'

My wife Lucy, on the other hand, was appalled that I had dropped so much cash on a present for my agent.

'What is this?' she said. 'You finally get a deal – at WGA minimum, I might add – and you're suddenly Robert Towne?'

'It was just a gesture, that's all.'

'A $375 gesture.'

'We can afford it.'

'Oh, can we? Do the math, David. Alison gets a fifteen per cent commission from the forty grand. The IRS will skim thirty-three per cent off the balance, which will leave you just under twenty-three grand, plus change.'

'How do you know all this?'

'I did the math. I also did the math on our combined debt to Visa and MasterCard – twelve grand, and rising monthly. And on the loan we took out to cover Caitlin's tuition last term – six grand, and also rising monthly. I also know that we're a one-car family in a two-car town. And the car in question is a twelve-year-old Volvo that really needs transmission work which we can't really afford, because –'

'All right, all right. I was recklessly generous. *Mea maxima culpa*. And, by the way, thanks for pissing on my parade.'

'Absolutely no one is pissing on your parade. You know how thrilled I was yesterday when you told me. It's what you – *we* – have been fantasizing about for the last eleven years. My point, David, is a simple one: the money is already spent.'

'Fine, fine, point taken,' I said, trying to put an end to this.

'And though I certainly don't begrudge Alison her Mont Blanc pen, it would have been nice if you had maybe thought, in the first instance, about who's been keeping us out of Chapter 11 all these years.'

'You're right. I'm sorry. But hey, good times ahead. We're in the money.'

'I hope you're right,' she said quietly. 'We deserve a break.'

I reached out to stroke her cheek. She smiled a tight, tired smile. With good reason, because the last ten years had been, for both of us, one long slog up a steep incline. We'd met in Manhattan in the early nineties. I'd arrived there a few years earlier from my native Chicago, determined to make it as a playwright. Instead I found myself stage-managing off-off-Broadway and paying the rent by stacking inventory at the Gotham Book Mart. I did get an agent. He did get my plays seen. None were produced, but one script – *An Ordinary Evening in Oak Park* (a dark satire on suburban life)

– did get a staged reading by the Avenue B Theatre Company (at least it wasn't Avenue C). Lucy Everett was in the cast. Within a week of the first reading, we decided we were in love. By the time the play had its three performances, I had moved into her studio apartment on East 19th Street. Two months later, she landed a role in a pilot sit-com for ABC that was being shot on the coast. Being wildly in love, I didn't have a moment's hesitation when she said, 'Come with me.'

So we moved to LA and found ourselves a cramped two-bedroom apartment on the King's Road in West Hollywood. Lucy made the pilot. I turned the tiny second bedroom into my office. The pilot was ditched by the network. I wrote my first speculative screen-play, *We Three Grunts* – which I described as a 'darkly comic heist caper' about a bank job pulled off by a bunch of ageing Vietnam vets. It went nowhere, but it did get Alison Ellroy in my corner. She was one of the last of an endangered species – the independent Hollywood agent, operating not out of some hyper-architectural monolith, but from a small suite of offices in Beverly Hills. After reading this 'darkly comic' screenplay, and my earlier unproduced 'darkly comic' stage stuff, she took me on as a client – but also gave me the following piece of advice:

'If you want to scratch a living writing in Hollywood, remember that you have to write generic . . . with the occasional "darkly comic" flourish. But only a flourish. Bruce Willis gets to crack wise, but he still blows away the chiselled-jawed German terrorist and then rescues his wife from the burning building. Got the idea?'

I certainly did. And over the next year, I turned out three spec scripts: an action film (Islamic terrorists seize a yacht in the Mediterranean, containing all three children of the President of the United States); a family drama film (mother dying of cancer tries to achieve closure with her grown children whom she was forced by her wicked mother-in-law to abandon when they were young); and a romantic comedy (a *Private Lives* rip-off, in which a newly married couple fall for each other's siblings while on honeymoon). All three scripts played by the genre rules. All three scripts had 'darkly comic' moments. All three scripts failed to sell.

Meanwhile, after the television pilot sank without trace, Lucy found that the casting doors weren't exactly swinging open in her direction. She got a commercial here and there. She came very close to landing a part as a sympathetic oncologist in a Showtime movie about a marathon runner battling bone cancer. She was also up for a role as a screaming slasher victim in some screaming slasher movie. Like me, she lurched from disappointment to disappointment. Simultaneously, our bank account began to hit the red zone. We had to find proper paying jobs. I talked my way into a low-impact thirty-hour week at Book Soup (probably the best independent bookshop in LA). Lucy was persuaded to try telemarketing by a fellow unemployed SAG member. Initially she hated it, but the actress in her responded to the 'hard sell' role she was forced to play on the phone. Much to her horror, she turned out to be an ace telemarketer. She made okay money – around thirty grand a year. She kept going up for auditions. She kept failing to connect. So she kept on telemarketing. Then Caitlin came into our lives.

I took time off from Book Soup to look after our daughter. I also kept writing – spec screenplays, a new stage play, a television pilot. Not one of them sold. Around a year after Caitlin's birth Lucy let her SAG membership lapse and graduated to the rank of telemarketing trainer. I was back at Book Soup. Our combined post-tax income just touched 40k per annum: chump change in a city where many a player spent 40k a year on his pumped pectorals. We couldn't afford to find a new apartment. We shared an ageing Volvo which dated back to the first Reagan administration. We felt cramped – not just by our lack of physical space at home, but also by the ever-growing realization that we were now trapped in small lives with ever-narrowing horizons. Of course, we delighted in our daughter. But as the years accelerated – and we both started to cruise into our late thirties – we began to regard each other as our respective jailers. We tried to cope with our varying professional failures and the knowledge that, while everyone else we knew was reaping the booty of the Clinton boom years, we were stuck in nowheresville. But though Lucy had given up all future hopes of an acting career, I kept churning out stuff – much to her exasperation, as she felt (rightly) that the major breadwinning burden was on her back. She kept urging me to give up the Book Soup gig –

to burrow my way into some proper job. And I resisted, telling her that the bookshop job suited my writing life.

'Your writing life?' she said with the sort of sarcastic edge that went way beyond withering. 'Don't talk crap.'

Naturally, this triggered one of those thermo-nuclear marital disputes, in which years of built-up resentments, enmities, and domestic frustrations suddenly scorch the earth beneath both pairs of feet. She said I was self-absorbed, to the point of putting my going-nowhere writing career in front of Caitlin's welfare. I countered that besides being a model of domestic responsibility (well, I was), my professional integrity was still intact.

'You've never sold a single script, and you dare talk to me about being a professional?' she said.

I stormed out. I drove all night and ended up just north of San Diego, walking the beach at Del Mar, wishing I had the reckless-ness to continue south across the border into Tijuana, and vanish from my disaster of a life. Lucy was right: as a writer I was a failure . . . but I still wasn't going to abandon my daughter on a furious whim. So I went back to my car, pointed it north, and arrived home just before sunrise. I found Lucy wide awake, curled up on the sofa in our cluttered living room, looking beyond forlorn. I collapsed into the armchair opposite her. We said nothing for a very long time. Finally she broke the silence.

'That was awful.'

'Yes,' I said. 'It was.'

'I didn't mean what I said.'

'Nor did I.'

'I'm just so damn tired, David.'

I reached for her hand. 'Join the club,' I said.

So we kissed and made up, and fed Caitlin her breakfast, and got her on the school bus, and then both went off to our respec-tive jobs – jobs that gave us no pleasure whatsoever, and didn't even pay well. By the time Lucy arrived home that night, domestic detente was re-established – and we never mentioned that malig-nant fight again. But once things are said, they are said. And though we tried to behave as if things were on an even keel, a chilly under-current now ran between us.

Neither of us wanted to confront this, so we both stayed busy. I knocked out a thirty-minute pilot for a sit-com called *Selling You*. It centred around the tangled internal politics at a public relations agency in Chicago. It was peopled by a group of smart, edgy neurotics. And yes, it was 'darkly comic'. Alison even liked it – the first script of mine she had praised for years . . . even though it was still a little too 'darkly comic' for her taste. Still, she gave it to the head of development at FRT. He, in turn, handed it to an independent producer named Brad Bruce, who was starting to make a name for himself as a generator of edgy, out-there sit-coms for cable. Brad liked what he read . . . and I got that phone call from Alison.

Then things began to change.

Brad Bruce turned out to be that rare species – a guy who believed that irony was the only way to cope with life in the City of Angels. He was in his late thirties, a fellow Midwesterner from Milwaukee (God help him) and we hit it off immediately. Better yet, we quickly established a fluid working style. I responded positively to his notes. We riffed well off each other. We made each other laugh. And even though he knew that this was the first script I'd managed to sell, he treated me like a fellow veteran of the television wars. In turn, I worked hard for him because I knew that I now had an ally . . . though I also understood that if the pilot didn't get made, his attention would move elsewhere.

Brad was a forceful operator, and he actually got the pilot made. What's more, it was everything a pilot should be: tightly acted and directed, stylishly shot and funny. FRT liked what they saw. A week later, Alison rang me.

'Sit down,' she said.

'Good news?'

'The best. I just heard from Brad Bruce. He'll be calling you in a nanosecond, but I wanted to be the messenger. So listen to this: FRT are commissioning an initial eight-episode series of *Selling You*. Brad wants you to write four of them, and be the overall script supervisor on the series.'

I was speechless.

'You still there?'

9

'I'm just trying to pick my jaw up from the floor.'

'Well, keep it there until you hear the numbers on offer. Seventy-five grand per episode – that's 300k for the writing. I figure I can get you an additional 150k for supervising the other episodes, not to mention a "Created By" and between five and ten per cent equity in the entire show. Congratulations: you are about to become rich.'

I quit Book Soup that night. By the end of the week, we had put a down payment on a delightful little Spanish vernacular house in mid-Wiltshire. The geriatric Volvo was traded in for a new Land Rover Discovery. I leased a Mini Cooper S, promising myself a Porsche Carrera if *Selling You* made it to a second series. Lucy was dazzled by our change in circumstances. For the first time ever, we were awash in material comforts. We could buy proper furniture, spiffy appliances, designer labels. As I was under extreme deadline pressure – I had only five months to deliver my four episodes – Lucy took over the decoration of the new house. She had also just started training an entire new platoon of telemarketeers – which meant that she too was working twelve-hour days. The only free time we had was devoted to our daughter. This was no bad thing – because as long as your days are ultra-full you can continue to gloss over the telltale cracks in a structurally damaged marriage. We both kept busy. We talked about the wondrousness of this lucky break, and acted as if everything was back on track between us . . . even though we both knew that this was hardly the case. And there were many melancholic moments when I often found myself thinking, far from making things better between us, the money has pushed us even further apart.

Nearly a year later, when the first episode of *Selling You* was screened and became an instant critical hit, Lucy turned to me and said, 'I suppose you'll leave me now.'

'Why would I do that?' I said.

'Because you can.'

'It's not going to happen.'

'Yes, it will. Because it's what the success scenario demands.'

Of course she was right. But it didn't happen for another six months, by which time I had traded my Mini Cooper for that Porsche I had promised myself. Not only had the show been renewed, but I suddenly found myself the subject of considerable public attention – as *Selling You* had become the hip, cutting-edge, must-see show of the season. The reviews were fantastic. *Esquire* ran a 500-word story about me in their 'Guys We Like' section, which referred to me as 'the Tom Wolfe of cable television'. I didn't exactly object. And I didn't say no when the *Los Angeles Times* asked to interview me for a piece which detailed my long years in professional purgatory, my extended stint at Book Soup, and my sudden ascendancy into 'that small select league of smart LA writers who don't do Generic'.

I had my assistant clip this story and messenger it over to Alison. Attached to it was a Post-It, on which I'd scribbled, 'Thinking of you generically. Love and Kisses. David.'

An hour later, a messenger arrived at my office with a padded envelope from Alison's agency. Inside was a small gift-wrapped box, and a card: 'Fuck you . . . Love, Alison.'

Inside the box was something I had coveted for years: a Waterman Edson fountain pen . . . the Ferrari of Writing Instruments, with a list price to match: $675. But Alison could afford it, as the deal she'd closed for my 'creative participation' in the second series of *Selling You* was worth just under $1 million . . . less her fifteen per cent of course.

Alison was quoted in that *LA Times* profile of me. Per usual, she was deeply droll, telling the interviewer that the reason she never dropped me as a client during all the bad years was because 'He knew when to not call – and believe me, there are few writers in this town with that skill.' She also surprised me by saying something touching: 'He's living proof that talent and extreme perseverance can sometimes triumph in Hollywood. David kept at it long after many another aspiring writer would have folded. So he deserves everything: the money, the office, the assistant, the recognition, the prestige. But most of all he's now getting his phone calls returned, and I'm fielding constant requests for meetings with him. Because everyone who's smart wants to work with David Armitage.'

As I was deep in the planning stage of the second season of *Selling You*, I was turning down most requests for meetings. But, at Alison's urging, I did go to lunch with a young executive at Fox Television named Sally Birmingham.

'I only met her once,' Alison said, 'but everyone in the industry is earmarking her for the big time. She has a big war chest at her disposal. And she absolutely adores *Selling You*. In fact, she adores it so much she told me that she would be prepared to give you a quarter of a million for any thirty-minute pilot of your choice.'

That made me pause for thought.

'250k for one pilot?' I asked.

'Yep – and I'd make certain it was pay or play.'

'She knows I couldn't even look at any new projects until the new series is wrapped?'

'She anticipated that. And she told me she's willing to wait. She just wants to sign you up for the pilot now – because, let's face it, it would also up her market value to have snagged David Armitage. Think about it – all going well, you'll be taking six weeks off between series two and three. How long is it going to take you to knock out a pilot?'

'Three weeks max.'

'And the other three weeks, you sit on a beach somewhere, if you can actually sit still so long, thinking to yourself that you just made a quarter of a million in twenty-one days.'

'All right – I'll do the lunch.'

'Smart guy. You'll like her. She's super-bright and beautiful.'

Alison was right. Sally Birmingham was super-bright. And she was beautiful.

Her assistant had called my assistant to set up the lunch date at The Ivy. Thanks to the usual tailback on the 10, I arrived a few minutes late. She was already seated at a very good table. She stood up to greet me, and I was instantly captivated (though I worked damn hard not to show it). Sally was tall, with high cheekbones, flawless skin, cropped light brown hair, and a mischievous smile. At first, I pegged her as the sort of dazzlingly patrician product of East Coast education and high-end breeding who undoubtedly had her own horse by the age of ten. But fifteen minutes into our conversation, I realized that she had managed to undercut the Westchester County WASP background with a canny mixture of erudition and street smarts. Yes, she had been raised in Bedford. Yes, she had gone to Rosemary Hall and Princeton. But though she was ferociously well read – and something of a cinephile – she also had an astute understanding of Hollywood in all its internecine glory, and told me she actually delighted in playing the 'player' game. I could see why the big *cojones* at Fox Television so valued her: she was a class act, but one who spoke their language. And she also had the most amazing laugh.

'Want to hear my favorite LA story?' she asked me.

'I'm game.'

'All right – I was having lunch last month with Mia Morrison, head of corporate affairs at Fox. She calls the waiter over, and says: 'So tell me your waters.' The waiter, a real pro, doesn't blanch. Instead he starts listing them: 'Well, we've got Perrier from France, and Ballygowan from Ireland, and San Pellegrino from Italy . . .' Suddenly, Mia interrupts him: 'Oh, no, not San Pellegrino. It's too rich.'

'I think I'll steal that.'

'"Immature poets imitate, mature poets steal."'

'Eliot?'

'So you really did go to Dartmouth?' she asked.

'I'm impressed by your background research.'

'I'm impressed by your knowledge of Mr Eliot.'

'But surely you've picked up the references from "Four Quartets" throughout my show?'

'I thought you'd be more of a "Waste Land" kind of guy.'

'Nah – it's too rich.'

Not only did we have instant rapport, but we also talked widely about just about everything. Including marriage.

'So,' she said glancing at the ring on my finger, 'are you married or are you *married*?'

Her tone was light. I laughed.

'I'm married,' I said. 'Without the italics.'

'For how long?'

'Eleven years.'

'That's impressive. Happy?'

I shrugged.

'That's not unusual,' she said. 'Especially after eleven years.'

'You seeing someone now?' I said, trying to sound nonchalant.

'There was someone . . . but it was a minor diversion, nothing more. We both ended it around four months ago. Since then . . . just flying solo.'

'You've never taken the conjugal plunge?'

'No . . . though I could have done something disastrous – like marrying my boyfriend at Princeton. He certainly pushed the issue – but I told him that college marriages usually only have a two-year life span. In fact, most relationships burn out when passion turns prosaic . . . which is why I've never lasted more than three years with anyone.'

'You mean, you don't believe in all that "there is one person meant for you" destiny crap.'

Another of her laughs. But then she said, 'Well, actually I do. I just haven't meant the guy yet.'

Once again, the tone was blithe. Once again, a glance passed between us.

But it was only a glance, and we were quickly back in our conversational whirl. I was astonished by the way we couldn't stop talking, how we riffed off each other, and shared such a similar world-view. The sense of connection was astonishing . . . and a little terrifying. Because – unless I was reading things very wrong – the mutual attraction was enormous.

Eventually, we got down to business. She asked me to tell her about my proposed pilot. My pitch was a sentence long:

'The harassed professional and personal life of a middle-aged female marriage counsellor.'

She smiled. 'That's good. First question, is she divorced?'

'Of course.'

'Troubled kids?'

'A teenage daughter who thinks that Mom is a serious jerk.'

'Nice. Does our marriage counsellor have an ex-husband?'

'Yes – and he ran off with a twenty-five-year-old yoga instructor.'

'We're obviously talking about an LA setting.'

'I was thinking San Diego.'

'Good call. The Southern California lifestyle without the LA baggage. Is the marriage counsellor dating?'

'Relentlessly – and with disastrous results.'

'And meanwhile, her clients . . . ?'

'They'll raise a smile, believe me.'

'A title?'

'*Talk It Over.*'

'Sold then,' she said.

I tried not to smile too broadly.

'You know I can't start work until after the second season . . .'

'Alison briefed me on that already . . . and that's fine with me. The important thing is: I've got you.'

She briefly touched the top of my hand. I didn't move it away.

'I'm pleased,' I said.

She met my stare. And asked, 'Dinner tomorrow night?'

We met at her place in West Hollywood. As soon as I was through the door, we were tearing each other's clothes off. Much later, as we lay sprawled across her bed, sipping a post-coital glass of Pinot Noir, she asked me, 'Are you a good liar?'

'You mean, about something like this?'

'That's right.'

'Well, it's only the second time it's happened in the eleven years I've been with Lucy.'

'When was the first time?'

'A one-night stand back in '99 with an actress I met in the book shop one night. Lucy was back east at the time, visiting her parents with Caitlin.'

'That's it? Your only extramarital transgression?'

I nodded.

'My, my – you do have a conscience.'

'It is a weakness, I know – especially out here.'

'Are you going to feel guilty now?'

'No,' I said without hesitation.

'Why's that?'

'Because things between Lucy and myself are now very different. And also . . .'

'Yes?' she asked,

'. . . because . . . well, because it's you.'

She kissed me softly on the lips.

15

'Is that a confession?'

'I guess it is.'

'Well, I have one too. Ten minutes after meeting you yesterday, I felt: this is the guy. I felt it all last night and all today as I counted down the hours to seven o'clock, and you walking through my door. And now . . .'

She ran her right index finger down the curve of my jaw.

'. . . now I'm not going to let you go.'

I kissed her. 'Is that a promise?' I asked.

'Girl Scout's honor. But you know what this means . . . in the short term, anyway?'

'Yes – I'm going to have to start learning how to lie.'

Actually I had already started, having covered my first evening with Sally by telling Lucy that I was flying to Vegas overnight to do a little look-around for a future episode. Sally didn't even mind when I used her phone at eleven to call home and tell my wife that I was happily ensconced in The Bellagio and missing her terribly. When I arrived home the next evening, I studied Lucy carefully for any telltale signs of suspicion or doubt. I also wondered if she had perhaps called The Bellagio to see if I was actually registered there. But she greeted me pleasantly, and didn't drop any hints about my whereabouts last night. In fact, she couldn't have been more affectionate, pulling me off to bed early that night. And yes, the guilt chord did ring between my ears. But its reverberations were silenced by an even louder realization: I was madly in love with Sally Birmingham.

And she was in love with me. Her certainty was overwhelming. I was the man with whom she wanted to spend the rest of her life. We would have brilliant fun together. We would have great careers, wonderful children. And we'd never lapse into the passionless ennui that characterized most marriages – because how could we ever be anything but ardent about each other? We would be golden – because we were meant to be.

There was only one problem, though – I was still married to somebody else. And I was desperately worried about the effect that any future domestic decampment might have on Caitlin. Sally was completely understanding.

'I'm not telling you to walk out now. You should only make that move when you're ready – and when you think Caitlin's ready. I'll wait. Because you're worth the wait.'

When you're ready. Not *if.* An explicit *when.* But Sally's definitiveness didn't disturb me. Nor did I think events were moving too quickly after just two weeks. Because I shared her certainty about our future together. Just as I privately fretted about the pain and damage I was about to inflict on my wife and child.

To Sally's credit, she didn't once pressure me into leaving home. Or, at least, not for another eight months – by which time all my work on the second series was finished, and I had become completely expert in covering my extramarital tracks. When deadline pressure on the three episodes I was writing became particularly intense, I decamped for two weeks to the Four Seasons Hotel in Santa Barbara, on the pretext of needing to lock myself away for a concentrated work blitz. And work I did – though Sally spent one of the weeks with me, not to mention both weekends. When the show moved to Chicago for a week of exterior filming, I decided to stay on for a few days afterwards to catch up with my old network of friends, though, in truth, that weekend Sally and I hardly left our suite at the W. Through careful juggling of our respective schedules – not to mention the use of a room at the Westwood Marquis – we were able to spend two lunchtimes a week with each other, and at least one evening at her apartment.

I was often amazed at just how good I had become at covering my tracks and inventing storylines. Granted, it could be argued that, as a professional storyteller, I was simply practising my craft. But in the past I had always considered myself an appalling liar – to the point where, a few days after my one previous extramarital encounter in '96, Lucy turned to me and said, 'You've slept with someone else, haven't you?'

Of course, I blanched. Of course, I denied it all vehemently. Of course, she didn't believe a word I said.

'Go on, tell me I'm hallucinating,' she said. 'But I can see right through you, David. You're transparent.'

'I am not lying.'

'Oh, please.'

'Lucy . . .'

But she walked out of the room, and didn't mention the matter again. Within a week, my intense guilt (and my equally intense fear of discovery) had dissipated – cushioned by my silent vow never to be unfaithful again.

It was a vow I kept for the next six years – until I met Sally Birmingham. But after that first night at her apartment, I felt little guilt, little anguish. Perhaps because my marriage had become governed by the law of diminishing returns. Or perhaps because, from the outset of my romance with Sally, I knew that I had never felt so ardent about anyone before.

This certainty made me an expert in subterfuge – to the point where Lucy never once questioned me about my whereabouts on a night when I was 'working late'. In fact, she couldn't have been more affectionate, more supportive during this time. No doubt our improved material circumstances had enhanced her affection for me (or, at least, that was my interpretation). But once I delivered the final drafts of my episodes, and began editing the four other scripts that had been written for the new series, Sally began to make increasingly loud noises about 'regularizing' our situation, and moving in together.

'This clandestine situation has to end,' she told me. 'I want you for myself . . . if you still want me.'

'Of course I want you. You know that.'

But I also wanted to postpone the final day of reckoning – the moment when I sat down with Lucy and broke her heart. So I kept stalling. And Sally started getting impatient. And I kept saying: 'Just give me another month.'

Then, one evening, I got home around midnight – after a long pre-production dinner with Brad Bruce. When I walked in, I found Lucy sitting in the living room. My suitcase was by her armchair.

'Let me ask you something,' she said. 'And it's a question I've wanted to know for the past eight months: Is she a moaner, or is she one of those ice-maiden types who, despite the drop-dead looks, really hates the idea of anyone touching her?'

'I honestly don't know what you're talking about,' I said, trying to sound bemused.

18

'You mean, you honestly don't know the name of the woman you've been fucking for the last seven – or is it eight – months?'

'Lucy, there is no one.'

'So, Sally Birmingham is no one?'

I sat down.

'That certainly gave you pause for thought,' she said, her voice even-tempered.

I finally spoke. 'How do you know her name?'

'I had someone find out for me.'

'You what?'

'I hired a private investigator.'

'You spied on me?'

'Don't play the moral outrage card, asshole. You were obviously seeing someone else . . .'

How did she know that? I had been so careful, so circumspect.

'. . . and when it was clear from your constant absences that this was something more than just a little ego-enhancing fling, I hired a private eye . . .'

'Wasn't that expensive?'

'Thirty-eight hundred dollars . . . which I will reclaim, one way or another, in the divorce settlement.'

I heard myself saying: 'Lucy, I don't want a divorce.'

Her voice remained steady, strangely calm. 'I don't care what you want, David. I am divorcing you. This marriage is finished.'

I suddenly felt a desperate fear – even though she was doing the dirty work for me, and instigating the beginning of the end. I was getting exactly what I wanted . . . and it scared the hell out of me. I said, 'If you had only come to me at the outset . . .'

Her face tightened. 'And what?' she said, the anger now showing. 'Tried to remind you that we had eleven years' history, and a daughter, and that, despite all the crap of the last decade, we'd actually come through and were finally living well.'

She broke off, on the verge of tears. I reached for her. She immediately pulled away.

'You're never touching me again,' she said.

Silence. Then she said, 'When I found out the name of your squeeze, do you know what I first thought? "He's really trading upwards, isn't he? The senior head of comedy at Fox Television. *Magna cum laude* from Princeton. And a babe to boot." The private investigator was a very thorough guy. He even supplied pictures of Ms Birmingham. She's very photogenic, isn't she?'

'We could have talked this out . . .'

'No, there was nothing to talk out. I certainly wasn't going to play the poor little woman in some country-and-western song, begging her faithless husband to come on home.'

'So why did you stay silent all this time?'

'Because I was hoping you might come to your senses...' She broke off again, clearly trying to keep her emotions in check. This time I didn't reach for her.

'I even gave you a deadline,' she said. 'Six months. Which, like a fool, I extended to seven, then to eight. Then, around a week ago, I could see you had decided to leave . . .'

'I hadn't reached that decision,' I lied.

'Bullshit. It was written all over you . . . in neon lights. Well, I decided to make the decision for you. So, get out. Now.'

She stood up. So did I.

'Lucy, please. Let's try to . . .'

'What? Pretend the last eight months didn't happen?'

'How about Caitlin?'

'My, my, you're finally thinking about your daughter . . .'

'I want to talk to her.'

'Fine – you can come back tomorrow . . .'

I was going to argue my case for staying the night on the sofa, and trying to discuss everything in the saner light of day. But I knew she wouldn't listen. Anyway, this was what I wanted. Well, wasn't it?

I picked up my suitcase. I said, 'I'm sorry.'

'I don't accept apologies from shits,' Lucy said and stormed up-stairs.

I sat in the car for ten minutes, immobile, wondering what I should do next. Suddenly, I found myself on my feet, racing back to my front door, and pounding my fist against it, yelling my wife's name. After a moment, I heard her voice behind the door.

'Go away, David.'

'Give me a chance to –'

'What? Tell me more lies?'

'I've made a terrible mistake . . .'

'Too bad. You should have thought about that months ago.'

'I'm just asking for the opportunity –'

'There is nothing more to say.'

'Lucy . . .'

'We're done here.'

I dug out my house keys. But as I tried putting the first one into the lock, I heard Lucy throw the inside bolt.

'Don't think about trying to get back in here, David. It's over. Just leave. Now.'

I must have spent the next five minutes thumping the door again, pleading my case, begging her to take me back. But I knew that she was no longer interested in hearing what I had to say. Part of me was absolutely terrified at this realization – my little family, destroyed by my own vanity, my new-found success. Yet another part of me understood why I had travelled down this destructive path. I also knew what would happen if the door suddenly opened now and Lucy beckoned me inside: I would be returning to a life without edge. And I remembered something a writer friend told me after he left his wife for another woman. 'Of course the marriage had a few problems – but none that were so overwhelming. Of course there was a bit of ennui – but that's also par for the course after twelve years of togetherness. Fundamentally, there was nothing that wrong between us. So why did I go? Because a little voice inside my head kept asking me one simple question: *is this everything life is going to be?*'

But this recollection was superseded by a voice bellowing inside my head: *I can't do this.* More than that, I thought: you're so conforming to male cliché. And you're also upending everything that is important in your life for a headlong dash into the unknown. So I fished out my cellphone and desperately punched in my home number. When Lucy answered, I said, 'Darling, I'll do anything . . .'

'Anything?'

'Yes, anything you ask.'

'Then fuck off and die.'

The line went dead. I glanced back at the house. All the lights downstairs were off. I took a deep steadying breath, then walked to my car and got inside. I dug out my cellphone and stared at it, knowing if I made the call I was about to make I would be crossing the frontier marked 'No Way Back'.

I made the call. Sally answered. I told her that I had finally done what she'd been asking me to do: I had told my wife it was over. Though she asked all the touchy-feely questions about how Lucy took the news ('Not well,' I said), and how I was faring ('I'm glad it's behind me'), she sounded genuinely thrilled. For a moment I wondered if she saw all this as some sort of victory – the ultimate merger and acquisition. But the moment passed when she told me how much she loved me, how hard this must have been for me, and how she would always be there for me. But though I was reassured by these declarations, I still felt a desperate hollowness – to be expected under the circumstances, but disquieting nonetheless.

'Get over here now, darling,' she said.

'I have nowhere else to go.'

The next day, Lucy and I agreed in a terse phone call that I would pick up Caitlin after school.

'Have you told her?' I asked.

'Of course I told her.'

'And?'

'You've just destroyed her sense of security, David.'

'Hang on,' I said. 'I'm not the one ending the marriage. That was your decision. Like I said last night, if you'd just give me a chance to prove . . .'

'No sale,' she said, and hung up.

Caitlin wouldn't let me kiss her hello when she saw me outside her school. She wouldn't let me hold her hand. She wouldn't speak to me when we got into the car. I suggested a walk along the seafront at Santa Monica. I suggested an early dinner at Johnny Rockets in Beverly Hills (her favorite restaurant). Or maybe a trip to FAO Schwartz in the Beverly Center. As I reeled off this list of potential options, the thought struck me: I'm already sounding like a divorced dad.

'I want to go home to Mommy.'

'Caitlin, I'm so sorry about –'

'I want to go home to Mommy.'

'I know this is awful. I know that you must think I'm –'

'I want to go home to Mommy.'

I spent the next five minutes trying to talk her into hearing me out. But she wouldn't listen to me. She just kept repeating the same line over and over again: 'I want to go home to Mommy.'

So, eventually, I had no choice but to do as she asked.

When we reached the front door of our house, she fled into Lucy's arms.

'Thanks for brainwashing her,' I said.

'If you want to talk to me, do it through a lawyer.'

Then she went inside.

Actually I ended up talking to Lucy through two lawyers from the firm of Sheldon and Strunkel, who came highly recommended from Brad Bruce (he'd used them for his previous two divorces, and had them currently waiting in the wings if Marriage Number Three tanked). They, in turned, talked to Lucy's lawyer – a woman named Melissa Levin, whom my guys described as an exponent of the 'Let's eviscerate the sonofabitch' school of legalistic practice. From the outset, she didn't simply want to seize all my material assets; she also wanted to make certain that I came out of the divorce hobbled, and boasting a permanent limp.

Eventually, after much expensive wrangling, my guys managed to curb her scorched-earth tendencies – but the damage was still pretty formidable. Lucy got the house (and all my equity in it). She also received a whopping $11,000 per month alimony and child support package. Given my new-found success, I could afford this – and I certainly wanted Caitlin to have everything and anything she wanted. But it did appal me to think that, from this moment forward, the first $200k of my gross income would be spoken for. Just as I wasn't pleased about the clause that Levin the Impaler also included in the settlement: allowing Lucy the right to move with Caitlin to another city, should her career require it.

Four months after our fast-track divorce was finalized, she exercised that option when she landed a job heading the Human Resources division of some software company in Marin County. Suddenly, my daughter was no longer down the road. Suddenly, I couldn't play hooky from my desk for an afternoon, and take off with her after school to Malibu, or to the big ice-skating rink in Westwood. Suddenly, my daughter was an hour's flight away from me – and as the series went into production, I found it impossible to see her more than once a month. That bothered me to the point where, on those frequent nights when I couldn't sleep, I'd pace the floors of the large West Hollywood loft that Sally and I rented and ponder why I had fractured my family. I knew all the reasons: a marriage that had become inanimate . . . the dazzling style and brilliance of Ms Birmingham . . . the seductive momentum that accompanies success (and the desire to slam the door on all those past years of failure). But in those four-in-the-morning moments of private despair, I couldn't help but think: I shouldn't have fallen so easily when pushed. Surely I could have talked Lucy into taking me back. Surely we could have made a go of it again.

But then, come morning, there would be a script to finish, a meeting to take, a deal to ink, an opening to attend with Sally on my arm – in short, the relentless forward momentum of success. It was a momentum which would allow me to temporarily dodge the lingering guilt; the silent, ever-present uncertainty about everything in this new life of mine.

Of course, news of my changed domestic set-up was on the Hollywood bush telegraph within moments of my departure from the family home. Everyone said all the right solicitous things (to my face, anyway) about the difficulties of ending a marriage. The fact that I had 'run off' (to use that meretricious expression) with one of the most high-profile young television executives in town didn't do my standing any harm. I had traded upwards – and, as Brad Bruce told me, 'Everyone knew you were a smart guy, David. Now everyone's going to think you're a really smart guy.'

My agent's reaction, however, was typically caustic. Alison knew and liked Lucy – and in the wake of the deal for the first series of *Selling You*, she had warned me to dodge all home-wrecking temptations. So, when I broke the news that I was about to start a new life with Sally, she fell silent. Finally she said, 'I guess I should congratulate you for waiting over a year before doing something like this. Then again, it's what always happens out here when somebody has the big breakthrough.'

'I am in love, Alison.'

'Congratulations. Love is a wonderful thing.'

'I knew you were going to react this way.'

'Sweetheart – don't you know that there are only ten stories in the world . . . and, right now, you're acting out one of them. But I will say this – at least your story has a different twist to it.'

'How's that?'

'In your case, the writer's fucking the producer. In my jaded experience, it's always the other way around. So bravo – you're defying the laws of Hollywood gravity.'

'But Alison – it was you who got us together in the first place.'

'Tell me about it. But don't worry – I'm not going to demand my fifteen per cent on your future joint earnings.'

Alison did point out, however, that as Sally and I were now an item, it was best if we let the proposed Fox pilot (which I still hadn't written) lapse.

'Face fact, it's going to look like her wedding gift to you – and I can just imagine some Peter Bart wannabee making a big issue out of it in *Daily Variety*.'

'Sally and I have discussed this already. We agreed that it's best if we forget the pilot for Fox.'

'What charming pillow talk you must have together.'

'It was over breakfast.'

'Before or after working out?'

'Why do I put up with you?'

'Because, "as a friend" I really am your friend. And also because I watch your back . . . to the point where the advice I have just given you is going to cost me almost forty grand in commission.'

'You're such an altruist, Alison.'

'No – just plain stupid. Still, here's one final piece of counsel from your fifteen per cent big sister: Keep your head down in the coming months. You've had it too good recently.'

I tried to heed her advice but Sally and I were playing the 'power couple' game. We were 'the perfect exemplars of the New Hollywood': the sort of Ivy League, literate folk who also happened to thrive in the combustible world of television. Well-heeled, but trying to look like we abhorred all ostentation. Our loft was minimalist in design; my Porsche and Sally's Range Rover were symbolically astute vehicles – 'upscale, but smart' cars driven by 'upscale, but smart' people who have obviously achieved a significant level of professional success. We got invited to the right parties, the right premieres. But whenever I was interviewed, I spoke about how we weren't seduced by the lure of celebrity or the need to maintain a high public profile. Anyway, we were both far too busy to crave the fast lane. Los Angeles is largely an early-to-bed city. So – with Sally planning on the new comedy slate for the autumn, and with the second season of *Selling You* now deep into production – we hardly had time for social pursuits, let alone each other. And Sally, as I discovered, lived her life as if it was a perpetual time-and-motion schedule: to the point where, though she never said it, I knew that she had even silently scheduled three 'love-making windows' per week. Even those random moments when she suddenly jumped my bones started to feel curiously pre-meditated – as if she had almost calculated that, on a rare morning when she wasn't doing breakfast with someone, we could just about find the ten or so minutes required to reach mutual orgasm before she started her workout.

Still, I wasn't complaining. Because – bar the constant twinge of regret I felt about Lucy and Caitlin – everything was going my way.

'We all should have your problems,' my new friend Bobby Barra told me on a rare late night (well, it was a Friday) when I drank one martini too many, and confided in him that I was still being nagged with silent guilt about busting up my marriage.

Bobby Barra loved the fact that I was using him as Father Confessor. Because that meant we were tight. And Bobby Barra liked the idea of being tight with me. Because I was now a name, a personage; one of the few true winners in a city of desperate aspiration and pervasive failure.

'Look at it this way. Your marriage belongs to that segment of your life when nothing you did really worked. So naturally, you had to jettison it once you crossed over to the charmed side of the street.'

'I guess you're right, I said, sounding unconvinced.

'Of course I'm right. A new life means new everything.'

Including new friends like Bobby Barra.

Two

Bobby Barra was rich. Seriously rich. But not 'fuck you' rich.

'What do you mean by "fuck you" rich?' I once asked him.

'You talking attitude or numbers?' he said.

'The attitude I can figure out. Give me the numbers.'

'Hundred mil.'

'That much?'

'It's not that much.'

'Sounds like enough to me.'

'How many millions in a billion?'

'Actually I don't know.'

'One thousand.'

'One thousand million makes a billion?'

'You've got the math.'

'So a billion's "fuck you" rich?'

'Not just "fuck you" rich – "fuck you and ten generations of your family" rich.'

'That's pretty rich. But if you've only got one hundred mil . . . ?'

'You can still say "fuck you" but you've got to choose your audience more carefully.'

'You must be "fuck you" rich by now, Bobby.'

'"Fuck you" adjacent.'

'That sounds pretty good to me.'

'It's still not "fuck you". I tell you – you start hanging with the really big boys – Bill Gates, Paul Allen, Phil Fleck – and a hundred mil is kids' stuff. A tenth of a billion. What's that to guys who are worth thirty, forty, fifty bil?'

'Chump change?'

'Bingo. Chump-fucking-change. Nickel-and-dime productions.'

I allowed myself a smile.

'Well, speaking as a mere mortal who only earned a million last year . . .'

'Yeah – but you'll get there . . . *if* you let me help you.'

'I'm all ears.'

Bobby Barra was full of advice when it came to the market – because that's what Bobby Barra did for a living. He played the market. And he played it so well that now, at the age of thirty-five, he really was 'fuck you adjacent'.

What made his new-found wealth all the more impressive was that it was completely self-created. Bobby referred to himself as 'the Dago from Detroit': the son of an electrician at the Ford Dearborn plant who hauled himself out of Motor City as soon as he passed his driver's test. Before that – at an age when most kids were thinking about the indignities of acne – Bobby was ruminating about high finance.

'Let me guess what you were reading at age thirteen?' Bobby Barra asked me around the time we became friends. 'John Updike.'

'Give me a break,' I said. 'I've never worn a Shetland sweater in my life. But Tom Wolfe . . .'

'That figures.'

'And you? What were you reading at thirteen?'

'Lee Iaccoca . . . and don't fucking laugh.'

'Who's laughing?'

'Not just Iaccoca, but Tom Peters, and Adam Smith, and John Maynard Keynes, and Donald Trump . . .'

'Quite a cultural cross-section there, Bobby. Do you think Trump ever read Keynes?'

'Nah – but the guy knows how to build a casino. And he is seriously "fuck you". Which, from the moment I read his book, is what I decided I wanted to be.'

'So why didn't you go into the building game?'

'Because you got to play the *goombah* thing – you know, cousin Sal's got an Uncle Joey who's got a nephew Tony who can put the muscle on the Hebrew who owns the vacant lot which you want to buy . . . Get the picture?'

'Sounds very white shoe to me.'

'Listen, corporate assholes play the same fucking game – only they do it with Brooks Brothers suits and Wharton MBAs and leveraged buy-outs. Anyway, I didn't want the *goombah* thing and I also knew that Wall Street wasn't going to like my vowels and my grease-monkey background. So the way I figured it, LA was a

29

far better gridiron for a guy like me. Because, face fact, this is the "money talks, bullshit walks" capital of the world. Plus: out here, no one gives a shit about whether you sound like John Gotti's mutant son. The bigger the bank account, the bigger the dick.'

'As John Maynard Keynes himself once remarked.'

Full credit to Bobby: he paid his way through USC by working three nights a week as a general dogsbody for Michael Milken in the last-gasp glory days of his junk-bond bonanza. Then, after college, he got hired by some dubious character named Eddie Edelstein, who ran his own small brokerage house in Century City and eventually got shipped off to a Club Fed for a major SEC no-no.

'Eddie was my guru – the best fucking broker west of the continental divide. The guy had a nose for an IPO like a pit bull. And when it came to calling a margin . . . take it from me, this guy was a total artist. Of course, the dumb putz then has to go fuck it all up by pocketing 100k after slipping this South African broker – a fucking Afrikaner Nazi – the inside dope on some smelting-and-refining company IPO. Turns out the Nazi was actually a SEC guy in disguise. Under-fucking-cover. I told Eddie to scream entrapment – but it was no use. Three-to-five – and even though it was one of those open prisons where he was allowed to bring a tennis racket, it still killed him. Cancer of the prostate, aged fifty-three. You floss your teeth, Dave?'

'Sorry?' I said, a little bemused by the sudden change of conversational direction.

'On his deathbed, Eddie gave me two pieces of advice: never trust a guy who says he's an Afrikaner, but sounds like he was raised in New Jersey . . . and if you want to avoid prostate cancer, always floss your teeth.'

'I'm not following this.'

'You don't floss, all that plaque and shit trickles down your throat and ends up lodging in your prostate. That's what happened to poor Eddie: ace broker, ace guy . . . but he should've flossed.'

I started flossing seriously after this conversation with Bobby. I also frequently questioned why on earth I liked hanging with him so much.

I knew the answer to that question: because (a) as a broker, he'd started making me some money, and (b) he was never less-than-entertaining.

Bobby had come into my life during the first season of *Selling You*. After the show's third episode was aired, he wrote me c/o FRT on his official company stationery, to say that my program was the smartest thing he'd seen in years, and also offering his services as a broker. 'I am not some *I promise you the earth* gonnif. I am not some *I will make rich by the time you eat that brownie* operator. But I am the smartest broker in town – and, in time, I *will* make serious money for you. Also, I am completely honest, and if you don't believe me, please call . . .'

And the letter listed a bevy of A and B list Hollywood types who had allegedly become Roberto Barra clients.

I scanned this letter. Before tossing it into my circular file, however, I did smile. Because of the two dozen or so pitch letters I'd received since *Selling You* hit the small screen – letters from upscale car dealers, real estate agents, tax consultants, personal trainers, and the usual *come channel with me* New Age goons, all congratulating me on my new-found success and offering their services – Bobby's was the most brazen, the most downright immodest. Its final sentence was ridiculous:

I'm not just good at what I do. I am brilliant at what I do. If you want to see your money make money, you've got to call me. If you don't, you will regret this for the rest of your life.

The day after opening this pitch, I received a copy of the same letter, with a Post-It attached to it:

Figuring that you probably threw away the letter you received from me yesterday, here it is again. Let's make money, Dave.

Well, I had to admire the guy's neck . . . though I did find the daily phone calls he subsequently made to my office rather tedious (on my instructions, my assistant, Jennifer, made certain that I was permanently in a meeting whenever he phoned). Just as I wasn't swayed when he sent me a case of Au Bon Climat wine. Of course I did the polite thing – I dropped him a brief thank you note – and then a week later, a case of Dom Perignon arrived. With a card.

You'll be drinking this stuff like 7-Up if you let me make you some real money.

Brad Bruce happened to be in my office when the champagne arrived.

'Who's the admirer . . . and does she have a phone number?' he asked.

'Actually, she's a he.'

'Forget about it.'

'Nah – it's not like that. The guy wants to get me into bed financially. He's a broker. A very persistent broker.'

'Name?'

'Bobby Barra.'

'Oh yeah, him.'

This stopped me short.

'You know him?'

'Sure. Ted Lipton uses him,' he said, mentioning the vice-president of FRT. 'Ditto . . .'

He reeled off a bunch of names, many of whom had been listed in that initial letter he sent me.

'So the guy's legitimate?' I asked.

'Highly – from what I've heard. And he obviously knows how to hustle. Wish my broker would send me champagne.'

That afternoon, I called Ted Lipton. After talking a little shop, I asked him for an opinion on Roberto Barra:

'Got me a twenty-seven per cent return last year. And yeah – I trust the little fucker.'

I didn't have a broker at the time – because in the insane rush of events since the first series was commissioned, I hadn't had a moment to consider such niceties as how to invest my new-found money. So I asked my assistant to find out everything she could about Roberto Barra. Within forty-eight hours, she came back with the inside dope: satisfied clientele, no criminal record, no business with bad guys, SEC Seal of Good Housekeeping.

'Okay,' I said after reading her report. 'Set up lunch.'

Bobby Barra turned out to be vertically challenged – five foot two, tight black curly hair, immaculately dressed in a black suit of Italianate cut (surprise, surprise). He took me to Orso. He talked fast and funny. He surprised me with his literacy – both in terms of films and books. He flattered me – and then joked about flattering me. He said, 'I'm not going to give you that *as a friend* LA bullshit,' then five sentences later deliberately dropped '*as a friend*' into the conversation. '*You're not just a TV writer, you're a serious TV writer . . . and in your case, that's not an oxymoron.*' He was brilliant company – a world-class spiel merchant who mixed erudition with tough-guy repartee ('You ever need someone's legs broken,' he said sotto voce, 'I know two Mexican kids who will do it for three hundred bucks, plus their car fare'). Listening to him talk, I couldn't help but think that he was like one of those Chicago sharpies about whom Bellow wrote so brilliantly. He was slick. He was smart, and just a little dangerous. He name-dropped relentlessly, but also sent himself up for being 'such an unapologetic star-fucker'. I could see why all those A and B listers wanted to do business with him. Because he exuded mastery over his chosen domain. And because in this, the ultimate enclave of self-salesmanship, he stood out as the biggest self-promoter of them all.

'All you need to know is this: I'm obsessed with making money for my clients. Because money is about choice. Money is about the ability to *exercise one's discretion*. To confront the random nature of destiny with the knowledge that, at least, you have the necessary arsenal to counteract life's endless complexities. Because money – *real money* – allows you to make decisions without fear. And say to the world: fuck you.'

'Wasn't that Adam Smith's argument in *The Wealth of Nations*?'

'You like Adam Smith?' he asked.

'I've only read the coverage.'

'Fuck Machiavelli, fuck *Success is a Choice*. Smith's *The Wealth of Nations* is the greatest of all capitalist manifestos.'

Then he took a short intake of breath and began to speak in a voice which could be best described as Detroit Stentorian:

'*All systems either of preference or of restraint, therefore, being thus completely taken away, the obvious and simple system of natural liberty establishes itself of its own accord. Every man, as long as he does not*

33

violate the laws of justice, is left perfectly free to pursue his own interest his own way, and to bring both his industry and capital into compe-tition with those of any man or order of man . . . Defense, however, is of much more importance than opulence.'

He paused, took a sip from his glass of San Pellegrino, then said, 'I know I'm not exactly Ralph Fiennes, but . . .'

'Hey,' I said, 'I'm impressed. And you did it all without an autocue.'

'Here's the thing: we're living in the biggest era of "natural liberty" known to man. But what Smith said is so damn true: before you go lavish, make certain you've got the cash to watch your back. And that's where I come in. Financially speaking, I'm not just going to watch your back, I'm going to build you a fortress made of capital. Which means that, no matter what cards you are dealt in the future, you will still be in a position of strength. And let's face it, as long as you're in a position of strength, nobody's going to be using you as a doormat.'

'So what are you proposing exactly?'

'I'm going to propose *nothing*. I'm simply going to show you how I achieve results. So, here's how I'd like to play this: if you are willing to trust me with a nominal sum of money – say, fifty grand – I promise you to double it within six months. You write my company a check for fifty grand, I send you the neces-sary paperwork, six months later you get a check for 100k minimum . . .'

'And if you fail . . .'

He cut me off. 'I don't fail.'

Pause. I asked, 'Let me ask you something: why have you put all this effort into snagging me?'

'Because you're hot, that's why. And I like hanging with the A-team. Here I go name-dropping again, but have you ever heard of Philip Fleck?'

'The multi-billionaire recluse? The film director *manqué*. Who hasn't heard of Phil Fleck? He's infamous.'

'Actually, he's just a guy like the rest of us. A guy with twenty billion dollars . . .'

'That's certainly "fuck you" in your book, Bobby.'

34

'Phil is *Hall of Fame* "fuck you" – and a seriously good friend of mine.'

'That's nice.'

'He's a big fan of yours, by the way.'

'You kidding me?'

'"Smartest writer on TV," he told me just last week.'

I didn't know whether to buy this line or not. So I just said, 'Say thanks for me.'

'You think I'm talking star-fuckng shit again, don't you?'

'If you say you're a friend of Phil Fleck's, I believe you.'

'Do you believe me enough to write me a check for fifty grand?'

'Sure,' I said, sounding uneasy.

'So write me the check.'

'Right now?'

'Yeah. Take the check book out of your jacket pocket . . .'

'How do you know I've got my check book with me?'

'Well, in my experience, the moment a guy makes some serious money – especially after years in the swamps – he starts carrying his checkbook around with him. Because he can suddenly buy a lot of big stuff that he couldn't buy before. And there's something a lot classier about writing a check than tossing down some platinum-dyed piece of plastic . . .'

I inadvertently touched the breast pocket of my jacket.

'Guilty as charged,' I said.

'So, write the check.'

I pulled out the checkbook and my pen. I placed them on the table. I stared down at them. Bobby impatiently tapped the checkbook with his index finger.

'Come on, Dave,' he said. 'It's time to deal. This is one of those critical moments that helps define the future. And I know what you're thinking: "Can I trust the guy?" Well, I'm not going to sell myself any more. Just let me ask you this: do you have the courage to be rich?'

I picked up the pen. I opened the book. I wrote the check.

'Smart guy,' Bobby said.

A few days later, the official documentation for my investment arrived from Roberto Barra and Partners. Two months went by before I heard from him again: a quick 'Hey, how's it going?' call, which told me that the market was buoyant and 'we were winning.' He promised to call again in another two months. He did so – almost to the day. Another fast, pleasant conversation, in which he sounded rushed but upbeat about the market. Then two months later, a Fedex envelope arrived at my office. It contained a bank check made payable to me, for the sum of $122,344.82. A note was attached to it.

'We actually did a little better than 100 per cent. Now let's party.'

I had to admire Bobby's style. After pitching me successfully, he then backed off completely . . . until he had results. In the wake of this amazing return, I immediately reinvested the lot with Bobby, then threw another 250k his way when the second series came through. We started hanging out together on an occasional basis. Bobby still wasn't married ('I make a bad prisoner,' he told me), but he always had some piece of arm candy in tow: usually a model or a wannabe actress. Inevitably she was blonde and sweet and Princess-Not-So-Bright. I used to give him shit about conforming to 'money dude' archetype.

'Hey, once I was just a short wop from Motor City. Now I'm a short wop from Motor City *with money*. So, naturally, I'm going to use that fact as a way of *schtupping* all those cheerleaders who used to consider me a grease monkey.'

After spending one or two evenings with Bobby and his *squeeze du jour*, I let it be known that I wasn't really interested in his idea of the fast lane. So we restricted our monthly boys' night out to a low-key dinner *à deux* – during which I'd sit back and let Bobby regale me with his non-stop spiel on just about everything. Sally couldn't understand why I liked him. Though she approved of the way he was investing my money, her one and only meeting with Bobby was something of a social disaster. Having been very supportive during my break-up with Lucy, he was keen to meet Sally once the proverbial dust had settled . . . especially as he was well aware of her player status at Fox Television. So, around three months after we officially became an item, he suggested dinner at La Petite Porte in West Hollywood. From the moment we all sat down together, I could tell that Sally had instantly filed him away under '*peasant*'. He tried to charm her with his usual palaver. 'Everyone who's anybody knows the name of Sally Birmingham,' he fawned. He attempted to show off his bookish credentials, asking her to name her favorite Don DeLillo novel 'I don't have one,' she shot back. 'Life's too short for his brand of literary self-importance.' He even played his 'I know A-List people' card, mentioning how Johnny Depp had phoned him from his home in Paris yesterday to discuss some stock options. Once again, Sally narrowed him in her sights and said, 'What an interesting life you lead.'

It was an unnerving spectacle, watching Sally quietly puncture Bobby's manic attempts to win favor. Yet what was most intriguing about this demolition job was the patrician smile Sally retained throughout. Not once did she say, 'You're full of shit.' Not once did she raise her voice. But by the end of the evening, she had cut him down to Toulouse Lautrec size and let it be known, in her own quiet way, that she considered him low grade, *petit bourgeois*, and not worth her time.

On the way home that night, she reached over to me in the driver's seat, and stroked the back of my head, and said, 'Darling, you know I adore you, but never put me through something like that again.'

Long silence. Finally I said, 'Was it that bad?'

'You know what I'm saying. He may be a brilliant broker . . . but socially speaking, he's a fool.'

'I find him amusing.'

'And I can understand why – especially if you ever end up writing something for Scorsese. But he's a people collector, David – and you're this month's *objet d'art*. If I were you I'd let him handle my investments and nothing more. He's cheap and meretricious: the sort of hustler who might splash on Armani aftershave in the morning, but still stinks of Brut.'

I knew that Sally was being cruel – and didn't like seeing this unsympathetic side to her. But I said nothing. I also said little to Bobby when, a few days after the dinner, he called me at my office to announce that he was projecting a twenty-nine per cent return this year.

'Twenty-nine per cent,' I said, stunned. 'That sounds positively illegal.'

'Oh, it's legal all right.'

'Just joking,' I said, picking up his defensiveness. 'I'm very pleased. And grateful. Next time I'll buy dinner.'

'Is there going to be a next time? Sally really thought I was a jerk, didn't she?'

'Not to my knowledge.'

'You're lying, but I appreciate the sentiment. Believe me, I know when I strike out with someone.'

'The chemistry just didn't work between you guys, that's all.'

'You're being polite. But hey, as long as you don't share her sentiments . . .'

'Why should I? Especially when you're making me twenty-nine per cent.'

He laughed. 'It's always the bottom line, isn't it?'

'You're asking me that?'

Bobby was shrewd enough to never again mention the subject of that disastrous dinner, though he always asked after Sally whenever we spoke. And once a month, I had dinner with him. Twenty-nine per cent *is* twenty-nine per cent, after all. But I genuinely liked Bobby, and saw that behind all the gimcrack salesmanship, the slick bravura, he was just another guy travelling hopefully, trying to make his own mark in a deeply indifferent world. Like the rest of us, he filled the time with his own turbo-charged ambitions and worries, in an attempt to believe that, somehow, what we do during that momentary spasm called life actually counts for something.

Anyway, I was so damn busy with the second series that, aside from our monthly dinner, I was out of touch with Bobby. By the time *Selling You* Season Two went into production, I'd reached the conclusion that my life was one big time-and-motion study: fourteen-hour work days, seven days a week. The few hours left over in the day were dedicated entirely to Sally. But she wasn't exactly complaining about our lack of quality time together. For Sally anything less than a seventeen-hour day was lazy.

The only real highlights in this breakneck schedule were the two weekends a month I'd spend in Sausalito with Caitlin. The breach between us didn't take long to heal. On my first visit to her new home, she was distant with me. But we had a terrific day out in San Francisco, and her initial aloofness melted a bit. Early that evening, as we were having dinner in a restaurant on Fisherman's Wharf, she said, 'I have to ask you a question, Daddy.'

'Shoot,' I said.

'Do you miss me and Mommy?'

I felt an immense sadness come over me.

'Only every hour of every day,' I said, taking her hand. She didn't pull away, but instead squeezed mine back.

'Can't you live with us again?' she asked.

'I wish that was possible, but . . .'

'Is it because you don't love Mommy any more?'

'I'll always love your mother . . . but sometimes people who love each other find it difficult to live together. Or they grow apart. Or . . .'

'You could grow back together again,' she said.

I smiled at the great turn of phrase.

'It's never that simple, Caitlin. People can do things that others find hard to forgive. Or they realize that they need to lead a different kind of life now.'

She withdrew her hand and stared down at the table.

'I don't like not having you around.'

'And I don't like not having *you* around,' I said. 'And I wish I could wave a magic wand and make it all better. But I can't. Still, we will be together two weekends a month. During all your vacations you can spend as much time as you like with me . . .'

'You'll be working during my vacations.'

'I'll make certain I'm not.'

'You promise?'

'I promise.'

'And you'll visit me every two weeks?'

'Without fail.'

And I never missed a visit. On the contrary, there was no damn way that anything was going to get in the way of my twice-monthly trip to see my daughter.

Another six months shot by. The second series was in the can.

Early reaction within FRT was tremendous. Alison had already started taking calls from Brad Bruce and Ted Lipton about the third series – and we were still two months away from the launch of our second season. Life was chaotic, but good. My career was cruising. My ardour for Sally hadn't dimmed . . . and she still seemed entranced by me. My money was making money. And though Lucy still cold-shouldered me whenever I visited Sausalito, at least Caitlin seemed delighted to see her daddy, and had even started spending one weekend a month with us in LA.

'What's wrong with you?' Alison asked me over lunch one day. 'You seem happy.'

'I am.'

'Should I alert the media?'

'Is there anything wrong with being happy?'

'Hardly. It's just . . . you've never really done happy, Dave.'

She was right. Then again, until very recently, I'd never gotten what I'd wanted before.

'Well,' I said, 'maybe I can start doing happy now.'

'That would make a change. And while you're at it: take a little time off. Success has made you look seriously wrecked.'

Once again, she was right. I hadn't made acquaintance with that thing called 'a vacation' in over fourteen months. I was tired and in deep need of a break. So much so that when Bobby rang up in mid-March and said to me, 'Feel like going to the Caribbean this weekend . . . and you can bring Sally,' I instantly said yes.

'Good,' Bobby said. 'Because Phil Fleck wants to meet you.'

40

Three

A COUPLE OF facts about Philip Fleck. He was born in Milwaukee, forty-four years ago. His father owned a small paper-packaging plant. When Dad dropped dead of a heart attack in 1981, Philip was recalled home from NYU film school to take over the family business. Though he was reluctant to shoulder this responsibility – as he was determined to become a movie director – he acceded to his mother's wishes and became the company boss. Within ten years, he had turned this minor regional company into one of the major retail packaging players in the United States. Then he took the company public and made his first billion. After that, he started to dabble as a venture capitalist, deciding in the early nineties to back an obscure horse called 'the Internet'. He chose his investments wisely – and by 1999, he was worth over $20 billion.

2000 was the year of his fortieth birthday. And it was also the year that he suddenly decided to vanish from view. He resigned the chairmanship of his family packaging company. He stopped being seen in public. He hired a security company to make certain that his privacy wasn't invaded. He eschewed all requests for interviews or public appearances. He fled behind the large apparatus which ran his entrepreneurial empire. He vanished from view, disappearing so completely that many thought he was either dead, crazy, or J.D. Salinger.

Then, three years ago, Philip Fleck reappeared in public. Correction: he himself didn't reappear, but his name suddenly became common currency again when his first film, *The Last Chance*, hit the screens. He wrote, directed and financed the thing himself – and in the one interview he gave to *Esquire* before the film's release, he called it 'the culmination of ten years' planning and thought'. The film was an apocalyptic tale about two couples on an island off the Maine coast who face a crisis of metaphysical proportions when a nuclear accident wipes out most of New England. They are trapped offshore, hoping that the deadly toxins will not be blown their way. As they fight and argue and fuck, they

41

begin to debate 'the true meaning of temporal existence' . . . and, *natch*, their impending deaths.

The film received suicidally bad reviews. Fleck was accused of being portentous and risible; a talentless rich guy who had bankrolled one of the most absurd vanity films ever made.

After this warm critical reception, Philip Fleck dropped out of sight again – only seeing a very few members of his so-called inner circle of pals . . . though his name did appear briefly in the news again when word leaked out that he had finally gotten married . . . to his script editor on *The Last Chance*. (A quick aside – when Brad Bruce saw the marriage notice in the Milestones section of *Time*, he turned to me in our production office and said: 'Maybe the guy married her because she was the only person who didn't laugh at his fucking awful script.')

Though the critics may have dented Philip Fleck's pride, they still couldn't do much harm to his bank account. In last year's *Forbes* survey of the 100 Richest Americans, he came eighth, with a current net value of $20 billion. He owned homes in Manhattan, Malibu, Paris, San Francisco, and Sydney, not to mention his own private island near Antigua. He had his very own 767 jet. He was an avid art collector, with a penchant for twentieth-century American painters – specifically, sixties abstractionists like Motherwell, Philip Guston, and Rothko. Though he gave widely to charity, he was best noted for his obsession with the movies – to the point where he had heavily funded such well-known organizations as the American Film Institute, the Cinémathèque Française, and the film department at NYU. He was a true cinephile – someone who, in that *Esquire* interview, admitted that he had seen over 10,000 movies during his lifetime. On rare occasions, he'd even been spotted haunting such famous small Parisian Left Bank cinemas as the Accatone and the Action Christine – though, from all accounts, it was difficult to pick him out in a crowd, as he was a notoriously ordinary looking guy.

'Forget the designer wardrobe upgrade [as the *Esquire* journalist wrote in that spiky profile of Fleck]. Up close and personal, he's a chunky average Joe with a personality bypass. The guy is Mr Taciturn. You can't tell if he's suffering from terminal diffidence, or the sort of misanthropic arrogance which comes with stratospheric wealth. But with his mega-millions, he has no real need to engage with the rest of the world. You meet Philip Fleck, you survey his domain – his vast financial muscle – in all its infinite grandeur, and then you look him over carefully, and you think: occasionally, the Gods do smile down on geeks.'

After Bobby had proposed the weekend at Fleck's Caribbean hideaway, I had my assistant find me that *Esquire* interview. As soon as I finished reading it, I called Bobby at his office and asked him, 'Is that journalist still alive?'

'*Just* . . . though I gather the city desk at the *Bangor Daily News* doesn't really compare with the heady world of Hearst Magazines.'

'If I'd gotten those reviews, I would have signed up as a kamikaze pilot.'

'Yeah, but if you had $20 billion in the bank . . .'

'Point taken.'

'Surely, after the shit flung at him over *The Last Chance*, he doesn't want to get back into the directing game again.'

'If there's one thing I know about Phil, it's this: he may be Mr Brooding . . . but the guy doesn't give up, and he *never* gives in. He's relentless. If he wants something, he gets it. And right now, he wants you.'

Yes, this was the underlying reason – the *subtext* – behind my summons to Fleck's Caribbean retreat. I yanked this out of Bobby during his initial phone call, inviting me to meet the great recluse.

'Here's the deal,' Bobby said. 'He's hanging out for a week at his place off Antigua. It's called Saffron Island – and, I'm telling you, it's paradise *de luxe*.'

'Let me guess,' I said. 'He's built his very own Taco Bell on the island . . .'

'Hey, what's with the sarcasm?'

'I just like giving you shit about your mega-rich friend.'

'Listen, Phil's really an original, a one-off. And though nowadays he guards his privacy like a nuclear test site, among his pals, he's a regular guy.'

And (according to Bobby) he really liked Bobby. 'Because I'm also such a likeable guy.'

'No offense,' I said, 'but I still don't get how you managed to infiltrate his inner circle. I mean, he makes the late Mr Kubrick sound accessible.'

So Bobby explained that he'd been 'put together' with Fleck three years ago during the pre-production for his movie. As Fleck was completely footing the bill, he was working on ways of turning the whole set-up into an enormous tax write-off. One of Fleck's associate producers had been one of Bobby's clients – and recognizing his financial genius (yes, those were Bobby's exact words), he suggested that Fleck speak with him. So Bobby got the summons to San Francisco to 'a modest little mansion on Russian Hill'. They eyed each other up. They schmoozed. Bobby outlined a plan whereby, if Fleck made the movie in Ireland, he could jettison the entire $20 million budget from his return the following year. And the IRS wouldn't be able to say dick about it.

So *The Last Chance* was made on some godawful little island off the coast of County Clare, with interior work shot in a Dublin studio. Though it was a disaster for all involved, at least Bobby Barra came away with a major prize: his friendship with Philip Fleck.

'Believe it or not, we talk the same language. And I know he respects my financial judgement.'

Enough to let you play with his money? I was about to ask – but I held my tongue. Because I was pretty certain that a man of Philip Fleck's mega-means probably had twelve Bobby Barras on his payroll. What I couldn't figure out exactly was what such an isolated figure saw in a hustler like Barra. Unless, like me, he found him diverting, and considered him potential material.

'What's the new wife like?' I asked Bobby.

'Martha? Very New England. Very bookish. Not bad looking, if you like the Emily Dickinson type.'

'You know Emily Dickinson?'

'We never dated, but . . .'

I had to hand it to Bobby. He was fast.

'I'll tell you this, *entre*-fucking-*nous*,' he said. 'No one was surprised when Phil decided she was the one. Before that, he was into arm candy in a big way – though he always looked awkward with some model who had trouble spelling her own name. Despite all the money, he's never been much of a babe magnet.'

'How nice that he met someone then,' I said, thinking that, despite her alleged Belle of Amherst credentials, this Martha woman must be one shrewd gold digger.

'Anyway, the point of this invitation is a simple one,' Bobby said. 'As I told you before, Phil loves *Selling You*, and he simply wants to meet you, and he thought you might like a couple of days with your lady under the Saffron Island palms.'

'Sally can come too?'

'That's what I just said.'

'And this is simply a meet-and-greet, nothing more?'

'Yeah, that's right,' Bobby said, a slight note of hesitancy slipping into his voice. 'Of course, he may want to speak with you a bit about the business.'

'That's okay by me.'

'And if you wouldn't mind reading a script of his before heading out there.'

'I knew there was a catch.'

'It's not much of a catch. All he's asking for is a "courtesy read" of a new script.'

'Look, I'm not a script doctor . . .'

'Bullshit. That's exactly what you do on all the episodes of *Selling You* which you don't write.'

'Yeah – but the difference is: it's *my* series. Sorry to sound up-my-ass, but I really don't administer CPR to other people's work.'

'You *are* up your ass – but the thing here is: no one's asking you to play doctor. Like I said, it's a courtesy read, no more. More to the point, the writer in question is Mr Philip Fleck. And he is willing to fly you in his own private jet to his own private island, where you will have your own private suite with your own private swimming pool, your own private butler and the kind of six star service you will never find anywhere else, and in exchange for this week of absolute sybaritic luxury, all that is asked of you is that you read his screenplay – which, I should point out, is a mere 104 pages, because I have the damn thing in front of me – and after you read it, you simply have to sit down with him sometime under the Saffron Island palms, sip a Pina Colada, and talk for around an hour to the eighth richest American about his screenplay . . .'

He paused for breath. And also for effect.

'Now I ask you, Mr Armitage – is that such a fucking stretch?'

'All right,' I said. 'Messenger the script over.'

It arrived two hours later . . . by which time Jennifer had pulled the *Esquire* profile off the Internet, and I was definitely intrigued. There was something so irresistible about the paradox that was Philip Fleck. So much money. So little creative ability. And – if the *Esquire* writer was to be believed – such a desperate need to show the world that he was a man of genuinely creative gifts. 'Money means nothing without validation,' he told the journalist. But say it turns out that, for all your billions, you are actually talentless? What then? And I guess there was a schmucky part of me that thought it would be rather amusing to spend a few days observing this supreme irony.

Even Sally was intrigued by the idea of spending a week in the proximity of such extreme wealth.

'Are you absolutely sure this is not some ruse that little Bobby Barra has cooked up?' she asked me.

'For all his big time talk I doubt that Bobby actually has access to his very own 767, let alone a Caribbean island. Anyway, I did get a copy of Fleck's script – and I had Jennifer run a WGA check on it. Fleck is registered as the author – so, yeah, the whole thing seems perfectly legit.'

'What's it like?'

'Don't know. I only got it right before leaving the office.'

'Well, if we're leaving on Friday, you'd better find the time to do some serious notes on it. You are going to have to sing for our supper, after all.'

'So you are coming?'

'A free week on Phil Fleck's island idyll? Damn right I am. I can dine out on this for months.'

'And if it all turns out to be utterly tacky?'

'It'll still be a story worth telling around town.'

Later that night, after insomnia sprung me out of bed at two in the morning, I sat in our living room and cracked open Fleck's screenplay. It was called *Fun and Games*. The opening scene read:

INT. PORNO SHOP, NIGHT

BUDDY MILES, fifty-five, lived-in face, cigarette permanently screwed into the side of his mouth, sits behind the counter of a particularly scuzzy porno shop. Though pin-ups and the lurid covers of assorted magazines bedeck the area where he sits, we quickly notice that he's reading a copy of Joyce's *Ulysses*. The opening movement of Mahler's Symphony 1 is being played on the boom box next to the cash register. He lifts a mug of coffee, tastes it, grimaces, then reaches below the counter and brings up a bottle of Hiram Walker bourbon. He unscrews the top, pours a shot into the coffee, replaces the bottle, and sips the coffee again. This time it passes muster. But as he looks up from the mug, he notices that a man is standing in front of the counter. He is dressed in a heavy winter parka. A balaclava helmet covers his face. Instantly BUDDY notices that the hooded figure is pointing a gun at him. After a moment, the hood speaks.

LEON	That Mahler you playing?
BUDDY	(nonplussed by the gun)
	I'm impressed. Ten bucks says you can't guess the symphony.
LEON	You on. It's Symphony Number-the-one.
BUDDY	Double or nothing you can't guess the conductor.
LEON	Treble-or-nothing.
BUDDY	That's a little steep.
LEON	Yeah, but I'm holding the gun.
BUDDY	Can't argue with that. Okay, treble or nothing. Who's the guy waving the stick?

LEON pauses for a moment, listening carefully to the recording.

LEON	Bernstein.
BUDDY	No sale. Georg Solti and the Chicago Symphony.
LEON	You fucking with me?

47

BUDDY   Check it out yourself.

LEON – still training the gun on BUDDY – opens the top of the boom box, pulls out the disc and studies its label with distaste, eventually chucking it away.

LEON   Damn. I never get that Chicago sound.
BUDDY   Yeah, it takes a while to adjust your ears to it. Especially all that big brass. Listen, are we going to get done whatever you want to get done?
LEON   You read my fucking mind. (He moves closer to Buddy). So go on, open up the register and make me happy.
BUDDY   No problem.

BUDDY opens the register. LEON leans over, using his free hand to grab the cash. As he does so, BUDDY slams the drawer on his hand and simultaneously pulls out a sawed-off shotgun from beneath the counter. Before LEON knows it, he has a shotgun at his head and his hand trapped in the cash register. He moans in pain.

BUDDY   I think you should drop the gun, don't you?

LEON does as ordered. BUDDY lets go of the drawer of the cash register, but still keeps the gun at LEON's head as he reaches over and pulls off his balaclava helmet. LEON is now revealed to be an African-American, also in his mid fifties. BUDDY stares at LEON, wide eyed.

BUDDY   Leon? Leon Wachtell?

Now it's LEON's turn to look wide-eyed. Suddenly the penny drops for him too.

LEON   Buddy Miles?

BUDDY lowers the gun.

BUDDY	Sergeant Buddy Miles to you, asshole.
LEON	I don't believe it.
BUDDY	And I don't believe you didn't recognize me.
LEON	Hey, it's a long time since 'Nam.

CUT TO:

I stopped reading. I put the script down. Immediately I was on my feet, heading towards the large closet off the entrance of our loft. After digging around assorted boxes, I found what I was looking for: a footlocker, crammed with my old scripts from all those years in Nowheresville. I opened the locker. I plunged into the deep pile of failed screenplays and never-produced television pilots and eventually I unearthed *We Three Grunts* – one of the first scripts I wrote after Alison took me on as a client. I returned to the sofa. I opened my script. I read page one.

INT. PORNO SHOP, NIGHT
BUDDY MILES, fifty-five, lived-in face, cigarette permanently screwed into the side of his mouth, sits behind the counter of a particularly scuzzy porno shop. Though pin-ups and the lurid covers of assorted magazines bedeck the area where he sits, we quickly notice that he's reading a copy of Joyce's *Ulysses* and the opening movement of Mahler's Symphony 1 is being played on the boom box next to the cash register. He lifts a mug of coffee, tastes it, grimaces, then reaches below the counter and brings up a bottle of Hiram Walker bourbon. He unscrews the top, pours a shot into the coffee, replaces the bottle, and sips the coffee again. This time it passes muster. But as he looks up from the mug, he notices that a man is standing in front of the counter. He is dressed in a heavy winter parka. A balaclava helmet covers his face. Instantly BUDDY notices that the hooded figure is pointing a gun at him. After a moment, the hood speaks.

LEON   That Mahler you playing?
BUDDY   (nonplussed by the gun)
I'm impressed. Ten bucks says you can't guess
the symphony.

And the scene went on exactly as it was written in Philip Fleck's
screenplay. I grabbed Fleck's script. I balanced it on one knee, while
opening my own script on the other knee. I did a page-by-page
comparison. Fleck had completely copied my original screenplay,
written some eight years before the one he had registered with the
Screen And Television Writers Association last month. This wasn't
mere plagiarism; this was *word-by-word, punctuation mark-by-
punctuation mark* plagiarism. In fact – given that the two scripts
were printed in the same typeface – I was pretty damn certain that
he simply had some minion type a new title page with his own
name on it before submitting it to the Association.

I couldn't believe it. What Fleck had done wasn't simply outrageous; it was downright scandalous – to the point where, with
SATWA backing, I could have easily exposed him publicly as a
literary pirate. Surely someone as hyper-conscious of his privacy as
Fleck would realize that the press would love to draw-and-quarter
him on a plagiarism charge. And surely he also knew that, by
sending the script to me, he was inviting (at best) my outrage. So
what asshole game was he playing?

I glanced at my watch. Two forty-one. I remembered something
Bobby once said to me: 'I am here 24/7 if you need me.' I picked
up the phone. I called his cell number. He answered on the third
ring. In the background, I could hear blaring techno-music and
the sound of an accelerating engine. Bobby sounded buzzed out of
his head: either nose candy or something from the Ritalin school
of pharmacology.

'Dave, you're up late,' he said.

'Is this a good moment?'

'If I told you I was doing ninety on the 10 with a Hawaiian
babe named Heather Fong copping my joint as we speak, would
you believe me?'

'No.'

'And you'd be right. I'm just heading home now after a long night discussing the Nasdaq with a couple of very bright Venezuelans . . .'

'And I've been up reading. What the fuck does Fleck think he's doing, copying my script?'

'Oh, you got that, did you?'

'Oh, I got it all right – and Mr Fleck's in big trouble. To begin with, I could get Alison to file a lawsuit . . .'

'Hey, I know it's almost three-in-the-am, but get an irony check, huh? Fleck was paying you a compliment, asshole. A major compliment. He wants to make your script. It's gonna be his next project. And he's going to pay you big time for it.'

'And is he also going to palm the script off as his own?'

'Dave, the dude is worth $20 billion. He ain't no dumb cracker. He knows that your script is *your script*. All he was doing was telling you, in his own skewed way, that he really digs it . . .'

'Wouldn't it have been just a little bit easier if he had simply called me up and told me how much he liked the script . . . or if he'd done the usual thing of having his people talk to my people?'

'What can I say? Phil keeps everybody guessing. But hey, if I was you, I'd be pleased. Alison can now screw vast amounts of money out of him for the script.'

'I'm going to have to think about this.'

'Oh, bullshit. Now listen – go take a sense of humor pill and get some sleep. This will all seem pretty damn amusing in the morning.'

I hung up. I suddenly felt very tired. So tired that I didn't want to think any more about the game that Philip Fleck was playing. But before falling into bed, I did leave the two scripts on our kitchen counter. They were both open to page one. Beside them was a note to Sally:

Darling:
Your thoughts, please, on this curious case of duplication.
   Love you . . .
   D xxx

Then I crept into our bedroom, got back into bed, and passed right out.

When I woke five hours later, I found Sally sitting at the end of our bed, proffering me a cappuccino. I muttered incoherent early morning words of thanks. She smiled. I noticed that she was already showered and dressed. Then I also saw that she had the two scripts under her arm.

'So, you really want to know what I think of this?' she asked.

I took a sip of coffee, then nodded.

'Well, to be honest about it, the whole thing's a bit generic, isn't it? Quentin Tarantino meets one of those dumb caper movies of the seventies.'

'Thanks a lot.'

'Look, you asked for an opinion, I'm giving you one. Anyway, it's a piece of juvenilia, right? And let's face it, the opening scene is overwritten. I mean, maybe you find references to Mahler amusing, but face fact, they're not going to work with the multiplex crowd.'

I took another sip of coffee, then said, 'Ouch.'

'Hey, I'm not saying it's talentless. On the contrary, it's got all the hallmarks that have made *Selling You* such a winner. The thing is, you've come on a long way since then.'

'Right,' I said, sounding hurt.

'Oh, for God's sakes, you don't expect me to praise something which really isn't that good, do you?'

'Of course I do.'

'But that wouldn't be honest.'

'What does honesty have to do with it? All I was asking for was your thoughts about Fleck's attempted plagiarism.'

'Plagiarism? Will you listen to yourself? You're like every writer I've ever met. Totally humorless when it comes to their own work. So he played a little hoax on you and decided to see how you'd react to his "purloining" of your script? Don't you get it? Don't you see what's he's trying to tell you?'

'Of course I do: he wants co-credit on my screenplay.'

She shrugged. 'Yes – you're right. That's the price you're going to pay if you let him make the script. And you should give him half-credit.'

'Why?'

'You know why: because that's the way the game is played. And also because – if truth be told – it's not the best movie ever written . . . so why not give him partial credit?'

I said nothing. Sally came over and kissed the top of my head.

'Don't sulk now,' she said. 'But I'm not going to lie to you. It's a stale old product. And if the eighth richest man in America wants to buy it off you, take his big bucks . . . even if it means that he ends up with a co-writing credit. Believe me, Alison's going to agree with me on this one.'

'Well, you've got to hand it to the guy,' Alison said when I called to tell her about Fleck's little stunt. 'It's a perversely original way of getting your attention.'

'And of telling me that he expects to be the co-writer.'

'Big deal. This is Hollywood. Even the valet parking guys think they deserve co-credit on a screenplay. Anyway, it's not your best work.'

I said nothing.

'Oh dear, a *sensitive* silence,' Alison said. 'Is the *auteur* a little touchy this morning?'

'Yeah. A little.'

'FRT has spoiled you, David. You now think you're Mr Creative Control. But remember: if this script gets made, we are talking about the big screen. And the big screen means the big compromises. Unless, of course, Fleck decides to turn your movie into some art house shit . . .'

'It's a caper movie, Alison.'

'Hey – in Fleck's hands, it could still be a candidate for existential dread. You ever see *The Last Chance*?'

'Not yet.'

'Give yourself a laugh and go rent it. It's probably the most unintentionally hilarious film ever made.'

I did just that, picking up the movie from my local Blockbuster that afternoon and watching it alone before Sally got home. I slipped the DVD into the player, opened a beer, sat back and waited to be entertained.

I didn't have to wait long. The opening shot of *The Last Chance* is close-up of a character named Prudence – a lithe, willowy babe, dressed in a long flowing cape. After a moment, the camera pulls back and we see that she's standing on a rocky promontory of a barren island, staring out at a mushroom-cloud explosion on the distant mainland. As her eyes grow wide at the intensity of this nuclear holocaust, we hear her saying, 'The world was ending . . . and I was watching it.'

Hell of an opening. A few minutes later, we're introduced to Prudence's island companion, Helene – another willowy babe (albeit with horn-rimmed glasses) who's married to a mad artist named Herman, who paints huge abstract canvases, depicting apocalyptic scenes of urban carnage.

'I came here to escape the material bonds of society,' he tells Helene, 'but now that society has totally vanished. So we've finally gotten our dream.'

'Yes, my love,' Helene says. 'That is true. We have gotten our dream. But there is a problem: we are going to die.'

The fourth member of this jolly quartet is a Swedish recluse named Helgor, who's doing a Walden Pond/Thoreau thing in a backward cottage on a corner of the island. Helene has the hots for Helgor, who has sworn off sex, not to mention electricity, electronically amplified sound, flush toilets, and anything that hasn't been grown in organic soil. But, upon hearing that the world is ending, he decides to stop the fornication abstinence thing, and lets himself be seduced by Helene. As they slide to the stone floor of his hovel, he tells her:

'I want to sup of your body. I want to drink your life force.'

Of course, it turns out that Mad Herman is schtupping Prudence, and that she is with child. In a brilliantly observational moment, she tells him, 'I feel a life expanding within me while death envelops everything.'

Helene finds out about Herman's adultery with Prudence, and Helgor spills the beans about screwing Helene, and there are fisticuffs between the two boys, followed by half an hour of brooding silences, followed by an eventual reconciliation, and a long-winded debate on the nature of existence, shot on a large outdoor stone patio, with the characters moving from white squares to black squares like (*duh*) figures in a chess game. As the post-nuclear fires rage on the mainland, and the toxic nuclear clouds begin to descend on the island, the quartet decide to meet their destiny head-on.

'We should not end life by suffocation,' Mad Herman argues. 'We should embrace the flames.'

With that, they all pile into a boat and head off into the inferno, with the strains of *Siegfried's Rhine Journey* escorting them into their very own *Götterdämmerung*.

Fade to Black. Credits.

When the movie was finished, I sat in my armchair for several minutes stupefied. Then I called my agent, and launched into a rant about its inherent badness. Alison finally said, 'Yeah, it's a real doozy, isn't it?'

'I can't work with this guy. I'm cancelling the trip.'

'Hang on for a moment,' she said. 'There's no reason *not* to meet Fleck. After all, it's some fun in the sun, right? More to the point, why not sell him *We Three Grunts . . .* or *Fun and Games* or whatever the hell he wants to call it? I mean, if you hate what he does with it, we can get your name taken off the credits. In the meantime, I know I can fuck him out of a lot of money. I'm going pay-or-play on this one, Dave. A cool million. And I promise you he'll pay it. Because even though we both know that registering your script under his name was a form of sweet talk, he still won't want that made public. Without us even asking, he'll pay big time to keep it quiet.'

'You really have a low opinion of human nature.'

'Hey, I'm an agent.'

After I finished talking to Alison, I called Sally. Her assistant put me on hold for around three minutes, then got back on the line, sounding tense, saying that 'something had come up' and Sally would call me back in ten minutes.

It was nearly an hour before she did ring me back. From the moment she got on the line, I knew that something was wrong.

'Bill Levy's just had a heart attack,' she said, her voice shaky.

'Jesus Christ,' I said. Levy was her boss – and the man who'd brought Sally into Fox Television. He was her corporate father figure, and one of the few professional people she felt she could trust. 'How bad is he?' I asked.

'Pretty bad. He collapsed during a planning meeting. Fortunately, there was a company nurse on the premises, and she was able to administer CPR before the ambulance came.'

'Where's he now?'

'UCLA Medical. In intensive care. Listen, everything's been thrown into chaos here by what's happened. I'm going to be home late.'

'Fine, fine,' I said. 'If there's anything I can do . . .'

But all she said was 'Got to run' and hung up.

She didn't arrive back until after midnight, looking drawn and enervated. I put my arms around her. She gently disengaged herself from my grip, and flopped on the sofa.

'He made it – just,' she said. 'But he's still in a coma, and they are worried about brain damage.'

'I'm so sorry,' I said, offering her something strong and alcoholic. But she only wanted Perrier.

'What makes this situation even shittier,' she said, 'is the fact that Stu Barker has been put in charge of Bill's division for the time being.'

This was bad news – Stu Barker was an ultra-ambitious asshole who had been gunning for Levy's job for the past year. He also didn't think much of Sally, because she was such a Levy partisan.

'So, what are you going to do?' I asked.

'What I have to do in a situation like this – draw my forces around me and keep that bastard Barker from undermining everything I've built up at Fox. And, I'm afraid, this also means that the week at Chez Fleck is definitely out for me.'

'I thought as much. I'll call Bobby now and say we can't make it.'

'But you should go.'

'With you facing a crisis like this one? No way.'

'Listen, I'm going to be working flat out for the next week. I mean, with Barker in charge of the division, the only way I'm going to keep things together is by being at the office fifteen hours a day.'

'Fine. But at least I'll be waiting home for you at night, with tea, sympathy and a martini.'

She reached over and squeezed my hand.

'That's very sweet of you. But I want you to take this trip.'

'Sally . . .'

'Listen to me. I really am better off on my own. It means I don't have to be focusing on anything else – and I can put all my energy into keeping my job. More to the point, you can't turn this opportunity down. Because, at worst, it will be a laugh . . . and a very luxurious one at that. At best, the paycheck will be huge. Given that Stu Barker would like nothing better than to push me out of the company, the money might come in handy for us, right?'

I knew that Sally was talking garbage. She was one of the most employable television executives in town. But though I tried to argue her into letting me stay, she was adamant.

'Please don't take this the wrong way,' she said.

'I'm not,' I said, trying to sound sanguine about her need to get me out of the house. 'If you want me to go to Planet Fleck, so be it.'

'Thank you,' she said, kissing me lightly on the lips. 'Listen, sorry to do this, but I've set up a late-night conference call with Lois and Peter,' she said, mentioning two of her closest Fox associates.

'No problem,' I said, getting up from the sofa. 'I'll be waiting for you in the bedroom.'

'I shouldn't be too long,' she said, picking up the phone.

But when I fell asleep two hours later, she still hadn't come to bed.

I woke at seven the next morning. She was already gone.

There was a note on the pillow beside me: 'Off to an early strategy meeting with my team. I'll call later.'

And she scrawled an 'S' at the bottom. No term of endearment. Just her initial.

An hour or so later, Bobby Barra phoned to arrange for one of Fleck's chauffeurs to pick us up tomorrow morning and bring us to Burbank Airport.

'Phil took the 767 when he left for the island on Sunday,' he said. 'So I'm afraid it's just the Gulfstream.'

'I'll live. But it looks like I'm coming alone.' And I explained Sally's career crisis at Fox.

'Hey, fine by me,' Bobby said. 'I mean, no offence, but if she has to stay behind, I'm not exactly going to be crying into my Margarita.'

Then he told me to expect the chauffeur to arrive at my door by eight tomorrow morning.

'Party, party, guy,' he said, hanging up.

I packed a small bag. Then I went to the *Selling You* production office and looked at the early assembly of the first and second episodes. Sally never called once. When I got home that night, there were no messages from her on our voice mail. I spent the evening re-reading *We Three Grunts*. I scribbled some notes about ways I would like to improve its structure, its narrative pacing – and make it a little more up to date. Using a red felt-tip pen, I started excising some of its bulkier dialogue. In screenwriting, the less you say the better you say it. Keep it economic, keep in simple, let the pictures do the talking – because the medium you're writing for is *the pictures*. And when you have pictures, who needs a lot of words?

By eleven that night, I had worked my way through half the script. Still no call from Sally. I considered ringing her cellphone. I dismissed the idea. She might interpret the call as either clingy, needy, or paternalistic (in a *why aren't you home?* sort of way). So I simply went to bed.

When the alarm went off at seven the next morning, I found another note on the pillow beside me.

'Crazy time. Got home at one last night, and I'm now running out to a six-thirty breakfast with some of the Fox legal people. Call me at eight on my cell. Oh . . . and get a suntan for me.'

This time she did scrawl *Love, S.* at the end of the note. That cheered me up. But when I rang her an hour later (as requested), she was brisk.

'This isn't a good time,' she said. 'Will you be taking your cell with you?'

'Of course.'

'I'll get back to you then.'

And she hung up. I forced myself not to be troubled by her brusqueness. Sally was a player. And this was how players behaved when things went to the mat.

A few minutes later, the doorbell rang. I found a liveried chauffeur waiting outside next to a shiny new Lincoln Town Car.

'And how are you today, sir?'

'Ready for some fun in the sun,' I said.

Four

BOBBY AND I were the only passengers on the Gulfstream. However, there were four crew: two pilots and two hostesses. The hostesses were both blonde, both in their twenties, and both looked as if they were one-time drum majorettes. They were named Cheryl and Nancy, and they both worked exclusively for 'Air Fleck,' as Bobby referred to the gentleman's fleet of planes. Before we took off, Bobby was already on the make with Cheryl:

'Do you think I might be able to get a massage en route?'

'Sure,' Cheryl said. 'I'm studying osteopathy part time.'

Bobby flashed her a sly smile. 'And say I wanted a very *localized* massage?'

Cheryl's smile tightened. Then she turned to me and said, 'Sir, would you like a drink before take-off?'

'That would be nice. Do you have any sparkling water?'

'Come on, Dave,' Bobby said, 'you've got to toast a trip like this with a little French fizz. Air Fleck only serves Cristal . . . isn't that right, dear?'

'Yes, sir,' Cheryl said. 'Cristal is the champagne on board.'

'Two glasses of Cristal then, dear,' Bobby said. 'And please . . . make them king-size.'

'Yes, sir,' she said. 'And should I ask Nancy to take your breakfast order before take-off?'

'That would work,' Bobby said.

As soon as Cheryl disappeared into the galley, Bobby turned to me and said, 'Cute ass, if you like the pert cheerleader type.'

'You're a total class act, Bobby.'

'Hey, I was just flirting.'

'You call asking for hand relief a form of flirting?'

'I didn't ask *directly*. I was being subtle.'

'You're about as subtle as a car crash. And who asks for a king-sized Cristal? This isn't Burger King, you know. Rule Number One of being a good guest, Bobby: don't try to sleep with the help.'

'Hey, Mr Hoity-Toity, you're the guest here.'

'And what does that make you, Bobby?'

'The *habitué.*'

Cheryl showed up with the two glasses of champagne. Accompanying them were small triangles of toast, dappled with black fish eggs.

'Beluga?' Bobby asked.

'It's *Iranian* Beluga, sir,' Cheryl said.

The pilot came on the tannoy, asking us to buckle up for take-off. We were seated in thick overstuffed leather armchairs, bolted to the floor, but fully swivelable. According to Bobby, this was the small Gulfstream – a mere eight seats in the forward cabin, with a small double bed, a work station, and a sofa adorning the rear cabin. The plane was being flown this morning solely for our benefit. But I wasn't complaining. I sipped my Cristal. The plane finished its taxi and came to a halt. Then it gathered up momentum and charged down the runway. Within seconds we were airborne, the San Fernando Valley disappearing beneath us.

'So what's it going to be?' Bobby asked. 'A movie or two? A little high-stakes poker? A Chateaubriand for lunch? They might even have lobster tails . . .'

'I'm going to do some work,' I said.

'You're a lot of fun.'

'I want this script in improved shape before our host sees it. Do you think he's got a secretary on the island?'

'Phil's got an entire business services division there. You want the script typed up, no problem.'

Nancy came out for our breakfast order. Bobby asked, 'Could you do a fluffy egg-white omelette with scallions and just a touch of Gruyère?'

'Sure,' Nancy said, nonplussed. Then she graced me with a smile. 'And for you, sir?'

'Just grapefruit and toast and black coffee, please.'

'Since when did you become a Mormon?' Bobby asked.

'Mormons don't drink coffee,' I said, then excused myself to work in the back cabin.

I dug out the script of *We Three Grunts,* and my red pen. I set up shop at the desk. I read through the first half, reasonably pleased with the changes I had made to date. What struck me most about the original 1993 draft was the way I needed to spell everything out – to ram home a point with a pile driver. There were decent patches of dialogue, but God, how I needed to show my cleverness, my bravado. At heart, this was nothing more than a generic heist movie. But I'd tried to disguise the fact by decorating the action with smart-assed repartee – which did nothing but call attention to itself. It oozed self-consciousness. And continuing the work I had done to date, I stripped it right back – excising vast chunks of over-explanatory dialogue and unnecessary plot points – turning it into something tougher, grittier, more sardonic . . . and definitely sharper.

I worked steadily for five hours. My only interruptions were the arrival of breakfast, and the sound of Bobby's Hugh Hefner smoothie voice placing further ludicrous orders ('I know this might be a stretch, dear . . . but could you do a banana daiquiri for me?'), or working the phones, barking orders to some minion back at Barra HQ in LA. Cheryl made the occasional appearance in the back cabin to top up my coffee cup and ask if I needed anything.

'Do you think you might be able to gag my friend?'

She smiled. 'With pleasure.'

In the forward cabin, I could hear Bobby shout into the telephone, 'Listen, you dumbshit guinea, if you don't sort out our little problem *pronto*, I'm not just going to fuck your sister, I'll fuck your mother too.'

Cheryl's smile tightened again. I said, 'You know, he's really not my friend. He's just my broker.'

'I'm sure he makes you a lot of money, sir. May I get you anything else while I'm here?'

'I'd just like to use the phone once he's off it.'

'No need to wait, sir. We've got two lines.'

She picked up the phone on the desk, punched in a code, then handed it to me.

'Just dial the area code and the number, and you'll get straight through.'

As Cheryl left the cabin, I dialled Sally's cellphone. After two rings, I was connected to her voice mail. I tried to conceal my disappointment by leaving an up-tempo message.

'Hey there, it's me at 33,000 feet. I do think we should buy ourselves a Gulfstream for Christmas. It's the only way to travel – though preferably without Bobby Barra, who's trying to win an Oscar for Best Performance by a Sleazy Male. Anyway . . . the point of this call is to see how everything is going at Fortress Fox, and also to tell you that I really wish to hell you were seated opposite me right now. I love you, darling . . . and when you've climbed out of the corporate trenches for a minute, give me a call on my cell. Later, babe . . .'

I hung up, feeling that empty feeling which always accompanies speaking to an answerphone. Then I went back to work.

Five hours later, as we were beginning our descent into Antigua, I had finished my overhaul of the script. I flicked through the changes I had made, generally pleased with its tighter narrative structure, its punchier dialogue . . . though I knew that, as soon as I read the retyped version, I'd immediately start wanting to make more changes. And if Philip Fleck really decided to film it, he would, no doubt, demand a completely new draft, which would lead on to a second draft, a polish, a third draft, another polish, the arrival of a script doctor, his draft, his polish, then a third writer brought in to beef up the action, then a fourth writer to hone plot points, then Fleck might suddenly decide to shift the entire action from Chicago to Nicaragua, and turn the entire thing into a musical about the Sandinista Revolution, replete with singing guerrillas . . .

'Mr Greta-fucking-Garbo returns,' Bobby said as I re-entered the front cabin. 'Remind me never to travel with you again.'

'Hey, work is work – and Fleck will have a new draft of the script to look at tomorrow. Anyway, from the sound of it, you were busy too. Was that an associate you were threatening?'

'Just a guy who screwed up a little deal for me.'

'Remind me to never get on the wrong side of you.'

'Hey, I don't fuck clients – and I'm using the "literal-and-figurative" definition here too.' He flashed me one of his smiles.

63

'Unless, of course, the client fucks me. But why should that happen, right?'

I smiled back. 'Why indeed?' I said.

The captain came on the tannoy, asking us to buckle up for landing. I peered out the window and saw a large swathe of blue defining the landscape below. Then we banked sharply as sea gave way to a shanty town – dozens of small grim cubed dwellings, looking like a sprawl of corrupted dice. After a moment, they vanished too – and we were descending fast through the palms, the pot-marked tarmacadam rising up to meet us, the sun incandescent, unforgiving.

We taxied to a stop far away from the main terminal building. As Cheryl opened the door and pressed the electronic button that lowered the stairs, we were hit by a rush of rank tropical heat. I noticed two men waiting for us: a heavily tanned blond guy dressed in a pilot's uniform, and an Antiguan policeman. He had an ink stamp and pad in one hand. As soon as we disembarked, the pilot said, 'Mr Barra, Mr Armitage . . . welcome to Antigua. I'm Spencer Bishop, and I'll be piloting you to Saffron Island this afternoon. But first, we need you to clear Antiguan immigration. Would you show this gentleman your passports, please?'

We handed them over to the immigration officer. He didn't bother to check our photographs or even notice whether our respective travel documents were valid. He simply stamped an entry visa on the first blank page he found, then handed them back to us. The pilot thanked the officer, and proffered his hand. As the officer shook it, I noticed that he palmed a folded American bank note. Then the pilot touched me lightly on the shoulder and pointed to a small helicopter, parked one hundred yards from the plane.

'Let's get you guys on board,' he said.

Within minutes, we were strapped into our seats, talking to each other via headsets, as the rotary blades did their loud concussing thing, and the pilot pulled down the throttle, and the airport vanished, and the blue began again. I stared out of the window at the aquamarine horizon, dazzled by its purity of color, its sheer boundlessness. As we flew closer, this fragment became more visually defined – an island around half a mile in circumference, dappled by thick palms, with a sprawling low-level house smack in the middle. I glimpsed an extended dock, against which a few boats were moored. There was a long strip of sand near the dock. And then, suddenly below us, was a circle of tarmacadam, with a large X in its centre. It took a moment or two for the pilot to manoeuvre us above it. Then he landed us right on the X with a light, but noticeable, bump.

Again, two functionaries were awaiting us – a man and a woman, both in their late twenties, both blond, and heavily tanned, and wearing the same tropical uniform – khaki shorts, white Nikes with white socks, a mid-blue polo shirt with the words *Saffron Island* discreetly monogrammed in italics. They looked like upscale camp counsellors. They were standing next to a new dark blue Land Rover Discovery. When they smiled, they showed off perfect dental work.

'Hey there, Mr Armitage,' the guy said, 'Welcome to Saffron Island.'

'And welcome back, Mr Barra,' the woman said.

'And welcome back to you too,' Bobby said. 'It's Megan, right?'

'You've got a great memory.'

'I never forget a beautiful woman.'

I cast my eyes heavenward, but said nothing.

'I'm Gary,' the guy said. 'And, as Mr Barra already said, this is Megan . . .'

'But you can call me Meg.'

'And we're going to be looking after you both during your stay here. Anything you want, anything you need, we are the people to call on.'

'Who's assigned to who?' Bobby asked.

'Well,' Gary said, 'since Meg looked after you the last time, Mr Barra, we thought that we'd let her take care of Mr Armitage during this visit.'

I glanced at Megan and Gary. Their fixed smiles betrayed nothing. Bobby pursed his lips. He looked disappointed.

'Whatever,' he said.

'So let's get your bags on board,' Gary said, moving quickly on.

'How many bags did you bring, Mr Armitage?' Megan asked me.

'Just one . . . and, please, my name is David.'

Bobby and I sat in the Land Rover – the motor running, the air conditioning already cranked up – as the two camp counsellors loaded up our bags.

'So, let me guess,' I said, 'you put the moves on Meg the last time you were here.'

Bobby shrugged. 'Hey, it comes with having a penis, right?'

'She's really the pumped pectorals type, isn't she? Did she get you in a half-nelson when you tried to grab her ass?'

'It didn't get that far . . . and can we drop this?'

'But Bobby, I love hearing about your romantic exploits. They're so touching.'

'Put it this way – I wouldn't come on to her, if I was you. She's got biceps like GI Joe.'

'Why would I want to come on to her, when I've got Sally waiting for me back home?'

'Oh, Mr Monogamous Virtue here. Mr Great Husband and Father.'

'Fuck you,' I said.

'Hey, it was a joke.'

'Sure it was.'

'Touchy, touchy.'

'Did you take lessons in being a moron, or does it just come naturally?

'Sorry if I hit a sensitive spot.'

'I am not sensitive about . . .'

'Leaving your wife and kid?' he said with a smile.

'You shithead.'

'The prosecution rests.'

Meg opened the front passenger door.

'How are you guys doing?' she asked.

'We're having our first fight,' Bobby said.

Gary climbed in the driver's seat and put the car into gear. We travelled down an unsealed road, the canopy of trees quickly closing over us. After a minute or so, I turned around and looked behind me. The little landing strip had vanished. Up ahead of us was nothing but jungle.

'Now gentlemen,' Gary said, 'I have some news. Mr Fleck is delighted you're with us, and he wants you both to have a great stay on the island. Unfortunately, however, he's had to go away for a few days . . .'

'What?' I said.

'Mr Fleck left yesterday for a few days.'

'You've got to be kidding?' Bobby said.

'No, Mr Barra – I am definitely not kidding.'

'But he knew we were coming,' Bobby said.

'Of course he did. And he regrets he had to leave on such short notice . . .'

'Did some big business thing come up?' Bobby asked.

'Not exactly,' Gary said with a slight laugh. 'But you know how keen he is on fishing. And when we got word that the marlin were biting down off the coast of St Vincent . . .'

'St Vincent?' Bobby said. 'But that's, like, a two day cruise from here.'

'More like thirty-six hours.'

'Terrific,' Bobby said. 'So, if he gets there tonight and fishes tomorrow, he won't be back for another three days.'

'I'm afraid that's about right,' Gary said. 'But Mr Fleck wants you to kick back and enjoy everything Saffron Island has to offer.'

'But we came – *at his request* – to see him,' Bobby said.

'And you will see him,' Gary said. 'In a couple of days.'

Bobby nudged me with his elbow. 'What the hell do you think of this?'

I knew what I wanted to say: '. . . *and you kept telling me you were his great friend.*' But I didn't want any more verbal fisticuffs with Bobby. So instead I just said, 'Well, if I had to choose between a writer and a marlin, I'd definitely go for the marlin.'

'Yeah, but fish don't have to worry about a client base and the current fucked-up state of the Nasdaq.'

'Now, Mr Barra – you know that our Business Services Center can patch you right into the centre of any market you want. And we can open a dedicated line for you and your clients on a 24/7 basis, should you want one. So, really, there's nothing to panic about.'

'And,' Meg interjected, 'the weather forecast for the next week is perfect. Not a hint of rain, light southerly breezes, and the mercury should hold steady at eighty-five degrees.'

'So you can keep track of the market *and* get a tan,' Gary said.

'Are you pissed off?' Bobby asked me.

Of course I was. But, once again, I decided to play it nice and temperate. So I shrugged and said, 'I guess I could use some sun.'

The Land Rover continued to bump along the jungly track. Then it came to a clearing. We parked next to an open-air shed, beneath which were three other Land Rovers and a large white transit van. I was going to ask why there was a need for four Land Rovers and a transit van on a tiny island . . . but, once again, I said nothing. Instead, I followed Meg as she led us up a small footpath, paved in chunky pebbles. After ten yards, we came to a small footbridge which traversed a large ornamental pond. I glanced down and noticed that it was loaded with a wide variety of tropical fish. Then I looked up and gasped. For there, in front of me, was the massive expanse of Chez Fleck.

From the air, it appeared to be a large timber structure. Up close, it revealed itself as an extravagant piece of modern design – a low-level sprawl of huge windows and lacquered wood. At either end of this tropical mansion were two cathedral-like towers, framed on all sides by four towering panes of glass. Between these two wing-like structures was a smaller series of V-shaped towers, each with a large picture window. We followed a wooden boardwalk to the opposite side of the house. As we turned the corner, I suppressed another gauche gasp – as a vast natural rock swimming pool had been set directly in front of the mansion. Beyond this, the blue began – as the house had a clear, unimpeded view of the Caribbean Sea.

'Good God,' I said. 'That's some view.'

'Yeah,' Bobby said. 'It's serious Fuck You.'

His cellphone started ringing. He answered it. After muttering a hello, he was instantly engaged in business.

'So what's the margin? . . . Yeah, but this time last year they were trading at twenty-nine . . . Of course I've been monitoring the Netscape guys . . . do you really think I'm going to walk you into a sucker punch? . . . you remember the market blip way back in '97 . . . February 14th, 1997, right after the Lewinsky stupidity hit the fan, and there was a minor correction for around seventy-two hours. But the long-term implications . . .'

I listened on, dazzled by Bobby's mastery of fact and figures, and the smooth delivery which he used for clients (as compared to the ferocious way he bullied minions). I noticed Gary and Meg also listening in to his consummate salesmanship. I wondered if they were thinking what I was thinking: how could such a sharp man of the marketplace turn into such a crass clown when faced with serious money? And why did he insist on playing the Neanderthal when it came to women? Then again, money and sex make fools of us all. Perhaps Bobby had decided that he didn't mind letting the world see how – when it came to his obsessions – he was positively naked in his stupidity.

He snapped shut his cellphone, then unclenched his shoulders and said, 'Never take on a dermatologist as a client. Every blip in the market is a melanoma to them. Anyway . . .' he said, nudging Gary, '. . . you heard me promise the prick an answer in ten . . .'

Gary picked up the walkie-talkie on his belt and spoke into it.

'Julie, I've got Mr Barra en route. He'll want the full Nasdaq index up on screen by the time we reach you . . . in about three minutes. Over?'

A voice crackled on the walkie-talkie's speaker. 'He's got it.'

'Lead the way,' Bobby said to Gary, then swerved his head towards me and added: 'Catch your act later, if you still deign to talk to a low-grade like me.'

As soon as they were gone, Meg said, 'Shall I show you to your room now?'

'Fine by me.'

We went inside. The main entrance hall was a long, airy corridor, with white walls and bleached wood floors. As I walked in, I found myself immediately face to face with one of the key works of twentieth century American abstract art: an arresting canvas of mathematical equations set amidst a brilliantly textured grey surface.

'Is that Mark Tobey's *Universal Field*?' I asked Meg.

'You know your art,' she said.

'I've only seen it in books. Amazing.'

'If you like art, you should check out what we call the Big Room around here.'

'Do we have the time now?'

'This is Saffron Island – there's as much time as you want.'

We turned left and walked down the corridor, past a long framed collection of classic Diane Arbus photographs. the Big Room was just that – one of the two vast, cathedral-like wings, with a forty-foot ceiling, completely clad in glass, and a massive indoor palm tree sprouting from the floor. Like everything I had seen so far, the Big Room was a testament to expensive good taste. There was a Steinway grand piano. There were long sofas and overstuffed armchairs in discreet off-white shades. There was a massive aquarium, built flush into one of the white stone walls. There was artfully subtle lighting. And there was a lot of art on the walls . . . the sort of work that you generally expected to encounter at MOMA or the Whitney or the Getty or the Art Institute of Chicago.

I moved around the room like a visitor at a museum, boggled by the work on show. Hopper. Ben Shahn. Two mid-period Philip Gustons. Man Ray. Thomas Hart Baker. Claus Oldenberg. George L.K. Morris. And a collection of Edward Steichen's landmark *Vanity Fair* photographs from the thirties.

On and on it went. There must have been at least forty works hanging on the walls of the Big Room. I couldn't even begin to fathom the amount of money expended to create such a collection.

'It's unbelievable what he's got here.'

A voice out of nowhere said:

'You should see what's on display at the other houses.'

I looked up and found myself staring at a small squat guy, in his mid forties, around five-foot-five, with long shoulder-length hair, braided into a greasy ponytail. He wore a pair of denim cut-offs, Birkenstock sandals and a tee shirt stretched over his pot

70

belly, with a picture of Jean-Luc Godard, beneath which was the quotation: 'Cinema is truth at 24 frames per second.'

'You must be Dave Armitage,' he said.

'That's me,' I said.

'Chuck Karlson,' he said, walking over and proffering his hand. I took it. It was wet to the touch. 'I'm a big fan of yours.'

'That's nice to hear.'

'Yeah – *Selling You* is, for my bucks, the best thing on television. Phil thinks so too.'

'You're a friend of his?'

'An associate, actually. I'm his film guy.'

'And what does a "film guy" do?'

'Primarily I look after his archive.'

'He's got a film archive?'

'You bet – with around 7,000 films on celluloid and another 15,000 split between video and DVD. Outside of the American Film Institute, it's the best archive in the country.'

'Let alone the Caribbean.'

Chuck smiled. 'He only keeps around 2,000 movies here on Saffron.'

'I guess with no multiplex in town . . .'

'Yeah – and, you know, Blockbuster doesn't exactly ship Pasolini movies out here.'

'You like Pasolini?'

'To me, he's a god.'

'And to Mr Fleck?'

'He's God the Father. Anyway, we've got all twelve of his films – so whenever you like, the screening room's yours.'

'Thanks,' I said, thinking that *The Gospel According to St Matthew* (the only Pasolini I'd seen) was about the last thing I wanted to watch on a Caribbean island.

'By the way, I know Phil's really looking forward to working with you.'

'That's nice.'

'If you don't mind me saying so, it's a great script.'

'Which one? His or mine?'

Another of his major smirks. 'They both have equal validity.'

That's certainly diplomatic of you, I thought, considering they're both the same.

'Listen, speaking of the script,' I said, 'I've done a bit of work on it over the past few days and was wondering if I might get it typed up.'

'No problem. I'll get Joan to drop over to your room and pick it up. See you at the movies, Dave.'

Meg now led me to my room. En route, I asked her about herself. She said that she was from Florida, and had been part of 'The Saffron Island Crew' for the past two years. She used to work on a cruise ship out of Nassau, but this was a lot more pleasant. And easy – because, by and large, the crew were the only people here.

'You mean, Mr Fleck doesn't use the island very often?' I asked.

'Only about three or four weeks a year.'

'And the rest of the time?'

'It's empty . . . though, occasionally, he might lend the island to one of his friends. But that's maybe another four weeks a year maximum. Otherwise, we've got the place to ourselves.'

'How many are you?'

'A full time staff of fourteen.'

'Good God,' I said, thinking what the annual wage bill must be like . . . especially given that the island was in use less than two months per year.

'Well, Mr Fleck's got the money,' she said.

My room was in one of the smaller V-shaped turrets that defined the centre section of the house. 'Small' was an inaccurate way of describing this loft-like space. White stone walls. Hardwood floors. Floor-to-ceiling windows, looking out directly on the water. A huge king-sized Mission bed. A large living area, with two enormous sofas. A full bar, stocked with everything upscale. A bathroom with a sunken bath tub, a sauna, and one of those showers – encased in clear plexiglass – which shot water at five different corners of the body. Above the bedroom, accessed by a circular metal staircase, was a complete office area, with all the requisite communications gadgets.

But, without question, the gadgety *coup de théâtre* was the three flat computer screens in my room. They were conveniently located on the desk, on an end table in the living room, and by the bed. Each screen was completely interactive. You touched it with your finger and it came to life, informing you that this was your very own in-room audio and video centre. I tapped the screen, and then the prompt marked *Video Library*. The letters of the alphabet were then displayed. I touched A – and a list of thirty films appeared on the screen: everything from Godard's *Alphaville* to Joseph Mankewicz's *All About Eve* to Joseph Strick's *Ulysses*. I touched *Alphaville*. Suddenly, the state-of-the-art Panasonic flat-screen television (suspended on a wall) came to life. After a second, Godard's skewed futuristic classic filled the screen. I hit the back button on the screen. The alphabet appeared again. I touched *C* and selected *Citizen Kane*. Within seconds, *Alphaville* had ended, and I was watching Welles's classic opening tracking shot – the high sequestered walls and gates, behind which lurks the vast mansion of a modern day Kubla Khan.

But Charles Foster Kane never had a toy like this on-command movie system.

A knock came at the door. When I shouted 'Come in,' Meg entered.

'Mind if I unpack your things now?' she asked.

'Thanks, but I can do that myself.'

'It's all part of the service,' she said, hoisting my bag. 'I am your butler.'

She shot me the slightest of smiles – one which just hinted at a trace of irony behind the casual, yet highly professional, facade.

'See you've figured out the movie system. Kind of nifty, isn't it?'

'Just a little. It's an amazing selection of films.'

'Mr Fleck has everything,' she said, disappearing into the adjoining dressing room with my bag. I went upstairs to the office area. I unpacked my laptop and plugged it directly into the Internet link. As Meg had promised, this fibre-optic system was just a little faster than a single exhalation of breath. Within a nanosecond, I was online and retrieving my e-mail. Among the messages from Brad Bruce and Alison was the one I was hoping for.

Darling:
It's crazy here. But I am still holding my own.
    Missing you.
    S.

I had several immediate thoughts about this e-mail. The first was: *well, at least she did make contact.* The second was: *well, at least she did say she was missing me.* And the third was: *why didn't she sign it 'love'?*

Then the rational side of me kicked in, and I reminded myself once again that she was in a major L.A.-style *sturm und drang.* And in Hollywood, a professional crisis of this ilk was immediately transformed by all involved into something approaching the siege of Stalingrad.

In other words, she was preoccupied.

There was another knock on the door. A woman in her early thirties, with short-cropped black hair and a deep tan, walked in. She was also dressed in the regulation *Saffron Island* tee shirt and shorts. Like Meg, she also looked like one of those clean-limbed, fresh-faced women who probably once did time as a sorority sister at some Big Ten University, and no doubt dated a fullback named Bud.

'Hey there, Mr Armitage,' she said. 'I'm Joan. You settling in okay?'

'Just fine.'

'Hear you've got a script for us to type up.'

'That's right,' I said, grabbing the screenplay out of my computer bag and heading downstairs to the living room. 'I'm afraid I don't have the original disk . . .'

'No worries about that. We can retype the whole thing.'

'Won't that be a lot of work?'

She shrugged. 'Things have been a little slow here recently. I could use the work.'

'You're going to have to decipher my hieroglyphics,' I said, flipping open to the third page and pointing to my numerous excisions and additions.

'I've seen worse. Anyway, you're going to be here for a few days, right?'

'So I've been told.'

'Well, if you don't mind, I'll call you if I get stuck anywhere.'

As she left, Meg came out of the dressing room, carrying two pairs of my trousers.

'These got a little crushed in your bag, so I'll get them freshly pressed. Now are you in the mood for a proper dinner or just something light?'

I glanced at my watch. It was nearly nine pm, though my brain was still four hours behind on LA time. 'Something very light, if it's no trouble . . .'

'Well, Mr Armitage . . .'

'David, please.'

'Mr Fleck likes us to use Mr with his guests. So how about a dozen oysters and a bottle of . . .'

'Gewurztraminer. But just a glass.'

'I'll get the sommelier to bring a bottle. If you don't drink it all, no big deal.'

'There's a sommelier here?'

'Every island should have one.' Another of her little smiles. 'Back in a bit with your oysters.'

Then she left.

A few minutes later, the sommelier rang. His name was Claude. He said that he was happy to help me choose a Gewurztraminer – and he had around two dozen in his cellar. I asked him to suggest one. He began an elaborate *goût-par-goût* rundown on his *choix preferés*, informing me that he especially favoured a 1986 Gisselbrecht: 'un Vin d'Alsace *exceptionnel*,' with a perfect balance of fruit and acidity.

'You know I just want a glass,' I said.

'We will still send up the bottle.'

As soon as I was off the phone, I went online, found a website for vintage wines and typed: *Gisselbrecht Gewurztraminer* 1986. A photograph of the wine in question appeared on my laptop screen, along with a detailed description, informing me that among *premier cru* Gewurztraminers, this was top of the pops.

And I could order a bottle for a mere $275 'at a *special discount price*'.

As I was beginning to discover, life on Fleck's Caribbean retreat was played according to a *money-no-object* set of rules.

I sat forward again in the desk chair and punched out a fast e-mail to Sally:

Darling:

Greetings from the nouveau riche land of Oz. This place is both wonderful and absurd. It's the high-rent version of 'Lifestyles of the Rich and Famous'. I have to admit it: the guy's got taste . . . but after just a half-hour here, I'm already thinking: there's something deeply skewed about having everything you want. Of course, just to let us know who's got the ultimate upper hand in life, Fleck is not *in situ* just at the moment. Instead, he's playing Hemingway and chasing some big white fish somewhere, leaving yours truly to cool his heels here. I don't know whether to be affronted, or to simply consider this the ultimate freebie. For the moment, I've decided to adopt the second mindset, and do useful, hyperactive things like work on my tan and catch up on my sleep. I only wish I was catching up on my sleep in bed next to you. I can be reached directly at 0704.555.8660. Please call when you manage to find a moment's break in the chariot race. Knowing you, I'm certain you've worked out a strategy that will see you through this little crisis. You're smarter than smart, after all.

I love you. And I wish you were here.

David.

I sent the e-mail. Then I picked up the phone and called my daughter in Sausalito. My ex-wife answered the phone. She was as friendly as usual.

'Oh, it's you,' she said tonelessly.

'That's right, it's me. And how are you?'

'What does that matter?'

'Look Lucy, I don't blame you for still being pissed with me . . . but isn't there a statute of limitations for this kind of thing?'

'No. And I don't like being palsy with assholes.'

'Fine, fine, have it your way. The conversation's closed. May I speak to my daughter, please?'

'No, you can't.'

'And why not?'

'Because it's Wednesday evening – and if you were a responsible parent, you would remember that, on Wednesday evening, your daughter has ballet class.'

'I *am* a responsible parent.'

'I am not even going to go there.'

'Fine by me. Now I'm going to give you a number where I'm staying in the Caribbean . . .'

'My, my, how well you treat that Princeton slut . . .'

My hand tightened around the phone.

'I'm not going to dignify that reprehensible comment with an answer. But if you want to know the truth . . .'

'Not particularly.'

'Then just take the number and ask Caitlin to call me back.'

'Why does she need to call you when you're seeing her the day after tomorrow.'

My anxiety level – already high, courtesy of this warm, cordial conversation – jumped a notch or two.

'What are you talking about?' I said. 'I'm not due a visit until two weeks from Friday.'

'Oh, don't tell me you fucking forgot . . .'

'Forgot what?'

'Forgot that, *as agreed between us*, you'd be taking Caitlin this weekend because I'm going away to a conference . . .'

Oh shit. Oh shit. Oh shit. She was right. And this was not going to be pretty.

'Hang on . . . when did we discuss this? Six, eight weeks ago?'

'Don't try to play that "*it was so long ago*" amnesia card with me.'

'But it's the truth.'

'Bullshit.'

'What can I say – except a major *mea maxima culpa*.'

'Not accepted. Anyway, a deal's a deal – so you've got to be back here in thirty-six hours.'

'Sorry, but that's not possible.'

'David – you are coming back, *as agreed.*'

'I wish I could, but . . .'

'Don't fuck with me here . . .'

'I am about five thousand miles from you. I have business to do here. I cannot leave.'

'If you don't do this . . .'

'I'm sure you can fly your sister down from Portland. Or hire a nanny for the weekend. And yes, I will pick up the tab.'

'You really are the most selfish pig in history.'

'You are entitled to your opinion, Lucy. Now here's my number out here . . .'

'We don't want your number. Because I doubt if Caitlin will want to speak with you.'

'That's for her to decide.'

'You killed her sense of security the day you walked out. And, I promise you, she'll end up hating you for it.'

I said nothing, as the phone was shaking in my hand. Finally Lucy spoke again.

'I'm really going to get you back for this.'

And she hung up.

I put down the phone. I put my head in my hands. I felt an appalling wave of guilt.

But I still wasn't going to rush back across the continent, just so Lucy could attend a conference for a day and a half. Yes, the matter had slipped my mind. But Jesus, it was nearly two months since she'd mentioned it. And it wasn't as if I had ever missed any of my designated weekends with Caitlin. On the contrary, she'd been asking to spend more time with Sally and myself in LA. So much for her *I doubt she'll want to speak with you* crap. Lucy's sense of grievance knew no frontiers. As far as she was concerned, I was Mr Bad Guy – and though I might have acted selfishly by deciding to end the marriage, she would never confront her own structural weaknesses which helped push our marriage over the edge (or, at least, that's what I was told by the therapist I saw during the divorce).

Another knock at the door. I shouted, 'Come in.' Meg arrived, wheeling in an elegant stainless steel cart. I came downstairs. My dozen oysters were accompanied by a basket of brown bread, and a small green salad. The bottle of Gewurztraminer was in a clear plexiglas cooler.

'Here it is,' she said. 'How 'bout I set it up on the balcony? You can catch the last of the sunset.'

'Sounds fine to me.'

She opened the French doors off the living room. I found myself staring at a blood orange sun turning liquid and trickling slowly into the darkened waters of the Caribbean Sea.

I slumped into a chair on the balcony and tried to block out the jumble of emotions I was feeling in the wake of that vitriol-charged phone call with Lucy. I must have been radiating stress, because as soon as she finished setting up the table, Meg said, 'You look like you could use a drink.'

'How right you are.'

As she uncorked the wine, I asked, 'What's Mr Barra been getting up to?'

'He's been on the phone non-stop. And he's been shouting all the time.'

'Please tell him I've gone to bed early tonight,' I said, thinking that I really couldn't take another dose of Bobby today.

'You've got it.'

She uncorked the wine. She poured a tiny amount into the long fluted glass.

'Off you go,' she said cheerfully.

I lifted the glass. I did all the standard operating stuff: swirling the wine, giving it a good sniff, and then letting just the smallest drop touch my tongue. Immediately I felt something close to a high-class electrical charge. It tasted so damn good.

'That really works,' I said. *But it should, at $275 a bottle.*

'Glad to hear it,' she said, filling the glass. 'Anything else I can get you?'

'Nothing at all . . . but thanks for everything.'

'Hey, it's all part of the service. Just pick up the phone anytime you need anything.'

'You're spoiling me.'

'That's the idea.'

I raised my glass. I looked out at the waning sun's final melt-down. I took a deep breath and caught that frangipani-and-eucyalptus aroma that announces life in the tropics. I sipped the absurdly expensive, absurdly wonderful wine. And I said, 'You know, I really do think I could get used to all this.'

I SLEPT LIKE the dead and woke with that curious elation which accompanies nine comatose hours of rest. Propping myself up against the pillows, I realized just how piano-wire taut I had been ever since my breakthrough and its resulting cataclysms. Success is supposed to simplify your life. Inevitably, it complicates it further – and perhaps we need the complications, the intrigues, the fresh strivings for even greater success. Once we've achieved what we've always wanted, we suddenly discover a new need, a new sense of *something lacking*. And so we travail on, in search of this new accomplishment, this new change-of-life, in the hope that, this time, the sense of contentment will be permanent . . . even if it means upending everything else we've built up over the years.

But then, when you've reached this new plateau of achievement you find yourself wondering: can you sustain all this now? Might it slip away from you? Or – worse yet – might you tire of it all, and discover that what you had in the past was actually what you wanted all along?

I snapped out of my melancholic reverie, reminding myself that – in the words of that well-known Hollywood insider, Marcus Aurelius – change is nature's delight. And most guys I know (especially writers) would sell their mothers to be in my position right now. Particularly when I was able to press a button to raise a blind, behind which lay the azure blue of a Caribbean morning. Or when I could lift the phone and have anything I wanted sent to my room.

And then there was the pleasant discovery that Bobby Barra had suddenly left town in a hurry.

I found out this little piece of information when I finally forced myself out of bed to use the bathroom, and noticed an envelope pushed under my door. I opened it and discovered the following scrawled note:

Asshole:
I was going to ring you last night, but Meg said you'd

already gone to bed with your teddy bear. Anyway, five minutes after we arrived yesterday word came from Wall Street that the chairman of some new armaments outfit due to IPO next week had just been indicted by the Fed for everything from embezzlement and fraud to sodomizing a dachshund. Anyway, as luck would have it, my associates and I have around $30 million riding on this IPO, which means that I have to hightail it to New York right away and play fireman before the entire fucking deal goes up in smoke.

Which, in turn, means that you will be denied my company for the next couple of days. I'm certain you're heartbroken, bereft, and popping champagne corks as you read this. We seem to have gotten on each other's wick yesterday. Of course, you were totally in the wrong. Of course, I also hope that we're still friends.

Enjoy the island. You're a complete jerk if you don't. I'll try to get back here in a couple of days – by which time Herr Host should be back with all the minnows he's snagged.

Go easy. You really do look like shit – so a couple of days in the sun should make you look less shitty.

Later,
Bobby

I couldn't help but smile. Bobby really knew how to reel in his friends just when they were about to permanently write him off.

Breakfast arrived, accompanied by a bottle of Cristal 1991.

'Drink as much or as little as you want,' said Meg, setting up the plates on my balcony.

I actually drank two glasses, and ate the plate of tropical fruit, and sampled the basket of exotic muffins, and drank the coffee. I listened to Grieg's Lyric Pieces for Piano as I ate, discovering that there was a discreet speaker built into the balcony wall. The sun was at full wattage. The mercury seemed to be in the mid-eighties. And, bar a quick check of my e-mail, there was nothing on the agenda for today – except sitting in the sun.

I regretted my decision to go online. Because the morning's

communiqués from cyberspace were anything but cheery. First came a strident missive from Sally:

David

I was surprised and hurt by your description of my current imbroglio at Fox as nothing more than a 'little crisis'. I am fighting for my professional life right now, and what I need more than anything is your support. Instead, you were patronizing, and I was so incredibly disappointed by your response. I so want to know that I have your confidence and your love.

I have to fly to New York this morning. Don't try to buzz me, but do send me an e-mail. I want to believe that this is all just a bad call on your part.

Sally

I read her e-mail twice, stunned by her complete misinterpretation of my words. I went into my AOL filing cabinet and reread my e-mail of the previous night, trying to figure out how the hell she could have taken offence. After all, all I'd written was:

Knowing you, I'm certain you've worked out a strategy that will see you through this little crisis. You're smarter than smart, after all . . .

Oh, I get it. She hated the idea that I would consider her battle royal to be *little* – whereas my attempted implication was that, in the great scheme of things, this crisis would eventually seem like small beer.

Jesus Christ, talk about touchy. But I was in a no-win position here, and I knew it. To date, Sally and I had had that rare thing: a relationship free of misunderstandings. I certainly didn't want this to be the first. So, knowing that she would not react well if I told her, 'You totally misread my meaning', I decided it was best to fall on my sword. Because if there was one thing that many long years of marriage had taught me, it was this: if you want to sweeten the atmosphere after a disagreement, it's always best to admit you were wrong . . . even if you think you were right.

So I clicked on the Reply button and wrote:

Darling:

The last thing in the world I want to do is upset you. The last thing in the world I think is that anything you do is little. All I meant was you're so brilliant at anything you tackle that this crisis – though large right now – would eventually be regarded in the future as small, because you'll manage to work it out so well. My fault was not expressing this sentiment clearly. I realize I've hurt you. And I now feel awful.

You know I think you are wonderful. You know you have my complete love and support for everything and anything you do. I am so damn sorry that my inappropriate choice of words sparked this misunderstanding. Please forgive me.

I love you.

David.

All right, I was grovelling a bit. But I knew that, for all her professional stridency, Sally had a most permeable ego – and one which needed constant bolstering. More to the point, at this early stage of our relationship, stability was all. I repeated my mantra of the past few days: *She's under extreme pressure. Asking her the time of day right now would probably be misinterpreted. But she will calm down when the situation calms down.*

Or, at least, that's what I was banking on.

Once I dispatched that e-mail, I turned to the next one. It was from Lucy, which essentially was straight out of the 'Fuck You, Strong Letter Follows' school of communication:

David:

You will be pleased to know that Caitlin was in floods of tears yesterday when I told her that you wouldn't be coming this weekend. Congratulations. You've broken her heart again.

I have managed to convince Marge to fly down from Portland to look after Caitlin for the two nights I will be away. However, she could only find a Business Class ticket at the last moment, and she must also put Dido and Aeneas in the local cattery for the weekend – and the total cost, including airfare, comes to $803.45. I will expect a check from you imminently.

I think your behavior on this occasion underlines everything I've felt about you since you became acquainted with that bitch goddess called success: you are completely motivated by self-interest. And what I said to you last night on the phone still holds: I will get you back for this.

Lucy.

Instantly I reached for the phone and punched in some numbers. I glanced at my watch. 10.14am in the islands. 7.14am on the coast. With any luck, Caitlin wouldn't have left for school yet.

My luck held. Better still, my daughter answered herself. And she sounded thrilled to speak to me.

'Daddy!' she said happily.

'Hey kiddo,' I said. 'Everything okay?'

'I'm going to be an angel in our Easter play at school.'

'You're already an angel.'

'I'm not an angel. I'm Caitlin Armitage.'

I laughed.

'I'm sorry I'm not coming this weekend.'

'But this weekend Auntie Marge is coming to stay with me. But her cats have to go to a cat hotel.'

'So you're not angry at me?'

'You're coming next week, right?'

'Without fail, Caitlin. I promise.'

'And can I stay in your hotel with you?'

'Absolutely. We'll do whatever you want all weekend.'

'And will you bring me a present?'

'I promise. Now can I talk to Mommy?'

'Okay . . . but as long as you don't fight.'

I sucked in my breath.

'We'll try not to, sweetie.'

'I miss you, Daddy.'

'I miss you too.'

A pause. Then I could hear the phone being handed over. There was a long silence, which Lucy finally broke.

'So, what do you want to talk about?' she asked.

'She really sounded devastated, Lucy. I mean, totally gutted.'

'I have nothing to say to you . . .'

'Fine by me. I don't really want to talk to you either. But don't you ever try to lie to me about her emotional state again. And I warn you, if you try to turn her against me . . .'

The line went dead as Lucy slammed down the phone. So much for a mature, adult exchange of views. But, at least, I did feel so damn relieved that Caitlin hadn't at all been distressed by my inability to make it up to see her this weekend. The issue of Aunt Marge and her $803 weekend tariff was another matter. Marge was a circumferentially challenged New Age goof who lived by herself with her beloved cats and her crystals and her recordings of Nepalese goat chants in her one-bedroom ashram. I will say this for her – she did have a good heart. And she adored her only niece, which made me happy. But eight hundred bucks to cart her size 42 waist down to San Francisco . . . not to mention providing five-star accommodation for her precious feline friends (who the hell christens a pair of cats 'Dido and Aeneas'?). Anyway, I knew that, like it or not, I'd have to fork over the dough – just as I also knew that Swami Marge was probably going to pocket half the $800. But I wasn't going to argue. I had already effectively won the argument with Lucy. Just to hear Caitlin tell me she missed me wiped out all of the morning's accumulated angst, and put me in a good mood again. And now I had an entire Caribbean island to myself.

I picked up the phone. I asked if a newspaper might be available. I was informed that the *New York Times* had just arrived by helicopter. 'Please send it on up.' I touched the audio/video screen. I went to the music library. I chose some piano sonatas by Mozart. The paper arrived. Meg set up a sunbed for me on the balcony. She disappeared into the bathroom and re-emerged with six different brands of sun cream, covering all the potential burn factors. She refilled my champagne glass. She told me to call when I wanted lunch.

I read the paper. I listened to the Mozart. I toasted gently in the sun. After an hour, I decided it was time for a swim. I picked up the phone. I was connected with Gary.

'Hey there, Mr Armitage. Having a good day in paradise?'

'Not bad at all. I was just wondering, is there a specific place for swimming on the island? Besides the pool, that is?'

'Well, we've got a great little beach. But if you were in the mood for snorkelling . . .'

Twenty minutes later, I was aboard the *Truffaut* (that's right, like the French director) – a forty-foot Cabin Cruiser, with a crew of five. We steamed along for around thirty minutes until we came to a coral reef near an archipelago of tiny islands. Two of the crew helped me into a wetsuit ('It's a little chilly in the water today,' one of them explained), then kitted me out with flippers, mask and snorkel. One of the crew was also dressed in scuba gear.

'Dennis here is going to guide you around the reef,' Gary told me.

'Thanks, but there's really no need,' I said.

'Well, Mr Fleck kind of insists that guests never swim alone. Anyway, it's all part of the service.'

That was an expression I heard over and over again on Saffron Island. *It's all part of the service.* Having my very own swim-along guide to the coral reefs was all part of the service. Having an entire four man crew looking after me on the Cabin Cruiser was all part of the service. So too was the shelled lobster they served me (and me alone) on board the boat, accompanied by a Chablis *premier cru*. When we were back on dry land later that afternoon, and I asked if they had this week's copy of the *New Yorker* on hand, they dispatched the helicopter to Antigua to buy a copy for me (even though I strenuously attempted to persuade them not to go to all that trouble – *and expense!* – for one damn magazine). But, once again, I was told that it was *all part of the service*.

I returned to my room. Laurence, the island's chef, called me, and asked what I would like for dinner. When I asked him to suggest something, he simply said: 'Anything you want.'

'Anything?'

'Just about.'

'Suggest something.'

'Well, my specialty is Pacific Rim cuisine. And since we have plenty of fresh fish . . .'

'I'll leave it up to you.'

Minutes later, Joan called from Business Affairs. She was half-way through my script, and had around ten queries regarding my appalling handwriting. We went through them all. Then she told me that the script would be retyped by midday tomorrow, as Mr Fleck was due back in the late afternoon – and as soon as he heard that I had revised the screenplay, he'd want to read it immediately.

'But won't you be up half the night typing?' I asked.

'All part of the service,' she said, adding that, with my permission, she'd have a copy of the newly revised script brought in with my breakfast tomorrow. If I could read it through, she could make any amendments later that morning.

I stretched out on the bed. I nodded off. When I came to, an hour had slipped by . . . and a note had been slipped under my door. I went to retrieve it.

Dear Mr Armitage:

We didn't want to disturb you, but outside your door you'll find the copy of the *New Yorker* you requested, as well as the catalogue for the island's film library. We thought you might like to set up a screening of something tonight. If so, give me a call at extension 16. Also – when it suits you, could you please call Claude the sommelier. He wants to discuss your wine choice for dinner tonight. You can also tell him when you'd like to eat. The kitchen is completely flexible on this matter. Just let them know.

Once again, it's a pleasure having you with us. And, as I said last night, I really do hope to see you at the movies . . .

Best

Chuck

I opened the door. I collected the film catalogue and the copy of the *New Yorker* which had been airlifted in at my request. I flopped back on the bed, wondering how they knew that I was napping –

and therefore shouldn't be disturbed. Was the room bugged? Was there a hidden camera somewhere? Or was I just being paranoid? After all, maybe they simply deduced that, after a strenuous, workaholic day in the sun, I needed a little siesta. Maybe I was over-reacting to all the attention I was being paid.

An old literary anecdote suddenly came to mind: Hemingway and Fitzgerald sitting in a Paris café, watching a bunch of swanky folks sauntering by. 'You know, Ernest,' Fitzgerald said grandly, 'the rich are different from you and me.' To which Hemingway gruffly replied: 'Yeah – they've got more money.'

But now I realized what that money actually bought them was a *cordon sanitaire*, within which you could fend off all the tedious mundanities with which the rest of the world had to grapple. Of course, it gave you power as well – but ultimately, its dominion was to be found in how it separated you from the way everyone else lived their lives. *$20 billion.* I still kept trying to grapple with that figure – and with the statistic (quoted to me, naturally, by Bobby) that Fleck's weekly interest from his fortune was around $2 million . . . and that was after tax. Without touching a penny of his fortune, he had a net income of around $100 million per annum to play with. What a complete absurdity. $2 million a week as spending money. Did Fleck remember what it was like to worry about making the rent? Or having to scramble about to pay the phone bill? Or putting up with a ten-year-old car which never shifted into fourth gear, because you couldn't afford to get the busted transmission fixed?

Did he have any sort of aspirations . . . when all his earthly wants had been already met? And how did a lack of material ambition alter one's world view? Did you concentrate on the more cerebral things in life, aspiring to great thoughts and deeds? Maybe you became a latter-day philosopher king, a Medici Prince? Or did you turn into a Borgia Pope?

I was becoming pampered after just one day at Chez Fleck. And – dare I say it – I was liking it. My latent entitlement complex was coming to the fore – and I was rapidly accepting the idea that there was an entire staff on this island ready to meet just about any request I made. On the boat, Gary told me if I felt like going to

Antigua for the day, he'd be happy to arrange a trip on the chopper. Or, for that matter, if I needed to go farther afield, the Gulfstream was sitting idle at Antigua Airport, and could be summoned whenever required.

'That's very kind of you,' I said. 'But I think I'll just stay here and kick back.'

And kick back I most certainly did. That night after the chef's exquisite Pacific Rim-style bouillabaisse (accompanied by an equally astonishing Au Bon Climat Chardonnay) I sat alone in the cinema and watched a double bill of two classic Fritz Lang films: *Beyond a Reasonable Doubt* and *The Big Heat*. Instead of popcorn, Meg popped in occasionally with a tray of Belgian chocolates and a 1985 Bas Armagnac. Afterwards, Chuck came into the screening room and went into a long spiel about Fritz Lang's adventures in Hollywood. He was so damn knowledgeable regarding just about everything on celluloid that I encouraged him to join me in an Armagnac and tell me a bit about himself. It seemed he'd first met Philip Fleck when they were both students together at NYU back in the early seventies.

'This was way, *way* before Phil was anything like rich. I mean, I knew his dad owned this paper-packaging place back in Wisconsin – but mainly, he was just another guy who wanted to direct, living in a crappy apartment on 11th and 1st Avenue. He spent his free time at the Bleecker Street Cinema or the Thalia or the New Yorker, or any of those other long-vanished Manhattan revival houses. That's how Phil and I became friends – we kept running into each other at these little cinemas, and we thought nothing of watching four films a day.

'Anyway, Phil was always determined to do the *auteur* thing, whereas my big dream was simply to run my very own cinema, and maybe get the occasional article into some fancy European film magazine like *Sight and Sound* or *Cahiers du Cinema*. Then, during our second year at NYU, Phil's dad died, and he had to head back to Milwaukee to run the family business. We lost contact with each other completely, though I certainly knew what was going on with him – because when he made his first cool billion by taking the paper company public, it was all over the papers. And then, when he pulled off all those investment coups and became . . . well, *Philip Fleck* . . . I couldn't get over it. My old cinephile pal, now a multi-billionaire.

'Then, one day, out of the blue, I get this phone call from Phil himself. He'd tracked me down to Austin where I was, like, the assistant film archivist at U Texas. Not a bad job, even though I was only making about twenty-seven grand a year. I couldn't believe it was him on the phone.

'"How the hell did you find me?",' I asked him.

'"I've got people who do that sort of stuff for me," he said. And then he got right to the point: he wanted to create his very own film archive . . . the biggest private one in America . . . and he wanted me to run it for him. Before he even told me what he was going to pay me, I accepted. I mean, this was the chance of a life-time – to create a great archive . . . and for one of my best buddies.'

'So now you go where he goes?'

'You've got it in one, pal. The chief archive is at a warehouse near his place in San Francisco, but he's also got divisions of it at each of his other houses. I'm in charge of a team of five who run the main archive, but I also travel with him wherever he goes, so he can have me on tap whenever he wants me. He takes film very seriously, Phil.'

I bet he does. Because you've got to be an extreme movie buff to employ your very own full-time archivist to cart along behind you, just in case you get a late-night craving for an early Antonioni, or simply must talk about Eisenstein's theory of montage while watching the sun set over the Saffron Island palm trees.

'Sounds like a great job,' I said.

'The best,' Chuck said.

I had another seamless night's sleep – a true sign that, after just a day here, I really was beginning to unwind. I didn't set an alarm clock or book a wake-up call. I simply woke when I woke – which was close to eleven am again, and discovered another note shoved under my door.

Dear Mr Armitage

I hope you slept really well. Just to let you know that we heard from Mr Fleck this morning. He sends you his best wishes, and his regrets that he is going to be delayed for another three days. But he will definitely be back here on Monday morning, and hopes you will continue to enjoy the run of the island until then. He said, should you want to do anything, go anywhere in particular, set up any activities of any kind, we should accommodate you.

In other words, Mr Armitage, pick up the phone and phone me whenever. We're at your service.

Hope we can make this another great day for you in paradise.

Best

Gary

So the marlin were biting and Philip Fleck had decided that I still wasn't as important as a bunch of fish. For some strange reason, I didn't care. If he wanted to keep me waiting, so be it.

Before I tackled such demanding things as deciding what to order for breakfast, I steeled myself for a brief encounter with my e-mail. But this morning's communiqués didn't bring grief. On the contrary, there was a most reconciliatory e-mail from Sally:

Darling

Apologies, apologies. In the midst of battle, I forgot who my true ally was – to the point where I was feeling irascible about everything. Thank you for your wonderful e-mail. Thank you even more for understanding.

I'm in New York, billeted at the Pierre . . . which isn't exactly the worst address imaginable. I came here at the behest of Stu Barker, who needed to go to New York to meet some of the major suits at Fox's corporate HQ. And he wanted me to be there, to discuss our planned autumn slate. Anyway, we flew domestic (he shrewdly didn't want to come across like some big swinging arriviste by insisting on a company jet the moment he stepped into Levy's shoes). All the way to New York, he couldn't have been more charming – a complete *volte face*. And he told me that he really wanted to work with me, really needed me on his team – and he wanted to put the years of enmity behind us. 'My *mishegas* was with Levy, not you,' he told me.

Anyway, we've got the big Fox meeting a couple of hours from now. Naturally, I'm anxious – because (to be blunt about it) it's important that I shine – both in front of the big boys and my new boss. I wish you were here to hug me (and do other things as well . . . but I won't get crude in cyberspace). I'll try to call later today, but I think we're going to fly back to the Coast right after the meeting. I hope you're getting a tan for the two of us. Fleck Island sounds amazing.

I love you.
Sally

Well, that was an improvement. Obviously, Stu Barker turning palsy-walsy also improved her spirits – but there's nothing like an apology from the woman you love to kick off the morning on a high note.

But there was even better news to come – because while I was online, the New Mail prompt began to flash on my screen. I switched over and found the following message from Alison:

Hey, Superstar
Hope you're pleasantly sunstruck and lolling in a hammock right now – because I've got some major good news:
You've just been nominated for an Emmy.
God help all of us who will now have to contend with your even more inflated ego (joke).
I'm thrilled for you, David. I'm also thrilled for me, because I know I can jack up your fee for the next series by 25 per cent. Which, if you do the math . . .
To quote King Lear, you've done good, fella. Can I be your date for the awards . . . or will Sally throw a hissy?
Love
Alison

By the end of the day, I was pleasantly delirious from all the congratulations I'd received. Brad Bruce rang me on the island, telling me how delighted the entire *Selling You* team was for me . . . even though they were still rather pissed at the Emmy people for making me the show's one nomination. The head of FRT comedy – Ned Sinclair – also rang. Ditto two of the actors. And I received congratulatory e-mails from around a dozen friends and associates in our so-called industry.

Best of all, Sally ducked out of her meeting in New York to phone me.

'Halfway through the meeting, an assistant to one of the Fox guys came in with a list of the Emmy nominations. Of course, the suits immediately pored over it, to see how many nominations the network received. Then, one of them looked up at me and said: "Isn't your boyfriend David Armitage?" And that's when he told me. I nearly screamed. I am so damn proud of you. And I have to tell you, it also made me look pretty damn good in front of the big boys.'

'How's it going in there?'

'I can't really talk right now . . . but, by and large, we're winning.'

We? As in Sally and the delightful Stu Barker – the guy she once described as the Heinrich Himmler of television comedy?

'Sounds like the two of you have really bonded,' I said.

'I still don't trust him whatsoever,' she said in a whisper. 'But, at the same time, it's better to have him on my side than aiming his tactical nukes in my direction. Anyway, I don't want to bore you with office politics . . .'

'You never bore me, my love.'

'And you are the sweetest, most talented man alive.'

'Now I really will get a swelled head.'

'Do. You deserve it.'

'Listen,' I said, 'Mein Host is still big-fish hunting in the adjacent islands, and he won't be back until Monday. But I've been given carte blanche on the island, which means that I could actually get them to send the Gulfstream to New York to pick you up and bring you back down here.'

'Oh God, I'd love to, sweetheart . . . but I've got to go back to

LA with Stu. It's kind of critical that I keep this bonding thing going. And he wants to do some serious planning stuff with me at the office on Sunday.'

'I see,' I said.

'If it hadn't been for this crisis at work, you know I'd be there with you right now.'

'I do understand.'

'Good,' she said. Anyway, I just wanted to say how fantastic your news is . . . and that I love you . . . and that I really do have to get back to this meeting. I'll call you tomorrow when I'm home.'

And before I had a chance to say goodbye myself, the line went dead. My five-minute window with Sally had closed.

My insecurity was quickly subdued by another night of being waited on, and by drinking an absurdly good Morgon '75, and by watching another double feature (Billy Wilder's *Ace in the Hole* and Kubrick's *The Killing*), and by being presented with a cake (personally designed by the island's pastry chef) in the shape of an Emmy Award.

'How did you know about my nomination?' I asked Gary when he brought the cake into the screening room, accompanied by six of the staff.

'Hey, news travels fast.'

This was a world where everything was known about you, where all requests were granted, where no detail was considered too small. You received exactly what you wanted, when you wanted it. In the process, you became the walking equivalent of a detached retina – blinded to external realities.

Not that I minded being a tourist in such a rarefied realm. But though I vowed not to do any work on the island, when Joan from Business Affairs showed up with my freshly typed script, I found myself quickly sprawled in the hammock on my balcony, red pen in hand. The new version was around eight pages shorter. Its pace was brisk, jazzy. The dialogue was snappier – and less self-knowing. The plot points were hit with ease. But – on a second reading – I found much of the third act now felt contrived: the aftermath of the robbery and the way all involved turned on each other seemed just a little *by the book*. So, over the course of the weekend, I redrafted the entire final thirty-one pages – and fell into the self-absorbed chasm of work. Despite the continued gorgeous weather, I locked myself in my room for all but three hours a day, and finished the job by six pm Sunday night. Joan from Business Affairs showed up shortly thereafter, and collected the forty or so pages of yellow legal foolscap upon which I had drafted the reworked Act Three. I celebrated with a slug of champagne. I spent an hour lolling in a hot tub. Then I dined on soft-shell crab and drank half a bottle of some wonderful New Zealand Sauvignon Blanc. Around ten that night, Joan showed up with the retyped pages.

'You'll have them back by midnight,' I said.

'Thank you, sir.'

I delivered the pages by the deadline required and fell into bed. I slept late. The newly bound screenplay arrived with breakfast, along with a note:

'We've just heard from Mr Fleck. He's received your screenplay and he's planning to read it as soon as possible. Unfortunately, he is again delayed at sea, but will be returning on Wednesday morning, and looks forward to seeing you then.'

My first reaction to this missive was a simple one: *Go fuck yourself, pal. I'm not going to sit around here, waiting for you to grace me with your presence.* But when I called Sally on her cellphone in LA and told her that Fleck was yanking my chain by delaying his return, she said, 'What do you expect? The guy can do what he wants. So, of course, he *will* do what he wants. Anyway, my love, you are just the writer . . .'

'Hey, thanks a lot.'

'Come on, you know how the food chain works. The guy might be an amateur, but he's still got the money. And that makes him king of the hill . . .'

'Whereas I'm the serf in this scenario.'

'Hey, if you're that pissed at the guy, throw a tantrum and demand the Gulfstream back to LA . . . but don't expect to see me for the next three nights, as I'm up paying a house call on our affiliates in San Francisco, Portland and Seattle.'

'When did that come up?'

'Yesterday evening. Stu decided we should go on a little inspection tour of our leading Pacific markets.'

'You and Stu seem to have *really* bonded.'

'I think I've won him over, if that's what you mean.'

That's not what I meant – but I didn't want to press the issue for fear of sounding possessed by the proverbial green-eyed monster. But Sally knew exactly what I was talking about.

'Do I discern a hint of jealousy in your voice?' she asked.

'Hardly.'

'You know why I have to schmooze this guy, don't you?'

'Of course, of course . . .'

'You know I am trying to keep the barbarians from the gate, right?'

'I know . . .'

'. . . and you should also know that I am incredibly in love with you, and wouldn't dream of –'

'All right, all right . . . Apologies.'

'Accepted,' she said crisply. 'And I've got to get back to this meeting. Talk to you later.'

And she hung up.

Jerk. Jerk. Jerk. *You and Stu seem to have really bonded.* What a brilliant comment. Now you'll have to do a little bit of extracurricular grovelling to keep her happy.

I picked up the phone and called Meg. I asked about sending a bouquet of flowers to LA. No problem, she told me. And no, I didn't need to give her a credit card number: 'We'll be happy to take care of that for you.' Did I have any preference? No – just something stylish. And the message on the card? I needed something reconcilatory and fawning, but not too deferential, so I decided upon:

You are the best thing that ever happened to me. I love you.

Meg assured me that the flowers would be delivered to Sally's office within the hour. Sure enough, ninety minutes later, an e-mail arrived from Ms Birmingham:

Now that's what I call a stylish apology. Love you too. But try to lighten up, eh?

Sally

I attempted to follow her advice. I called Gary and arranged for a day of sailing around a small nearby archipelago of islands. Fleck's Cabin Cruiser was crewed up for this voyage. Scuba gear was also onboard in case I wanted to go diving. And the assistant chef came along to whip up lunch. They also rigged a hammock between the masts, upon which I napped for an hour. When I woke to the offer of a cappuccino (instantly accepted), I was also handed a print-out of an e-mail from Chuck-the-Movie-Guy:

Hey, Mr Armitage!

Hope you've not got anything planned tonight, because I've just heard from Mr Fleck, and he wants me to set up a screening of a very special film for you this evening. Could you let me know what time would suit, and I'll have the popcorn ready.

When I said to the yacht's steward that I'd like to speak with Chuck personally, he patched me in on the ship-to-shore telephone.

'So what's the movie?' I asked him.

'Sorry, Mr Armitage – but that's a surprise. Mr Fleck's orders.'

So I presented myself at the screening room at 9pm that night. I sank into one of the overstuffed leather armchairs, balancing a Waterford Crystal bowl of popcorn between my legs. The lights went down – and the projector flickered into life. The soundtrack played a lush, 1940s recording of *These Foolish Things*, then the screen was filled with a title card in Italian, announcing that I was about to sit through Pier Paolo Pasolini's *Salo – The 120 Days of Sodom*.

Of course, I'd heard about Pasolini's infamous last movie – a postwar reworking of the Marquis de Sade's deranged novel. But I'd never seen it. Because after its initial screenings during the mid-seventies, the film was banned just about everywhere in the States . . . including New York. And when you get banned in

New York, you know you've concocted something that's just a little too hot to handle.

Within about twenty minutes, I understood why the New York authorities had a few moral qualms about this movie. Set in the Fascist republic of Salo (created by Mussolini during his last stand at the end of the war), the movie kicked off with four Italian aristocrats (of largely seedy demeanour) agreeing to marry each other's daughters. This was the mildest of moral transgressions instigated by this quartet – because they were soon scouring the northern Italian countryside for young nubile adolescent boys and girls, who'd been rounded up for them by fascist guards. Their victims were then transported to a stately home where their captors announced that they were now living in a realm above the law – a place where they would be required to participate in an orgy every night, and where anyone caught in a religious act would be put to death.

And so, the aristos began to have their way with their victims. They buggered boys and staged a mock wedding between a virginal girl and one of the adolescent boys, forcing the couple to consummate the 'marriage' in front of them. But just when the guy was about to penetrate his bride, the aristos rushed forward, deflowering these children themselves.

It got worse. During one 'orgy', the chief aristo defecated on the floor, then insisted that the child bride from the previous scene eat his faeces. Believing that everybody should join the party, they forced all their captives to defecate into bedpans and then served up a banquet of turds on fine china. But just when I started imagining that things couldn't turn even more warped, they tortured and annihilated all their victims in the courtyard of the stately home – gouging out eyeballs, garrotting a young woman, burning another's breasts with a candle, cutting off tongues. And as the strains of *These Foolish Things* returned to the soundtrack, two fascist male guards begin to slow-dance with each other.

Fade to black. Final credits.

As the lights came up, I found myself in an actual state of shock. *Salo* wasn't just *out there* . . . it was completely *beyond there*. What disturbed me even more was that this was not some cheap-ass snuff movie, made by a couple of low-lifes for five thousand bucks in a San Fernando Valley warehouse. Pasolini had been an ultra-sophisticated, ultra-serious director. And *Salo* was an ultra-serious exploration of totalitarianism, taken to the outer limits of taste. I had just borne witness to the worst imaginable excesses of human behavior, while sitting in a lushly appointed screening room on a private Caribbean island. And I couldn't help but wonder: *what the fuck was Philip Fleck trying to tell me?*

But before I could come to grips with this, I heard a voice behind me.

'You could probably use a drink after that.'

I turned around and found myself staring at a woman in her early thirties – attractive in a severe New England sort of way, with horn-rimmed glasses and long brown hair pulled up in a bun.

'I think I need a very strong drink,' I said. 'That was . . .'

'Horrendous? Appalling? Nauseating? Abominable? Or maybe just good old-fashioned gross?

'All the above.'

'Sorry about that. But, I'm afraid, that's my husband's idea of a joke.'

I was immediately on my feet, my hand outstretched.

'So sorry I didn't recognize you. I'm . . .'

'I know who you are, David,' she said, proffering me a small smile. 'And I'm Martha Fleck.'

Six

'SO . . . WHAT'S IT like being talented?'

'Sorry?' I said, taken slightly aback.

Martha Fleck smiled at me and said, 'It's just a question.'

'A very direct question.'

'Really? I thought it was a rather nice question.'

'I'm not particularly talented.'

'If you say so,' she said with another smile.

'But it's the truth.'

'Well, modesty is an admirable thing. But the one thing I know about writers is that they're normally a mixture of doubt and arrogance. But the arrogance usually wins out.'

'Are you saying that I'm arrogant?'

'Hardly,' she said, shooting me another smile. 'Then again, anyone who gets up in the morning and faces a blank screen needs a fantastic sense of his own self-importance. Drink? I'm certain you need one after watching *Salo* . . . though my husband considers it to be a flat-out masterpiece. Then again, he did make *The Last Chance*. I presume you've seen it?'

'Uh, yes. Very interesting.'

'How diplomatic of you.'

'It's good to be diplomatic.'

'But it makes for less-than-lively conversation.'

I said nothing.

'Come on, David. It's time to play *To Tell the Truth*. What did you really think of Philip's movie?'

'Not the . . . uh . . . best thing I've ever seen.'

'You can do better than that.'

I scanned her face for a sign. But all I saw was that amused smile. I said:

'Okay, if you want the truth, I thought it was pretentious crap.'

'Bravo. And now you get that drink.'

She reached down and touched a small button on the side of her chair. We were sitting in the 'great room' of the house, having adjourned there at her suggestion. She was seated underneath a late Rothko – two large merging squares of black offset by a thin, centrally positioned crease of orange; a slight hint of dawn promise amidst all the darkness.

'Are you a Rothko fan?' she asked me.

'Yes.'

'So's Philip. Which is why he had to own eight of them.'

'That's a lot of Rothkos.'

'And a lot of money – around $74 million for the set.'

'An impressive sum.'

'Pocket money.'

Again another of her little pauses, in which she watched me watching her. Yet her tone was constantly light and coy. Much to my surprise, I was finding her seriously attractive.

Gary arrived.

'Nice to have you back, Mrs Fleck. How was New York?'

'Fun.' She turned to me. 'Shall we do some serious drinking, David?'

'Well . . .'

'I'll take that as a yes. How many brands of vodka do we keep, Gary?'

'Thirty-six, Mrs Fleck.'

'Thirty-six vodkas. Isn't that droll, David?'

'Well, it is a lot of vodkas.'

She turned back to the help. 'So Gary, reveal all: what is the ultra-supreme of all our supreme vodkas?'

'We have a triple-filtered Stoli Gold from 1953.'

'Let me guess – it was Stalin's reserve stock.'

'I can't vouch for that, Mrs Fleck. But it is supposed to be quite remarkable.'

'Then please serve it up . . . with a little Beluga on the side.'

Gary gave a slight bow of the head, then left.

'You weren't on the boat with your husband, Mrs Fleck?' I asked.

'My name is Martha . . . and as I've never had an affinity with Hemingway, I saw no need to spend several days at sea, chasing whatever big fish Philip was after.'

'So New York was a business trip?'

102

'I really *am* impressed with your diplomacy, David. Because when your husband is worth $20 billion, most people wouldn't expect you to have any work whatsoever. But yes, I was in New York to meet with the board of a little foundation I run to help indigent playwrights.'

'I never knew such a species existed.'

'Aren't most playwrights down on their luck . . . unless they bump into luck? Like you did.'

'Yes . . . but it was still luck.'

'I am getting terribly worried about your extreme modesty, David,' she said, lightly touching my hand.

'You were a script editor, right?' I asked, withdrawing my hand.

'Oh, you are a well-informed gent. Yes, I was what's known in the regional theater trade as a *dramaturg* – which is a pretentious Germanic way of saying that I doctored scripts and worked with writers, and occasionally found an interesting play worth developing in the slush pile of submissions.'

'And that's how you met . . . ?'

'Mr Fleck? Yes, that's where I bumped into my marital fate. In that place of twinkling lights and romantic allure called Milwaukee, Wisconsin. Do you know Milwaukee, David?'

'I'm afraid not.'

'A charming town. The Venice of the Midwest.'

I laughed. 'Then why were *you* there?'

'Because there's a half-way decent repertory theater there. They were in need of a script editor. I was in need of a job – and they offered me one. The money wasn't bad either – twenty-eight thousand a year. More than I made anywhere else. But, then again, the Milwaukee Rep was pretty well funded, thanks to their local boy-made-good Mr Fleck, who was on a personal crusade to turn his hometown into his very own Venice. A new art gallery. A new communications centre at the university, with – *naturellement* – its very own film archive. Just what Milwaukee was craving. And, of course, a spanking new playhouse for the local professional theater. I think Philip spent around $250 million on all three projects.'

'That's very benevolent of him.'

'And very shrewd as well since he managed to offset everything against tax.'

Gary returned, wheeling in a trolley upon which sat a small bowl of caviar artfully surrounded by chipped ice, a plate of small pumpernickel bread rounds, the bottle of vodka, and two stylish shot glasses. Gary removed the bottle from the ice and formally presented it to Martha. She glanced at the label. It looked venerable and Cyrillic.

'Do you read Russian?' she asked me. I shook my head. 'Nor do I. But I'm sure 1953 was a vintage year. So, go on, Gary, pour away.'

He did as commanded, handing us each a brimming glass. Martha raised hers and clinked it against mine. We threw back our shots. The vodka was very cold and very smooth. I felt myself wince with pleasure as it frosted the back of my throat and then travelled straight to my brain. Martha seemed to have a similar reaction.

'That works,' she said.

Gary refilled our glasses, then offered us each a pumpernickel round piled with caviar. I tried mine. Martha asked, 'Does it meet your approval?'

'Well . . . it does taste like caviar.'

She told Gary she could wield the bottle herself now. After he withdrew, Martha poured me another shot and said, 'You know, before I met Philip, I never knew a thing about luxury brand names, or the difference between . . . I don't know . . . a bag by Samsonite or by Louis Vuitton. That stuff never seemed important to me.'

'And now?'

'Now I possess all sorts of arcane mercantile knowledge. I know about the price of Iranian caviar – $160 an ounce. I also know the glass in your hand is Baccarat, and the chair you're parked on is an original Eames design, which Philip bought for $4,200.'

'Whereas before you knew all these things . . . ?'

'I was taking home $1,800 a month, living in a small one-bedroom apartment, and driving a twelve-year-old VW Rabbit. To me a designer label meant The Gap.'

'Did it bother you, having no money?'

'It never really crossed my mind. I was in the non-profit sector, so I dressed like a drabbie and I thought like a drabbie, and it didn't worry me in the slightest. But would I be wrong in thinking that you hated being broke?'

'Having money is easier.'

'That is true. But when you were working at Book Soup, didn't you envy all those successful writers you saw browsing around the shop, with their seven-figure deals and their Porsches in the parking lot, and their Cartier watches, and –'

'How did you know about Book Soup?' I asked, interrupting her.

'I read your file.'

'My file? You have a file on me?'

'Not exactly. More of a dossier – which Philip's people put together when you agreed to come out here.'

'And what exactly was in this file?'

'Just press clippings, and an up-to-date biography, and a list of all your credits, and a bit of background information that Philip's people gleaned here and there . . .'

'Such as?'

'Oh, you know – basic *need-to-know* stuff like what you prefer to drink, the kind of movies you like to watch, the state of your bank accounts, your investment portfolio, the name of your therapist . . .'

'I am *not* in therapy,' I said angrily.

'But you were. Right after you left Lucy and moved in with Sally, you spent six months talking with a Dr – what was his name again? – Tarbuck, perhaps? A Donald Tarbuck who practices right off Victory Avenue in West LA. Sorry . . . am I talking out of turn?'

I suddenly felt very uneasy. 'Who told you all that?' I asked.

'No one told me anything. I just read it . . .'

'But somebody must have told *your people* all this. So who was it?'

'Honestly I haven't a clue.'

'I bet it was that little bastard, Barra.'

'I've obviously upset you, which certainly wasn't my intention. But let me assure you that Bobby's no stool pigeon, and you haven't landed yourself in the former East Germany. My husband simply happens to be a very thorough guy who wants to have a very thorough rundown on anyone he's thinking of hiring.'

'I didn't apply for any job.'

'Point taken. Philip was simply interested in working with you, and thought he should find out a few basic details . . . as everyone does these days. End of story. Okay?'

'I'm not being paranoid . . .'

'Of course not,' she said, pouring us both another shot. 'Now get that down you.'

We clinked glasses again and drank. This time the vodka slipped down with ease — a hint that my throat and my brain had both started to go numb.

'Happier now?' she asked gently.

'It's good vodka.'

'Do you consider yourself a happy type, David?'

'What?'

'I was just wondering if, deep down, you doubt your success, and wonder if you really deserve it?'

I laughed. 'Do you always play the *agent provocateur*?'

'Only with people I like. But I'm right, am I not? Because I sense that you don't believe in your accomplishments, and you secretly rue leaving your wife and child.'

A long silence, during which I reached for the vodka bottle and poured two fresh shots.

'I think I ask too many questions,' she finally said.

I lifted my drink and threw it back.

'But may I be permitted to ask you one more?' she said.

'Which is what?'

'Tell me what you *really* thought of Philip's movie.'

'I did tell you . . .'

'No, what you said was, "*It's pretentious crap.*" What you didn't explain was *why* you considered it pretentious crap.'

'You really want to know?' I asked. She downed her drink and nodded. So I told her exactly why it was the worst film I'd ever seen, taking it apart scene by scene, explaining why the characters were fundamentally absurd, why the dialogue gave new meaning to the word 'artificial', and why the entire enterprise was nothing short of ludicrous. The vodka must have triggered some garrulous switch in my brain, because I talked non-stop for around ten minutes, pausing only to accept two additional refills from Martha. When I finally finished, there was a massively long silence.

'Well . . . you did ask me for my opinion,' I said, the words slightly slurring.

'And you certainly gave it.'

'Sorry.'

'Why apologize? Everything you said is absolutely right. In fact, what you just said is exactly what I told Philip before the film went into production.'

'But I thought you worked closely with him on the script?'

'I did – and, believe me, compared to the original draft the final shooting script was a vast improvement . . . which is not saying much, as the film itself was such a disaster.'

'Didn't you have any sway with him?'

'When does a lowly script editor ever have sway with a director? I mean, if 99.5 per cent of all writers in Hollywood are treated like the hired help, then the script editor is considered virtually subhuman.'

'Even by the guy who's fallen for you?'

'Oh, that didn't happen until way after the movie.'

She then explained how Fleck showed up one day at the theater he'd built in Milwaukee for a little *meet-and-greet* with the staff . . . *his* staff to be specific, as his annual subsidy was meeting the wage bill. Anyway, during the course of this royal walkabout, the theater's artistic director whisked him in to the small cubbyhole which Martha called her office for a fast '*Hello, nice to meet you*'. When they were introduced – and Fleck heard that she was the theater's script editor – he mentioned that he'd just finished writing a movie, and could use a professional's advice about its alleged strengths and weaknesses.

'Of course I instantly told him I would be honored to read it – because what else was I going to say? I mean, he was our patron saint, our Man Upstairs. Secretly, I thought, Oh God, a vanity script, written by Joe Super Rich. But I also really didn't think that he'd actually ever send the script around . . . because as the gentleman had so much money, he could probably buy script advice from Robert Towne or William Goldman. But the next morning, *bang* – the script landed on my desk. There was a Post-It attached to the front page: "I'd greatly appreciate it if you give me your honest appraisal of this by tomorrow morning." And it was signed: *P.F.*'

So Martha had no choice but to spend the rest of the day reading the damn thing, and then spend the entire night in a state of ever-heightening anxiety, as she realized that though Fleck's script was, without question, garbage, if she wrote exactly what she thought, she could kiss her job goodbye.

'I was up until five in the morning, trying to fashion a report which somehow got the message across that this was hopeless, but managed to do so in as neutral a way as possible. But the fact was – I just couldn't think of a single good thing to say about it. Eventually, with the sun coming up, I ripped up my fourth attempt at an impartial report, and thought: I'm going to treat the guy like any other bad aspiring writer, and tell him exactly why he'd gotten it so wrong.'

So she sat down and wrote a killer of a report, had it messengered over to the theater and went to bed, thinking that when she woke up, she'd have to start looking for a new job.

But instead, the phone rang at her apartment at five that afternoon. It was one of 'Fleck's people' – telling her that Mr Fleck himself wanted to see her, and the Gulfstream would be taking her to San Francisco that evening. Oh . . . and the theater had been informed that she wouldn't be in for the next few days.

'Now, up until this point, I had never flown anything but coach, so the limo to the airport and flight on the Gulfstream were just a little out of the ordinary. So too was Philip's town house in Pacific Heights, with the staff of five and the screening room in the basement. Of course, all the way to San Francisco, I was wondering why he wanted to see me – and wondered whether he was flying me out west as a sort of power trip: "I'm bringing you here by private jet so I can have the luxury of firing you face to face."

'But when I reached his house, he couldn't have been more charming . . . which, given Philip's natural taciturnity, is something of a stretch. Holding up my report, he said: "You certainly don't kiss ass, do you?" Then he asked me to spend the next seven days working with him to improve the script. And he asked me to name my price. I told him I was already getting paid by the theater in Milwaukee, so I didn't expect anything from him . . . except hard work. "To me, you're just another writer, and one with a script that needs a major overhaul. So if you're willing to listen, I'm willing to help you."

'So we spent the next seven days pulling the thing apart and putting it back together again. Philip placed his entire life on hold to work with me – and he really did listen. He also seemed to be responding to my criticisms – because, by the time the week was over, we'd managed to cut most of the bilge from the screenplay, tighten up the structure and make the characters semi-believable. I told him I still thought that the entire enterprise was far too high-falutin. But there's no doubt that it was a better script than before.

'And there was also no doubt that there was an unspoken thing between us. Philip may be preternaturally reticent . . . but once he gets to know you, he can be quite funny. And I really liked his smarts. For a guy who'd built up a multi-billion-dollar empire, he knew so much about movies and books, and he really was determined to throw a lot of money at the arts. Anyway, on our last night together, we got into a marathon drinking session . . .'

'Vodka?' I asked.

'Of course,' she said, raising her eyebrows playfully. 'My poison of choice.'

I met her stare. 'And let me guess what happened next?'

'Yes. Only when I woke the next morning, Philip was gone . . . though there was a really romantic note on the pillow: 'I'll be in touch.' At least he didn't sign it *P.F.*

'So back I went to Milwaukee, and I never heard a damn word from him. Six months later, I read somewhere that *The Last Chance* had gone into production in Ireland. Eight months later, it opened at the only art house in Milwaukee – and, naturally, I went to see it, and couldn't believe what Mr Fleck had done. Not only had he thrown out eighty per cent of the changes we made, but he'd also put back half the bad dialogue we'd managed to cut.

Of course, I wasn't the only person who thought he'd made the wrong choices, as the papers were full of truly derogatory stuff about the movie, and how Philip had just broken up with a super model whom he'd been seeing for the last year . . . which immediately explained why I hadn't heard from the gentleman after that one night in his bed.

'Anyway, I was so disgruntled – both by the way he'd undermined all the work we'd done, and the fact that he'd never called me again – that I sat down and punched out a tough letter which expressed considerable displeasure at his professional and personal ill-treatment of me. I really didn't expect to get a reply. But then, about a week later, he showed up on my doorstep one night. And the first words out of his mouth were: "I was wrong about everything. Especially you."

'And after that?'

'We were married within six months.'

'How very romantic,' I said.

Another of her little smiles as she poured us the final two shots from the bottle.

'So the moral of this story is . . . what?' I asked. 'You're not to blame for your husband's lousy movie?'

'Touché, again.'

I threw back the shot. Now I didn't even feel it trickle down my throat. Because I was feeling nothing at all.

'Let me let you in on a secret. The reason my husband is keeping you waiting here is that he can't stand being around anyone who's talented.'

'I think anyone who's made as much money as he has deserves to be called talented.'

'Perhaps. But the talent he craves – the gift he dreams about having – is the talent you have. I hugely admire it too. Why do you think I flew back here tonight? It was the chance to meet you. I really think *Selling You* is a landmark show.'

'I'm flattered.'

'My pleasure.'

She looked directly at me, and smiled again. I glanced at my watch. She said: 'If it's way after your bedtime, don't let me keep you up. I can get Gary to bring you in some warm milk and cookies. And I'm sure we have a spare teddy bear around here somewhere, in case you need companionship.'

She arched her eyebrows slightly, more amused than amorous. Or maybe more amorous than amused. Or maybe she was just raising her eyebrows for no reason whatsoever. Hell, I couldn't tell anything anymore, as I was now dead drunk.

'I think I just need to see my bed,' I said. 'Thank you for the vodka.'

'All part of the service,' she said. 'Sweet dreams.'

I said goodbye, and staggered towards my room.

I don't remember how I got there. Nor do I remember passing out, fully clothed, on the bed. But I certainly do remember jolting awake around four in the morning, and just about making it to the toilet, and retching non-stop for around five minutes, and stripping off all my clothes and standing under a hot shower, and eventually staggering back to bed, still dripping wet, and sliding under the covers, and thinking about my conversation with Martha Fleck, and eventually passing out again, and not waking up until sometime around midday, and thinking that my brain was now suffering from near-nuclear meltdown, and also trying to make sense of everything that happened the night before: from being force-fed *Salo* in all its shit-eating glory, to that flirty booze-fuelled conversation with Martha.

But as I struggled to reassemble the skewed jigsaw that was last night, I also reached a decision: I was going to leave the island today. I'd been kept waiting around for too long, and for no particular reason, and I didn't want to indulge a rich man's whims any longer. So I picked up the phone and rang Gary, and asked him if it was possible to arrange my transfer to Antigua this afternoon, with an onward connection to Los Angeles. He said he'd get back to me. Then, five minutes later, the phone rang. It was Martha.

'Have you ever made the acquaintance of something called Berocca?'

'Hello, Martha.'

'Good morning, David. You sound a little shell-shocked.'

'I wonder why. But you sound amazingly awake.'

'That's because of the wonderful restorative properties of Berocca. It's a soluble vitamin, with a horse-sized dose of Vitamin B & C – and it's the only known cure for a hangover I've ever encountered. They make them in Australia, where they know about hangovers,'

'Please send two over right away.'

'They're en route as we speak. Just don't chop them up with a credit card and snort them up a rolled $50 bill.'

'I don't do that sort of thing,' I said, sounding defensive.

'That was a joke, David. Lighten up, please.'

'Sorry . . . and, by the way, I really did enjoy the evening.'

'Then why do you want to leave us this afternoon?'

'News obviously travels fast.'

'I hope this decision wasn't prompted by anything I said.'

'Hardly. I think it's more to do with the fact that your husband has kept me waiting here for just over a week. And I have a life to be getting on with . . . and a daughter I need to visit in San Francisco this Friday.'

'That's easily taken care of. I'll have the Gulfstream booked to fly you direct on Friday morning. With the time change in your favor, you'll get there by mid-afternoon, no problem.'

'But that means cooling my heels here for another two days.'

'Look, I understand why you're peeved at my husband. As I said last night, he is playing a game with you . . . like he plays games with everybody. And I feel very bad about all this, because it was me who suggested that he should try to work with you. I'm such a great fan of yours. Besides *Selling You*, I've actually read all your early theater stuff . . .'

'Really?' I said, trying not to sound flattered, but failing.

'Yes, I got one of my assistants at the foundation to track down all your play scripts . . .'

That must have taken some work, I thought . . . considering that none of those plays were ever published. But if there was one thing I now knew about the Flecks, it was this: if they wanted something they got it.

'. . . and I also really want to talk with you about the rewrite you've just done on the movie for Philip.'

Which, evidently, Joan had slipped to her.

'You've read it already?'

'First thing this morning.'

'How about your husband?'

'I wouldn't know,' she said. 'We haven't talked for a few days.'

I was about to ask why but thought better of it. So, instead I said, 'Did you really come back from New York to meet me?'

'It's not very often that we have a writer I admire staying on the island.'

'And you *really* like the new version of the script?'

She let out a dark laugh. 'Searching for reassurance?'

'Absolutely,' I said.

'Well, I think the job you've done is terrific.'

'Thank you.'

'Believe me, I'd tell you otherwise.'

'I've no doubt about that.'

'And if you do stay, I promise not to force vodka down your throat again . . . unless, of course you want it forced down your throat.'

'Not a chance.'

'Then we'll be alcohol-free Mormons all day. In fact, I'll even call you Elder David if you wish . . .'

Now it was my turn to laugh. 'All right, all right. I'll stay one more day. But if he's not here tomorrow, I'm gone.'

'It's a deal,' she said.

The Berocca arrived a few minutes later – and much to my surprise, it actually did lessen my hangover agony. But so too did the afternoon I spent with Martha. Given the amount of Stoli she'd thrown back the night before, she looked damnably alert, almost radiant. She arranged lunch on the main balcony of the house. The sun was high, but a light breeze tempered the heat. We ate cold lobster and drank Virgin Marys and talked our heads off. Martha had dropped the coquettish tone which had characterized the previous night, and revealed herself to be funny, erudite, and someone who could talk about a dozen different subjects with great intensity and brio. More tellingly, she really knew her stuff when it came the business of play writing – and she had a lot of smart, intelligent points to make about the new version of *We Three Grunts*. Much to my amazement, she really had read the entire David Armitage oeuvre . . . including two forgotten plays of the early 1990s which had been given one-off readings by obscure off-off-Broadway companies, and which had been gathering dust in their script archives since then.

'Hell, even I haven't read those plays in years,' I said.

'Well, when Philip told me he wanted to work with you, I thought it would be smart to see what you'd been up to before you were famous.'

'And is that how you'd managed to find *We Three Grunts*?'

'Yes, I'm to blame for putting it into Philip's hands.'

'And was it also your idea to put his name on my script?'

She looked at me as if I was deranged. And said, 'What on earth are you talking about?'

I explained about her husband's little stunt with my screenplay . . . how it had arrived (via Bobby) with his name on the title page.

She exhaled slowly – through clenched teeth.

'I am so sorry, David,' she said.

'Don't be. It's not exactly your fault. And the fact is, I still accepted his offer to come out here . . . which shows you just what a fool I am.'

'Everyone gets suckered in by Philip's money. And it allows him to play the games he loves to play. Which is why I feel bad about this. Because when he called me to ask about you, I should have known that he'd start messing you around too.'

'He *called you* to talk about me? Aren't you kind of married?'

'Actually, we're kind of separated.'

'Oh, right.'

'It's not official or anything. And it's certainly something that neither of us wants to be made public. But, for around the last year or so, we've essentially been living apart.'

'Sorry to hear that.'

'Don't be. Because it was my decision. Not that Philip exactly begged me to reconsider, or pursued me to all four corners of the earth. That's not his style, anyway. Not that he has any style to begin with.'

'Do you think it's permanent?'

'I don't know. We talk from time to time – maybe once a week. If he needs me for a public appearance – a big charity benefit, some heavyweight business dinner, or the annual invitation to the White House – I put on the appropriate dress and the appropriate fixed smile, and let him hold my arm, and play-act the happy couple. And, of course, I live in all his houses, and use all his planes – but only when he's not using them. The fact that he has so many houses and so many planes means that it's easy to avoid each other.'

'It's gotten that bad between the two of you?'

She paused for a moment and stared out at the interplay of sunlight and water on the glistening surface of the Caribbean Sea.

'From the outset, I knew that Philip was just a little odd. But I fell in love with his oddness. And his intellect. And the vulnerability which he keeps hidden behind his taciturn rich man facade. For the first couple of years, we really did get along. Until, one day, he started going into retreat. I couldn't figure it out at all. Nor would he explain it to me. The marriage was like a shiny new car that, one morning, simply refuses to start. And though you try everything to get it moving again, you start worrying: might this be a lemon? And what makes this worry even worse is the realization that, despite everything, you still love the idiot you've married.'

She fell silent, staring out again at all that water.

'Of course,' she said, 'looking at that view, you must think: everyone should have her problems.'

'A bad marriage is a bad marriage.'

'Was yours very bad?' she asked.

Now it was my turn to avoid eye contact.

'You want the facile answer or the honest answer?' I asked.

'That's your call.'

I hesitated for a moment, then said, 'No, in retrospect, it wasn't that awful. We'd lost our way a bit – and I think there was a certain amount of built-up resentment on both sides because she had been carrying us financially for so long. And my success didn't really simplify matters between us. Instead, it just created more of a gulf . . .'

'And then you met the astonishing Ms Birmingham.'

'Your researchers are very thorough.'

'Are you in love with her?'

'Of course.'

'Is that the facile or the honest answer?'

'Put it this way . . . it's very different from my marriage. We're a "power couple", with all that that implies.'

'That sounds like a pretty honest answer to me.'

I glanced at my watch. It was nearly four o'clock. The afternoon had slipped by in a nanosecond. I glanced up at Martha. The sun had angled itself in such a way that her face was bathed in a soft glow. I looked at her carefully, and suddenly thought: she is actually beautiful. So smart. So damn witty. And (unlike Sally) so self-deprecating. More to the point, we were so attuned to each other's sensibility. Our rapport was instant, all-pervasive, so . . .

Then a second thought immediately popped into my head: *don't even think about going there.*

'Penny for them,' she said, interrupting my reverie.

'Sorry?'

'Your thoughts, David. You seemed to be somewhere else.'

'No – I was definitely here.'

She smiled and said, 'That's nice to know.'

At that moment I realized . . . *what*? That she'd been watching me watching her . . . that there was 'an unspoken thing' between us? . . . the makings of a really messy *coup de foudre*? . . . '*Grow up, you idiot*' (I heard the Voice of Reason whisper in my ear). '*So what if there's an attraction? You know what would happen if it was acted upon. Terminal fallout, followed by the longest nuclear winter imaginable.*'

Now it was her turn to glance at her watch.

'My God, look at the time,' she said.

'Hope I haven't kept you from anything,' I said.

'Hardly. Anyway, time flies when the conversation flies.'

'I'll drink to that.'

'Is that a cue to break our vow of sobriety and order us something French and fizzy?'

116

'Not just yet.'

'But later, perhaps?'

I heard myself saying, 'If you're not doing anything . . .'

'My social diary isn't exactly full down here.'

'Nor mine.'

'So if I suggested something . . . a little outing, perhaps . . . you'd be game?'

Don't do it, Mr Voice of Reason hissed in my ear. But, of course, I said, 'Fine by me.'

An hour later, with the sun in steep decline towards night, I found myself sitting with Martha on the deck of the Cabin Cruiser, sipping a glass of Cristal and steaming towards the horizon. Before we embarked, she told me to bring a change of clothes and a sweater.

'Where, exactly, are we going?' I'd asked her.

'You'll see,' she said.

Around half an hour later, a tiny island came into view: hilly, verdant, festooned with palms. From the distance, I could make out a dock, a beach, behind which was a trio of simple buildings – built in pseudo-Easter Island style, with thatched roofs.

'Quite a little hideaway,' I said. 'Who does it belong to?'

'Me,' Martha said.

'You serious?'

'Absolutely. It was my wedding present from Philip. He wanted to buy me some huge, absurd Liz Taylor-style rock. But I said that I wasn't really a Star of India gal. So he said: "How about an island?" And I thought: well, that's pretty damn original.'

When we docked, Martha led me ashore. The beach wasn't large, but it was perfectly white and sandy. We walked up to the little development of buildings. The main structure was circular, with a comfortable lounge (all bleached wood and bleached fabrics), and a large verandah, with sun-loungers and a large dining table. A kitchen took up the rear of the building. On either side of this central structure were two burees: Polynesian-style cottages, each furnished with a king-sized bed, stylish cane armchairs, more bleached fabrics, and a bleached-wood bathroom. *House and Garden Goes Tropical.*

'Quite a wedding gift,' I said. 'I presume you had a hand in the design of the place?'

'Yes, Philip flew in an architect and a builder from Antigua, and essentially gave me carte blanche. And I told them that, of course, I wanted a five-star facsimile of Jonestown . . .'

'You mean, you're going to start your own cult?'

'I think there's a clause in my prenup that specifically forbids me from founding my own religion.'

'You have a prenuptial agreement?'

'When you marry a fellow worth $20 billion, his people definitely insist that you sign a prenuptial agreement . . . which, in our case, was about the same length as the Gutenberg Bible. But I hired an exceptionally tough lawyer to negotiate my end of the deal . . . so, if things do fall apart, I am well covered. Ready for a little island tour?'

'Isn't it getting dark?'

'That's the point,' she said, taking me by the hand. On our way out of the buree, she grabbed a flashlight positioned by the door. Then she led me up a narrow path that began behind the main building and headed straight uphill through a jungly thicket of palms and labyrinthine vines. The sun was still casting a fading glow, but the nocturnal tropical soundtrack of insects and ornithology was in full swing . . . an echo chamber of hisses and unearthly shrieks which brought out my deep city-boy fears about the call of the wild.

'Are you sure this is a smart thing to be doing?' I asked.

'At this time of the night, the pythons aren't out yet. So . . .'

'Very funny,' I said.

'You're safe with me.'

Up and up we climbed – the flora and fauna now so thick that the path felt like an ever-darkening tunnel. But then, suddenly, we emerged on top of the hill we'd been ascending. The foliage gave way to a cleared summit. Martha had timed our arrival perfectly . . . because there before us was the incandescent disc of the sun: perfectly outlined against the darkening sky.

'Good God,' I said.

'You approve?' she asked.

'It's quite a floor show.'

We stood there in silence. Martha turned to me and smiled and took my hand in hers and squeezed it. Then, in an instant, the world was dark.

'That's our exit cue,' Martha said, turning on her flashlight. We headed slowly downhill. She continued holding my hand until we reached the compound. Then, just before we went inside, she let go — and went off to speak to the chef. I parked myself on the verandah, staring out at the darkened beach. After a few minutes, Martha returned, accompanied by Gary. He was carrying a tray with a silver cocktail shaker and two frosted martini glasses.

'And I thought we were going to practise abstinence tonight?' I said.

'You didn't exactly say no to the two glasses of champagne on the boat.'

'Yes — but martinis are in a different league to champagne. It's like comparing a Scud missile to a BB gun.'

'Once again, no one's forcing it down your throat. But I figured you wouldn't mind yours made with Bombay Gin, straight up with two olives.'

'Did your people research that one as well?'

'No — that was just a straightforward guess.'

'Well, you were right on the money. But I promise you — I'm just drinking the one.'

Of course, Martha didn't have to twist my arm to down a second martini. Nor did she have to bribe me into sharing the bottle of another absurdly wonderful wine and grilled fish. By the time we were working our way through a half-bottle of Muscat from Australia, the two of us were in riotous form, trading absurd stories about our respective adventures in the movie and theater games. We talked about our childhoods in Chicago and the Philadelphia suburbs, and Martha's failed attempts to become a theater director after graduating from Carnegie-Mellon, and my fifteen years of endless professional setbacks, and the assorted romantic confusions that characterized our twenties. When we started swapping bad date tales, we were on our second half-bottle of Muscat. It was late and Martha had told Gary and the rest of the staff to call it a night. So they all retired back to their quarters behind the kitchen, and she said, 'Come on, let's take a walk.'

'I think, at this point, it might be a stagger.'

'Then a stagger it is.'

She grabbed the second half-bottle of Muscat and two glasses and led me down the hill from the compound, and on to the beach, Then she sat down on the sand and said:

'I promised you a short stagger.'

I joined her on the sand, looking up at the night sky. It was an exceptionally clear night, and the cosmos seemed even more vast than usual. Martha filled our glasses with the sticky golden wine and said:

'Let me guess what you're thinking as you gaze upwards? It's all trivial and meaningless, and I'm going to be dead in fifty years . . .'

'If I'm lucky . . .'

'All right, *forty* years. Ten less years of insignificant endeavour. Because, in the year 2041, what will anything we do now matter? Unless either of us starts a war, or writes the defining sit-com of the new millennium . . .'

'How did you know that was my ultimate ambition?'

'Because it's been clear from the moment I clapped eyes on you . . .'

She paused, and touched my face with her hand, and smiled, then thought better of whatever she was about to say.

'Yes . . . ?' I asked.

'. . . from the moment I saw you,' she said, her tone flippant again, 'I knew you had your mind firmly fixed on being the Tolstoy of the sit-com.'

'Do you always talk such nonsense?'

'Absolutely. It's the only way to keep cosmic irrelevance at bay, which is why I want you to tell me something about your wife.'

'Like what?'

'Was Lucy one of those real *at first sight* romances?'

'Absolutely.'

'And was she the first great love of your life?'

'Yes. Without question.'

'And now?'

'Now the great love of my life is my daughter, Caitlin. And Sally, of course.'

'Yes. Of course.'

'And Philip . . . ?'

'Philip was never the great love of my life.'

'Okay – but before him?'

'Before him was someone named Michael Webster.'

'And he was *it*?'

'Hook, line, and sinker. We met when we were undergraduates at Carnegie. He was an actor. When I first laid eyes on him, I thought: he's the one. Fortunately, it was mutual. So mutual that, from sophomore year on, we were inseparable. After college, we tried to make it in New York for seven years – but spent most of the time scrambling. Then he got a job for a season at the Guthrie – a fantastically lucky break, made even luckier by the fact that I managed to wangle a position in their script department. Anyway, we both really took to Minneapolis; the director of the Guthrie really liked Michael and renewed his contract for a second season. Some casting director from LA wanted him for a role in a Movie of the Week thing. We were talking about maybe starting a family . . . in other words, everything was finally panning out for us. And then, on a really snowy night, Michael decided to run down late to the local 7–11 for a six pack of beer. Coming home, his car hit a patch of black ice and slammed into a tree at forty miles an hour, and the idiot had forgotten to put on his seat belt . . . and he went right through the windscreen and head-first into the tree.'

She reached for the bottle of Muscat. 'A refill, perhaps?'

I nodded. She topped up our glasses.

'That's a terrible story,' I said.

'Yes. It is. Made even more terrible by the four weeks he spent on life-support, even though he was officially brain-dead. Both his parents were long gone, his brother was stationed with the Army in Germany, so it came down to me to make the decision. And I couldn't bear the idea of letting him die. Because I was so out of my mind with grief that I was under the delusion there would be some miraculous resurrection, and the great love of my life would be restored to me whole.

'Eventually, some battle-axe nurse – a real tough old broad who'd seen it all on the Intensive Care ward – insisted I join her for an after-work drink at the local bar. At the time, I was spending twenty-four hours a day by Michael's bedside – and hadn't slept in about a week. Anyway, this broad all but frogmarched me to the nearest boozer, insisted I throw back a couple of stiff whiskies, and then gave it to me straight: 'Your guy is never going to wake up again. There's going to be no medical miracle. He's dead, Martha. And for your own sanity, you've got to accept that awful fact, and pull the plug.'

'Then she bought me a third whisky and got me home. Whereupon I fell completely apart, and finally passed out for around twelve hours. When I woke up late the next morning, I called the hospital and told the resident in charge that I was prepared to sign the necessary papers to turn off Michael's life support.

'And a week after that – in a moment of complete sorrow-deranged misjudgment – I made an application for the script-editing job that had just opened at the Milwaukee Rep. The next thing I knew, I was offered the job and en route to Wisconsin.'

She drained her glass.

'I mean, traditionally, you're supposed to go to Paris or Venice or Tangier if you're unhinged by grief. What did I do? I went to Milwaukee.'

She broke off and stared out at the sea.

'Did you meet Philip shortly afterwards?'

'No – about a year later. But during the week we spent together working on his script, I got around to telling him about Michael. Philip was the first man I'd slept with since his death – which made the way he dropped me afterwards about ten times worse. I'd written him off as beyond arrogant . . . especially after I saw what he'd done to our script . . . until he showed up at my door that night, my irate letter in his land, begging forgiveness.'

'Did you instantly forgive him?'

'Hardly. I made him pursue me. Which he did – with extreme diligence and, dare I say it, great style. Much to my surprise, I actually found myself falling for him. Maybe because he was such an isolated character – yet one who, I gradually discovered, liked me for what I was, for how I thought, and saw the world. And he also needed me. That was the biggest surprise of them all – the fact that this guy, with all his money and the ability to get anything he wanted, told me that he knew I was the best thing that could happen to him.'

'So he won you back?'

'Yes, he eventually did – the way Philip eventually wins everything . . . through sheer bloody-minded persistence.'

She drained her glass.

'The problem is,' she said, 'once he's won something, he loses interest.'

'Foolish man.'

'Ha.'

'No, it's the truth,' I heard myself saying. 'How could anyone lose interest in you?'

She held me in her gaze, then reached out and stroked my hair. And said:

> *Dominion lasts until obtained –*
> *Possession just as long –*
> *But these – endowing as they flit*
> *Eternally belong.*

'If you name the writer, you get a kiss,' she said.

'Emily Dickinson,' I said.

'Bravo,' she said, then put her arms around my neck, and drew me close and kissed me gently on the lips. Then I said, 'My turn. Same deal applies.'

> *Confirming All who analyze*
> *In the Opinion fair*
> *That Eloquence is when the Heart*
> *Has not a Voice to spare –*

'That's a toughie,' she said, draping her arms back around my neck. 'Emily Dickinson.'

'I'm impressed.'

We kissed again. A slightly longer kiss.

'Back to me now,' she said, still keeping her arms around me. 'You ready?'

'Absolutely.'

'Pay close attention,' she said. 'This is a tricky one.

> *How soft this prison is*
> *How sweet these sullen bars*
> *No despot but the King of Down*
> *Invented this repose.*
>
> *Of Fate if this is All*
> *Had he no added Realm*
> *A Dungeon but a Kinsman is*
> *Incarceration – Home.*

'That is a stumper,' I said.

'Go on, take a wild guess.'

'But say I get it wrong? What then?'

She drew me even closer. 'I'm counting on you to get it right.'

'It wouldn't be . . . Emily Dickinson?'

'Bingo,' she said and pulled me right down on to the sand. We began to kiss deeply, passionately. After a few unbridled moments, however, the Voice of Reason began to sound air-raid warning signals between my ears. But when I tried to disentangle myself from her embrace, Martha pinned me down against the sand and whispered, 'Don't think. Just . . .'

'I can't,' I whispered back.

'You can.'

'No.'

'It'll be just for tonight.'

'It won't – and you know it. These things always have repercussions. Especially . . .'

'Yes?'

'Especially when . . . you know and I know this will not be just one night.'

'Do you feel that way too?'

124

'What way?'

'*That way . . .*'

I gently removed her arms from mine, and sat up.

'What I feel is . . . *drunk.*'

'You don't get it, do you?' she said softly. 'Look at all this: you, me, this island, this sea, this sky, this night. Not *a* night, David. *This night.* This unique, unrepeatable night . . .'

'I know, I know. But . . .'

I put my hand on her shoulder. She took it and held it tightly.

'Damn you for being so sensible,' she said.

'I wish . . .'

She leaned over and kissed me lightly on the lips.

'Please shut up,' she said. Then she got to her feet. 'I'm going to take a walk,' she said.

'Can I join you?'

'I think I'll make it a solo walk, if you don't mind.'

'You sure?'

She nodded.

'Are you going to be okay out here?'

'It's my island,' she said. 'I'll be fine.'

'Thank you for tonight,' I said.

She gave me a sad smile and said, 'No – thank you.'

Then she turned and headed off down the beach. I thought about chasing after her, about taking her in my arms again and kissing her, and blurting out a lot of jumbled thoughts about love and the nature of timing and how I didn't want to complicate my life any further, and how I so wanted to kiss her . . .

But instead, I did the rational thing and forced myself up the hill. Once inside my hut, I sat on the edge of the bed, put my face in my hands and thought: *this has been one strange week.* That's all I thought, however, because my cognitive abilities were numbed by the alcoholic equivalent of toxic shock. Had I been able to properly fathom what had just transpired – not to mention the massively unsettling thought that, maybe, *just maybe,* I was a little in love with her – I might have started to feel unhinged.

But I didn't get an opportunity to indulge my guilt. Because, for the second night running, I passed out fully clothed on my bed.

Only this time, my exhaustion was so complete that I didn't stir until 6.30am, when there was a light tapping on the door. I muttered something vaguely resembling English, then the door opened and Gary walked in, carrying a tray with a coffee pot, and a large glass of water. I noticed that, though still wearing last night's clothes, I had been covered by a blanket. I wondered who'd been in earlier to play the Good Samaritan.

'Morning, Mr Armitage,' Gary said. 'How are we feeling this morning?'

'Not good.'

'Then you need two of these,' he said, popping a pair of Berocca tablets into the water. When they were fully dissolved, he handed me the glass. I downed the contents in one long gulp. As it sped down my gullet, images of the previous night's endeavours began to play across that vacant lot better known as the inside of my head. As I replayed our embrace on the beach, I had to resist the temptation to shudder. I didn't succeed . . . though Gary pretended not to notice, and instead said:

'Might a cup of very strong black coffee be most useful right now?'

I nodded. He poured the coffee. I sipped it, nearly gagging on the first mouthful. But the second sip went down easier, and by the time I was working on the third, the Berocca was starting to lift the fog from my brain.

'Did you have an enjoyable night, sir?' Gary asked me. I studied his face with care, wondering if the obsequious little bastard was trying to tell me something . . . if he had been on the verandah with a pair of binoculars, watching us imitate a pair of goofy adolescents on the beach. But his face betrayed nothing. Nor would I.

'Yeah, great,' I said.

'I'm sorry to be getting you up so early, but – as you requested – the Gulfstream will be flying you to San Francisco this morning. Would you mind if I just briefly run through travel arrangements?'

'Go ahead . . . but you might have to repeat them a couple of times.'

He gave me a thin little smile, and said, 'Now Mrs Fleck told

us that you need to be in San Francisco by around four this afternoon to meet your little girl after school.'

'Yeah, that's right. How is Mrs Fleck this morning?'

'En route to New York right about now.'

I didn't think I was hearing this clearly. 'She's what?'

'Heading to New York, sir.'

'But how . . . ?'

'The way she usually gets to New York, sir. By one of our
airplanes. She left the island last night. Shortly after you went to
bed.'

'Really?'

'Yes. Really.'

'Oh.'

'She did, however, leave you a note,' he said, proffering a small
white envelope with my name written on the front. I resisted the
temptation to open it, and simply put in on the pillow beside me.

'She also asked me to make all the arrangements for your flight
to the Coast. So, here's what we've organized – we'll get you back
to Saffron by around nine, with the helicopter to Antigua scheduled for ten-thirty and departure on the Gulfstream to San Francisco
at eleven-fifteen. The pilot's informed me it's a seven-hour-forty-
minute flight, but with the four-hour time change, you should
arrive around three-ten. We've arranged for a limo to collect you
at the airport, and to be at your disposal all weekend. And we've
also arranged, with our compliments, a suite for you and your
daughter at the Mandarin Oriental.'

'That's far too extravagant of you.'

'You can thank Mrs Fleck – she set it up.'

'I'll do that.'

'One final thing – during the ninety minutes you're back on
Saffron, Mr Fleck will look forward to meeting you.'

'What?' I said, my hands suddenly cold and clammy.

'Mr Fleck will be meeting you at nine.'

'He's back on the island?'

'Yes, sir. In fact, he arrived back late last night.'

Great, I thought. Just great.

Seven

As the boat sped back towards towards Saffron Island, my anxiety level began to rise. No doubt, this had something to do with finally meeting the guy who had been keeping me waiting for the past seven days. But it also probably had something to do with my host arriving home to discover that his wife and his guest had taken off to her own private island for the night. Then there was the little matter of my drunken beachside embrace with Martha. The fact that she had returned to Saffron late last night would have assuaged any suspicions that we spent the night together, but I did wonder whether one of the staff had seen us kissing in the sand, and had dutifully informed Fleck that his wife and his guest had been re-enacting the famous Burt Lancaster/Deborah Kerr surfside clinch in *From Here to Eternity* – a scene which Fleck the film buff would know only too damn well.

Cut!

I gripped the bars that encircled the deck of the Cabin Cruiser, and told myself to calm down. I reminded myself that a hangover always left me feeling vulnerable and prone to paranoid fantasies. In the great, expansive catalogue of sexual stupidities – drunken necking on a beach rated as a minor misdemeanour. Hell, I had met temptation and resisted it. So give yourself a pat on the back, and stop this self-flagellation. And while you're at it, stop postponing the inevitable, and open Martha's letter.

So I did just that. It was a card, written in neat, cramped writing. On the first side of it was the following:

> I can wade Grief –
> Whole Pools of it –
> I'm used to that –
> But the least push of Joy –
> Breaks up my feet –
> And I tip – drunken –
> Let no Pebble – smile –

128

Temptation

Twas the New Liquor—
That was all!

I turned the card over and read:

I think you know the poet, David.
And yes, you're right: timing is, sadly, everything.
  Take care,
  Martha

My first reaction was, Well, that could have been a lot worse. My second reaction was, She is wonderful. And my third reaction was, Forget all about it . . .

When the boat docked at Saffron Island, Meg was there to greet me. She had packed up all my things, she said, and had everything ready to load aboard the chopper. But if I wanted to check my suite before leaving . . .

'I'm sure you've found everything,' I said.

'Then Mr Fleck is waiting for you in the Great Room.'

I followed her up the dock, into the house, and down the corridor to that vast, cathedral-like lounge. Before entering the room, I took a deep steadying breath. But as I walked in, I found that I was alone.

'Mr Fleck must have stepped away for a moment. Could I get you something to drink?'

'Just a Perrier, please.'

Meg left, and I parked myself in the same Eames chair which Martha told me cost $4200. After a minute or so, I stood up and began to pace the room, glancing at my watch, telling myself I shouldn't be getting anxious, because, after all, this guy was just *a guy*. Though he might be a guy with big bucks, nothing he said or did or thought about me would have any impact on my career. More to the point, he'd sent for me. I was *the talent*. He was the buyer. If he wanted what I was selling, fine. If not, I'd live.

Two minutes went by, then three, then five. Then Meg returned, carrying a tray. But instead of my Perrier, there was a tall glass of tomato juice, adorned with a celery stalk.

'What's that?' I asked her.

129

'It's a Bloody Mary, sir.'

'But I ordered a Perrier.'

'Yes, but Mr Fleck felt you should have a Bloody Mary first.'

'He *what*?'

Suddenly, I heard a voice from on high: specifically, from the balcony that overhung this room.

'I thought you might be in need of a Bloody Mary,' the voice said in a low, slightly hesitant voice. After a moment, I heard footsteps on the circular steel stairs that led to the balcony. Philip Fleck walked down the steps slowly, favouring me with a vague smile. Of course, I knew his face from countless press photographs, but what initially surprised me was his chunky stature. He couldn't have been more than five-foot-five, with sandy brown hair flecked with grey, and a boyish face that showed all the signs of high-carbohydrate over-consumption. He wasn't exactly fat – but he was most definitely fleshy. His clothes were hip-preppy-casual – a faded blue button-down shirt, worn loosely over a pair of well-washed tan chinos, with white Converse low-top sneakers on his feet. Though he'd allegedly just spent a week on a fishing boat under a sizzling Caribbean sun, he was surprisingly pale, making me wonder if he was one of those skin cancer obsessives who feared melanomas lurking behind even the slightest darkening of his pigment.

He proffered his hand. I took it. His grip was soft, unforceful – the grip of someone who didn't care whether or not you liked the impression he was making.

'You must be David,' he said.

'That's me.'

'Then, from what I hear, a Bloody Mary is definitely in order.'

'Really? And what precisely did you hear?'

'I heard from my wife that the two of you did some serious drinking last night.' He looked in my direction, but not directly at me – as if he was a bit myopic, and couldn't focus on any near-distant object. 'Did I hear right?'

I chose my words with care. 'It was a slightly wet evening,' I said.

'Slightly wet,' he said, his voice still soft, and ever so tentative. 'What a nice turn of phrase you have. But given the "slight wetness" of the previous night . . .'

He motioned towards Meg and the drink on the tray. Part of me wanted to refuse it. But the other part told me to play along . . . especially as I really was in sudden need of a hangover cure.

So I took the Bloody Mary off the tray, raised it in Fleck's direction, and downed it in one long gulp. Then I replaced it on the tray and smiled directly at him.

'You were obviously thirsty,' he said. 'Another, perhaps?'

'No thanks. One did the job.'

He nodded to Meg and she withdrew. He motioned for me to sit in the Eames chair. He took up a position opposite me on the sofa, but situated himself in such a way that he didn't have to look at me, but instead could talk in the diagonal direction of the nearest wall.

'So . . .' he said quietly, '. . . a question for you . . .'

'Fire away,' I said.

'Do you think my wife's an alcoholic?'

Oh boy . . .

'I wouldn't know.'

'But you spent two evenings drinking with her.'

'Yes, that's true.'

'And she drank heavily on both occasions.'

'But so did I.'

'So are you an alcoholic too?'

'Mr Fleck . . .'

'You can call me Philip. And you should know that Martha spoke quite highly of you. Mind you, she herself was quite high at the time. But that's part of Martha's charm, wouldn't you agree?'

I said nothing. Because I didn't know what the hell to say.

And Fleck was content to let us lapse into uncomfortable silence for the better part of a minute before I finally broke it.

'How was the fishing?' I asked.

'Fishing? I wasn't fishing.'

'You weren't?'

'No.'

'But I was told . . .'

'You were misinformed.'

'Oh. So if you weren't fishing . . . ?'

'I was elsewhere. São Paulo to be exact.'

'Business?'

'No one ever goes to São Paulo for pleasure.'

'Right.'

Yet again, the conversation seized. Yet again, Fleck stared diagonally at the opposing wall.

Finally, after another endless minute of silence, he spoke.

'So . . . you wanted to see me,' he said.

'I did?'

'That's what I was told.'

'But . . . *you* invited me here.'

'Did I?'

'Absolutely.'

'Oh. Right.'

'I mean, I thought you wanted to see me.'

'About what?'

'The script.'

'What script?'

'The script I wrote.'

'You write scripts?'

'Are you trying to be funny?'

'Do I sound like I'm trying to be funny?'

'No – you sound like you're trying to play a game with me.'

'And what sort of game would that be?'

'You know why I'm here.'

'Tell me again . . .'

'Forget it,' I said, standing up.

'Pardon?'

'I said – forget it . . .'

'Why did you say that?'

'Because you're messing me about.'

'Are you angry?'

'No – I'm just leaving.'

'Have I done something wrong?'

'I'm not going to get into it.'

'But if I've done something wrong . . .'

'This conversation's closed. Goodbye.'

And I headed towards the door. But Fleck's voice stopped me.

'David . . .'

'What?' I said, turning around. Fleck was now looking straight at me, a big mischievous smile on his face, holding a copy of my script in his right hand.

'Gotcha,' he said. And when I didn't immediately break into a hundred watt *hey, what a great joke* grin, he said: 'Hope you're not too pissed at me now.'

'After waiting here for a week, Mr Fleck . . .'

He cut me off.

'You're right, you're right – and for that, my apologies. But hey, what's a little Pinteresque banter between colleagues.'

'We're colleagues?'

'I certainly hope so. Because, speaking personally, I want to make this script.'

'You do?' I said, trying to sound neutral.

'I think what you've done in the new rewrite is quite remarkable. Because it's like a deconstructed caper movie with a really rigorous political underpinning. And what you're really getting at is the malaise inherent in laissez-faire consumerism; an ennui that has become such a defining mainstay of contemporary American life.'

This was news to me – but if there was one thing I'd learnt about the writing trade it was this: when a director started enthusiastically telling you what your movie was about, it was always best to nod your head in sage agreement . . . even if you thought he was talking utter shit.

'Of course,' I said, 'first and foremost, it *is* a genre movie . . .'

'Precisely,' Fleck said, motioning for me to sit back down in the Eames chair. 'But it subverts the genre – the way Jean-Pierre Melville redefined the existential hit man legend in *Le Samourai*.'

The existential hit man legend? Sure.

'At heart, though,' I said, 'it is about a couple of guys in Chicago trying to rob a bank.'

'And do I know how to film that bank job.'

For the next half an hour, he gave me a shot-by-shot storyboard of how he'd film the bank job (using Steadicam – and grainy color film stock 'to get a real sense of guerrilla film making'). Then he talked casting ideas.

'I only want unknowns. And for the leads, I'm really considering these two amazing actors I saw last year at the Berliner Ensemble . . .'

'How's their English?' I asked.

'We can work on that,' he said.

I could have mentioned the slight credibility problem of having heavily accented Germans playing a pair of grizzled Vietnam vets, but I held my tongue. In the course of his epic monologue, he mentioned that he was thinking of budgeting the film at around $40 million – an absurd sum for an alleged piece of guerrilla film-making. But who was I to question the way he wanted to squander his money? And I remembered what Alison told me before I came out here.

'*I know I can fuck him out of a lot of money. I'm going pay or play on this one, Dave. A cool million. And I promise you he'll pay it. Because even though we both know that registering your script under his name was a form of sweet talk, he still won't want that made public. And without us even asking, he'll pay big time to keep it quiet.*'

I was actually succumbing a bit to his zealousness; the way he made me feel as if I hadn't written a mere frolic, but one of the great defining human documents of the age. Martha was right – when Fleck wanted something he pursued it with complete fervour. But I also remembered what she said about how he lost interest once he had gotten what he wanted. And I was still a little bemused by the way he'd tried to unsettle me at the beginning of our conversation – though, to his credit, he did stop halfway through his oration to apologize for 'pulling my chain'.

'I'm afraid it's a bad habit of mine,' he said. 'When I meet someone for the first time, I like to wrong-foot them a bit . . . just to see how they'll react.'

'And did I pass the test?'

'An A+. Martha told me you were a class act – and she knows her writers. Thanks again for spending so much time with her over the last couple of days. She's such a big fan of yours, and I know she really enjoyed the opportunity to talk with you at such great length.'

Not to mention playing a kissing game with me involving the

poems of Emily Dickinson. But Fleck's face betrayed no knowledge of such events. Anyway (I told myself), they were unofficially separated. He probably had mistresses in each of his many ports of call. So what if he found out I'd been necking with his wife? He loved my screenplay. If he imposed his goofy ideas on it, I'd pull my name from the credits . . . after cashing his check.

But before we could speak any further on the subject of his wife, I decided to change the subject.

'I meant to thank you for introducing me to Pasolini's *Salo*,' I said. 'It might be the worst first date movie of all time, but it's still quite a film, and one you certainly don't get out of your brain easily.'

'For me it is, without question, the greatest film made since the War. Wouldn't you agree?'

'That's a big statement . . .'

'. . . and I'll tell you why it deserves that accolade. Because it deals with the foremost issue of the last century . . . which is the need to exercise absolute control over others.'

'I don't think that was just a twentieth-century preoccupation.'

'True – but in the last century, we made a great leap forward in terms of human control . . . we harnessed the power of technology to establish total hegemony over others. The German concentration camps, for example, were the first supreme example of hyper-technological death – for they created an exceedingly efficient apparatus for human extermination. The atomic bomb was also a triumph of human control, not only for its capability for detached mass destruction, but also as a political tool. Face fact, we all bought into the Cold War apparatus of the Secret Security State, thanks to the threat of the bomb . . . and it allowed governments on both sides of the ideological divide the perfect means for keeping the *hoi polloi* constrained, while also giving them the *raison d'être* for setting up a vast intelligence network to stifle dissent. Now, of course, we have the vast information capabilities necessary for even greater control over individuals. Just as Western societies use consumerism – and the endless cycle of acquisitiveness – as a means by which to keep the populace preoccupied, subdued.'

'But what does this have to do with *Salo*?'

'It's simple, really – what Pasolini was showing was fascism in its purest pre-technological form: the belief that you have the right, *the privilege,* to exert complete control over another being to the point of completely denying them their dignity and essential human rights; to strip them of all individuality and treat them like functional objects, to be discarded when they have outserved their capability. Now the demented aristocrats in the film have been replaced by larger powers: governments, corporations, data banks. But we still live in a world where the impulse to dominate another individual is one of the foremost of all human motivations. We all want to impose our own world-view on everyone else, don't we?'

'I suppose so . . . but how does this whole, uh, *thesis,* relate to my . . . *our* . . . heist movie?'

He looked at me and smiled the smile of someone about to impart a fantastic, highly original suggestion – and had been just waiting for the right moment to spring it on me.

'Say . . . and this is just a suggestion, but one I want you to consider very seriously . . . say our two Vietnam vets manage to pull off an initial bank job, but then make the mistake of getting a little ambitious, and decide to go after the loot of an ultra-secretive billionaire.'

Takes one to know one, I thought. But Fleck didn't flash me a grin of self-irony. He just kept talking.

'Anyway,' Fleck continued, 'let's say that this billionaire lives in a hilltop fortress in northern California . . . with one of the largest private art collections in the States, which our guys have decided to rip off. But when they finally break into this guy's citadel, they are immediately taken prisoner by his platoon of armed guards. And they discover he's set up a libertine society for himself and a bunch of his chums – with his very own sex slaves, both male and female. As soon as they're captured, our two guys are enslaved themselves . . . but immediately start plotting a way of liberating themselves and everyone else from this draconian regime.'

He paused and smiled at me. 'What do you think?' he asked.

Careful now. You don't want him to see you wince.

'Well,' I said, 'it sounds a bit like *Die Hard* meets The Marquis de Sade. A question, however: do our two guys get out alive?'

'Does that matter?'

'Of course it does . . . if you want this to be a somewhat commercial movie. I mean, given that you're thinking about spending $40 million, you are going to want to aim it at the multiplex crowd. Which means that they are going to have to have someone to root for. Which means that one of the vets walks out of there after blowing all the bad guys away . . .'

'And what happens to his other friend?' he asked, his voice suddenly terse.

'You let him die heroically . . . and preferably at the hands of the demented billionaire. Which, of course, gives the Bruce Willis character an even bigger personal grudge against his captor. At the end of the movie, after blowing away all his minions, Willis and the billionaire finally square off. Naturally, Willis has to walk away from the ruins of the mansion with some babe on his arm . . . preferably one of the sex slaves whom he's emancipated. Roll credits. And you've got a guaranteed $20 million opening weekend.'

Long pause. Philip Fleck pursed his lips.

'I don't like that,' he said. 'I don't like that at all.'

'Personally speaking, nor do I. But that's not the point.'

'What is the point then?'

'If you want to turn this heist movie into a "two guys get captured by a rich loony" movie, and you also want the film to make money, then you are going to have to play by certain mainstream Hollywood rules.'

'But this is not the movie you wrote,' he said, a hint of annoyance in his voice.

'Tell me about it,' I said. 'As you well know, the film I wrote – *and rewrote* – is a dark, funny, slightly dangerous Robert Altman-style comedy; the sort of thing that would be a perfect vehicle for Elliott Gould and Donald Sutherland as the old Vietnam vets. What you're proposing . . .'

'What I'm proposing is also dark and dangerous,' he said. 'I don't want to make some generic piece of shit. I want to re-interpret *Salo* in a twenty-first-century American context.'

'When you say "reinterpret" . . . ?' I said.

'I mean . . . lure the audience into believing that they are

137

watching a conventional heist movie, and then . . . *bam!* . . . throw them into the blackest heart of darkness imaginable.'

I studied Fleck with care. No, he wasn't being ironic or wry or even grimly fanciful. The guy was absolutely serious.

'Define what you mean by "heart of darkness"?' I said.

He shrugged. 'You saw *Salo*,' he said. 'What I'd be aiming for is the same extreme cruelty . . . pushing the boundaries of taste and audience tolerance to the furthest extremes.'

'Like, say, the turd banquet . . . ?'

'Well, naturally, we wouldn't want to directly ape Pasolini . . .'

'Of course *we* wouldn't . . .'

'But I do think there should be some sort of terrible degradation involving faecal matter. Because there's nothing more primal than shit, is there?'

'I'd certainly agree with that,' I said. I kept expecting him to say *Gotcha!* again, and give me a hard time about wrong-footing me for the second time. But he was deadly earnest. So I said, 'But you do know that if, say, you actually show a guy taking a dump on the floor, you won't just fail to get the movie passed by the ratings people . . . you might fail to get it released.'

'Oh, I'd get it released,' he said. True . . . because he could pay to get anything done. Just like he could also drop $40 million on an another extremist vanity project. The guy could do whatever he wanted . . . because his money insulated him from the usual run-of-the-mill worries about returning a profit on a movie (let alone getting the damn movie widely seen).

'You know, however, that the sort of film you're proposing will only play in Paris or maybe in some art house in Helsinki, where the suicide rate is high . . .'

Fleck tensed slightly. 'That's a joke, right?'

'Yeah. I was joking. All I'm saying is . . .'

'I know what you're saying. And I am aware that what I am proposing is radical. But if someone like me – given the resources at my disposal – plays it safe, how will art ever progress? Face fact, it has always been the wealthy elite who have funded the avant-garde. I'm simply funding myself. And if the rest of the world chooses to revile what I've done, so be it. As long as it's not ignored . . .'

'You mean, like your first movie?' I heard myself saying. Fleck tensed again, then glared at me in a way that made him seem simultaneously wounded and dangerous. Oops. I had just put my foot in it . . . big time. So I quickly said, 'Not, of course, that it deserved such treatment. And I doubt what you're proposing now – with our script – would be ignored. You might have the Christian Coalition burning effigies of you, but I'm certain attention would be paid. In a major way.'

Now he was smiling again, and I was relieved. Then he hit a button on the table. Meg arrived within seconds. He asked for a bottle of champagne.

'I think we should toast our collaboration, David,' he said.

'Are we collaborating on this?'

'That's what I'm assuming. I mean, you are interested in continuing to work on the project, aren't you?'

'That depends . . .'

'On what?'

'The usual stuff: our mutual schedules, my other professional obligations, the contractual terms your people work out with my people. And then there's the issue of money.'

'Money wouldn't be an issue.'

'Money's *always* an issue in the movie business.'

'It's not with me. Name your price.'

'Sorry?'

'Name your price. Tell me how much you'd want to rewrite the script.'

'This is an area I never really dabble in. You'll have to talk to my agent . . .'

'I'm going to say it again, David: *Name your price.*'

I took a deep, nervous breath. 'You're talking about one rewrite to your specifications?'

'Two drafts and a polish,' he said.

'Then you're asking for a substantial commitment of time,' I said.

'And I'm sure you'll charge accordingly.'

'And we'd be talking about your "Salo in Napa Valley" scenario?'

A tight little smile. 'I suppose one could refer to it as that,' he said. 'So . . . the price, please.'

Without flinching, I said, '$2.5 million.'

He studied his fingernails. And said, 'Sold.'

Now I did flinch. 'You sure about that?'

'It's a done deal. So, shall we get started?'

'Well . . . *uh* . . . I don't usually start work until a contract is signed. And I'd have to talk things over with my agent.'

'What's to talk about? You named a price. I've accepted it. Let's go to work.'

'Now?'

'Yes – this instant.'

But an hour from now, I'm supposed to be aboard one of your private jets, heading west to see my daughter; a weekend together that I can't (and won't) miss.

'Well, I know my agent's out of town right now . . .'

'But surely we can track her down somewhere. And if not, I'll still arrange for half of the $2.5 million to be transferred to your bank account this afternoon.'

'That's incredibly generous – and honorable – of you. But that's not really the problem. The thing is, I've got an important family commitment back on the Coast.'

'Is it life or death?' he asked.

'No – but if I don't show up, it's going to really upset my daughter – and my ex-wife will use my no-show as a way to legally flay me.'

'Fuck her,' he said.

'It's not that easy.'

'Yes, it is. Anyway, $2.5 million will buy you a lot of legal assistance.'

'But there's a child involved too.'

'She'll live.'

Perhaps. But I might not be able to handle the guilt.

'Here's what I propose,' I said. 'Let me go to San Francisco now, and I can be back here first thing Monday morning.'

He started regarding his fingernails again. 'I won't be here,' he said.

'Well then, I could meet you wherever you are.'

'Next week's impossible.'

'How about the week after?' I said, and suddenly regretted making that offer. Because I had violated Rule Number One of Writing for the Movies: I'd sounded far too eager . . . which, in turn, meant that I appeared to need the work or really wanted the money. Which was true – but in Hollywood (and especially around a tricky guy like Fleck), you had to behave as if you could live without the million-dollar deal. So much of the game was about striking an attitude of complete self-command, and never admitting doubt or (horror of horrors) actually needing someone else. In this instance, I didn't *need* this writing gig – and, in fact, had grave doubts about its creative legitimacy. But how could I resist the absurd paycheck . . . especially when I would also get Alison to structure the contract in such a way that I would have no problems with taking my damn name off the screenplay, and could subsequently deny all knowledge of Fleck's warped, faecal-obsessive tamperings with my original baby.

The thing was, Fleck himself now realized that he had me in a delightful conundrum: stay the weekend and get working on a $2.5 million writing contract. Or leave and . . .

'I'm afraid this is the only weekend I have free,' he said flatly. 'And, to be blunt about it, I'm rather disappointed by your attitude, David. I mean, you came out here to work with me, didn't you?'

I adopted a calm, reasonable tone of voice.

'Philip . . . just to set the record straight again. You flew me out here to discuss my script. You also kept me waiting seven days . . . an entire week, during which we could have done a vast amount of work on the script. Instead . . .'

'You were actually waiting here seven days?'

Oh God. Back we go into the Twilight Zone.

'I did mention this at the start of our conversation,' I said.

'Then why didn't anyone tell me?'

'I have no idea, Philip. But I was certainly given to believe that you did know I was cooling my heels here.'

'Sorry,' he said, suddenly all vague and distant again. 'I didn't have a clue . . .'

What a complete, total liar. I couldn't believe his ability to suddenly disengage, and to act as if he was suffering from memory lapse or a strange interlude . . . to the point where he hardly even acknowledged my presence. It was as if he abruptly blacked you out once you said (or did) something which didn't fit in with his plan, his world-view. As soon as that happened, he pressed a mental *Erase* button, and you were consigned to the bin marked 'nowhere'.

'Well . . .' he said, glancing at his watch. 'Are we done here?'

'That's up to you.'

He stood up. 'We're done. Anything else you need to tell me?'

Yeah – you're an asshole supreme.

'I think the next move is yours,' I said. 'My agent's name and number is on the pad. I'm happy to proceed with the rewrite on the terms discussed between us. Since I won't be starting work on the next series of *Selling You* until two months from now, this is a good moment to get the work you want done. But, once again, it's your call.'

'Fine, fine,' he said, looking over my shoulder at one of his functionaries who was holding a cellphone in one hand, silently motioning that he needed to take this call. 'Listen . . . thanks for coming out. I hope it was useful to you . . .'

'Oh, absolutely,' I said, a noticeable edge of sarcasm entering my voice. 'It was *so* useful.'

He gave me a quizzical look. 'Are you being sarcastic?'

'Hardly,' I said, sounding even more sarcastic.

'You know what your problem is, David?'

'Enlighten me.'

'You can't take a joke, can you?'

And he broke into another of his *Gotcha!* grins.

'You mean, you *do* want to work with me?' I asked.

'Absolutely. And if it means waiting a month, so be it.'

'Like I said, I can get going whenever . . .'

'Then let my people talk to your people, and once all the contractual stuff is sorted out, we'll arrange a free weekend somewhere, during which the two of us can thrash out the entire rewrite. Does that sound good to you?'

'Yeah, fine,' I said, not knowing what to think anymore.

'Well, if you're pleased, I'm pleased,' pumping my hand. 'Nice to be in business with you. And I really think we're going to come up with something truly *out there*. Something they won't forget in a hurry.'

'I'm sure.'

He patted my shoulder. 'Have a good flight back, my friend.'

And he was gone.

Meg – standing quietly in a corner of the room – stepped forward and said, 'The chopper's ready when you are, sir. Anything else we can do for you before you go?'

'Absolutely nothing,' I said, but then thanked her for looking after me.

'I hope the time here was useful to you, sir,' she said, the smallest flicker of a smile crossing her lips.

The chopper got me to Antigua. The Gulfstream got me to San Francisco. We landed on schedule just after three pm. As promised, a limousine was waiting, and brought me to Lucy's house in Sausalito. Caitlin came running down the path and threw herself into my arms. Her mother emerged from the house, glowering at me, glowering at the limousine.

'Are you trying to impress us?' she asked, handing me Caitlin's weekend bag.

'Lucy, when have I *ever* been able to impress you?' I asked.

Caitlin looked anxiously at each of us, her eyes imploring us not to start. So I ushered her into the limousine, informed Lucy that we'd be back at six on Sunday evening, and then told the driver to take us to the Mandarin.

'Why do you have this big car?' Caitlin asked me as we crossed the bridge back into San Francisco.

'Someone who likes my writing gave it to me for the weekend.'

'Will you be able to keep it?'

'No – but we can make the most of it this weekend.'

Caitlin seriously approved of the penthouse suite at the Mandarin Oriental. So did I. It overlooked the Bay, the two bridges, the lustrous downtown skyline, the entire melodramatic sweep of the city. As we pressed our noses against the suite's vast windows and peered out, Caitlin asked me, 'Can we stay here every weekend you visit me?'

'I'm afraid this is a one-off.'

'The rich man again?'

'The very one.'

'But if he keeps liking you . . .' she said hopefully.

I laughed. 'Life doesn't work that way,' I said, wanting to add: *Especially in the movie business.*

Caitlin didn't want to go out for the evening; she was very content to be in this room with a view. So we ordered up room service. As we waited for it to arrive, the phone rang – and I heard a voice I hadn't heard for over a week.

'How's it hanging?' Bobby Barra said.

'Well, what a pleasant surprise,' I said. 'You still in New York?'

'Yeah – still trying to fight a rearguard action to save this fucking IPO. But it's like trying to put a Band-Aid on a sliced jugular vein.'

'Nice image, Bobby. And let me guess how you found out I was here.'

'Yeah – Phil's people told me. But I talked to The Man Himself. And I've got to tell you, guy . . . he loved you.'

'Really?'

'Hey, what's with the quizzical tone?'

'He kept me waiting a week, Bobby. *A week*. Then he showed up an hour before I had to leave, and first made like he never knew me, and then made like he wanted to work with me and then played a variety of other head games. He yanked my chain, and I didn't like it.'

'Listen, what can I say? Between ourselves, he's a little weird. Like there are times when I think the guy is Plan Nine from Outer Space. But he's also $20 billion worth of weird, and he told me he really wants to make this movie with you . . .'

'His creative ideas are shit, you know,' I said, interrupting. 'In fact, he's actually obsessed with shit.'

'So what? I mean, shit has its own integrity, right? Especially when it comes with a seven figure price tag. So forget about the guy's bad manners, enjoy the Mandarin, have a great time with your daughter, and tell that agent of yours to expect a call from Fleck's people next week.'

But when I got back to LA late Sunday night and told the whole story to Sally she said that, in her opinion, there was less than no chance I'd hear from him again.

'He toyed with you, as if you were last week's trinket. But at least you got a suntan out of it. You meet anyone else on the island?'

I decided it was best not to mention my evening with Mrs Fleck, so I said no, and then changed the subject back to the subject Sally wanted to get back to – her triumphant management of the Stu Barker crisis . . . turning her one-time adversary into her great ally and protector within the course of a week. So much so, in fact, that he was giving her carte blanche with the autumn prime time lineup, and was making it known in top Fox circles that she was *the* player to watch right now.

Oh, and somewhere in the midst of her heroic account of this latest professional conquest, she did mention that she missed me and loved me madly. I kissed her and told her the exact same things.

'Everyone has their moment,' she said. 'This is ours.'

And, in a way, she was right. Because, to my immense surprise, Fleck's lawyer did call Alison a week later to discuss the terms and conditions of the contract. It was all very straightforward and businesslike. There was no argument about the $2.5 million tab for my services. There was no argument about a clause allowing me to remove my name from the script.

Alison said, 'Let's face it, a two-point-five deal would make anyone sit up and salivate . . . me especially. But if he is going to push ahead with all his excrement fantasies we're definitely not going to want your name attached to that sort of insanity . . . which is why I insisted on this take-the-money-and-run clause.'

'Do you think I'm crazy to be getting into this?' I asked her.

'From what you've told me, the guy is from the David Koresh School of Mental Stability. But as long as you know that – and as long as we've got you fixed up with a contractual parachute – the price is right. However, you better keep this job down to a couple of months maximum, because I've no doubt that you are about to be in even greater professional demand.'

Sure enough, Alison was right. When the second season of *Selling You* hit the small screen a month later, it was an instant hit.

'If the opening two episodes prove anything,' the *New York Times* wrote, 'it's that David Armitage isn't simply a flash in the pan. His brilliantly structured, mordant, corrosive scripts for these first two installments of the new series show that he is one of the great comic writers of our time, with an absurd eye that still manages to grasp the inherent social complexity of the contemporary American workplace.'

Thank you very much indeed. The reviews – coupled with great word of mouth (and a considerable number of fans from the first season) – guaranteed terrific ratings. So terrific that, after Episode Three, FRT greenlit a third season, and Alison negotiated a $2.5 million writing-producing package for me. Around the same time, Warner Brothers offered me a cool million-five to write a movie of my choosing. Naturally, I accepted.

I mentioned this Warners deal to Bobby Barra during a phone call right after the season premiere of *Selling You*. He congratulated me – and asked if I would like to be one of the privileged few who would be allowed to invest seriously in a sure-fire IPO for an Asian search engine that was guaranteed to become the number one player in China and all of Southeast Asia?

'This is like backing Yahoo with slopey eyes,' he told me.

'How politically correct of you, Bobby.'

'Listen – we're talking about the biggest untapped market in the world. And it's the chance to get in at ground level. But I've got to know fast . . . you interested?'

'You've never steered me wrong yet.'

'Smart guy.'

Actually, I really did feel like something of a smart guy – because everything was going my way.

And then there was the little matter of the Emmy Awards, which I attended with both Sally and Caitlin (whom everyone thought was charming). When they reached the award for Writing for a Comedy Series, and the envelope was opened, and my name was called, I embraced my two girls and raced to the stage and accepted the award with a short speech in which I thanked 'all the far more talented people than myself who brought my scribblings to remarkable televisual life', while also acknowledging the fact that the only way you ended up winning an award like this was through pure, dumb luck.

'And so, when I look back on the extraordinary professional experience that was *Selling You*, I know I'll think that this was one of those rare, peerless moments in professional life when all the planets were in alignment, when the Gods of Happenstance smiled, when I learned that Providence wasn't just a town in Rhode Island . . . or when, in plain English, I simply got lucky.'

It was the climactic moment to an astonishing two years. That night, falling into bed with Sally, my brain tingling with far too much champagne, I found myself thinking, *You once dreamed of a life like this. Now it's yours.*

Congratulations: you have arrived.

Part Two

One

THE TROUBLE ALL started with a phone call. A very early morning phone call on the Wednesday after the Emmy Awards. Sally had already left the apartment for a breakfast confab with Stu Barker, and I was still deep in Never-Never Land when the phone suddenly sprang into life. As I jolted awake, one thought filled my clouded brain: a phone call at this hour is never good news.

The phone call was from my producer, Brad Bruce. He sounded tense – producers always do – but from the moment he started talking, I could tell that he wasn't simply his normal edgy self; something was definitely wrong.

'Sorry to be calling at this time,' Brad said, 'but we've got a problem.'

I sat up in bed. 'What sort of problem, Brad?'

'Are you familiar with a rag called *Hollywood Legit*?' he asked, mentioning a free, alternative paper that had come on the scene in the last year, in competition with *LA Reader* – and one which prided itself on its tough investigative reporting, and its distaste for all the usual Hollywood overpaid self-importance.

'Has the series made the pages of the *Legit*?' I asked.

'It's you who's made the pages, David.'

'Me? But I'm just a writer.'

'A very high profile writer . . . which makes you a target for all sorts of accusations.'

'I've been accused of something?'

'I'm afraid so.'

'What exactly?'

I could hear him sucking in his breath, then accompanying the exhalation with one word: 'Plagiarism.'

My heart missed three beats. '*What?*'

'You've been accused of plagiarism, David.'

'That's insane.'

'I'm glad to hear it.'

'I don't plagiarize, Brad.'

'I'm sure you don't . . .'

'So if I don't plagiarize, why am I being called a plagiarist?'

'Because this shitbag journalist named Theo McCall wrote some-thing in his this week's column, which is due to hit the streets tomorrow morning.'

I knew Theo McCall's column. It was called 'The Inside Dirt' – and it certainly dished it. Week in, week out, this guy dug up all sorts of unpleasant, scandalmongering stuff about the enter-tainment community. It was the sort of column that I took prurient delight in reading. Because we all love gossip . . . until the moment that we ourselves become the subject matter.

'I'm not in *that* column, am I?' I said.

'The very one. Want me to read you the item? It's rather long.'

That didn't sound promising. 'Go on,' I said.

'Okay . . . here it is: "*Congrats are in order to* Selling You *writer-and-creator, David Armitage. Besides scooping up an Emmy last week for Comedy Writing, he's now basking in a sensational set of reviews for the new series which, it must be admitted, is even better than its premiere season . . .*"

I interrupted him.

'"It must be admitted" . . . What a begrudging, petty-assed thing to say.'

'It gets worse, I'm afraid. "*Without question, Armitage must be regarded as one of the great discoveries of the past few years . . . not just for his wickedly skewed comic observations, but also for the bril-liant stream of one-liners mouthed by his hyper-anxious characters, week after week. But though no one questions Mr Armitage's droll orig-inality, one sharp-eared informant enlightened this column last week with the intriguing news that an entire exchange of dialogue from Armitage's Emmy-award-winning episode is a near-verbatim lift from Ben Hecht and Charles McArthur's classic journalism comedy,* The Front Page . . .*"

Once again I interrupted Brad.

'This is complete bullshit,' I said. 'I haven't seen *The Front Page* in . . .'

Now Brad interrupted me. 'But you *have* seen it?'

'Sure – both the Billy Wilder film and the Howard Hawks version with Cary Grant and Rosalind Russell. I even acted in a college production of the play at Dartmouth . . .'

'Oh, that's fucking wonderful . . .'

'We're talking nearly twenty years ago . . .'

'Well, you obviously remember *something* from *it*. Because the passage you allegedly lifted . . .'

'Brad, I lifted *nothing* . . .'

'Hear me out. This is what McCall writes: "*The repartee in question can be found in the* Selling You *episode – 'Shtick Happens' – for which Armitage won his Emmy. In it, Joey – the fast-and-loose dogsbody for Armitage's fictitious PR agency – runs smack into a police van while driving a big-deal client (a mega-egoistic Soul diva) across town for a taping of* The Oprah Show. *He then comes staggering back into the office to inform Jerome – the company's founder – that their diva is in the hospital, screaming police brutality. In Armitage's script, there is the following exchange:*

JEROME   *You actually ran into a cop car?*

JOEY   *What can I say, boss? It was an accident.*

JEROME   *Were any of the cops hurt?*

JOEY   *I didn't stick around to find out. But you know what happens when you hit a cop car. They all roll out like lemons.*

'*Now compare and contrast this clever banter with the following dialogue from* The Front Page, *in which Louis – the henchman of wheeling-dealing editor, Walter Burns – races into the newsroom to tell his boss that, in the course of whisking the future mother-in-law of ace reporter, Hildy Johnson, across town, he's collided with a van filled with Chicago's finest:*

WALTER   *You actually ran into a police van?*

LOUIE   *What can I say, boss? It was an accident.*

WALTER   *Were any of the cops hurt?*

LOUIE   *I didn't stick around to find out. But you know what happens when you hit a cop van. They all roll out like lemons.*

'Oh, Jesus . . .' I whispered. 'I never . . .'

'You better listen to McCall's final paragraph: "*Without question, this virtual reproduction by Armitage is one of those unintentional examples of what the French call an 'hommage' . . . better known in plain English as being a copycat. No doubt, this is the only example of plagiarism in the Armitage 'oeuvre'. But it's clear that this clever, talented writer has, in this instance, embraced that famous T.S. Eliot diktat: 'Immature poets imitate; mature poets steal.'"*'

Long pause. I suddenly felt as if I had just walked into an empty elevator shaft.

'I don't know what to say, Brad.'

'There's not much to say. I mean, to be blunt about it, he caught you red-handed . . .'

'Now wait a damn minute. Are you saying that I *deliberately* lifted that dialogue from *The Front Page*?'

'I'm saying nothing. I'm just looking at the facts. And the fact is the dialogue he quoted from your script *and* from that play are one and the same . . .'

'Okay, okay, maybe the dialogue is the same. But it's not as if I sat down and opened the script of *The Front Page* and copied . . .'

'David, believe me, I'm not accusing you of that. But you have been caught with the smoking gun in your hand . . .'

'This is trivial stuff . . .'

'No, this is deeply serious stuff . . .'

'Look, what are we dealing with here? A joke from a seventy-year-old play that somehow ended up, *by osmosis*, in my script. But we're not talking about an intentional case of literary theft. We're talking about my inadvertent use of someone else's joke, that's all. Who doesn't purloin jokes? It's the nature of the game.'

'True – but there's a difference between using some guy's "*take my wife . . .*" gag, and having four lines of dialogue from a famous play pop up in *your* script.'

Long pause. My heart was pounding, as the realization hit me: *I am in big trouble here.*

'Brad, you've got to know that this was completely unpremeditated on my part . . .'

'And David, you've got to know that, as your producer, I am

going to go to the wall with you on this one. Of course, I know you would never do anything so insane and self-destructive. Of course, I can fully understand how a couple of lines from someone else's work can be unintentionally absorbed into your own work. And, of course, I know that every writer has, at one time or another, been accidentally guilty of this petty misdemeanor. The problem is – you got caught.'

'But it's a minor-league offense.'

'And so say all of us. But . . . I've got even more bad news. You know Tracy Weiss . . .' he said, mentioning FRT's head of public relations.

'Of course I know Tracy.'

'Well, at nine-thirty last night, she got a call from this *Variety* journalist, Craig Clark, who wanted an official comment from FRT. Thank Christ Tracy knows Clark pretty well. Because she convinced the guy to hold on the story until today . . . on the understanding that he'd get an exclusive statement from FRT *and* from you . . .'

'Great.'

'Listen, we're into damage control mode. So anything we can do to lessen the shit storm . . .'

'Understood, understood.'

'So when Tracy called me last night . . .'

'If you knew about this last night,' I said, 'why did you wait to call me until now?'

'Because Tracy and I knew that, if you'd been told last night, you wouldn't have slept. And we both decided that, given what you're about to face into today, you definitely needed a good night's sleep.'

'So what am I facing into today, Brad?'

'You need to be at the office by eight, no later. Tracy and I will be there. Ditto Bob Robison . . .'

'Bob knows?' I said, sounding edgier.

'Bob's the Head of Series. Of course, he knows. What Tracy's hoping for is that we can all craft a statement in which you admit that this was an unpremeditated goof; that you regret the mistake, and that you're simply guilty of telling a good joke twice. Anyway, after we figure out the statement, you're meeting for ten minutes with the *Variety* hack . . .'

'I have to go face-to-face with this guy?'

'If you want a sympathetic hearing, there's no other way around it. And what Tracy's banking on is that, if he gives you the benefit of the doubt, we can get our side of the story out there simultaneously with McCall's turdy column, and cauterize this thing fast.'

'And if the *Variety* guy doesn't buy my side of the story, what then?'

Once more, I could hear my producer take a slow, steadying inhalation of breath.

'Let's not go there yet.'

Long pause. Then he said, 'Look, I know this is bad . . .'

'Bad? It's much ado about nothing.'

'*Exactly*. And that's the way we're going to play it. Which is why I know we'll get through this. But David, I just need to ask you one thing . . .'

I knew what was coming. 'No,' I said, 'I have never, *ever* intentionally plagiarized anything. And *no*, to the best of my knowledge there are no further unintentional paraphrases or quotes from other people's work, in any of my *Selling You* scripts.'

'That's exactly what I wanted to hear. Now get your ass down here fast. It's going to be a long day.'

In the car on the way to the office, I called Alison at home.

'That is the slimiest thing I've heard in my life,' Alison said after I paraphrased McCall's column, 'and I've encountered a lot of slimy stuff.'

'Any way you look at it, it's bad . . .'

'It's petty bullshit, dressed up as scandal. Fucking journalists. They all have the morality of a tom cat. They'll spray anything that moves.'

'What am I going to do?'

'Whatever happens, you'll live.'

'That's very reassuring.'

'What I'm saying here is: don't panic. Get yourself safely to the office in that Hun-mobile of yours. I'll meet you there. And believe me: I won't let them fry you, David. I won't even let them sauté you. Hang in there.'

As I edged my way through traffic, my mood vacillated from fear to belligerence. All right, my subconscious had possibly betrayed me . . . but I had done nothing deliberately wrong. More to the point, this creep McCall was taking a few inconsequential lines and transforming them into a burning-at-the-stake offense. As far as I was concerned, the only way to combat such malicious journalistic behavior was to come out of the corner, swinging.

'That's exactly what we *won't* do,' Tracy Weiss said when I proposed this take-no-shit approach at the start of our meeting. We gathered in Brad's office, sitting around the circular 'ideas table' where we usually brainstormed stuff for the series. But this morning, I was greeted by Brad, Tracy and Bob Robison with supportive words and edgy faces which betrayed their fear – and which also let it be known that, ultimately, this was not going to be a communal *we'll share the guilt together* situation. On the contrary, from the moment I faced the three of them around that table, I realized that – though this was, corporately speaking, their problem – I was the defendant here. And if punishment was meted out, I'd take the brunt of it.

'The fact is, David,' Tracy said, 'though McCall may be, at the best of times, a vindictive scumbag, he still has you by both *cojones*. Which means that, like it or not, we've got to soft-pedal this thing.'

Alison, seated next to me, lit up a Salem and said, 'But McCall is trying to hang David for jay-walking.'

'Cut the melodrama, Alison,' Bob Robison said. 'The guy's got evidence. And – take it from an ex-member of the California bar – evidence is all you need to convict someone. Motives count for shit if you've been nabbed in the act.'

'But there's a difference here,' I said. 'The alleged plagiarism was subliminal . . .'

'Big fucking deal,' Bob Robison said. 'You didn't mean to do it, but you still did it.'

'That *is* a big fucking deal,' Alison said, 'because half the time, writers don't know where their stuff comes from.'

'Unfortunately,' Robison said, 'Theo McCall worked that one out for David.'

'I didn't mean this to happen,' I said.

'My sympathies,' Robison said, 'and I mean that. Because you know how highly I rate you. But the fact remains: *it happened*. You plagiarized. You may not have intended to plagiarize, but you still plagiarized. Do you see the point I'm trying to make here, David?'

I nodded.

'And once again,' Brad said, 'I want both you and Alison to know that we are completely behind you on this. We will not abandon you.'

'That's very touching, Brad,' Alison said dryly, 'and I hope I never have to quote that promise back to you.'

'We *are* going to fight this,' Tracy said, 'but in a way that doesn't seem either aggressive or defensive. The idea is to close down any further lines of argument – or inquiry – by issuing a statement in which David admits accidental culpability . . .'

'Good phrase,' Robison said.

'. . . but in which he also doesn't prostrate himself. The tone is going to be very important. So too is the tone you bring to the interview with Craig Clark.'

'Do you think he'll be sympathetic?' Brad asked him.

'First and foremost, he's an entertainment journalist. And a story like this . . . well, my hope is that he has enough insight into the business to understand how something like this could unwittingly happen. At the same time, he's not a malicious creep like McCall. We'll be giving him exclusive access to David, and he does love the show. So let's hope that he decides this story is a sidebar, nothing more.'

We spent the next hour working on the FRT statement – in which the company acknowledged that I had inadvertently transposed a few lines from *The Front Page* into my script, that I greatly regretted this 'undevised error' (Tracy's words, not mine), and had been genuinely appalled when it was pointed out to me. There was a quote from Bob Robison stating that he fully accepted my explanation for the 'transposition', and that they completely supported me – to the extent that, as widely reported in the entertainment press last month, they had just signed me for the next series of *Selling You*. (It was Alison who insisted that they put this line in the press release – just to remind everyone they weren't just sticking by me, but would continue to 'further our relationship'.)

Finally, there was a quote from me, in which I sounded contrite as hell, but also genuinely bemused as to how this could have happened in the first place:

'Writers are like sponges – they soak everything up, and then recycle it all again . . . sometimes without even realizing it. Certainly this was the case with the four lines of dialogue from *The Front Page* which managed to end up in an episode last season of *Selling You*. I'll admit it: *The Front Page* is one of my favorite plays, and one which I acted in during college. But that was in 1980, and I haven't seen or read it since then. How then did a handful of Ben Hecht and Charles MacArthur's peerless lines find their way into my script? I honestly don't know. That doesn't excuse this accidental transposition [Tracy's words again] – which has caused me acute embarrassment, as it would any writer. I have never intentionally used another writer's words. This is a once-off error – and all I can plead is mental misadventure; pulling a joke out of the jumbled filing cabinet of my brain, and not remembering where I'd heard it in the first place.'

We talked at length about this confessional statement. Bob Robison wanted it to be a flat out *mea culpa* (well, he is a Catholic). Alison wanted me to strike a quasi-apologetic, yet still defiant pose – pointing out that this was small beer . . . and, for God sakes, don't other people's jokes always end up in other people's material? But it was Tracy who encouraged me to balance contrition with wit.

'This is also the tone you need to strike with Craig Clark,' Tracy said after we finished writing my quote. Sorry, embarrassed, yet also 'ironically knowing' . . . whatever that meant.

As it turned out, Craig Clark was decent enough for a journalist. After ushering the others out of Bob's office, Tracy discreetly sat in a corner while Craig fired questions at me. He was in his early forties – slightly stocky, slightly harassed in demeanor, but wholly professional and (I was relieved to discover) relatively sympathetic.

'Let me say from the outset that I'm a huge fan of *Selling You*.'

'Thank you,' I said.

'I really do think it's a breakthrough in television comedy; a total original. Which is why this . . . uh . . . disclosure must be so hard for you. Just to kick things off, can I ask you this: do you think most writers at one time or another have accidentally borrowed someone else's lines?'

Praise the Lord! The guy was in my corner. He didn't want to eviscerate me, or to wreck my career. He asked a couple of tough questions – about whether even an accidental crib was a forgivable offense (to which I replied, 'No – it's not,' in the hope that the *I'm making no excuses for myself* approach would impress him), and if I deserved severe censuring from my fellow writers ('Probably,' I said, maintaining the *I'll take my punishment like a man* tone). I also made him laugh – saying that if I had to accidentally borrow from something, thank God it was *The Front Page* and not *Gilligan's Island.* I also said that, as penance, I was going to write the next Jackie Chan movie. In short, I seemed to strike the *okay sorry, but this isn't a federal offense* tone which Tracy wanted from me. At the end of our twenty minutes (Tracy let it overrun, as Clark appeared to be enjoying himself), he shook my hand and said, 'Well, I do hope this turns out to be a minor glitch on your career chart.'

'Thanks,' I said. 'And I really appreciate the thoughtful interview.'

'You gave good copy.'

I reached into my pocket and took out a little notebook, and wrote my home and cellphone numbers on a page. Then I tore it out and handed it to him.

'If you need to ask me a few more questions, just give me a ring at either of those numbers. And once all this dust has settled . . . maybe we can have a beer.'

'That would be great,' he said, pocketing the paper. 'I . . . uh . . . have written a couple of spec television comedy scripts . . .'

'Let's talk.'

He shook my hand again. 'You're on,' he said.

Tracy opened the door for him and said, 'I'll walk you to your car.'

As soon as they were gone, Alison came back into the office.

160

'Tracy gave me the thumbs up on the way out. You happy with how it played?'

I shrugged. 'Right now, I feel numb.'

'You're about to feel even number. While I was sitting in your office, Jennifer took a call from Sally. She said it was urgent.'

Oh, wonderful. She'd found out . . . before I had a chance to tell her.

I went to my office and called Sally. Her assistant put me straight through. Her first words were, 'I'm stunned by this.'

'Darling, can I –'

'And what's hurt me the most is the fact that I found all this out second hand.'

'But I only found out myself just before seven.'

'You should have called me immediately.'

'But I knew you were doing breakfast with Stu.'

'I would have taken your call.'

'And the thing was, I had to race straight down here, and I've been in crisis meetings ever since, not to mention an interview with some guy from *Variety*.'

'*Variety* knows already?' she said, sounding anxious.

'Yeah – but Tracy Weiss, the head of PR here, got a call last night from this journo who writes for *Variety* and she decided . . .'

'So she knew about this last night . . .'

'Yes, but, *believe me,* I was only told this morning. And to get our side of the story out, she decided to offer this hack an exclusive with me . . .'

'It's in tomorrow's *Daily Variety?*'

'Absolutely.'

'And have FRT issued a statement?'

'Yeah – with a contrite quote from me.'

'You'll get them to email it to me?'

'Of course, darling. But please, don't go all cold and professional on me. I need you right now.'

'If you needed me, you should have called me immediately. I am supposed to be the love of your life.'

'You know you are. It's just . . . oh Christ, Sally, this is just a little overwhelming.'

'Can you imagine what it was like for me . . . to be shown that *Hollywood Legit* column by some minor minion from our press office, and to be told "What a shame about your guy" . . . and not to know a thing about it.'

'I'm sorry, I'm sorry, I'm . . .'

I broke off, suddenly feeling steamrollered by everything.

'David . . . ?'

'Yeah . . .'

'You all right?'

'No. I am definitely not all right.'

'Now I feel terrible . . .'

'You know how much I adore you . . .' I said.

'And you know how much I adore you. It's just . . .'

'You're right, you're right. I should have called. But everything went chaotic. And . . .'

'You don't have to explain. I overreacted. But I was just so upset. And, I mean, it does look very bad. It was accidental, wasn't it?'

'It certainly wasn't premeditated.'

'Well, that's something. And you're certain . . . ?'

Here came that question again – the one everybody needed to ask me.

'Believe me, that's the only time someone else's lines have ended up in a script of mine.'

'Of course, I believe you, darling. And because it's a one-off, it will be forgiven and forgotten.'

'I am not an intentional plagiarist,' I said, sounding vehement.

'I know that. Within a week, it will be old news.'

'I hope to hell you're right.'

'I'm always right,' she said lightly, and I laughed for the first time since waking up.

'You know what would be great?' I said. 'A long boozy lunch with you. I think I need a martini anaesthetic fast.'

'Darling, you know I'm back off to Seattle this afternoon . . .'

'I'd forgotten that.'

'It's that new series of ours . . .'

'Fine, fine.'

'But I will be back first thing Saturday. And I will call lots.'

'Good.'

'It's going to be okay, David.'

After the call, I poked my head out of the office. Alison was sitting behind Jennifer's desk, working the phones. I nodded towards her to come in to the office. She finished her call and walked in, closing the door behind her.

'So how did that go?' she asked me.

'She was eventually supportive.'

'That's something,' she said neutrally.

'Don't say it . . .'

'Say what?'

'What you're thinking about Sally.'

'I'm thinking nothing about Sally.'

'Liar.'

'Guilty as charged. But at least she came around . . . after probably working out that this isn't going to harm her as well . . .'

'Now that's bitchy,' I said.

'But completely accurate.'

'Can we move on?'

'With pleasure. Because I've got some good news. I just spoke to Larry Latouche at SATWA,' she said, using the acronym of the Screen and Television Writers' Association. 'He already knew about the McCall piece.'

'He *did*?'

'What can I say – it's a slow week for showbiz gossip. Maybe if we get lucky, in the next forty-eight hours, some hot actor will get caught with an under-aged illegal Mexican babe, and he'll deflect some of the heat. For the moment, however, you're about to become the town's talking point. And word is spreading fast.'

'Wonderful.'

'But the good news is that Latouche is outraged by McCall's accusations – especially as he himself can cite at least two dozen other examples of a few lines from someone else's script ending up being innocently used elsewhere. Anyway, he wanted you to know that the Association is fully behind you on this . . . and he's planning to issue a press release tomorrow morning, confirming this and also damning McCall for turning a trifle into bullshit news.'

'I'll call Latouche later to say thanks.'

'Good idea. We need heavy hitters in your corner right now.'

There was a knock on the door. Tracy entered, holding a copy of the press release.

'So here it is. The big suits at Corporate HQ in New York have just approved it.'

'How have they taken the news?' Alison asked.

'They're not pleased – because, they don't like *tsouris*. But they're completely supportive of David, and want this whole situation closed down a.s.a.p..'

Alison then mentioned the Latouche statement. Tracy wasn't happy.

'That's nice to have their support, Alison,' she said, 'and I appreciate you organizing this, but I wish you'd cleared it with me first.'

Alison lit up another Salem.

'I didn't realize I worked for you, Tracy,' she said.

'You know what I'm saying,' Tracy said.

'Yeah – you're a control freak.'

'Alison . . .' I said.

'You're right,' Tracy said. 'I am a control freak. And I want to control this situation in such a way that your client's career isn't damaged. Does that bother you?'

'No – but your tone does,' Alison said.

'And your cigarette's really bothering control freak me,' Tracy said. 'We're a smoke-free environment.'

'Then I'm just going to have to fuck off out of here,' Alison said.

'Alison, Tracy,' I said, 'let's all calm down a bit.'

'Sure,' Alison said, 'and while we're at it, we can all hug each other and shed a tear, and *achieve growth*.'

'I didn't mean to upset you, Alison,' Tracy said.

'This whole shitty situation upsets me . . . and yeah, that's my attempt at an apology too.'

'You free for dinner tonight?' I asked Alison.

'Where's your inamorata?'

'Checking up on a pilot being filmed in Seattle.'

'Then the martinis are on me. We need about six apiece. Come by the office around six.'

After she left, Tracy turned to me and said, 'If you don't mind me saying so, she's a total piece of work . . . and you're lucky to have her in your corner. I think she'd just about kill and maim for you.'

'Yeah, she is pretty feral . . . and insanely loyal.'

'Then you're a lucky guy. They expunged "loyalty" from the LA vocabulary long ago.'

'But I can count on your loyalty, can't I?'

'Sure,' she said quickly. 'That's all part of the package.'

'So what do I do now?'

'Wait and see how the McCall story plays.'

By noon the following day, there was a sense that we were winning the public relations war. Though the *LA Times* ran a small sidebar (in the Arts section) about McCall's column, the story wasn't picked up by any of the other major national papers – a sure sign that this item was being regarded as Hollywood tittle-tattle, nothing more. Yes, the *Hollywood Reporter* ran a large-ish page two story on those four damn lines; it was a balanced story, featuring my apologia (from the press release), and Larry Latouche's justification of my position. Better yet was Craig Clark's story in *Daily Variety*, pointing out that (during the course of our 'exclusive interview') I was completely open about this 'accidental plagiarism', and 'did not try to make excuses for his inadvertent error'. Then he went on to quote around five different leading television and film writers (whom he'd obviously chased down yesterday), all of whom leaped to my defense. But the real *coup de grâce* was a comment that Clark gleaned from Justin Wanamaker, a man who (along with William Goldman and Robert Towne) was considered one of the truly eminent screen-writers of the past thirty years.. In a prepared statement (which – as Clark revealed – Wanamaker e-mailed exclusively to *Variety*) he didn't simply put the knife into Theo McCall's back. He also twisted it several times:

'There are serious entertainment journalists, and then there are morally suspect pugilists like Theo McCall, who think nothing of undermining a writer's career by making suspect allegations of plagiarism, based on the flimsy premise that a borrowed joke constitutes a mortal sin, worthy of the Inquisition. There is something truly despicable about watching a Grub Street hack attacking one of the truly original comic talents in America today.'

Tracy was thrilled with the Craig Clark story. Ditto Brad and Bob Robison and, of course, Alison.

'Up until five minutes ago, I always thought Justin Wanamaker was a pompous prick,' she said. 'Now I'm going to nominate him for The Nobel Prize. What a great fucking Exocet of a quote. I hope it destroys the little shit's reputation.'

Sally also called me from Seattle, delighted with the *Variety* story.

'Everyone's been ringing me all morning, offering solidarity, telling me how horribly you've been treated, and how elegantly you came across in the *Variety* interview. I'm so damn proud of you, darling. You've handled it brilliantly. We are going to win this one.'

How nice to know that we were once again 'we'. But I couldn't really blame Sally for her anger yesterday. And now, she was right – we were turning a potentially disastrous situation around . . . to the point where my own voice and e-mail (at home and at the office) became flooded with messages of support from friends and professional associates. Better yet, by Saturday, the tide actually started turning against Theo McCall – with three letters on the *LA Times*'s editorial pages pointing out other incidents of accidental plagiarism, and also lambasting McCall's brand of smear journalism. Then, in the Sunday edition of the same paper, came a truly devastating left hook, in the form of a three-hundred-word piece in the Arts Miscellany column, which disclosed that, before he became a *Hollywood Legit* hack, McCall had spent five years trying to break into television comedy – without any success whatsoever. One NBC producer even went on the record to say that McCall had been briefly employed by him as a writer during the late nineties, but had been fired – and how's this for a vindictive quote – 'when it became clear that his meager talent would always remain meager'. It was also pointed out that, shortly after NBC fired his sorry ass, ICM also dropped him as a client.

'I wish life always worked this way,' Sally said after she read me the *LA Times* dismembering job on McCall. 'They're really declaring open season on the asshole.'

'With good reason – because the guy's made a career out of playing the feared Hollywood attack dog. Now he's been neutered, so everyone feels it's safe to kick him.'

'He deserves no less. And the brilliant thing is: you've not only been vindicated; you're also coming out of the entire incident looking like the wronged party . . . and something of a giant-killer to boot.'

Once again, Sally was spot-on. Over the weekend, I received a call from Jake Dekker, the head of production at Warner's, to assure me that *Breaking and Entering* was being fast-tracked toward a green light. Then, around noon on Sunday, Sheldon Fischer – FRT's Chief Executive Officer – also rang me at home, and told me the following anecdote.

'About a year ago, when I was named Entertainment Executive of the Year by the Orange County B'Nai Brith. At the ceremony, I thanked my wife, Babs, saying – and this is a direct quote – "She's always been there at three in the morning, when the rest of the world is asleep." Everyone afterwards complimented me on the turn of phrase, with the exception of Babs, who pointed out that that was the exact sentence used by that late playwright guy, August Wilson, when thanking his wife during his Tony Award acceptance speech back in the early nineties. And I'd been at those awards. And Wilson's line lodged in my brain . . . and then, all those years later, out it came again, masquerading as an original Sheldon Fischer comment.

'My point, David, is that I really felt for you when that poisonous accusation appeared. And, as I know from experience, what happened to you could happen to anyone.'

'Thank you, Mr Fischer,' I said. 'The support I've received from everyone at the network has been extraordinary.'

'Well, family is family, David. And please, call me Shel . . .'

Alison nearly coughed on a lungful of Salem smoke when I repeated this conversation to her the next morning.

'Did you know that your best new friend *Shel* is so into families that he just decamped from Wife Number Three to take up with – get this – his colonic irrigationist . . . who also happens to be a twenty-eight-year-old Serb with a pair of knockers that would have made the late Jayne Mansfield seem flat-chested.'

'How the hell did you find out all this arcane gossip?'

'From Theo McCall's column, naturally.'

'That's not funny.'

'Oh yes it is – since he's the joke now. This whole business has flattened that sucker. It's like you've kicked the biggest bully on the street right in the crotch . . . and everyone's delighted.'

'I didn't do anything special. I just told the truth.'

'Yeah – and you deserve a humanitarian award for character and principle, not to mention being such a swell guy.'

'You're not being cynical by any chance?'

'Me cynical? How could you say such a thing. But I'll tell you this, David: I am very fucking relieved. Because, I think you might just have won this one.'

'We're not out of the shit yet,' I said.

But later that morning, Tracy popped into my office, looking confident.

'I've just run a check on all the national and state papers: a mention in the *New York Times*, the *Washington Post* and *USA Today* on McCall's item about you, and the fact that the *LA Times* exposed him as a failed writer. The *San Francisco Chronicle* also ran a small item. Ditto local papers in Santa Barbara, San Diego and Sacramento. But all the coverage is incredibly biased towards you . . . thanks to Justin Wanamaker. By the way, we should probably send Wanamaker a discreet thank-you gift on your behalf.'

'Isn't he really into guns and stuffed rhino heads and all that retro-Hemingway stuff?'

'Yes, that's Mr Wanamaker's macho shtick. But if you think we're going to buy him an AK-47 assault rifle . . .'

'How about a case of good single malt Scotch? He's still a serious boozer, right?'

'Yep, and he also makes a point of lighting up a Lucky Strike whenever he's being interviewed, just to get the point across that he hates California Health Nazis. So I think a case of Scotch would be most welcomed. Any brand in particular?'

'Just make sure it's at least fifteen years old.'

'Done. And what do you want on the card?'

I thought about this for a moment, and said: 'How about . . . *Thank you.*'

'That just about says it all.'

'And while we're on the subject . . . thank *you*, Tracy. You played this all brilliantly. And you really saved my ass.'

Tracy smiled. 'All part of the job,' she said.

'But we're not totally in the clear yet, are we?'

'Put it this way: from what I hear from my spies at *Hollywood Legit*, McCall's been hobbled by that *LA Times* story – which has made him look like a despicable, talentless little jerk who uses his column as payback time for his own professional failure. None of the other coverage has attacked you or your position – which, quite simply, means that everyone's bought your side of the story. But the next couple of days are critical . . . just in case somebody does decide to make further noise about all this. My gut feeling is: *it's over*. But I want to wait until Friday to say that officially.'

And on Friday morning, the official call came from Tracy. I was at home, working on an outline for the opening episode of *Selling You*'s third series when the phone rang.

'Have you seen this morning's edition of *Hollywood Legit*?' she asked me.

'For some reason, I've crossed it off my Must Read list. Is that clown shoveling shit in my direction again?'

'That's why I'm calling you. His column this week is all about how Jason Wonderly . . .'

She was talking about this year's teen heart-throb who got caught shooting up in a toilet on the set of his deeply resistible hit show, *Jack the Jock*, in which he played a mischievous, but clean-living, high school quarterback who chases skirt, but also has a strong community conscience.

'. . . anyway, according to McCall, it seems that Wonderly's dealer was nabbed trying to sneak little Jason a nickel bag at Betty Ford . . .'

'But there's nothing about me or *Selling You*?'

'Not a word. Better yet, I had my assistant do a complete check through all the major papers. No follow-ups on the story. In fact, nothing anywhere since Monday. Which basically means that the story is yesterday's news . . . otherwise known as dead. Congratulations.'

Later that day, more good news came my way, when Jake Dekker from Warner Brothers called me up to say that Vince Nagel – the hot young director of the month – had finally read the first draft of *Breaking and Entering*, and he'd flipped about it. Though he was going to be in New York next week, he wanted to meet with me the week after . . . to give me some notes and move the project to the second draft stage.

'And, by the way,' Jake told me towards the end of the conversation, 'I was so happy to see that little creep McCall put in his place over what he tried to do to you. That guy was the journalistic equivalent of the Ebola virus. It's good to see him snuffed out . . . and, more importantly, to see that you have come through this unnecessary ordeal so well.'

Jake Dekker was right: it had been one long ordeal of a week. And besides the fact that someone had pointed an accusing finger at me in print (never a comfortable experience, believe me), what had unnerved me most was the realization that – had I not won my case in the court of Hollywood public opinion – the outcome might have been . . .

But let's not go there. Let's celebrate the fact that I got through the entire nasty business, virtually unscathed. In fact, as Sally was quick to point out, my position had been intriguingly strengthened by this short, sharp tribulation.

'Everyone loves a comeback,' Sally said. 'Everyone loves someone who fights their corner, and is vindicated.'

'I still feel like an idiot,' I said, lowering my head on to Sally's lap.

'That's not just dumb, it's also futile. Anyway, we've been through this a hundred times over the past week. It was a *subliminal mistake* . . . and not an uncommon one. So stop beating yourself up. You were found not guilty. *You walked.*'

Maybe Sally was right. Maybe, like someone in a potentially fatal accident, my entire professional life had passed in front of my eyes . . . and, just a week after the initial impact, I was still reeling. So much so that, for most of the weekend, I simply slept late, and lazed around the loft, and read the new Elmore Leonard novel, and tried to put everything else out of my mind.

In fact, I so enjoyed this indolent weekend that I decided to extend it into the first half of the new week. Though I probably should have been continuing to plan the next season of *Selling You*, I decided to assume the role of Los Angeles *flâneur* for a few days: loitering without much intent in West Hollywood cafes, meeting a writing friend for a long schmoozy lunch at a good Mexican joint in Santa Monica, buying far too many CDs, paying an acquisitive visit to my old haunt, Book Soup, ducking in and out of mid-afternoon movies, and generally putting all professional pressures on hold.

Monday melded into Tuesday which melded into Wednesday. And late that evening, as I cleared the dishes after an order-in sushi dinner at home, I told Sally, 'You know, I really could get used to this indolent life.'

'You're only saying that because you're not indolent. The counter-life always looks better when you have a round-trip ticket back to your own life. Anyway, you know what writers become when they get too indolent?

'Happy?'

'I was thinking more along the lines of 'impossible'. Or maybe: *completely* impossible.'

'All right, all right. I won't get *too* indolent.'

'That's nice to know,' she said dryly.

'But I tell you, in the future, I am definitely taking a week off every . . .'

The phone rang. I answered it. It was Brad Bruce. He didn't say hello, he didn't greet with me with any pleasantries. He simply asked, 'Is this a good time to talk?'

'What's wrong, Brad?' I said, causing Sally to immediately look at me with concern. 'You sound bad.'

'I am bad. Bad and very upset.'

'What's happened?'

Long pause.

'Maybe we should do this face to face,' he said.

'Maybe we should do *what* face to face?'

Another long pause. Finally he said, 'Tracy has just walked into my office with this Friday's edition of *Hollywood Legit*. And yes, yet again you feature prominently in Theo McCall's column. In fact, you're the entire column.'

'I am?' I said, my unease now edging into fear. 'But that's impossible. I've done nothing wrong.'

'That's not what his new evidence shows.'

'His new *evidence*? For what?'

'For plagiarism.'

It took me a moment or so to speak.

'That's crazy. I am not – repeat, *not* – a plagiarist.'

I glanced over at Sally. She was staring at me, wide-eyed.

'You said this last week,' Brad said in a low tone, 'and I believed you. But now . . .'

'Now *what*?'

'Now . . . He's found three other examples of plagiarism in your scripts for the show. Not only that, he's found a couple of lifted lines in all those plays you wrote before . . . before . . .'

Before I was famous, perhaps? Before I had it all? Before I was exposed as a literary thief . . . even though I never, ever intentionally stole anything. So how . . . ? *How* . . . ?

I sat down slowly on the sofa. The room was spinning. My professional life was, once again, passing before my eyes. Only this time I knew that the plunge wasn't like one of those falling dreams which concluded with me landing on my pillow. This time, the plunge was real – and the landing would be anything but soft.

Two

THANKS TO THE dubious wonders of technology, Tracy was able to scan Theo McCall's new column and have it dispatched to my home computer screen within minutes. Sally stood over me as I sat down to read it. But she didn't put a reassuring hand on my shoulder, nor did she utter any words of support. In the time between the end of my phone call with Brad and the arrival of the article, she said nothing. Nothing at all. She simply stared at me with something approaching incredulity . . . the same sort of disbelief that I saw in Lucy's face on the night I told her I was in love with someone else. The disbelief that accompanies a betrayal.

But I hadn't been trying to betray anyone. Not even myself.

I sat down at the computer. I went online. Tracy's dispatch was waiting for me. I opened it. There, in bold print, was the article in question. I wasn't just stunned by its length, but also by its headline:

THE INSIDE DIRT by Theo McCall
IS THE 'ACCIDENTAL PLAGIARIST' REALLY THAT ACCIDENTAL?
New Evidence Uncovers Selling You *Creator David Armitage's Penchant for the Borrowed Line*

As we all know, Hollywood is an industry that will overlook any venal or mortal sin committed by one of its own . . . as long as the individual in question is well connected and profitable. Whereas a mere mortal like you or me would find themselves permanently unemployable after being found in sizeable possession of a Class A drug – or caught *in flagrante delicto* with some jailbait minor – the entertainment industry closes ranks behind their own whenever such pesky little problems besmirch them. And whereas most self-respecting newspapers, magazines or centres of higher education would immediately dismiss (with extreme prejudice) any writer or academic who perpetrated the offence of plagiarism, in Hollywood they will go to excessive lengths to guard the reputation of a literary shoplifter. Especially if the shoplifter in question is the writer of one of the hottest television series of the past few years.

Two weeks ago, this column pointed out that David Armitage – the abundantly talented, Emmy-Award-winning creator of *Selling You* – had allowed a couple of lines of dialogue from the classic newspaper play, *The Front Page*, to end up in one of his scripts. Instead of simply acknowledging the error and moving on, Mr Armitage and his people at FRT went on the offensive, finding a sympathetic hack at *Variety* to write his side of the story . . . the same hack, by the way, who was, just last year, romantically involved with FRT's Head of Publicity while on sabbatical from his marriage. And before you could say 'nepotism', many of Hollywood's leading scribes were lining up to sing Mr Armitage's praises and to damn the journalist for daring to point out the transposition of four lines from one script to another.

Naturally, the most bellicose of all the writerly voices was the Papa Hemingway of Santa Barbara, Justin Wanamaker – the cutting edge radical screenwriter of the sixties and seventies who, in his twilight years, is now reduced to turning out lucrative, but generic, action scripts for Jerry Bruckheimer. And his Jeremiad not only provided a passionate defense of Mr Armitage, but also kicked off a character assassination campaign against the journalist in question – a campaign later furthered by the *LA Times*, who sought to make the Dollar Book Freud point that the journalist had had a brief unhappy career as a television writer, and was now simply wreaking vengeance on the first successful television writer he could get between his sights.

But, to quote Sgt Joe Friday from the first truly post-ironic cop show, *Dragnet*, this column deals with 'Just the facts, ma'am.' And the fact of the matter is that, in the two weeks since Mr Armitage's plagiarism was first revealed, his unnecessary fight back has forced 'The Inside Dirt' to commission a pair of researchers to trawl through the entire David Armitage *oeuvre*, just to make certain that the gentleman's cribbing offence was a mere one-off.

But, surprise, surprise . . . what did our researchers find:

1. In Episode Three of last season's *Selling You*, Bert – the skirt-chasing account executive – talks about his ex-wife, who's moved back to LA after taking him to the cleaners in court. 'You know what the real definition of capitalism is?' he tells his associate, Chuck. 'The process by which Californian girls become Californian women.'

    Virtually the same line can be found in Oscar-winning dramatist Christopher Hampton's play, *Tales from Hollywood*, in which the Austrian dramatist, Odon von Horvath, notes that 'Capitalism is the process by which American girls become American women.'

2. In Episode One of the new series, Tanya, the gum-snapping receptionist, informs Joey that she doesn't want to sleep with him anymore, because she's got a new guy who looks exactly like Ricky Martin. Later, Joey sees the new boyfriend at the office and tells Tanya: 'Ricky Martin? Get outta here. The guy looks like Ricky the Zit.'

    Ricky the Zit, as it turns out, is the name of a character in Elmore Leonard's novel, *Glitz*.

3. In the same episode, the company's founder, Jerome, has a particularly unpleasant run-in with a B-list Hollywood actor shooting a commercial for a client. Afterwards, Jerome tells Bert, 'The next time we ever do a commercial, no actors . . .'

    In Mel Brooks's classic film, *The Producers*, Zero Mostel turns to Gene Wilder and says, 'The next time we do a play, no actors.'

    Ah, but there's more examples of Mr Armitage's literary shoplifting. Our researchers sifted through some of his early stage plays – most of which never received anything more than staged readings off-off Broadway – and discovered two intriguing facts:

1. Armitage's 1995 play, *Riffs*, concerns a love triangle between a one-time jazz pianist – now a housewife, married to a doctor – who develops a passion for her husband's best friend, a jazz saxophonist. They start playing duets together – and, courtesy of the increasingly steamy music, their passion grows. Then, when hubby's out of town for a weekend, they finally consummate their passion . . . only to have hubby burst in on them. And in a tussle with the saxophonist, the wife intervenes, only to be accidentally stabbed through the heart by hubby.

    Intriguingly enough, the plot of *Riffs* is a virtual facsimile of the plot of Tolstoy's famous novella, *The Kreutzer Sonata*, in which a bored pianist housewife becomes enamored by her husband's best friend . . . who happens to be a violinist. When they play Beethoven's Kreutzer Sonata together, romantic sparks fly. But when they finally get it on while hubby's out of town, *shazam*, hubby shows up and, in a jealous rage, accidentally kills his beloved wife.

2. In Armitage's new screenplay, *Breaking and Entering* (currently in development at Warner Brothers, in a deal worth one-point-five million . . . leaked to us from an inside source), the central protagonist opens the film with the following voice-over line: 'The first time I robbed Cartier's, it was raining.'

    How strange to discover that a classic John Cheever story opens with the line: 'The first time I robbed Tiffany's it was raining.'

    As can be gathered, Mr Armitage isn't simply a one-off 'accidental plagiarist', as he and his supporters so passionately contend. Rather, he's a repeat offender. And though he might argue that the offenses in question simply add up to a borrowed joke here, a borrowed plot line there, the fact remains that plagiarism is plagiarism . . . and there's no way he can refute the obvious conclusion: the guy is guilty as hell.

By the time I finished reading, I felt so angry that I had to stop myself from putting my fist through the computer screen.

'Can you believe this bullshit?' I asked Sally, turning around to speak with her. But she was already seated on the couch, her arms wrapped around herself (seriously negative body language), looking very perturbed. She refused to look at me as I spoke.

'Yes, David – I can believe it. Because it's *there* – hard evidence, in black-and-white, that you are a habitual plagiarist.'

'Oh come on, Sally – what's the asshole accusing me of? A line here, a line there . . . ?'

'And how about the plot line of your play? Borrowed from Tolstoy . . .'

'But what he failed to mention was that, in the program note for the play, I acknowledged the debt to Tolstoy.'

'*What* program note? The play was only given a staged reading, right?'

'Okay – *had* it received a proper production, I would have very clearly acknowledged the debt . . .'

'You say that now.'

'It's the truth. Do you really think I would do something as moronic as steal from Tolstoy . . . ?'

'I don't know what to think anymore.'

'Well, I know this – that little shit McCall is doing his best to destroy my career. It's his way of making me pay for him being exposed by the *LA Times* as a failed writer.'

'That's not the point, David. The point is: he's nabbed you again. And this time, you're not going to get away with it.'

The phone rang. I answered it immediately. It was Brad.

'You've read the story?' he asked me.

'Absolutely – and I really feel that he's just taking a few minuscule examples and . . .'

Brad cut me off.

'David, we need to talk.'

'Of course,' I said. 'We can fight this. Just like . . .'

'We need to talk tonight.'

I glanced at my watch. It was 9.07pm. 'Tonight? Isn't it a bit late?'

'We have a crisis, and we must respond fast.'

I breathed a small sigh of relief. He wanted to talk strategy. He was still in my corner.

'I couldn't agree more,' I said 'Where do you want to meet?'

'Here at the office. At ten, if that's okay. Tracy's here right now. Bob Robison is on his way over as we speak.'

'I'll be there a.s.a.p.. And I'd like to bring Alison.'

'Sure.'

'Okay, see you at ten,' I said, hanging up. Then I turned back to Sally and said, 'Brad's on side.'

'Really?'

'He said we need to respond fast and he wants me to come to the office right now.'

Once again, she didn't look at me.

'So, go then,' she said. I approached her and attempted to put my arms around her. But she shrugged me off.

'Sally, darling,' I said, 'everything's going to be fine.'

'No, it isn't,' she said, then left.

I stood frozen to the spot, wanting to pursue her, to convince her of my innocence in all this. But instinct told me to leave. So I grabbed my jacket, my phone and my car keys, then headed out.

On the way over to FRT, I called Alison on her cellphone. But I got her voice mail and a message reminding all callers that she was going to be in New York until Thursday. I glanced again at my watch. It was well after midnight on the East Coast . . . which is why I was listening to her recorded voice. So I left her the following brief message: 'Alison, it's David. And it's urgent. Call me on my cell as soon as you get this.'

Then I put the pedal to the metal, and headed towards the office, rehearsing the arguments I was going to put against McCall's smear campaign . . . not to mention the broadside I'd send in the direction of Warner Brothers about finding the mole who leaked my script to McCall.

But when I got to FRT, Brad and Bob were looking grim, while Tracy had that red-eyed look that usually accompanies crying.

'I am so sorry about all this,' I said. 'But look, this maniac hired a pair of researchers to microscopically inspect all my scripts. And what did they find? Five lines which could be attributed to other writers. That's it. And as for his ridiculous charge about the Tolstoy story . . .'

Bob Robison interrupted me.

'David, we all hear what you're saying. And frankly, when I saw the piece, I pretty much thought the same thing: it's just a couple of lines here and there. As regards that old play of yours: fuck Tolstoy. I'm sure anybody with half a brain would realize that you were deliberately reinterpreting the guy's story . . .'

'Thank you, Bob,' I said, relief washing over me like a high intensity shower.

'I'm not through, David.'

'Sorry.'

'As I said, I don't think that McCall's case against you is either fair or just. The problem we have now, however, is one of credibility. And like it or not, once McCall's column hits the streets on Friday, you are going to be tainted merchandise . . .'

'But Bob . . .'

'Let me finish,' he said sharply.

'Sorry . . .'

'This is the situation as we see it. You can explain away one case of unintentional plagiarism. But *four* additional cases?'

'Four goddamn lines,' I said. 'Nothing more.'

'Four goddamn lines that McCall's pushed into print, following on the four lines from *The Front Page* . . .'

'But don't you see that this asshole is trying to be Kenneth Starr . . . taking the flimsiest of evidence and transforming it into Sodom and Gomorrah.'

'You're right,' Brad said, finally entering the conversation. 'He is an asshole. He's a character assassin. He's decided to fuck you over. And, I'm afraid, your scripts yielded just enough *minor* evidence for him to taint you with the plagiarism brush, and get away with it.'

Bob came in here. 'More to the point, I promise you that his very long article will be picked up by every news organization imaginable. It's not only going to leave you looking like damaged goods, it will also decimate the credibility of the show.'

'That's crap, Bob . . .'

'Don't you fucking dare tell me what's crap,' he said, the anger now showing. 'Do you have any idea of the damage this has done? And I'm not simply talking about yourself and your show, but also to Tracy? Thanks to that shithead McCall, her credibility has been wrecked too . . . to the point where we're having to accept her resignation . . .'

'You're resigning?' I said looking at Tracy, wide-eyed.

'I have no choice,' she said quietly. 'The fact that my one-time "adulterous" involvement with Craig Clark was revealed . . .'

'You've done nothing wrong, Tracy,' I said.

'Maybe – but the *perception* is that I called an ex-boyfriend to write a sympathetic puff piece on your behalf.'

'But *he* called you.'

'Doesn't matter – the perception's otherwise.'

'What does Craig say about all this?' I asked.

'He's got his own problems,' Tracy said. '*Variety*'s just fired him too.'

'You have not been fired,' Bob said sharply to her.

'No – I've just been given the bottle of whisky and the gun with one bullet, and told to do the honorable thing.'

She looked like she was on the verge of crying again. Brad squeezed her arm as an attempted gesture of support, but she shrugged him off.

'I don't need anyone's sympathy,' she said. 'I made a stupid call, and now I'm paying the price.'

'I'm appalled by all this,' I said.

'You should be,' Tracy said.

'I can't tell you how sorry I am. But as I said before, I didn't mean . . .'

'Understood, understood,' Bob said. 'But you also have to appreciate our tangled position right now. If we don't let you go . . .'

Even though I had been expecting it, the news still hit me like a slap across the face.

'You're firing me?' I asked, my voice hushed.

'Yes. With the deepest regret, I should add, but . . .'

'That's not fair,' I said.

'It might not be,' Brad said, 'but we have our own credibility to consider.'

'I have a contract with you . . .'

Bob shuffled some papers and pulled out a document.

'Yes, you do – and as I'm certain Alison will explain to you, there is a clause that voids the contract should you be found to have falsely misrepresented your work in any way. Plagiarism would certainly qualify as a major misrepresentation . . .'

'What you're doing is wrong,' I said.

'What we're doing is unfortunate, but necessary,' Bob said. 'For the good of the series, you have to go.'

'And say Alison and I take you to court?'

'Do what you want, David,' Bob said. 'But our corporate pockets are far deeper that yours. And you won't win this one.'

'We'll see about that,' I said, standing up.

'Do you think this is fun for us?' Brad said. 'Do you think anyone in this room is pleased with this situation? I know you're the creator of this show . . . and, believe me, you'll still get your creator credit and a cut of budget. But the fact is, there are seventy other people involved in *Selling You* – and I'm not jeopardizing their positions by fighting your corner. Your current position in indefensible. You didn't just get caught with the smoking gun, David; this time, it was a smoking bazooka . . .'

'Thank you, Mr Loyalty . . .'

Long silence. Brad's hand twisted tightly around a pen. He took a deep steadying breath, then said, 'David, I'm going to put that remark down to the high emotional temperature we're all running right now, as I have shown you loyalty to the nth degree. And before you start lashing out at any of us again, do remember one thing: this is a fuck-up of your own making.'

I was about to say something loud and emotional and incoherent, but instead I simply stormed out of the office, stormed out of the building, fell into my car, and started driving.

I drove for hours, roaming the freeways without plan or logic.

I did time on the 10, the 330, the 12, and the 85. My itinerary was a masterpiece of geographic illogicality – Manhattan Beach to Van Nuys to Ventura to Santa Monica to Newport Beach to . . .

And then, finally, my cellphone started ringing. As I grabbed it off the adjoining seat, I glanced at the dashboard and noticed it was three-ten. I had been driving aimlessly for five hours.

'David, are you okay?'

It was Alison, sounding half-awake, but worried.

'Hold on,' I said. 'Got to pull over.'

I turned the car into a lay-by and cut the engine.

'You're out? Driving?'

'Seems that way.'

'But it's the middle of the night.'

'Yeah.'

'I'm just up, and I just got your message. Where are you right now?'

'I don't know . . .'

'What do you mean, you don't know? What's the name of the road, the highway?'

'Don't know.'

'Now you have me worried. What's going on?'

That's when I started to sob . . . when the entire horror of what had happened finally hit home, and I suddenly couldn't deny it. I must have sobbed for an entire minute. When I eventually brought it under control, Alison spoke.

'David, my God, tell me, please . . . what the hell's happened to you?'

I told her everything – from the extensive plagiarism accusations in McCall's new column, to Sally's inimical reaction, to being fired by Bob and Brad.

'Jesus fucking Christ,' Alison said when I finally finished, 'this has gotten completely out of hand.'

'I feel like I've opened a door and walked straight off a skyscraper.'

'All right, first things first. Do you know where you are right now?'

'Somewhere in town.'

'You're sure you're in LA?'

'Yeah — that I'm pretty sure of.'

'You think you're okay to drive?'

'I guess so.'

'Right — here's what I want you to do. Get home. Safely, I should add. If you're in LA, you should be there within an hour. And as soon as you're home, e-mail me McCall's column. I'll be heading out to Kennedy — because I'm getting on the nine am flight back to LA. I should be able to go online at the airport and read the column, then I can use the AirPhone on board after we've taken off. All going well, I should land around noon LA time, so why don't you plan to meet me at the office by two. In the meantime, I want you to do one thing . . . which is sleep. Do you have anything at home to knock you out?'

'I think there's some Tylenol PM.'

'Take three.'

'Please don't tell me this is all going to look a lot better after sleep. Because it won't.'

'I know that. But, at least, you'll have had some rest.'

I made it home within forty minutes. I e-mailed the story to Alison. As I sat at the computer, the bedroom door opened and Sally came out. She was just wearing a pyjama top. My first thought was: she is so beautiful. My second thought was: will this be the last time I ever see her so intimately?

'You actually had me worried,' she said.

I kept staring at the screen.

'Would you mind explaining where you've been for the past seven hours?' she asked.

'I was at the office, and then I was driving.'

'Driving where?'

'Just driving.'

'You could have called me. You *should* have called me.'

'Sorry.'

'So what happened?'

'If I've been driving for half the night, you know what happened.'

'You've been fired?'

'Yes, I've been fired.'

'I see,' she said, her tone flat.

'Tracy Weiss has also gotten the bullet.'

'For giving the exclusive interview to her ex-guy?'

'That was the crime.'

'This is a tough business.'

'Thank you for that blinding glimpse of the obvious.'

'What do you want me to say, David?'

'I want you to come over here, put your arms around me and tell me you love me.'

Long silence. Finally she said, 'I'm going back to bed.'

'You think they're right to fire me, don't you?'

'I suppose they have a point.'

'Really – all for a couple of unintentionally borrowed lines?'

'Did they say anything about your compensation package?'

'That's Alison's department – and she's in New York right now.'

'But she knows?'

'We've spoken.'

'And?'

'She wants me to get some sleep.'

'That sounds like a very good idea.'

'You think I'm in the wrong here, don't you?'

'It's late, David . . .'

'Answer the question, please,' I said.

'Can we do this tomorrow?'

'No. *Now.*'

'All right then. I think you've blown it. And yes, I'm very disappointed. Happy now?'

I stood up and walked past her into the bedroom. I undressed. I found the Tylenol PM in the bathroom. I popped four tablets. I got into bed. I set my alarm clock for 1pm. I switched the phone on to voice mail. I pulled the covers over my head. I passed out within a minute.

Then the alarm went off. I saw a note on the pillow next to mine.

Off to Seattle tonight. Will be gone two days. Sally.

I squinted at the alarm clock. One pm. I forced myself to sit up in bed. I picked up Sally's note and read it again. It was the sort of note you leave the maid. I suddenly felt very alone, very scared, very desperate to see my daughter. I picked up the phone. There were none of the usual telltale beeps informing me that I had messages. I dialled my voice messaging system nonetheless. The recorded voice informed me what I already knew: '*You have no messages.*'

Surely, there must be some mistake. Surely some of my friends and colleagues, having already learned about the McCall column, had then called to show support.

But they all phoned two weeks ago. Now, in the face of multiple plagiarism charges, I was out on my own. Nobody wanted to know.

I picked up the phone again. I called Lucy's house in Sausalito. Even though I knew Caitlin was at school, her voice was on the answerphone and I wanted to hear it.

But after two rings, Lucy picked up.

'Oh, hi . . .' I said.

'What are you doing, calling in the afternoon? You know Caitlin's at school.'

'Just wanted to leave her a message, saying I missed her.'

'Suddenly all homesick for your former family, now that your career is dead?'

'How did you know . . . ?'

'You haven't seen a newspaper this morning?'

'I'm just up.'

'Well, if I were you, I'd go right back to bed. Because you're third page news in the *San Francisco Chronicle and* the *LA Times.* Nice one, David – stealing from other people's work.'

'I didn't steal . . .'

'Yeah – you just cheated. Like you cheated on me.'

'Tell Caitlin I'll call her later.' And I hung up.

I went out into the kitchen. There, on the counter, was our morning's copy of the *LA Times.* Sally had thoughtfully opened it to page three, where the top right hand corner headline read:

SELLING YOU CREATOR ACCUSED OF MORE PLAGIARISM

Beneath this was a short, five-hundred-word précis of the McCall demolition job . . . evidently rewritten at speed late last night (when the advanced copies of *Hollywood Legit* must have been leaked to the papers). After recounting all the charges McCall made against me, the paper stated that, contacted late last night, *Selling You* producer Brad Bruce said 'This news is a tragedy both for David Armitage and for the *Selling You* family' and that a formal statement from FRT would be issued later today.

Nice strategy, Brad. First come on touchy-feely about what had befallen me, before issuing the press release that I had been fired off the show.

I raced over to the computer. I went online. I checked out the *San Francisco Chronicle* website. The article was also a rushed job by their LA correspondent, featuring the same rundown of the accusations and the same quote from Brad. But what truly unnerved me was the discovery that, in my AOL letterbox, there were already half a dozen e-mail requests from assorted journalists, asking for an interview . . . or, at the very least, a comment about my reaction to McCall's column.

I picked up the phone and called my office. Check that: my *former* office. Jennifer, my *former* assistant, answered.

'I've been instructed to pack up your office,' she said. 'I presume you want everything delivered to your apartment?'

'Jennifer, you could at least say hello.'

'Hello. So is the apartment the place to send everything?'

'Yes.'

'Fine. Expect it all tomorrow morning. And what should I do about any calls for you?'

'Have there been any calls?'

'Fifteen this morning. The *LA Times*, the *Hollywood Reporter*, the *New York Times*, the *Seattle Times*, the *San Francisco Chronicle*, the *San Jose Mercury*, the *Boston Globe* . . .'

'I get the idea,' I said.

'Shall I e-mail you the list and all their contact numbers?'

'No.'

'So if anyone from the press wants to contact you . . .'

'Tell them I'm uncontactable.'

'If that's your decision . . .'

'Jennifer, what's with the Ice Age routine . . . ?'

'How do you expect me to act? Your departure means I've been given a week's notice . . .'

'Oh Jesus . . .'

'Please – no platitudes.'

'I don't know what to say, except I'm sorry. This is all as much a surprise to me as it is . . .'

'How can it be a surprise when you stole stuff?'

'I never intended . . .'

'What? To get caught? Well, thanks for catching me in your web too.'

And she slammed the phone down.

I hung up. I put my head in my hands. Whatever the huge personal damage I had suffered, it appalled me to think that I had unknowingly inflicted vast collateral damage on two innocent parties. It was appalling to think that fifteen journalists were chasing me for quotes. Because now I was *real news* – the great television success story who threw it all away. Or, at least, that's the spin they'd put on it. My side of the story played successfully last week. Now, however, with all this new trivial evidence (but evidence nonetheless), the tide would turn, the spin would change. I'd be held up as an example of a talented man besieged by self-destructive forces; a guy who'd created one of the most original television series of the last ten years, but *still* had to rob lines from other writers. And there would be the usual palaver about me being yet another victim of Tinseltown's ferocious cult of shallow success, blah, blah, blah.

The bottom line of all this editorial coverage would be a simple one: I'd be permanently unemployable as a writer.

I glanced at my watch. One-fourteen. I called Alison's office. Her assistant, Suzy, answered. She sounded genuinely upset. Before I could ask for my agent, she said, 'I just want to tell you this: I think what's happening to you is totally unfair.'

I gulped and felt my eyes sting.

'Thank you,' I said.

'How are you doing?'

'Not good.'

'You coming over?'

'Yeah – right away.'

'Good – she's expecting you.'

'Any chance I could talk to her now?'

'She's on the phone with FRT.'

'See you in a half-hour then.'

When I walked in the door of her office, I caught sight of Alison sitting behind her desk, staring silently out the window, looking war-weary and preoccupied. Hearing me enter, she swivelled around and walked out from behind her desk and put her arms around me and simply held me for a minute or so. Then she walked over to a cabinet and opened it.

'Does Scotch work for you?' she asked.

'It's that bad?'

She said nothing. Instead, she returned to the desk with the bottle of J&B, and two glasses. She poured each of us a large one. Then she lit up a cigarette, inhaled deeply, and tossed back half the drink. I followed suit.

'All right,' she said. 'Here it goes. I've never lied to you as an agent and I'm not going to start now. The situation right now is about as bad as it gets.'

I threw back the rest of my drink. She refilled it immediately.

'Now when I read the McCall story at the airport, my first reaction was: how could Brad and Bob take this seriously . . . especially when the charges he puts forward are so fucking minor? What he's accused you of is ridiculous. I mean, we're into the realm of *"If I had a nickel for every writer who's borrowed a joke."* And the shit about the Tolstoy story is just shit. He knows it too. However, the line from the Cheever story . . .'

'All I can say is this: I realized it was a direct "borrow", and one which, I also knew, would never make it on to the screen. What he got his hands on was a draft, that's all.'

'I know that, and you know that. The problem here is that, coupled with *The Front Page* stuff from last week . . . well, you're a smart enough guy to figure out that . . .'

'Guilty or not, I'm in deep trouble.'

'That's the essence of it.'

'And you've spoken with FRT, and they can't be in any way persuaded . . . ?'

188

'Not a chance. As far as they're concerned, you're burnt toast. But that's not all. As soon as I landed I spent an hour engaged in a screaming match with one of their lawyers. It seems that they are going to do their best to block any golden parachute for you.'

Worse and worse. 'But there's a clause . . .'

'Oh yes,' Alison said, pulling a file towards her, 'there is definitely a fucking clause. Clause 43b, to be precise, of your agreement with FRT – and the gist of this clause is that if you have done anything illegal or criminally malfeasant in relation to the show, your future profit participation in its proceeds will be curtailed.'

'They're trying to say that I've done something criminally malfeasant?'

'They're attempting to cut you off from any future creator fees by arguing that your plagiarism constitutes an illegal act . . .'

'This is such bullshit.'

'Absolutely – but they are determined to make it stick.'

'Can they?'

'I've just spent the last half-hour on the phone with my lawyer. He's going to look carefully at the contract tonight. But his gut instinct is . . . yeah, they can make this one stick.'

'So there'll be no compensation?'

'Worse than that . . . they have also informed me that they plan to sue you for the writing fees for the three episodes in which you allegedly plagiarized.'

'What are they trying to do? Disembowel me?'

'Absolutely. Because, let's face it, the money involved is serious. If they get rid of your creator fees, they're saving themselves around three hundred and fifty thousand per season. And if, as expected, the show runs a couple more seasons . . . well, do the math. For each of the three episodes, you are due one hundred and fifty thousand. Add it all up . . .'

'Surely we can fight them on that point . . .'

'Again, my lawyer guy says they have you on the clause in which the writer guarantees all work in the script is his alone. But the way I figure it, we can probably negotiate a settlement price . . .'

'Which means *I* have to pay *them* back?'

'If it comes to it, yes. My hope – and it is a hope – is that, in a few days, when everything cools down, they'll forget chasing you for the three episodes, if they know they've won the creator fees argument.'

'You're going to let them win that?'

'David, when have I ever *let* some shithead studio or network win anything against one of my clients? But we have a situation. Legalistically, you are *perceived* to have broken the terms of your contract. And if my $375-an-hour guy – who knows every damn loophole in the Hollywood legal book – tells me they've got you hog-tied, we're into the realm of trying to minimize the wreckage as much as possible.

'But I will get a second – and maybe even a third – legal opinion before talking to FRT's shysters again . . . let alone their slimy counterparts at Warners.'

'Can I have another Scotch?'

'I think that's a good idea,' she said, 'because I have some other difficult news.'

I poured myself a double. 'Go on,' I said.

'Some legal eagle from Warner Brothers was just on to me. They're putting *Breaking and Entering* into turnaround . . .'

'You mean, the meeting with Nagel is scrapped?'

'I'm afraid so. But it gets worse. They want the entire signature fee back.'

'That's insane. How can they do that?'

'They're screwing you on that John Cheever line you borrowed . . .'

'Come on. I was just trying the line out. In a *first* draft . . .'

'Hey, you don't have to sell *me* your position. The problem is that, like FRT, they're using that line to beat you over the head with the "writer guarantees all work in the script is his alone" clause. The other problem is, they've got corroboration . . . even though most of those assholes don't even know who John Cheever is.'

'Well, at least the Fleck script will cover those debts.'

She lit up another cigarette, even though there was one already burning in her ashtray.

'I'm afraid Fleck's lawyer called me this afternoon . . .'

'Please don't tell me . . .'

'"With regret, Mr Fleck cannot proceed with any further negotiations, owing to the current state of Mr Armitage's professional reputation." That's an exact quote, I'm afraid.'

I stared down at the floor. And said, 'Then there's no way I can pay back the two hundred and fifty grand to Warners.'

'Is it already spent?'

'A lot of it, yeah.'

'But you're not broke?'

'I may be dumb, but I'm not stupid. I've got around half a million invested with my broker. The problem is, half of that is owed to Uncle Sam. And if FRT and Warners want all their money back . . . then I am broke.'

'Let's not go to the abyss just as yet. I will play hardball with the bastards. I will get them to lower their demands on the payback. Meantime, you better talk to your broker and your accountant about how best to maximize what you still have invested . . .'

'Because I'm washed up in this town, right?'

'It's going to be difficult finding you work.'

'And say this thing doesn't blow over? If I'm permanently tainted by it, what then?'

'Honestly?' Alison asked.

'Absolutely.'

'I don't know. But, once again, let's see how the next few weeks play out. More to the point, you need to make a statement, in which you defend your corner, but also regret what's gone down. I've called Mary Morse – a PR gal I know. She's going to be over here in about ten minutes, to work out the statement with you, and to get it out to all concerned, so at least they have your angle on everything. If things don't improve in a few days' time, we're going to have to find a sympathetic journalist, who can tell your side of the story.'

'Well, that guy from *Variety* is definitely out of the frame, now that his career is fucked too. And poor Tracy . . .'

'That wasn't your fault.'

'Yeah, but if it hadn't been for this mess of mine . . .'

'Look – they're both professionals, and they should have known that their past involvement might go public if . . .'

'She was just trying to protect me.'

'True – but that was her job. You can't beat yourself up over their problems as well. You've got more than enough trouble on your plate.'

'Don't I know it.'

By the next morning, the entire world knew about it as well. McCall's accusations hit the streets. So too did FRT's press release, announcing (with regret, *natch*) my dismissal from the series. All the major national papers carried it on their arts and entertainment section, though the *LA Times* put the story on its front page. Worse yet, the tale also merited coverage on NPR's *All Things Considered, Entertainment Tonight*, and most of the early morning talk shows. Yes, everyone quoted from my statement – where I apologized for the upset caused to FRT and everyone involved in *Selling You*, and again said that I really didn't think I could stand accused of theft because of a mere couple of lines. 'The worst thing a writer can be accused of is theft,' I wrote in the statement, 'and I certainly don't consider myself a thief.'

That night, on HBO's *Real Time*, the host, Bill Maher, noted during his monologue:

'The big news in Hollywood today is that *Selling You* creator, David Armitage, used the famous Richard Nixon *I am not a crook* defense, after FRT sacked him for plagiarism. When asked whether everything he wrote was 100 per cent original, he said: "I did not have sex with that woman . . . "'

Maher got a big laugh with that one-liner. I watched his show alone in the loft. Sally was in Seattle, at an address unknown, as she hadn't left name the name of her hotel, nor had she phoned me all day. I knew that she usually stayed at the Four Seasons when visiting the Seattle set, but I feared that if I phoned her, I'd be appearing far too needy, far too desperate. Right now, my one hope was that, once the initial blitzkrieg of bad publicity died down, she'd remember all the reasons why we fell in love with each other in the first place, and would . . .

What? Come running back to me, telling me she'd stand by me, no matter what? Like Lucy? She'd stood by me . . . begrudgingly sometimes, but she was always there nonetheless. For all those years, when I was nowhere, and she was forced into telemarketing when her acting career failed and we needed to pay the rent. How did I repay her steadfastness? By doing the predictable mid-life, post-big-breakthrough thing. No wonder she so despised me. No wonder I was so scared now. Because I was finally admitting what I had known within months of moving in with Sally: her love for me was predicated on my success, my status within the entertainment community, and (in turn) the way it enhanced her own position within that High School With Money called Hollywood.

'*Everyone has their moment,*' she said just before I won the Emmy Award. '*This is ours.*'

Not anymore, babe.

Could everything I'd achieved in a few fast years be asset-stripped from me in a matter of days?

Come on people – I'm David Armitage! I felt like shouting from the nearest rooftop. But, then again, once you're on a rooftop, the only destination is down. Anyway, in Hollywood (as in life) all talent is ephemeral, expendable. Even those at the top of the pile were subject to this law of replication. No one out here was unique. We all played the same game. And the game operated according to one basic rule: your moment lasted for as long as your moment lasted . . . if, that is, you were lucky enough to have a moment at all.

But I still couldn't believe that my moment was now in the past tense. Surely Sally wouldn't be so mercenary as to abandon me right now. Just as I had to believe that, somehow, I would be able to convince Brad, and Bob, and Jake Dekker at Warners, and any other interested production company in this damn town, that I was worthy of their trust.

Come on people – I'm David Armitage! And I've made you all money!

Yet the more I tried to put an optimistic spin on my situation, the more I thought: the worst sort of bullshit is the bullshit with which you bullshit yourself.

So I opened a bottle of Glenlivet Single Malt and started watching it disappear. Somewhere after the fifth finger trickled down my gullet, I had a supremely moronic interlude, during which I entered a mood of introspective inspiration. I decided to bare my soul to Sally, to put it all on the proverbial table, and hope that she would, in turn, respond tenderly to this *cri de coeur.* So I staggered over to my computer, and wrote:

Darling
     I love you. I need you. Desperately, in fact. This is a bad business; an unfair business. Please, please, *please* don't give up on me; on us. I am desperate. Please call me. Please come home. Let's get through this together. Because we *can* get through it. Because we are the best thing that ever happened to each other. Because you are the woman with whom I want to spend the rest of my life, with whom I want to have children, whom I will still love when, years from now, we enter that twilight zone of decrepitude. I'll always be there for you. Please, please, *please* be here for me now.

Without reading through the thing again, I hit the Send button, and tossed back another two fingers of Glenlivet, and careened into the bedroom, and went down for the count.
     Then it was morning, and the phone was ringing. But in those few bleary seconds before I answered it, a sentence floated through my head. Not a sentence, actually . . . a phrase: *the twilight zone of decrepitude.*
     And then the rest of the ludicrous contents of that e-mail came back to me . . . in all its grisly, beseeching glory. And I thought: you *are* an idiot.
     I reached for the ringing phone.
     'David Armitage?' a very awake voice asked me.
     'I'm afraid so.'
     'Fred Bennett, *Los Angeles Times.*'
     'What the hell time is it?
     'Around seven-thirty.'
     'I don't want to talk.'

'Mr Armitage, if I could just have a moment?'

'How did you get my home number?'

'That's not the hardest thing in the world to find.'

'I've made a statement.'

'But have you heard about the motion tabled in front of the Screen and Television Writers Association last night?'

'What motion?'

'A motion to publicly censure you for plagiarism, to strip you of your Association membership, and to recommend that you be banned from all professional work for a minimum of five years . . . though some committee members were pressing for a lifetime ban . . .'

I put the phone back in its cradle, then I reached down and yanked the plug from the wall. Immediately it began to ring in another room, but I ignored it. Instead, I pulled the covers over my head, willing this day to vanish from view.

But sleep was now impossible, so I eventually staggered to the bathroom, and popped three Advil in an attempt to quell the jack-hammer currently excavating the inside of my head. Then I went into the living room and faced the computer. My e-mail box had twelve messages, eleven of which were from assorted journalists. I opened none of them. The twelfth was the one I was dreading . . . an e-mail from Sally:

David:

I hate the situation you've found yourself in. I too hate the fact that your career has been devastated by these reve-lations. But this is a situation of your own making; that, for reasons best known to yourself, you decided to be the archi-tect of your own undoing. This is what I can't fathom. It makes me wonder if I really even know you . . . a concern exacerbated by your deeply worrying e-mail. I realize that you are distressed by what has happened. But there is nothing so unattractive as someone begging for love – especially when they have undermined the trust needed to sustain love. Though I appreciate the fact that you are under severe emotional strain, that still isn't an excuse for heart-on-the-sleeve prose. And let's not even get into that 'twilight zone of decrepitude' line.

All this has left me even more confused and baffled and sad. I think a few more days apart might bring some clarity to our situation. I've decided to head off to Vancouver Island for the weekend. I'll be back Monday. We can talk then. In the meantime, let's agree not to communicate over the weekend, just so matters don't get further confused. I do hope you will consider, in the meantime, getting some professional support. If your e-mail was anything, it was an enormous cry for help.

Sally

Wonderful. Just wonderful.

The phone started ringing again. I ignored it. Then my cell-phone joined the cacophony. I reached for it and glanced at the incoming number on the display. It was Alison. I answered it immediately.

'You sound terrible,' she said. 'Were you drinking last night?'

'You're a very perceptive woman.'

'Have you been up long?'

'Ever since an *LA Times* hack rang me to let me know that SATWA was planning to ban me for life.'

'What?'

'That's what he said – a special meeting of the Politburo last night.'

'This thing has gone ga-ga. And it's about to get worse.'

'Tell me.'

'Theo McCall's about to be interviewed live from LA on the *Today Show*.'

'On the subject of *moi?*'

'It would seem that way.'

'Jesus Christ, this guy is relentless.'

'He's like any gossip columnist – completely ruthless. You're just a commodity to him. A very lucrative commodity right now, in terms of getting his name known nationally and appearing on *Today.*'

'He won't be satisfied until I'm drawn and quartered.'

'I'm afraid that's about right. Which is why I decided to wake you so early and tell you about his *Today Show* appearance. I think it's best if you watch it, just in case he says anything so outrageous or slanderous we can nail his vile little ass.'

Actually, there was nothing 'little' about Theo McCall. He was in his early forties – a Brit who'd crossed the Atlantic around ten years ago, and had one of those accents in which plummy rounded vowels mingled with Southern Californian nasality. He was also fat. His face reminded me of an oozy slab of Camembert which had been left for too long in direct sunlight. But he was shrewd about his size, in that he compensated for it by dressing like a dandy – a dark grey chalk-stripe suit, a spread-collar white shirt, a discreet black polka-dot tie. I sensed that, given the low-rent nature of *Hollywood Legit,* it was his only suit. But I had to grudg-ingly admire the way he was selling himself to the world – as an Anglo-American dandy, with the inside dope on Hollywood bad behavior. No doubt, he had dressed carefully for this interview, considering it an audition for the upscale gossip positions he was desperate to inhabit.

But Anne Fletcher – the journalist interviewing him from New York – wasn't totally buying his T.S. Eliot meets Tom Wolfe jour-nalism act.

'Theo McCall, many people in Hollywood consider you to be the most feared journalist in town,' she said.

A slight pleasurable smile crossed McCall's fat lips.

'How flattering,' he said in his best plummy voice.

'But others consider you to be nothing more than a scandal-monger, and someone who doesn't think twice about destroying careers, marriages, even entire lives.'

He blanched a little, but recovered quickly.

'Well, of course, certain people *would* feel that way. But that's because, if there's one great rule about Hollywood, it's that they protect each other . . . even when serious wrongdoing is involved.'

'And you think that the plagiarism that got David Armitage fired from the FRT show he created was "serious wrongdoing"?'

'Absolutely – the man stole from other writers' work.'

'But what did he really "steal"? A gag from one play, and a couple of one-line jokes from others. Do you really think he deserves losing his career for a couple of minor offenses?'

'Well, Anne, to begin with, I didn't decide on the punishment he received. That was the decision of his bosses at FRT. But, as to your question about whether I think plagiarism is a serious offense – well, theft is theft . . .'

'But what I asked you, Mr McCall, is whether such a petty misdemeanor like borrowing jokes . . .'

'He also lifted a plot line from Tolstoy . . .'

'But Mr Armitage did explain that his unproduced play was a deliberate reinterpretation of the Tolstoy story . . .'

'Of course, Mr Armitage would say that now. But I have a copy of his original script here . . .'

He held up the dusty playscript of *Riffs*. The camera zoomed in on the title page.

'As you can see here,' McCall said, 'the title page reads: *Riffs*, A Play by David Armitage . . . but there's nothing that says 'Based on *The Kreutzer Sonata* by Tolstoy', even though the entire plot is completely lifted from the Tolstoy story. And this raises an even bigger question: why did a man of David Armitage's talent and ability need to steal from other people in the first place? It's the one question that everyone in Hollywood wants to know: how he could have been so self-destructive, and so desperately dishonest. It's well known, for example, that as soon as *Selling You* was a hit, he walked out on his wife and child for a high-flying television executive. So this pattern of cheating which sadly ended up engulfing his career . . .'

I hit the off button, and flung the remote control at the wall. Then I grabbed my jacket and raced out the door. I jumped into my car, I revved the motor, I raced off. It took around a half-hour to reach the NBC studios. I was gambling that the slob would loll around the hospitality suite after his interview and spend time getting his face wiped clean of make-up. My gamble was spot-on, as McCall was just coming out the door and heading to a waiting Lincoln Town Car as I pulled up. Check that: as I roared to a halt right by the door, slamming on the brakes so hard that they shrieked, startling McCall in the process. Within seconds, I was out of the car, running towards him, screaming:

'You fat Limey fuck . . .'

McCall stared at me wide-eyed, his corpulent face registering terror. He looked as if he wanted to run, but was too paralyzed with fear to do anything. Which meant that I was all over the shithead within seconds, grabbing him by his chalk-striped lapels, shaking him forcibly and screaming an incoherent stream of invective, along the lines of: 'Trying to ruin my life . . . calling me a thief . . . shitting on my wife and child . . . going to break every fucking finger on both your hands, you ugly slob . . .'

In the middle of this discordant rant, two things happened, neither of them auspicious for me. The first was that a local freelance photographer – waiting in the NBC lobby – came running out when he heard my uproar, and took a bunch of rapid shots of me yanking McCall's lapels and doing an in-his-face harangue. The second was the arrival of a NBC security man – a tall muscular guy in his late twenties, who immediately waded into the fray, yelling, '*Hey, hey, hey . . . enough!*' before hauling me off McCall and getting me into a half-nelson.

'This guy assault you?' the guard shouted at McCall.

'He tried,' he said, backing off.

'You want me to call the cops?'

McCall stared at me with amused contempt . . . a nasty little 'I've got you, you sonofabitch' smile crossing his lips.

'He's in enough trouble as is,' McCall said. 'Just throw him off the lot.'

Then he turned and started talking to the photographer, asking his name, asking for his card, asking: 'So you managed to get all that?'

Meanwhile, the guard strong-armed me towards my car.

'That's your Porsche?'

I nodded.

'Nice car. Now, sir, I'm gonna offer you a special one-off deal. You get in your car and get lost, and we're going to forget this whole damn thing. If you come back . . .'

'I won't come back.'

'I've got your word on that?'

'I promise.'

'Okay, sir,' he said, slowly releasing me from his grip. 'Let's see you act on that promise and leave quietly.'

I opened the car door and slid in behind the wheel and started the engine. Then the security guard tapped on the window. I rolled it down.

'One last thing, sir,' he said. 'You might want to think about changing your clothes before going anywhere else today.'

It was only then that I realized I was still in my pajamas.

Three

THERE IS NO ESCAPING the laws of cause-and-effect . . . especially when a photographer is present to record you assaulting a journalist while dressed in your pajamas.

So it was that – two days after I made the front page of the *LA Times* – I found myself back in the news . . . with a photograph on page four of its Saturday edition, showing me berating Theo McCall. My face was contorted into an expression of deranged wrath. I was clearly clawing his suit. Then there was the matter of my night-time attire. Outside the bedroom, pajamas conjure up images of the loony bin. Worn by a clearly unsettled individual in the parking lot of the NBC Studios during daylight hours, they indicate that the gent in question might have a few psychological *issues* worth exploring under professional care. Certainly, had I been able to study the photograph with critical detachment, I would have reached the following conclusion: this guy has clearly lost it.

Beneath the photo was a short item, under the headline:

FIRED *SELLING YOU* WRITER ATTACKS JOURNALIST
IN NBC PARKING LOT

The story was straightforward – the facts of the NBC incident, the role of McCall in my downfall, a brief précis of my crimes against humanity, and the fact that, after being cautioned, NBC security allowed me to leave the lot once McCall declined to press charges. There was also a quote from McCall himself: 'I was simply trying to tell the truth . . . even though that truth clearly enraged Mr Armitage. Fortunately, NBC security intervened before he could cause me physical harm. But I do hope, for his own sake, that he seeks serious help. He is obviously a deeply troubled, disturbed man.'

May I kiss the hem of your *shmata*, Dr Freud (and yes, that *is* a borrowed line). But I really didn't have time to worry about McCall's mental assessment of me, as I had several far graver problems on my hands. It seems that the freelancer who caught me roughing up the clown managed to get his photo on the wire services. So the story went right around the country (everyone loves a good *'once he was famous, now he's ga-ga'* story). It even found its way north to the vast chilly expanses of Canada . . . more specifically, to Victoria, British Columbia, where Sally saw the story in the local rag. And she was not amused. So *not amused* that she rang me at nine-thirty Saturday morning and, without even a hello, said, 'David – I've seen the story . . . and I'm afraid that, from this point on, we're history.'

'Can I try to explain?'

'No.'

'But you should have seen what he was saying about me on *Today* . . .'

'I did see it. And quite frankly, I agreed with a great deal of it. What you did was positively insane. And I do mean *insane* . . .'

'Oh for Christ's sake, Sally, I simply lost my temper . . .'

'No – you lost your mind. How else did you end up in the NBC lot in your pajamas?'

'Things just got a little on top of me.'

'A *little* on top of you? I don't think so.'

'Please darling, let's talk this through before . . .'

'No chance. I want you out of the apartment by the time I'm back tomorrow night.'

'Hang on a minute, you can't order me to leave. We're co-tenants, remember? Two names on the lease.'

'According to my lawyer . . .'

'You've already been talking to your lawyer *this morning*? It's a Saturday?'

'He hadn't gone to *shul* yet. Anyway, considering that I'm in crisis . . .'

'Oh cut the fucking melodramatics, Sally.'

'And you say you're not disturbed . . .'

'I'm upset.'

'Well, that makes two of us . . . only you're the one who, according to California law, can be regarded as a physical danger to the co-lessee, which, in turn, allows the co-lessee to get a court order against the other party, barring them from occupying the same premises.'

Long silence.

'You're not really going to do that, are you?' I asked.

'No – I won't get the court order, as long as you promise me to be out of the apartment by six pm tomorrow night. If you are still there, I will call Mel Bing and get him to put the legal wheels in motion.'

'Please Sally, can't we . . . ?'

'This conversation's closed.'

'It's not fair . . .'

'You brought it on yourself. Now do yourself a favor and go. Don't make things any worse for yourself by making me get the courts involved.'

With that, the line went dead. I sat on the sofa, reeling with shock. First my name gets smeared. Then I get fired. Then I make the papers, looking like I'm auditioning for the role of Ezra Pound. Then I get handed my eviction notice – not only from my apartment, but also from the relationship for which I broke up my marriage.

What fresh hell was next?

Of course, it had to come courtesy of my dear ex-wife Lucy, via her own legal eagle, Alexander McHenry. He called me around an hour after the depth charge from Sally.

'Mr Armitage?' he said in a professional, neutral voice. 'It's Alexander McHenry from the firm of Platt, McHenry and Swabe. As you may remember, we represented . . .'

'I remember exactly who you represented. I also know that if you're calling me on a Saturday morning, you have unpleasant news to impart.'

'Well . . .'

'Cut to the chase, McHenry. What's Lucy upset about now?'

I knew the answer to that question, as I figured the *San Francisco Chronicle* had also run the story about the parking lot incident.

'Well, I'm afraid your ex-wife is most alarmed by your behavior yesterday in front of NBC. She is also particularly distressed at the amount of publicity that the incident received, especially as regards how Caitlin would handle the news.'

'I was planning to talk to my daughter personally this morning.'

'I'm afraid that's not going to be possible. Your ex-wife feels that, in the light of your actions yesterday, you could be considered a physical risk to herself and your daughter . . .'

'How can she believe that? I have never, *never* harmed . . .'

'Be that as it may, the fact is: you did attack Mr McCall in the NBC parking lot. You have just been released from your contract with FRT after being exposed as a plagiarist; a tragic incident which, as any psychologist would verify, could easily destabilize a man's mental state. In short, you could be considered a serious risk to your ex-wife and child.'

'What I was trying to say before you interrupted me is that never once have I harmed my wife or child. I lost my temper yesterday, end of story.'

'I'm afraid that's not the end of the story, Mr Armitage. Because we have taken out a banning order against you making any physical or verbal contact with Lucy or Caitlin . . .'

'You cannot keep me from my daughter.'

'It's done. And I must inform you that, should you attempt to contravene the order – either by trying to see Caitlin or Lucy, or even phoning them – you run the risk of arrest and possible imprisonment. Are you clear about that, Mr Armitage?'

I slammed down the phone and collapsed on the sofa, my head in my hands. Let them take away whatever the hell they wanted . . . but not Caitlin. They couldn't do that to me. They just couldn't.

There was a heavy knocking at the door.

'Come on, David. I know you're in there, so open the fucking door.'

Alison.

I went to the door and opened it halfway.

'What are you doing here?' I asked her quietly.

'I think the expression might be: trying to save you from yourself.'

'I'm fine.'

'Sure you are. And you looked wonderful this morning in the

LA Times. Loved the pajamas. Just what an agent wants to see her star client wearing in a parking lot, while trying to beat up . . .'

'I didn't try to beat him up.'

'Oh, that makes everything just hunky-dory again. Are you going let me in or what?'

I stopped blocking the door and went inside. She followed. I sat down on the sofa, and stared at the floor

'Fuck it,' I said. 'Fuck it all.'

'Is this just a reaction to the NBC thing?'

I told her about the fallout from that picture in the papers – and how Sally had evicted me from both our relationship and the apartment, and how Lucy was cutting me off from my daughter. Alison said nothing for a long time. Then, 'I'm getting you out of town.'

'You're *what?*'

'I'm hauling you out of Dodge to somewhere quiet and safe, where you can't do any more damage . . .'

'I am okay, Alison.'

'No, you are not. And the longer you hang around LA, the better the chance that you are going to turn into a total freak show . . .'

'Thanks a lot'

'It's the truth. Like it or not, you are now out of control. And if you continue to be publicly out of control, it'll make great copy for the papers, but will permanently put you out of commission as regards any future work . . .'

'I'm sunk already, Alison . . .'

'I'm not going to even get into that argument. When does Sally want you out of here?'

'By six pm tomorrow.'

'Okay, first things first. Give me your key to this place.'

'Why?'

'Because I'll be packing up all your stuff tomorrow.'

'I'll take care of that.'

'No, you won't. We're leaving here in thirty minutes.'

'To where?'

'A place I know.'

'You're not about to Betty Ford me, are you?'

'Hardly. I'm taking you to a place where you can't get into trouble, and where you'll have time to recuperate a bit. Believe me, what you really need right now is sleep and time to think.'

I thought: like it or not, she is right. I felt piano-wire-taut, and seriously wondered if I could make it through the weekend without resisting the urge to do something final and messy . . . like jumping out a window.

'All right,' I said. 'What do you want me to do?'

'Go pack a bag or two. No need to take any books or CDs – there'll be plenty where you're going. But you'd better bring your laptop, just so you can stay online. And then, take a shower and shave off that damn half-beard of yours. You're starting to look like a member of the Taliban.'

Within half an hour, I was washed, clean shaven, wearing fresh clothes, and lugging two large duffel bags and a computer case down to Alison's car.

'Okay, here's the deal,' she said. 'We're going to be driving up the Pacific Coast Highway for about two hours. I'll go in my car, you go in yours. But promise me you won't suddenly do a vanishing act, and drive off into oblivion . . .'

'Who do you think I am? Jack Kerouac?'

'I'm just saying . . .'

'I promise you, I won't go AWOL.'

'Good – but if we get separated, call me on my cell.'

'I'm a good tail,' I said.

As it turned out, I was able to follow her straight up the Pacific Coast Highway, eventually turning off at the small town of Meredith. We passed a narrow street of shops (including, I noticed, a bookstore and a small grocery), then continued down a winding two-lane blacktop until we came to an unpaved driveway which weaved its way through a dense little wood before dead-ending at a cottage of whitewashed wood, fronting a small pebbly beach, upon which lapped the waters of the Pacific. The cottage itself stood on less than a quarter-acre of land . . . but the coastal view was pretty damn sublime, and I liked the sight of a hammock strung up between two trees, allowing the occupant to recline, yet simultaneously enjoy the ocean view.

'Not a bad spot,' I said. 'Is this your little secret retreat?'

'I wish I owned it. Nah – it belongs to Willard Stevens, the lucky bastard.'

Willard Stevens was a screenwriter client of Alison's, who (like my boozy defender, Justin Wanamaker) had been hot stuff during the movie-brat era of the seventies, but now made a tidy living as a rewrite man.

'So where's Willard?'

'In London for three months, doing a polish on the new Bond film . . .'

'Three months for a polish?'

'I think he's planning to spend a little time on the Côte d'Azur while he's at it. Anyway, he gave me the key to this place while he's away. I've only used it once. And since he won't be coming back for another ten weeks . . .'

'I am *not* spending ten weeks here.'

'Fine, fine. It's not a padded cell. You've got your car. You're free to come and go as much as you want. All I ask is that, initially, you spend a week up here. Call it a little holiday – a chance to take stock, to clear your head away from all the bullshit back in town. So will you promise me to hang here for a week?'

'I haven't seen the inside of this place yet.'

Within two minutes of walking inside, I committed to the week. The cottage had stone walls, a stone floor, comfortable furniture. Lots of books and music and films on DVD.

'This will do just fine,' I said.

'Glad you approve. Anyway, there's only a phone – and the television deliberately gets no stations, because Willard decided he didn't want to watch anything here except old movies. But his film library's pretty damn good. And, as you see, there's plenty to read and to listen to. And the tuner on the stereo does pull in the local NPR affiliate, if you want to keep up with the news and with *Car Talk*. And you probably saw the grocery store in the little town. The nearest big supermarket's about fifteen miles away, but you should find everything you need . . .'

'I'm sure I'll be fine,' I said.

'Now listen,' she said, planting herself on the sofa and motioning for me to sit down in the armchair. 'I need a couple of assurances from you.'

'No, I won't wreck the place. No, I won't disappear . . .'

She interrupted, saying, 'And no, you won't set foot inside the Los Angeles city limits. And no, you won't call FRT or Warners or anyone else in the business. And no – and this is the biggest *no* of them all – you won't make contact with Sally or Lucy or Caitlin.'

'How do you expect me *not* to talk to my daughter?'

'You *will* talk to your daughter . . . but only if you let me handle it. What was the name of your divorce lawyer?'

'Forget that loser. He let Lucy's gal disembowel me.'

'Okay, then I'll call my legal eagle and ask him to find us a Nazi. But again, I've got to emphasize this . . .'

'I know, if I call Caitlin, I'm going to turn a catastrophic situation into an Armageddon situation.'

'Bingo. Also: I'm going to talk to your accountant guy . . . and get a complete up-to-date position on your tax liability and other fun stuff. And tomorrow, before the six pm deadline, I'll get all your stuff out of the apartment and into storage, and I'll deal with Sally on little things like your share of the deposit, the furniture you bought together, etc.'

'Let her have everything.'

'No.'

'I blew it with her. I blew it with everybody and everything. And now . . .'

'Now you're going to spend at least a week doing nothing but taking long walks, reading in the hammock, reducing your daily booze intake to a glass or two of decent Napa wine, and trying to sleep well. Are we clear about all that?'

'Aye, aye, doctor.'

'Speaking of doctors, one final thing . . . and don't scream about this . . . a therapist named Matthew Sims is going to be phoning you around eleven tomorrow morning. I've booked him for fifty minutes, and if you like him, he'll do a daily session with you on the phone. Take it from me: as therapists go, he's no bullshit . . .'

'He's *your* therapist?'

'Don't act so surprised.'

'It's just . . . I didn't realize . . .'

'Honey, I'm a Hollywood agent. Of course I have a therapist. And this guy gives good phone, and I think you know that you need to be talking to someone right now . . .'

'All right, I'll take the call.'

'Good.'

'Alison . . .'

'Yeah?'

'You didn't have to do all this.'

'Yeah, I think I did.'

'Now I'm afraid I've got to turn around now and head back to town. I've got a heavy date tonight.'

'Anyone exciting?'

'He's a sixty-three-year-old retired Chief Financial Officer for one of the studios. He's probably just had a triple bypass and is also in the early stages of Alzheimer's. But hey, I'm not going to say no to a little action.'

'Jesus, Alison . . .'

'Listen to you, Mr Prude. I may be fifty-seven years old, but I am not your mother. Which means I am allowed to have sex . . .'

'I'm saying nothing.'

'Damn right you're not,' she said, fixing me with a skewed smile. Then she reached out and took each of my hands. 'I want you to be all right.'

'I'll try.'

'And remember – whatever the hell happens professionally – one way or another you *will* live. Amazingly enough, life does go on. Try to keep that in mind.'

'Sure.'

'Now go get into that hammock.'

As soon as Alison drove off, I did as ordered, grabbing a copy of Hammett's *The Thin Man* off Willard Stevens's shelf and collapsing in the hammock. Although it was one of my favorite crime novels, the jumbled pressure and exhaustion of the past few days suddenly mowed me down, and I passed out after a page. When I woke there was a distinct chill in the air, and the sun was bowing out into the Pacific. I felt cold and disorientated . . . and within seconds, the entire appalling scenario came rushing back to occupy my brain. My initial urge was to run to the phone, call Lucy, tell her she was playing the vilest sort of hardball, then demand to speak to Caitlin. But I talked myself down from that furious position, reminding myself what happened when I decided to confront Theo McCall (and also realizing how the world would come tumbling down upon me if I did violate the court order). So I got out of the hammock and went inside and threw some water on my face and found a sweater. Then, realizing that the cupboard was bare, I jumped in the car and headed to the local grocery shop.

It wasn't just a grocery – it was also a general store-cum-delicatessen. Like everything I spied on the main street in Meredith (the bookstore, the shops that sold scented candles and upscale bath salts, the clothing store with Ralph Lauren shirts in the window) it suggested that this was a well-heeled weekend retreat for well-heeled Angelinos . . . albeit, I sensed, one of those places where everyone maintained a certain polite detachment from each other.

Certainly this was the case in Fuller's Grocery. After buying basic supplies for the house – as well as some fancy-assed pasta and pesto for dinner – the fiftysomething woman behind the counter (handsome, grey-haired, blue denim shirt – the archetypal upscale owner of an upscale grocers like this) didn't ask me if I was new in town, or just up for the weekend, or any of that other nosey neighbor stuff. Instead she quietly checked me out, and said, 'The pesto's a good choice. I made it myself.'

The pesto was a good choice. So too was the bottle of Oregon Pinot Noir. I restricted myself to two glasses. I was in bed by ten, but I couldn't sleep, so I got up and watched a video of Billy Wilder's *The Apartment* (one of my all-time favorite films). Even though I'd seen it a half-dozen times before, I still cried shamelessly when Shirley MacLaine ran through the Manhattan streets to profess her love for Jack Lemmon at the end. And when I couldn't sleep after that, I sat up some more and gawked at a great forgotten Cagney comedy of the thirties, *Jimmy the Gent*. By the time that was finished, it was nearly three. I staggered into bed and passed out.

I woke to a phone call – from Matthew Sims, the therapist with whom Alison had set me up. His voice sounded reasonable, calm: the standard issue therapeutic voice. He asked me if he'd woken me. When I confirmed this, he said that, given it was a Sunday, he wasn't exactly block booked, and would be happy to call back in twenty minutes. I thanked him and headed out to the kitchen to make a quick pot of coffee, and to get two cups into me before the phone rang again.

Alison was right: Matthew Sims was good news. No touchy-feely crap. No *inner child* nonsense. He got me talking about the last week, about how I felt like I was in free fall, and feared ever being able to recover from all this professional calamity, and still felt appalling guilt for breaking up my family, and now wondered whether or not I had somehow set myself up for this disaster. Naturally enough, Sims immediately fastened on to this comment, asking me, 'Are you saying that you believe you consciously or subconsciously willed yourself all this trouble?'

'Subconsciously, yeah.'

'Do you really believe that?'

'Why else did all those borrowed lines appear in my scripts?'

'Maybe you just accidentally borrowed them, David. That kind of assimilation of other people's jokes does happen sometimes, doesn't it?'

'Or maybe I wanted to be found out.'

'What is it that you wanted found out about yourself?'

'The fact . . .'

'Yes.'

'The fact . . . that I'm a fraud.'

'Do you really think that, especially given all the success you've had up until recently?'

'I think that now.'

And then our time was up, and we agreed to talk again at eleven the next day.

I spent much of the day in the hammock or walking the beach, thinking, thinking. And having all those silent mental arguments, in which I said all the things I wanted to say to Lucy; in which I convinced Sally to give me – *us* – another chance; and in which I was interviewed by Charlie Rose on PBS and gave such an intelligent, searing rebuttal to McCall's charges that Brad Bruce called me the next day and said: 'Dave, we made a big mistake. Get on down here and let's start working on the third season.'

Sure. In my dreams. Because there was no way that anything would be restored to me. I'd blown it . . . allowing an unintentional mistake to blossom into a personal conflagration. And so I started playing the *If only* . . . game. As in: if only I hadn't responded so vehemently to McCall's initial disclosure. If only I'd eaten humble pie and written McCall a letter thanking him for pointing out my little error. But I was both frightened and arrogant – just as I was around the time I started my affair with Sally Birmingham: frightened that all would be revealed and I'd lose my family; yet flush with my new-found success to believe that I deserved this 'prize'. And, of course, *if only* I'd stayed with Lucy, then I mightn't have reacted in such an extreme way when McCall appeared on *Today*. Because he would never have made that comment about me leaving my wife and child – the comment which sent me hurtling towards that ignominious scene in the NBC parking lot . . .

Enough, enough. To quote that famous needlepoint motto: you can't undo what's been done. Which, in turn, brings one to the blunt realization: *when you're fucked, you're fucked.*

But what was even more unnerving was the thought: was this the situation I really wanted? Did I so distrust my success that I somehow needed to fail. Was I – as Sally had said – the architect of my own ruinous denouement?

I brought this matter up with Matthew Sims when we spoke again on Monday morning.

'Are you saying you can't trust yourself?' he asked.

'Can anybody ever really trust themselves?'

'By which you mean . . . ?'

'Don't we all have our fingers on the self-destruct button?'

'Possibly – but most of us don't push it.'

'I did.'

'You keep coming back to that, David. Do you really think that everything which has happened to you was self-inflicted?'

'I don't know.'

Over the next few days, this became our central topic of conversation: had I set myself up for this spectacular fall? Matthew Sims kept encouraging me to believe that, sometimes, bad shit simply happened.

'And remember,' Sims said, 'we all do out-of-character stuff when we're under severe strain. I mean, you didn't physically harm the man . . .'

'But I did do enormous harm to my situation . . .'

'Okay,' he said. 'You made a bad mistake. What now?'

'I don't know.'

Sims's phone calls were the central point of my day. I spent the rest of the time walking and reading, and watching old movies, and resisting the temptation to make certain phone calls or to go online. I didn't even bother buying a newspaper. When Alison called every night at six, I didn't ask her if my name was still in the papers. Instead, I let her fill me in on the day's events. On Monday, she told me that all my belongings had been packed up and shipped to storage. On Tuesday, she said that she'd hired a well-considered divorce lawyer named Walter Dickerson to act on my behalf, and that the $5,000 she squeezed out of Sally for my portion of the deposit and the furniture we'd bought together would cover his work on the case.

'What did Sally say?'

'There was a lot of invective at first. A lot of "How dare you?" To which I replied, "How dare you break up a guy's marriage and then dump him when he hits hard times?"'

'Jesus Christ, you actually said that to her?'

'You bet.'

'How did she react?'

'More of the "how dare you" shit. So I pointed out that it wasn't just me who thought that . . . but all of Hollywood. Of course, I was simply talking out of my ass, but it made her sit up and write the check. We had to argue the price a bit – especially as I asked for $7,500 to begin with – but eventually she came around.'

'Well . . . thanks, I guess.'

'Hey, it's all part of the service. Anyway, now that she's given you the bullet, I'm going to speak the truth: I always thought she was Little Miss Ruthless. To her, you were just one rung on the ladder.'

'Now you tell me.'

'You knew that all along, David.'

'Yeah,' I said quietly. 'I guess I did.'

On Wednesday, Alison told me that my accountant, Sandy Meyer, was preparing a complete statement of my financial where-withal, but had been unable to get in contact with Bobby Barra . . . who, according to his assistant, was on business in China. No doubt, selling them their own Great Wall.

On Thursday, Alison told me that Walter Dickerson was in serious negotiation with Alexander McHenry, and should have some sort of news by the start of next week.

'Why the hell hasn't Dickerson called me?'

'Because I told him not to. I briefed him thoroughly on the situation and said you wanted to have proper access to your daughter again. Then I gave him McHenry's number and told him to rough him up. Would you have said anything more to him?'

'I guess not. It's just . . . ?'

'How are you sleeping?'

'Not badly, actually.'

'That's an improvement. And you're talking things through with Sims every day.'

'Oh yes.'

'Making progress?'

'You know what therapy's like: you keep saying the same old crap over and over again until you're so sick of it yourself, you think: I'm cured.'

'Are you feeling cured?'

'Hardly. Humpty Dumpty has not been put back together again.'

'But, at least, you're better than you were last week.'

'Yeah.'

'Then why not spend another week up there?'

'Why not? I have nowhere else to go.'

Nor did I have much to do during my second weekend, except

continue working my way through Willard's extensive film library, read, listen to music, hike along the shoreline, eat light meals, stick to two glasses of wine a day, and try to keep all the demons at bay.

Then Monday came. Shortly after I finished my telephonic confessional session with Matthew Sims, the phone rang. It was my lawyer, Walter Dickerson. He spoke smoothly.

'I'm going to give it to you straight, David,' he said. 'For reasons best known to herself, your ex-wife has decided to really go to town on this one. Her own lawyer admitted to me that he felt she was way overstepping the mark on the barring order, considering that there's no previous history of domestic violence, and also that, with the exception of one missed weekend, you've been very conscientious about your access to Caitlin. But though McHale explained all this to your ex, she is really determined to punish you . . . which means we have what's known in the trade as "*a situation*". And it comes down to this: in my experience, when someone is that angry, they will go even more ballistic if you try to throw a writ back in their face. In other words, we could go to court and do an entire song and dance about how you simply lost it with the guy who was trying to destroy your career, but didn't do the clown any harm . . . so how in the hell could you be of any danger to your ex-wife and child? But I promise you: once we do this, she'll just up the ante and start throwing all sorts of accusations at you – from Satanic abuse to keeping a voodoo doll under your bed . . .'

'She's not that crazy . . .'

'Maybe not – but she's awfully damn angry at you. If we fuel her anger, it's going to cost you – both financially and emotionally. So here's what I've discussed with McHenry – and though it may not be ideal, it's better than nothing. He thinks he can convince your ex-wife to initially allow you a daily phone call with Caitlin . . .'

'That's it?'

'Look, considering that she wants to deny you contact completely, getting her to agree to a phone call would be a step forward.'

'But will I ever see my daughter again?'

'Of that I have no doubt . . . but it might take a couple of months . . .'

'A couple of months. Come on, Mr Dickerson . . .'

'I'm not a miracle worker, David. And I have to listen to what my opposite number is saying about his client's intentions. And what he's saying to me is that, right now, a daily phone call with your daughter should be considered a gift. As I said, there is the litigation option . . . but it's going to cost you a cool twenty-five grand *minimum*. It'll also generate some publicity. From what Alison was telling me – and also from what I've been reading in the papers recently – the last thing you need is publicity.'

'Okay, okay, get me the daily phone call.'

'Smart guy,' Dickerson said, adding: 'I'll be back to you as soon as I have an answer from the other side. And by the way, I'm a big fan of *Selling You*.'

'Thanks,' I said weakly.

Sandy Meyer also called me on Monday, to tell me that the $250k owing to the IRS was due in three weeks, and that he was rather worried about my cash flow position.

'Now I checked with BankAmerica, and you've got about twenty-eight thousand in your checking account . . . which should cover the next two months' alimony and child support payments. After that . . .'

'All my other money is tied up with Bobby Barra.'

'I looked at his most recent account statement, which is for the last quarter. He's done pretty well by you, as your total balance as of two months ago was $533,245. The problem is, David – you have no other cash bar this investment portfolio.'

'I was supposed to be earning nearly $2 million this year, before this curve ball took off my head. Now . . . now, there's nothing else coming in. And you know what happened to most of my big first year earnings . . .'

'I know: your ex-wife and the IRS.'

'God bless them both.'

'So it looks like you're going to have to liquidate half your portfolio to meet that IRS demand. But Alison also said that FRT and Warners want around half a million back in writer's fees. If that demand becomes reality . . .'

'I know: the math doesn't work. But my hope is that Alison will be able to negotiate them down to about half of that.'

'Which means that your investment portfolio will essentially be wiped out. Is there any other money coming in?'

'Nope.'

'Then how are you going to find the eleven grand per month for Lucy and Caitlin?'

'Shine shoes?'

'Surely Alison can find you some work.'

'Haven't you heard? I'm supposed to be a plagiarist. And nobody hires plagiarists.'

'You have no other assets I don't know about?'

'Just my car.'

I could hear him shuffling more papers. 'It's a Porsche, right? Worth probably around $40k right now.'

'That sounds about right.'

'Sell it.'

'What am I going to drive?'

'Something a lot cheaper than a Porsche. Meanwhile, let's hope that Alison can get FRT and Warners to be reasonable. Because if they decide to press for the full sum, you know you're looking at Chapter 11 . . .'

'Oh yes.'

'But let's hope we never have to end up in that snakepit. First things first: according to his assistant, Bobby Barra is due back at the end of the week. I've left him an urgent message to contact me. I suggest you do the same. By the time he's back, we've only got seventeen days to pay Uncle Sam . . . and it does take some time to sell half a portfolio. So . . .'

'I'll chase Barra.'

I talked about my financial worries with Matthew Sims the next morning. Naturally he asked me how I felt about it.

'Scared to death,' I said.

'Okay,' he said. 'Let's take the absolute worst-case scenario. You lose everything. You're declared bankrupt. Your bank account is zip. Then what? Do you think you'll never work again?'

'Sure I'll work – in a job where I say stuff like: *"You want fries with the shake?"*'

'Come on, David, you're a clever guy . . .'

'. . . who's *persona non grata* in Hollywood . . .'

'Maybe for a little while.'

'Maybe for ever. And that's what's scaring me so badly. I might not be able to write again . . .'

'Of course you'll be able to write.'

'Yeah – but no one's going to buy the stuff. And writers live for an audience: readers, viewers, whatever. Writing's the one thing I'm good at. I was a crap husband, I'm a middling father, but when it comes to words I'm clever as hell. I spent fourteen long years trying to convince the world that I was a proper writer. And you know what? I finally won the argument. In fact, I won it beyond my wildest damn dreams. And now it's all going to be taken away from me.'

'You mean, the way you feel your ex-wife is going to permanently take Caitlin away from you?'

'She's trying her best.'

'But do you really think she'll succeed?'

And for the fifth (or maybe sixth) time running, our session ended with me saying: 'I don't know.'

I slept badly that night. I woke early the next morning, my sense of dread back to full operating speed. Then Alison called me, sounding just a little tense.

'Have you read the papers this morning?'

'I stopped reading newspapers when I came up here. What is it now?'

'All right, this is a good news/bad news call. What do you want to hear first?'

'The bad news, of course. But how bad is bad?'

'That depends.'

'On what?'

'How attached you are to your Emmy.'

'The bastards want it back?'

'That's what's happened. As reported in this morning's *LA Times*, the American Academy of Television Arts and Sciences passed a motion last night to strip you of your Emmy on the grounds of . . .'

'I know what the grounds are.'

'I'm really sorry, David.'

'Don't be. It's an ugly piece of tin. You collected the Emmy from the apartment?'

'Yeah.'

'Then ship it on back. Good riddance. So what's the good news?'

'Well, this was in the same *LA Times* report. It seems SATWA did pass a motion at their monthly meeting last night to censure you . . .'

'That's your idea of good news?'

'Hear me out. They did censure you, but by a two-to-one majority, they defeated a motion to recommend you being banned from work for any given amount of time.'

'Big deal. The studios and every damn producer in town will do that for them . . . with or without a SATWA resolution.'

'Look, I know I'm going to sound like some spin doctor . . . but the thing is, a censure is a slap on the wrist, nothing more. So we should take this as a good sign that, in professional writing circles, people are seeing this for what this really is: bullshit.'

'Unlike the Emmy people.'

'They're just playing a public relations game. When you come back . . .'

'I don't believe in reincarnation. Anyway, don't you remember what Scott Fitzgerald said, in one of his few sober moments towards the end: there are no second acts in American lives.'

'I operate according to a different theory: life is short, but writing careers are curiously long. Try to get some sleep tonight. You sound like shit.'

'I am shit.'

Of course, I didn't sleep . . . but instead watched all three parts of *The Apu Trilogy* (six hours of Hindi domestic life from the 1950s – brilliant, but only a manic insomniac would actually sit straight through it all). Eventually I staggered into bed, waking again to the sound of a ringing phone. What day was it? Wednesday? Thursday? Time had lost all value for me. In the recent past, my life had been one long workaday sprint – during which I crammed in so much: a couple hours of writing, a few production meetings, a few brainstorming sessions, endless phone calls, a business lunch, a business dinner, a screening here, a *must-be-seen-at* party there. Then there were the alternate weekends with Caitlin. On the weekends I was without her, I'd spend nine hours a day in front of the computer, grinding out part of a new episode, or a section of my script, pushing, pushing, pushing. Because, as I knew so damn well, I was on a roll. And when you're on a roll, you can't afford to stop. For if you do . . .

The phone kept ringing. I reached for it.

'David, it's Walter Dickerson. Did I wake you?'

'What time is it?'

'Around noon. Listen, I can call back.'

'No, no, tell me – do you have news?'

'Yes I do.'

'And?'

'It's pretty reasonable news.'

'By which you mean . . .'

'Your ex-wife has agreed that you can have phone contact with Caitlin.'

'That's a step forward, I guess.'

'Without question. However, she has insisted on a couple of conditions. You can only call every other day, with a maximum time limit of fifteen minutes.'

'She actually set those terms?'

'Absolutely. And according to her lawyer, it took some convincing to get her to agree to that limited amount of telephone access.'

'When can I make my first phone call?'

'Tonight. Your ex-wife suggested seven pm as the standard time for the call. Does that work for you?'

'Sure,' I said, thinking: my schedule isn't exactly full. 'But Mr Dickerson . . . Walter . . . how long do you think it'll be before I'll be able to actually see my daughter?'

'The honest answer to that is: it depends upon your ex-wife. If she wants to keep busting your balls . . . excuse my French . . . this could drag on for months and months. If that happened – and if your pockets were deep enough – we could take her to court. But let's hope that, once her temper cools down, she'll be willing to negotiate some proper physical access. But like I said, it's going to be a gradual process. I wish I had better news, but . . . as you've probably figured out by now, there is no such thing as an amicable divorce. And when there's a child involved, the disagreements are endless. So, at least we've got you talking with Caitlin again. It's a start.'

As scheduled, I made that first call at seven pm that night. Lucy must have had Caitlin positioned by the phone, as she picked up immediately.

'Daddy!' she said, sounding genuinely pleased to hear my voice. 'Why have you disappeared?'

'I had to go away to do some work,' I said.

'Don't you want to see me anymore?' she asked.

I swallowed hard.

'I'm desperate to see you,' I said. 'It's just . . . I can't right now.'

'Why can't you?'

'Because . . . because . . . I'm far away, working.'

'Mommy said you got into some trouble.'

'That's right, there was some trouble . . . but it's better now.'

'So you will be coming to see me?'

'As soon as I can.' I took a deep breath, and bit hard on my lower lip. 'And meantime, we will talk all the time on the phone.'

My composure cracked.

'Daddy, what's the matter?'

'I'm fine, I'm fine, I'm fine . . .' I said, pulling myself back from the precipice. 'Tell me what you've been doing at school.'

For the next fourteen minutes, we talked about a wide variety of issues . . . from her role as an angel in her school's upcoming Easter pageant to why she thought Big Bird was boring, but Cookie Monster was cool, to her desire for a Sleep-Over Barbie doll.

I timed the call with my watch. Precisely fifteen minutes after Caitlin picked up, I heard Lucy's voice in the background, saying: 'Tell Daddy it's time to stop.'

'Daddy, it's time to stop.'

'Okay, my darling. I miss you terribly.'

'I miss you too.'

'And I'll call you on Friday. Can I talk to your mother now?'

'Mommy,' Caitlin said, 'Daddy wants to speak with you. Bye, Daddy.'

'Bye, darling.' Then I heard the phone being handed over to Lucy. But without uttering a word, she hung up on me.

Naturally, this phone call took up my entire session with Matthew Sims the next day.

'Lucy so despises me, she'll never let me see Caitlin again.'

'But she did let you talk to her . . . which is an improvement over where we were last week.'

'I still brought this all on myself.'

'David, when did you leave Lucy?'

'Two years ago.'

'From what you told me during our first session, you were incredibly generous as regards the division of property.'

'She got the house – which I'd completely paid off.'

'Since then, you've made all your support payments on time, you've been a good dad to Caitlin, and you haven't done anything hostile or untoward towards your ex-wife.'

'No.'

'Well then, if she's still harboring enmity towards you a full two years after the divorce, that is her problem, not yours. And if she's using Caitlin as a weapon against you . . . she will soon be forced to confront the fact that she is acting selfishly. Because your daughter will tell her so.'

'I hope you're right. But I'm still haunted by something . . .'

'What?'

'The fact that I should have never left them; that I made a terrible mistake.'

'Would you really want to go back now?'

'That would never happen. There's too much crap under the bridge; too much bad blood. But . . . I still made a mistake. A terrible mistake.'

'Have you ever told Lucy that?'

When I called back on Friday, however, Lucy still wouldn't speak to me – and instead instructed Caitlin to hang up the phone at the end of our allotted fifteen minutes. The same thing happened on Sunday – but, at least, I was able to give Caitlin my phone number at the cottage, and asked her to tell Lucy that I would be staying at this number for the next few weeks.

The decision to remain at Willard's cottage had been an easy one to reach. I had few options – and as luck would have it, my need for longer term accommodation coincided with Willard's decision to stay on in London for an additional six months.

'He's got another big rewrite job, and he seems to like the grey gloom of that town, so it looks like you can stay up there until Christmas,' Alison said when she called me with the news. 'More to the point, he's happy to have you installed as caretaker . . . and he's not going to charge you anything, except the utilities.'

'Sounds fair to me.'

'He also wanted me to tell you that he feels what's happened to you has been totally over the top and wrong. He's even written to the Emmy people to tell them that they've acted like a bunch of shitbirds.'

'He actually used those words?'

'An approximation.'

'When you're taking to him again, please tell him how grateful I am. It's the first lucky break I've had in a while.'

But my run of good luck was short-lived. The next day, a megaton bomb landed in my lap after I finally made contact with Bobby Barra.

I rang him on his cellphone. He sounded more than a little hesitant when he heard my voice.

'Hey guy, how's it going?' he asked me.

'I've had better months.'

'Yeah, I heard things had been rough. Where you calling from right now?'

I explained about Sally kicking me out, and Alison finding me this coastal refuge.

'Man, you have hit Shit City,' Bobby said.

'Understatement of the year.'

'Well listen, guy – sorry I haven't been in touch, but you know I was over in Shanghai for this Search Engine start-up. And I know you're calling me to find out about how the IPO has shaken down.'

An alarm bell went off between my ears.

'What does that IPO have to do with me, Bobby?'

'What does it have to do with you, guy? C'mon . . . you're the one who told me to move your entire portfolio into this IPO.'

'I never said that.'

'The hell you didn't. Remember that conversation we had when I called you a couple of months ago to tell you about your portfolio dividend for the last quarter?'

'Yeah, I remember it . . .'

'And what did I ask you?'

He asked me if I would like to be one of the privileged few who would be allowed to invest seriously in a sure-fire IPO for an Asian search engine . . . a search engine that was guaranteed to become the number one player in China and all of Southeast Asia. And – with my detailed memory for all grisly details – I remembered our entire conversation at the time.

'This is like backing Yahoo with slopey eyes,' he said.

'How politically correct of you, Bobby.'

'Listen guy – we're talking about the biggest untapped market in the world. And it's the chance to get in at ground level. But I've got to know fast . . . you interested?'

'You've never steered me wrong yet.'

'Smart guy.'

Shit. Shit. Shit. The guy thought that was a directive to sell.

'Well, wasn't it?' Bobby asked me. 'I mean, I did ask you if you were interested. You did answer in the affirmative. So I took that to mean you wanted in.'

'But I didn't tell you to transfer my entire fucking portfolio . . .'

'You didn't say otherwise either. To me, "in" means *in.*'

'You had no right to transfer any shares of mine without my explicit written approval.'

'That's bullshit and you know it. How the hell do you think the brokerage business works? By a polite exchange of paper? This is a game which alters every thirty seconds, so if someone tells me to sell . . .'

'I didn't tell you to sell . . .'

'I made an offer to get you into the IPO, you accepted. And if you read the agreement you signed with my company when you became a client, you'll see that there's a clause authorizing us to buy or sell shares on your behalf with your *verbal* consent. But hey, if you want to take this to the SEC, go right ahead. They'll laugh you out of court.'

'I don't believe this . . .'

'Hey, it's not the end of the world. Nine months from now, the share price is going to quadruple, which means that not only will you make up the initial fifty per cent loss in share value . . .'

Three alarm bells started going off between my ears.

'What the fuck did you just say?'

He remained calm. 'I said: given the momentary downturn in technology stocks, the initial IPO didn't go as well as expected . . . and about half the value of your shares was wiped out.'

'That can't be true.'

'What can I say, except: it happens. Anyway, all this stuff is a gamble, right? I try to minimize your risk . . . but sometimes the market turns weird for a spell. The thing is: this is not a disaster. Far from it. Because by this time next year, I'm certain you'll be seeing . . .'

'Bobby, by this time next year, I'll be in debtor's jail. I owe the IRS around a quarter-million, and FRT and Warners are about to start chasing me for, *at best*, the same amount of cash. Do you understand what's happened to me? All my contracts have been cancelled. I am a Hollywood untouchable. The only money I have in the world is the money I've invested with you. And now you tell me . . .'

'What I'm telling you is to keep your nerve.'

'And what I'm telling you is that I have seventeen days to pay that IRS bill. The Internal Revenue Service doesn't adopt a grand-fatherly approach to anyone who's late with a big bill. They're the biggest bastards on the planet.'

'So what do you want me to do?'

'Get me all my money back.'

'You're going to have to be patient for that.'

'I *can't* be fucking patient.'

'Well, I can't get you what you want. Not immediately anyway.'

'So what can you get me immediately?'

'Just the current value of your portfolio – which is around the quarter-mil mark.'

'You've bankrupted me . . .'

'I think it's you who've bankrupted yourself. And as I have been trying to tell you, if you keep the money where it is for nine months . . .'

'I don't have nine fucking months. I have seventeen days. And once I pay off the Feds, I'll have nothing. You got that? Less that zero . . .'

'What can I say? A gamble's a gamble.'

'If you had only been straight with me . . .'

'I was straight with you, jerkoff,' he said, suddenly angry. 'I mean, let's face facts here. If you hadn't gotten your ass thrown off your show for stealing people's lines . . .'

'Fuck you, fuck you, fuck you . . .'

'That's it. We are done here. Literally and figuratively. I don't want your business. I don't want to deal with you.'

'Of course you don't, now that you've screwed me . . .'

'I am not continuing this dialogue. And I only have one final question for you: do you want me to liquidate the stock?'

'I have no choice.'

'That's an affirmative then?'

'Yes – sell it all.'

'Fine. Done. Expect the money in your account tomorrow. End of story.'

'Never call me again,' I said.

'Why would I do that?' Bobby said. 'I don't deal with losers.'

Naturally, my session the next morning with Matthew Sims kicked off with a discussion of that last line.

'Well, do you consider yourself a loser?' he asked me.

'What do you think?'

'You tell me, David.'

'I'm not just a loser. I'm a disaster zone. Everything, *everything*, has been taken from me. And it's all due to my own stupidity, my own self-absorption.'

'There you go again, down the self-hatred track.'

226

'What do you expect? I am now also heading toward financial collapse.'

'And you don't think you're clever enough to get yourself out of this?'

'How? Through suicide?'

'That's not the sort of joke you tell your therapist.'

Nor, for that matter, was my accountant in jocular form when I explained the Bobby Barra debacle.

'I don't want to say "I told you so", Sandy Meyer said, 'but I did warn you about centralizing your portfolio in the hands of one broker.'

'The guy did so well for me up until now. And I was expecting to make such big bucks this year . . .'

'I know, David. It's a tough situation. But okay, here's how I think we should play it. The $250k in liquidated stock goes to pay off Uncle Sam. Your credit cards are maxed out right now at $28k . . . so the $30k in your account goes to pay off that debt, leaving you two grand in cash. But Alison told me you're living rent free right now.'

'Rent free and cheap. If I spend $200 a week, it's an event.'

'Then that two grand will buy you ten weeks. But there's the problem of the eleven grand a month for Lucy and Caitlin. I spoke with Alison about this. She says you've got a tough new lawyer working your corner. I'm sure, given your considerably reduced circumstances, a court would agree to lower your monthly payment.'

'I don't want to do that. It's not fair.'

'But David, Lucy is earning very good money now . . . and the initial alimony and child support payment was, in my opinion, sky high. I know you were pulling down a million a year. But even so, the level of payment struck me as so excessive as to be . . . if you don't mind me saying so . . . guilt money.'

'It was guilt money. It still is guilt money.'

'Well, now you can longer afford to feel guilty. Eleven grand a month is out of your league.'

'I'll sell the car . . . as you suggested. I should get forty grand for it.'

'What are you going to drive?'

'Something cheap and well under seven thousand bucks. With the remaining thirty-three grand, I can afford the next three months' payments.'

'And after that?'

'I haven't a clue.'

'You better talk to Alison about finding you some work.'

'Alison is the best agent in town . . . but she won't be finding me any work.'

'With your permission, I'm going to give her a call,' Sandy said.

'Why bother? I'm a lost cause.'

A few days after Sandy's call, Alison rang me and said, 'Hello, Lost Cause.'

'I see you've been talking to my esteemed accountant.'

'Oh, I've been talking to lots of people,' she said. 'Including FRT and Warner Brothers.'

'And?'

'Well, it's another good news/bad news call. First I'm going to give you the bad news: both FRT and Warners are adamant that you pay back the fees.'

'That's me finished.'

'Not so fast – the good news is that both companies have agreed to halve their demand – which means one hundred and twenty-five thousand each.'

'I'm still ruined.'

'Yeah – Sandy explained everything to me. But the other good news is that I have convinced them to let you pay it off on the installment plan, with no payment due for the first six months.'

'Big deal. The fact is, I have no money to make these payments. And I'm out of work.'

'No, you're not.'

'What are you talking about?'

'I found you some work.'

'Writing work?'

'Absolutely. It's not particularly glamorous work, but it *is* work. And for the amount of time it'll take you to do it, it's well paid.'

'So cut to the chase.'

'Now I don't want you to groan when I tell you . . .'

'Just tell me, *please.*'

'It's a novelization.'

I tried not to groan. A novelization was hack work – in which you took a screenplay of a forthcoming movie and turned it into a short, easy-to-read novel, which was generally sold at supermarket checkouts and all outlets of K-mart. Professionally speaking, it was the lowest-of-the-lows – the sort of job you took because you either had low self-esteem, or had hit the bottom of the barrel and were desperate for cash. I qualified on all fronts, so I swallowed my protestations and asked:

'What's the movie?'

'Try not to groan again . . .'

'I didn't groan the first time . . .'

'Well, you might do now. It's a new teen movie that New Line are realizing.'

'Called?' I asked.

'*Losing It.*'

This time I did groan. 'Let me guess . . . it's about two pimply sixteen year olds who want to lose their virginity?'

'My, my, you are clever,' Alison said. 'Except that the kids are seventeen

'Late starters.'

'Hey, virginity is "in" these days.'

'What's the name of our two protagonists?'

'You're going to love this: Chip and Chuck.'

'Sounds like a pair of cartoon beavers. And the setting is some-where deeply banal and suburban, like Van Nuys?'

'Close: Orange County.'

'And does one of the kids turn out to be a slasher?'

'No – it's not *Scream*. But there is a dazzling twist in the tail: it turns out that the gal whom Chip finally *schtups* is Chuck's half-sister . . .'

'But Chuck doesn't know of her existence?'

'Bingo. It turns out that January . . .'

'Her name is January?'

'Hey, it's that kind of movie.'

'Clearly. And it sounds like total shit.'

'That it is. But they are also offering twenty-five thousand for the novelization, on the condition that it's delivered in two weeks.'

'I'm in,' I said.

The script arrived by Fedex the next morning. It was godawful: smug, full of smutty jokes about erections and clitorises and flatulence, with one-dimensional characters, the usual routine teen situations (including the requisite backseat blow-job), the requisite punch-up between the two boys after Chuck discovers that he's related to the girl Chip's been sleeping with, and the requisite '*growth*' finale, in which Chip and Chuck reconcile, Chuck and his estranged father reconcile, and January reveals to Chip that he was her first lover too . . . and though she doesn't want a 'hot-and-heavy romance', they'll always be friends.

I called Alison after I finished reading it.

'Well?' she asked.

'Garbage,' I said.

'So can you make the two-week deadline?'

'No problem.'

'Good. Now here are some ground rules that the publisher, Max Newton, asked me to give you. The length should be 75,000 words maximum. And remember this is for the moron market – so keep it fast, keep it simple, keep it basic . . . but also make certain the sex scenes are . . . how did he put this? . . . "hot, but not scorching". Does that make sense to you?'

'I suppose so.'

'One final thing: the publisher knows that it's you who's writing the novelization . . .'

'He didn't object?'

'He's in New York. And he thinks what goes on out here is, at the best of times, stupid. But we both agreed that – to protect him and yourself – it was best if you used a pseudonym. You don't mind, do you?'

'Are you kidding me? I don't want my name attached to such crap.'

'Then think up an assumed one.'

'How about John Ford?'

'Why the hell not? And David . . . one last thing: though you know it's shit, and I know it's shit, and even the publisher knows it's shit . . .'

'I know: be a pro.'

'That's my boy.'

Starting tomorrow, I would have exactly thirteen working days to get the job done. So, before I even started mapping out a chapter-by-chapter outline for the book (today's job), I did some simple arithmetic, dividing 75,000 by thirteen. This yielded a total of 4,230 – which, in turn, became the daily quota of words I would have to write, if I was to make the deadline on time. Given that there are around 250 words per double-spaced typed page, this meant I would have to be churning out just under seventeen pages per day. An insane amount of pages, save for the fact that the stuff I was dealing with deserved to be churned out fast, and without much in the way of deep thought.

But a job is a job – especially when you find all other work possibilities in your chosen field closed off to you. So I took the work seriously, determined to do the best I could with this low-grade material; to give the novelization the appropriate professional sheen, and to make the deadline without fail.

I devised a rigid schedule for myself and stuck to it. The two outside interruptions I'd allow myself would be my thrice-weekly phone call with Caitlin, and my daily session with Matthew Sims.

'You sound in better spirits,' Sims said about halfway through the novel.

'It's work. Trashy work, but . . .'

'You're still doing it diligently, which is admirable.'

'I need the money, and I also need to be filling the time with something constructive.'

'In other words, you're being responsible, and you're also demonstrating to yourself that you can go out and find work again.'

'This is not exactly the sort of stuff I want to be doing.'

'But it's a start. And it's reasonably well paid, isn't it? So, why not be pleased about the fact that this could be considered a positive new beginning?'

'Because writing a novelization is never a positive experience.'

Still, I kept at it. I met my quota of words every day. I stuck to my schedule. I didn't dumb down to deal with this dumb down material. I did a good job. And I made the deadline . . . even getting it to the nearest Fedex depot a full hour before the last pickup of the day.

I made three copies of the text, dispatching one each to the publisher in New York and to Alison, and keeping one for myself. Then I went out to an Italian joint in Santa Barbara (around forty minutes up the road) and treated myself to my first restaurant meal since decamping up here. But I felt I deserved a small indulgence after such a slog. And it did feel wonderful to be eating out – something I'd taken for granted over the past two years, but which now seemed like a rarefied pleasure. Afterwards, I took a long moonlit walk on the beach, delighting in the simple fact that I'd gotten a job done on time and reasonably well.

Or, as it turned out, more than reasonably well . . . as Alison called me three days later to tell me that the publisher in New York was enthusiastic about the end result.

'Do you know what Max Newton told me: "This guy has taken bad shit and turned it into quality shit." He really was very impressed . . . not just with the smoothness of the writing, but also that you made the deadline without hassle. Believe me, that makes you the rarest damn writer on the planet. But the really good news is that Max publishes one of these novelizations a month. In the past, he's assigned them as a one-off to a variety of writers – but that wasn't a particularly satisfactory arrangement. So he'd like to offer you a six-novelization contract. The same money – $25k per novelization. The same timetable – a book a month . . .'

'And I can keep using my pseudonym?'

'Yes, John Ford – no problems with that name. More to the point, this book contract alone means you can just about kill one of the debts to either FRT or Warner's.'

'You're forgetting about my alimony.'

'Yeah – Sandy talked to me about that. You must get that monthly burden reduced. It's crazy money. And Lucy can afford . . .'

'Let's not discuss this, please.'

'Your call, David.'

'But this is good news, Alison. Great news, in fact. I never thought I'd say that about a novelization, but . . .'

'It's a lot better than nothing,' Alison said.

I slept well that night. I woke the next morning, feeling curiously rested and curiously sanguine about things. If Max Newton was pleased with the first six adaptations, maybe Alison could convince him to keep me on as his resident screenplay-into-novel hack. At the current rate of pay – taking into account Alison's commission and tax – I could maintain my payments to Lucy and also manage to pay off the two debts to FRT and Warners in just over two years.

'It's great to hear you sounding so optimistic,' Matthew Sims said during our next session.'

'It's great to be off my knees.'

A week went by. The check from Max Newton arrived via Alison. I put it in the bank and immediately transferred the lot into Lucy's account, sending her an e-mail which simply said:

'Two months' maintenance payments should have reached your account today. It would be nice to talk with you sometime.'

The next night, when I was signing off on my conversation with Caitlin, I asked my daughter if I could speak with her mommy.

'Sorry Daddy, she says she's busy.'

I didn't press the matter further.

Another few days went by without sign of the new screenplay from Max Newton. So I e-mailed Alison, wondering what was going on. She e-mailed me back, saying she'd spoken with Max yesterday and all was well. In fact, he told her that his legal department would Fedex the contract to her tomorrow.

But when tomorrow arrived, there was a phone call from Alison, her voice brimming with 'bad news' tremors.

'I don't know how to tell you this . . . ,' she said.

I couldn't bring myself to yet again ask: 'What now?' So I stayed silent.

'Max cancelled the contract.'

'He *what*?'

'He cancelled the contract.'

'On what grounds?'

'Our old friend, Theo McCall . . .'

'Not again . . .'

'I'll read you the item. It's just a few lines:

'Oh, how the mighty have fallen. Selling You *creator, David Armitage – sacked by FRT for stealing other writer's lines (exposed first in this column), then publicly shamed for attacking a certain journalist (i.e., moi) in the NBC parking lot – has been reduced to the lowliest form of so-called "creative writing": better known as "novelizations". According to an inside mole at Lionel Publishing in Nueva York, the one-time Emmy winner (recently stripped of his award by the American Academy of Television Arts and Sciences) has been reduced to churning out instant book adaptations of forthcoming movies. And guess what film the one-time golden boy of television has just novelized: a grisly forthcoming New Line teen-flick,* Losing It *. . . which, rumor has it, makes* American Pie *look like late-period Bergman. Better yet is the pseudonym Armitage chose beneath which to hide: John Ford. Does he mean the great director of Westerns . . . or the Jacobean playwright, who wrote* 'Tis Pity She's A Whore *. . . though in Armitage's case, the title could be:* 'Tis Pity He's A Plagiarist.'

Long silence. I didn't feel sick or shell-shocked or devastated . . . because I'd been through those assorted phases before. Now I simply felt numb – like a boxer who'd taken one blow to the head too many, and could no longer feel anything.

Alison finally spoke, 'David, I cannot begin to tell you . . .'

'So Max Newton read this and cancelled the contract?' I said, my voice strangely calm.

'Yes, that's about it.'

'Okay,' I said flatly.

'Do understand, I am talking with a high-powered attorney I know about a possible defamation of character suit against McCall.'

'Don't bother.'

'Please don't say that, David.'

'Look, I know when I'm defeated.'

'We can easily fight this.'

'No need. But listen, before I hang up, I just want to say this: you haven't just been an agent extraordinaire . . . you've also been the best friend imaginable.'

'David, what the hell is that supposed to mean?'

'Nothing except . . .'

'You're not going to do something stupid, are you?'

'You mean, like twist my Porsche around a tree? No – I wouldn't give McCall the satisfaction. But I am giving up the fight.'

'Don't say that.'

'I am saying it.'

'I'll call you tomorrow.'

'Whatever.'

I put down the phone. I packed up my laptop and found all the ownership papers for my car, then made a call to a Porsche dealer in Santa Barbara I'd spoken with a week or so earlier. He said that he'd expect me within the hour.

I drove north. At the dealership, the salesman came out to meet me. He offered me coffee. I declined. He said he'd have a full service report and a purchase price within two hours. I asked him to call me a cab. When it arrived, I told the driver to take me to the nearest pawnbrokers. He eyed me warily in the rearview mirror, but did as I asked. When we reached the shop, I told him to wait. There was heavy-duty wiring on the window and a surveillance camera at the barred steel door. I was buzzed in and entered a tiny vestibule with scuffed linoleum, fluorescent lights, a window with bulletproof glass. This was a very nervous pawnbroker. An over-weight guy around forty appeared at the window. He was eating a sandwich while he talked to me.

'So whatcha got?' he asked.

'A top of the line Toshiba Tecra Notebook. Bought new for forty-five hundred.'

'Pass it through,' he said, lifting up the lower part of the window. He inspected it briefly, lifting it up, plugging it in, turning it on, gazing at the software application on the Windows desktop. Then he turned it off, shut it and shrugged.

'The thing about these things is this: six months after they're released on the market, they're outdated. And their retail value ain't much. Four hundred bucks.'

'A thousand.'

'Six hundred.'

'Sold.'

When I got back to the Porsche dealership, the salesman had the full report ready and an offer price of $39,280.

'I really was expecting forty-two, forty-three thousand,' I said.

'Forty is the absolute tops I could go.'

'Sold.'

I asked him for a cashier's check. Then I got him to call me another cab and had it bring me to the nearest branch of BankAmerica. I flashed a lot of ID. There was an extended phone call to my BankAmerica branch in West Hollywood. There were several forms to sign. But eventually they agreed to cash the $40,000 check and to forward the sum of $33,000 to Lucy's account in Sausalito. I left the bank with $7,000 cash and took another cab to a used-car lot not far from the Porsche dealership. This operation only dealt with lower-end vehicles. Still, for $5,000 cash, I managed to buy a 1994 Navy Blue VW Golf with 'only 98,000 miles on the clock' and a six-month service warranty. I used the dealer's phone to call my insurer. He sounded a little shocked when I told him I had switched the Porsche for a seven-year-old Golf, value $5,000.

'Well, you've still got another nine months to run on the Porsche insurance. But the Golf will only cost about a third of the price . . . which means there's about five hundred left over.'

'Send me a check, please.' And I gave him my address in Meredith.

I drove my new old car to a cyber café. I bought a coffee and logged on to my server. I sent an e-mail to Lucy:

The next three months' maintenance payments have been transferred to your account. I am now paid up for five months. I still hope that, one day, we will be able to talk again. In the meantime, I do want you to know one thing: I was very wrong to do what I did. I realize that now . . . and I am sorry.

After I sent the e-mail, I used the telephone in the café, and called American Express, Visa, and MasterCard. Each of the three companies confirmed that I had a zero balance on each of the cards (having taken Sandy's advice several weeks earlier and used the last of my checking account to clear all credit debts). Each of the three companies tried to convince me otherwise when I said that I wished to close my accounts down ('But there's no need, Mr Armitage,' the woman at American Express told me. 'We so hate to lose such a wonderful customer like you.') But I didn't budge from my position: cancel all accounts effective immediately . . . and send me the necessary forms to sign at my new address in Meredith.

Before leaving the café, I stopped by the main counter and asked if they had a pair of scissors. They did. I borrowed them, and cut all three of my Gold credit cards into quarter pieces. The guy behind the till watched me:

'Been upgraded to Platinum or something?' he asked me.

I laughed and dumped the dismembered cards in his hands. Then I headed out.

On my way back south to Meredith, I did some quick addition in my head. Seventeen hundred bucks in my bank account. Three thousand six hundred bucks cash in my pocket. A five hundred dollar check en route from the insurance guy. Five months' maintenance paid off. Five more months of free rent at Willard's cottage . . . and if I got lucky, he might decide to stay on even longer in London (but I wasn't thinking that far ahead). I had no debts. I had no bills outstanding – especially as Alison (bless her) insisted on using her commission from the novelization to cover Matthew Sims's tab (she said that she'd made so damn much from me during my two lucrative years, the least she could do was cover my shrink bill). My medical insurance was paid up for nine more months. I needed no clothes, no books, no fancy fountain pens, no compact discs, no videos, no personal trainers, no $75 haircuts, no teeth-bleaching sessions at the dentist (cost: $2,000 per annum), no $8,000 holidays in a charming little beachfront boutique hotel at the tip of Baja . . . in short, none of the costly paraphernalia that once crowded my life. My net worth was $5,800. Utilities in the cottage were no more than $30 a week, and I hardly used the phone. Between food, a couple of bottles of modest wine, a few six packs of beer, and the occasional trip to the local multiplex cinema, I could easily keep to my $200 per week budget. Which, in turn, meant that the next twenty-six weeks were paid for.

It was a curious feeling, having reduced everything down to this level. Not exactly liberating in that bullshit zen way . . . but definitely far less complex. The numbness that hit me the night Alison told me about McCall's last column continued to hold sway over me. I often felt as if I was just going through the motions, and making decisions on autopilot. Like cutting up all my credit cards. Or selling my laptop. Or walking into Books and Company on Meredith Main Street and asking for a job.

Books and Company was that rare thing: a small independent bookshop, still managing to function in a world of big monocultural chain stores. It was the sort of shop which reeked of polished wood, and had exposed timber beams and a parquet floor, and which stocked the usual mix of upmarket literary fiction, popular blockbusters, cookery books, and a nice-sized children's section. There had been a note in the window for the past weeks, informing the good citizens of Meredith that the shop needed a full time salesperson – and all interested parties should apply to the owner.

Les Pearson was a man in his late fifties: bearded, bespectacled, wearing a blue denim shirt and blue Levis. I imagined him haunting the City Lights bookshop in San Francisco during the Summer of Love, or once having been the proud owner of a pair of bongo drums. Now, however, he exuded settled middle-agedness . . . as befitted the owner of a small bookstore in a small exclusive beachfront town.

He was standing behind the counter when I entered the shop. I'd been in before, so his first question was:

'Can I find you anything?'

'In fact, I've come about the job.'

'Oh, really?' he said, now looking me over with care. 'You ever work in a bookshop before?'

'Do you know Book Soup in Los Angeles?'

'Who doesn't?'

'Well, I was there for thirteen years.'

'But you live here now. Because I've seen you around.'

'Yeah, I'm staying at Willard Stevens's place.'

'Oh right – heard that someone was down at his cottage. How do you know Willard?'

'We used to share the same agent.'

'You're a writer?'

'Used to be.'

'Well, I'm Les . . .'

'And I'm David Armitage . . .'

'How do I know that name?'

I shrugged.

'And you're really interested in the job here?'

'I like bookshops. I know my stuff.'

'It's a forty-hour week: Wednesday-through-Sunday, eleven-to-seven, with an hour off for lunch. And being a small independent bookshop, I can't really afford to pay more than $7 an hour – around $280 a week. There are no medical benefits, I'm afraid, or any perks like that . . . except bottomless free coffee and 50 per cent off anything you want to buy. Does $280 a week sound okay to you?'

'Yeah. No problem.'

'And if I wanted a couple of references . . . ?'

I took a notepad and pen out of my jacket pocket, and wrote the name of Andy Barron, the Book Soup manager (who I knew would be discreet enough not to blab to the world that I was trying to find work in a bookstore). I also gave him Alison's number.

'Andy used to employ me, Alison used to represent me,' I said. 'And if you want to get in touch with me . . .'

'I've got Willard's number in my address book.' He proffered his hand. 'I'll be in touch, okay?'

Later that afternoon, the phone rang at the cottage.

'What the hell are you doing, getting a job in a fucking bookshop?' Alison asked me.

'Hello, Alison. And how's life in Los Angeles?'

'Smoggy. Please answer the question. Because this Les Pearson guy rang me, saying he was considering you for a job in his shop.'

'Did you give me a good reference?'

'What do you think? But why the hell are you doing this?'

239

'I need to work, Alison.'

'And why the hell haven't you answered any of my e-mails of the past couple of days?'

'Because I got rid of my computer.'

'Oh, for Christ's sakes, David, *why*?'

'Because I'm not in the writing game anymore, that's why.'

'Don't say that.'

'It's true.'

'Look, I'm sure that, with a little looking around, we could find you . . .'

'What? A rewrite job on a Serbian soap opera? A quick polish on a Mexican vampire film? Face it, if I can't keep a novelization gig – because the publisher is too ashamed to be associated with me . . . even when I'm working under a pseudonym – then who the hell is going to hire me? The answer is: no one.'

'Not immediately, perhaps. But . . .'

'When? Remember that *Washington Post* reporter who had the Pulitzer stripped from her after it turned out she made up an entire story? You know what she's doing, ten years after her little transgression? Selling cosmetics in some department store. That's what happens when you're exposed as a literary cheat: you end up in retail.'

'But compared to that journalist, you didn't do anything that serious.'

'Theo McCall managed to convince the world otherwise . . . and now my writing career is over.'

'David, I don't like the fact that you sound so damn calm.'

'But I am calm. And very content.'

'You're not on Prozac, are you?'

'Not even St John's Wort.'

'Look, why don't I come visit you . . . ?'

'Give it a few weeks, please. To quote Ms Garbo: I *vant* to be alone right now.'

'You sure you're all right?'

'Never been better.'

'I don't like the sound of that,' she said.

Around an hour later, the phone rang again. This time it was Les Pearson.

'Well, you certainly got a glowing reference from Andy Barron and from your agent. When do you want to start?'

'Tomorrow's fine by me.'

'See you at ten then. Oh . . . one small thing: I really was sorry to learn about all the stuff you've been through.'

'Thanks.'

So, as agreed, I started work the next day. It was a straightforward job – between Wednesday and Sunday, I single-handedly ran the show at the bookshop. I was the guy behind the counter, helping customers. I was the guy in the back office, dealing with orders and inventory. I was the guy who swept the place, and ran a duster across the shelves, and cleaned the toilet, and counted the cash, and made a deposit every night in the local bank, and even had time every day to spend an hour or two behind the cash register, reading.

It was easy stuff – especially during the weekdays, when only the occasional local wandered in. The weekends were a bit busier – especially with all the Angelinos who flocked to town. But the work wasn't exactly taxing. I never knew if any of the Meredith regulars had found out who I was. I never enquired. Nor, to their credit, did anyone ever make a comment or shoot me a knowing look. In Meredith, there was an unspoken rule that you maintained a polite distance from everyone else. Which suited me just fine. And when the Angelinos came to town on Friday night, I never saw anyone from 'the industry' . . . because, with the absentee exception of Willard Stevens, Meredith attracted a weekend crowd of lawyers, doctors, dentists. To them, I was just the guy in the bookshop . . . and one who, in a matter of weeks, began to change in appearance.

To begin with, I dropped around fifteen pounds, bringing me down to a super-thin weight of 162 lbs. Stress initially had something to do with this. So too did reducing all alcohol intake to a beer or a glass of wine a day. And my diet was simple and low in crap. I also started jogging on the beach every day. At the same time, I decided to dispense with my morning shave. My hair also started to grow in. By the end of my second month in the bookshop, I looked like some emaciated holdover from the sixties. But neither Les nor anyone in Meredith commented on this new Haight-Ashbury look. I did my job. I did it well. I was diligent and straightforward and always polite. And things ticked over nicely.

Les, in turn, was an easy employer. He only worked Mondays and Tuesdays (the two days I had off). Otherwise, he spent his time sailing and playing the stock market on the Internet, hinting (in our occasional conversations) that a bit of family money came his way around ten years earlier, allowing him to open this book-shop (an old dream of his, during the many years that he was an ad man in Seattle) and to maintain a pleasant lifestyle on this corner of the Pacific Coast Highway. He once said that he was divorced, and that his two children were grown and living in the Bay Area. And when I mentioned on the day I started work that I needed to call my daughter every other night at seven, Les insisted that I use the bookshop phone. When I offered to pay for this regular fifteen minute call, he wouldn't hear of it.

'Call it a perk of the job,' he said.

Lucy still wouldn't speak with me. After two months, I finally called Walter Dickerson and asked if there was any way he could try to negotiate some sort of proper face-to-face access with Caitlin.

'If Lucy wants it supervised, I'm agreeable to that,' I said. 'I'm just desperate to see my daughter.'

But after a few days, Dickerson called me back.

'It's a no-change situation, David. According to her legal guy, your ex-wife is still 'uncertain' about the idea of physical access. The good news, however, is that (according to the lawyer) Caitlin is really pushing her mother on this issue – demanding to know why she can't see her Daddy. And the other good news is that, after some to-ing and fro-ing, I have managed to increase your phone access to one phone call a day.'

'That is good news.'

'Give it a little more time, David. Be on your best behavior. Sooner or later, Lucy will have to give way on this one.'

'Thanks for getting me the extra phone calls. You know where to send the bill?'

'Let's call this one on the house.'

By my third month at Books and Company, life had settled into a pleasant, compartmentalized routine. I jogged. I went to work. I closed up the shop at seven. I had my daily phone call with Caitlin. I went home. I read or watched a movie. On my days off, I often drove up the coast. Or I'd spend the evening at the local multiplex and maybe eat in a modest Mexican joint in Santa Barbara. I tried not to think what would happen eight weeks from now when I had to pay another $11,000 in alimony. I tried not to think about how I would deal with the FRT and Warner Brothers' paybacks – both of which were pending. And I also tried not to think about what would happen to me when Willard Stevens returned from London . . . which, according to Alison, would happen in three months' time.

For the moment, I decided to deal with things on a day-to-day basis. Because I knew that if I started really pondering the future, I'd slip into hyper-anxiety again.

Alison continued to call me weekly. She had no news to report, no pending prospects for work, no flurry of royalty payments or new syndication rights . . . because, of course, I lost all that when I lost my contract with FRT. But she still phoned me every Saturday morning, just to see how I was dealing with the world. I would tell her I was fine.

'You know, I'd really be much happier if you would tell me that things are genuinely shitty,' she said.

'But they're not shitty.'

'And I think you're having a world-class case of denial,' she said, 'which, one day, will come crashing down on top of you like King Kong.'

'So far, so good,' I said.

'And another thing, David – one of these days you might just surprise the shit out of me by dropping a dime and giving me a call.'

Two weeks later, I did just that. It was ten in the morning. I had just opened the shop. There were no customers, so after making myself a coffee and sorting through the mail, I decided to give the *LA Times* a quick glance (I had finally started to read newspapers again). And there, in a sidebar within the Arts and Entertainment section, was the following item:

Reclusive multi-billionaire Philip Fleck has decided to return to the director's chair, a full five years after his first, self-financed feature film – the $40 million dollar turkey, *The Last Chance* – was laughed off the few screens upon which it was released. Now Fleck announces that he's going relatively mainstream with a quirky new action-comedy, *We Three Grunts*. The plot concerns a pair of ageing Chicago Vietnam vets who, having hit bad times, develop a lucrative sideline by robbing banks. Once again, Fleck will be self-financing the film – which he also wrote himself – and which he says contains much of the same skewed humor which so characterized the great Robert Altman films of the 1970s. Fleck also promises some real surprises in the casting – to be announced shortly. Let's hope that Fleck – whose current net worth hovers around the $20 billion mark – won't try to turn this alleged comedy into some arty Swedish essay on angst. Existential angst never plays well against the Chicago skyline.

I put the paper down. I picked it up again, brimming with disbelief. My eyes singled out one specific sentence: *Once again, Fleck will be self-financing the film – which he also wrote himself.*

The bastard. The slimy talentless bastard. Not only had he stolen my script again. This time, he had the audacity to keep the original title.

I picked up the phone. I dialled Los Angeles.

'Alison?' I said.

'I was about to call you.'

'You saw it?'

'Yeah,' she said. 'I saw it.'

'He can't be serious.'

'He's worth $20 billion. He can be as serious as he fucking likes.'

Four

'DON'T WORRY ABOUT this,' Alison said.

'How can I *not* worry about this?' I said. 'He's stolen my script. I mean, it's the greatest dumb irony on earth. I lose everything because of a couple of misappropriated lines . . . and Mr Billionaire then puts his name to an entire 108-page script that *I* wrote.'

'He won't get away with it.'

'Damn right he won't,' I said.

'And I'll tell you why. Because you registered it with SATWA when you wrote it back in the mid-nineties. One quick call to them will confirm you are the legal author of *We Three Grunts*. Then another quick call to my lawyer will send an Exocet of a writ in the direction of Mr Fleck. Remember how he offered you $2.5 million for the script all those months ago? That's the price he's going to pay now . . . if he doesn't want his theft plastered over every front page from here to Tierra del Fuego.'

'I want you to stick it to this asshole. I mean, his pockets are virtually bottomless, so $2.5 million will be like a pack of Juicy Fruit to this guy. More to the point is the moral bankruptcy involved in trying to fuck me over when I'm down and out.'

Alison let out one of her tobacco-cured laughs.

'Nice to hear you in such good form,' she said.

'What the hell are you talking about?'

'The last couple of months, you went all zen and centred on me. I put it down to you reliving the Book of Job and finally succumbing to shock. But it's good to hear you back in tough guy mode.'

'Well, what do you expect? This is so beyond everything I've been subjected to . . .'

'Fear not,' Alison said. 'The shit will pay.'

She didn't call me the next day. She didn't call me the day after. I rang her on the third day, but her assistant said that she was out, but would definitely be getting back to me tomorrow. But the call never came. Then it was the weekend. I must have left her three messages on her home phone, but she failed to return my calls.

245

Monday came and went. Finally, on Tuesday morning, she rang me at the cottage.

'What are you doing today?' she asked me.

'Thanks for returning my calls.'

'I've been busy.'

'Do you have news?'

'Yes,' she said, sounding constrained. 'But it would be better if we could discuss it face to face.'

'Can't you tell me . . . ?'

'You free for lunch?'

'Sure.'

'Okay, I'll see you around one pm at the office.'

I showered, dressed, and climbed into the VW and headed south. I made the city in less than two hours. I hadn't been in Los Angeles in nearly four months – and cruising down Wiltshire, heading towards Alison's office, it struck me how much I missed the dump. Though the rest of the world derides the place for its alleged shallowness and its visual deformities ('New Jersey with better clothes,' as one of my wiseass Manhattan friends called it), I've always loved its hallucinatory sprawl; its intermingling of the industrial and the opulent; its aching gimcrack glamour; the sense that you were in a Paradise Trashed . . . yet still brimming with possibility.

Alison's assistant, Suzy, didn't recognize me at first.

'Can I help you?' she asked, squinting suspiciously at me when I came through the door. Then the penny dropped. 'Oh my God, David . . . uh, hello.'

Alison then came out from her inner office, and did a double-take when she saw me. My beard was now well below my chin, and I had my hair tied in a ponytail. She gave me a fast peck on the cheek, then sized me up once more and said, 'If I ever hear of a Charles Manson lookalike competition, I'm signing you up. You'll be a shoo-in.'

'And it's very nice to see you too, Alison,' I said.

'What sort of diet have you been on? Macro-neurotic?'

I ignored the comment and stared at the bulging file under her arm.

'What've you got there?'

'Evidence.'

'Of what?'

'Come on inside.'

I did as ordered, sitting down in the seat opposite her desk.

'We could go out to somewhere fancy,' she said. 'But . . .'

'You'd rather talk here?'

'Absolutely.'

'It's that bad?'

'It's that bad. So shall we order in?'

I nodded and Alison picked up the phone and asked Suzy to call Barney Greengrass, and get them to send over a platter of their best Nova, with the usual bagel and *schmeer* accompaniments.

'And a couple of celery sodas, just so we can pretend we're in New York,' Alison said.

She put down the phone. 'I take it you're not drinking?'

'Is it that obvious?'

'You're radiating anorexic good health.'

'Do I need a drink for what you're about to tell me?'

'Possibly.'

'I'll pass.'

'I am impressed.'

'Enough of the build-up, Alison. Tell me.'

She opened the file. 'I want you to think back to when you originally finished *We Three Grunts*. According to my files, it was sometime during the autumn of '97.'

'November, '97, to be exact.'

'And you're certain you registered it with SATWA?'

'Of course. I've always registered all my scripts with The Association.'

'And they always gave you a standard form letter saying it's been registered, right?'

'Uh huh.'

'Do you have the letter for *We Three Grunts*?'

'I doubt it.'

'Are you absolutely sure?'

'Well, I've always been pretty ruthless with my papers, throwing out non-essential stuff.'

'Isn't a SATWA letter of registration important?'

'Not when I know that, having registered the script with them, it *is* registered. What the hell are you getting at, Alison?'

'The Screen and Television Writers' Association does have a script entitled *We Three Grunts* listed in their books. But they only registered it last month, under the name of its author, one Philip Fleck.'

'But, hang on, they surely have a record of my script registration in November '97?'

'No, they do not.'

'But that can't be. I *did* register it.'

'Hey, I believe you. Not only that, I managed to dig out the original 1997 draft of the screenplay.'

She reached into the file and pulled out a battered, slightly yellowing copy of the script. The title page read:

WE THREE GRUNTS
A Screenplay
by
David Armitage
(First Draft: November 1997)

'There's the proof you need,' I said, pointing to the date on the title page.

'But David, who's to say that you didn't concoct this title page yourself recently? Who's to say you didn't decide to steal Philip Fleck's script and put your own name on the title page . . .'

'What are you accusing me of, Alison?'

'You're not listening to what I'm saying here. I *know* you wrote this movie. I know you're not a plagiarist. And I also know that you're not any more deranged than any other writer I represent. But I also know that SATWA have no record of your authorship of *We Three Grunts* . . .'

'How do you know that?'

'Because when the Guild told me last week that the script was only registered under the name of Philip Fleck, I contacted my lawyer who, in turn, put me in touch with a private investigator . . .'

'You hired a PI?' I asked, sounding shocked.

'Hell yes. I mean, we're talking about a serious theft here, and one which could be worth $2.5 million. So of course I got me a gumshoe. You should have seen this guy. Thirty-five years old, worst case of acne I've ever laid eyes on, and his suit looked like he'd stolen it off the back of some Mormon missionary. Believe me, he was no Sam Spade. But despite the looks, the guy was as thorough as a tax inspector. And what he turned up with . . .'

She dug deeper into the file, first bringing out the recent official SATWA registration of *We Three Grunts*, clearly under the name of Philip Fleck. Then she brought out the official SATWA registration of all my scripts. Every *Selling You* episode was listed. So too was *Breaking and Entering*. But none of my unproduced screenplays from the nineties was cited.

'Name one of those screenplays,' Alison said.

'*At Sea,*' I said, mentioning the generic ('but darkly comic') action script, in which Islamic terrorists seized the yacht containing the US president's three children.

Alison flipped a piece of paper in front of me.

'Registered under the name of Philip Fleck last month. Name another of your unproduced screenplays.'

'*A Time of Gifts,*' I said, mentioning the woman-dying-of-cancer film I wrote in '96.

'Registered under the name of Philip Fleck last month,' she said, handing me another official SATWA letter. 'And let's go for the hat trick. Name a third unproduced screenplay of yours . . .'

'*The Right Place, The Wrong Time.*'

'That was the honeymoon mix-up thing, right? Registered under the name of Philip Fleck last month.'

I stared down at the new document which Alison handed me.

'He's stolen every script of mine that's been unproduced?'

'That's the situation.'

'And there's no record of the scripts being registered under my name?'

'None whatsoever.'

'How the hell did Fleck engineer this?'

'Ah,' Alison said, digging even deeper into the file. 'Here's his real masterstroke.'

She handed me a Xerox copy of a small *Hollywood Reporter* article, dated four months ago:

FLECK FOUNDATION MAKES $8 MILLION DONATION TO SATWA BENEVOLENT FUND

The Philip Fleck Foundation today announced that it would be making an $8 million donation to the Screen and Television Writers' Association Benevolent Fund. Fleck Foundation spokesperson, Cybill Harrison, said that the gift was in recognition of the Association's sterling work in promoting and protecting the work of screenwriters, while also hopefully assisting those writers facing financial crises or serious illness. SATWA's executive director, James LeRoy, noted: 'This magnificent gift points up a simple fact: when it comes to supporting the arts in America, Philip Fleck is the closest thing the country has to a Medici. Every writer should have a friend like Philip Fleck.'

'Great last line, isn't it?' Alison said.

'I don't believe this. He bought the Association.'

'Effectively, yes. More to the point, he bought the ability to have the Association lose the registrations of your unproduced screenplays, and to register them in his own name.'

'But, Jesus, with the exception of *We Three Grunts*, none of the others is particularly distinguished.'

'But they're still pretty smart and clever, right?'

'Of course they're smart and clever. *I* wrote them.'

'There you go. Fleck now has four solid professional scripts to his name – one of which is so good that, according to this morning's *Daily Variety*, he's managed to get Peter Fonda and Dennis Hopper to play the two Vietnam vets, with Jack Nicholson in a cameo as . . .'

'Richardson, their lawyer?'

'You got it.'

'That's fantastic casting,' I said, suddenly excited. 'And the entire *Easy Rider* generation will definitely turn out to see it.'

'Without question. And Columbia has agreed to distribute the thing.'

'This really is a *go* then?'

'Hey, it's Fleck's money, so it's also his green light. The problem is, your name isn't going to be on the credits . . .'

'Surely there's a legal avenue we can take . . .'

'I've been round and round this thing with my lawyer. He says that Fleck has pulled off the perfect sting. Your old registrations have been expunged. Fleck has now become the official author of all your old work. And were we to go public – especially on the issue of *We Three Grunts* – Fleck's people would play the "He's a deranged plagiarist" card. They'd also let it be known that, when you were still "a legitimate writer", Fleck had you out to his island, to talk about writing a movie for him. But he got whiff of the fact that you were trouble and turned you down. So, naturally, you got up to your old psychotic tricks and convinced yourself that you were the real author of *We Three Grunts* . . . even though there's no record to show you as the actual writer, whereas there is official SATWA accreditation of Fleck's authorship.'

'Jesus Christ.'

'It's amazing what money can buy you.'

'But . . . hang on . . . couldn't we get Fleck on registering all four screenplays in the last month?'

'Who's to say that he didn't get around to submitting them to the Association until now? He could argue, for example, that he'd been writing these scripts privately for the last couple of years. The fact that he was going into production with *We Three Grunts* meant that he probably decided it was time to officially register every-thing with SATWA.'

'But how about the studio executive and development people who read my script . . . ?

'You mean, *five years ago*? Oh come on, David. Rule number one of development is: *you always forget the script you've just passed on, three minutes after you've passed on it.* More to the point, even if some damn D-gal or guy does remember reading your script, do you actually think they're going to take your side against the mighty Mr Fleck? Especially given your current position in this town. Trust me, the lawyer, the PI and I have tried to run all sorts of scenarios on how to fight this. We can't find any. Fleck has closed every damn loophole imaginable. Even the lawyer had to admire the elegance of the scam he's pulled. In pool parlance, you're *snookered.*'

I stared down at the pile of papers covering Alison's desk. I was still trying to fathom the hall of mirrors in which I currently found myself, and the realization that there was no way out of this situation – that my work was now Fleck's work. Nothing I could do or say would change that.

'There's something else you need to know,' Alison said. 'When I told the PI about the way that Theo McCall undid your career, he was immediately interested, and went off and did a little additional research.'

Again, she dug into the file and pulled out another couple of Xeroxes. Then she handed them to me and said: 'Get a load of these.'

I looked down and saw that I was holding a statement from Bank of California for the Money Management Account of one Theodore McCall of 1158 King's Road, West Hollywood, Ca.

'How the hell did he get these?'

'I didn't ask. Because I didn't want to know. But put it this way: where there's a will, there's a relative. Anyway, check out the credit column for the 14th of every month. As you'll notice, there's a deposit for $10,000 from a company called Lubitsch Holdings. Now my PI ran a check on this outfit, and it turns out it's some shell company registered in the Cayman Islands, traceable to no one. What's more, he found out that McCall makes a shitty thirty-four grand a year at *Hollywood Legit,* but also manages to pull in another $50k as the Hollywood stringer for some British rag. He's got no family money, no trust fund, no nothing. But for the last six months, he's been on this ten-grand-a-month retainer from a mysterious company named Lubitsch.'

Pause.

'When did you visit Fleck's island?' she asked me.

'Seven months ago.'

'Didn't you tell me he's something of a film buff?'

'The ultimate film collector.'

252

'Who is the only person you know named Lubitsch?'

'Ernst Lubitsch – the great film comedy director of the thirties.'

'And only a real film buff would find it amusing to name a Cayman Island holding company after a legendary Hollywood director.'

Long silence. I said, 'Fleck paid McCall to find something with which to destroy me?'

Alison shrugged. 'We don't have hard-and-fast evidence, because Fleck has covered his tracks so damn well. But the PI and I both agree: that seems to be the story.'

I sat back in the chair, thinking, thinking, thinking. The pieces of this skewed jigsaw were suddenly assembling in my head. For the past six months, I had believed that the entire appalling scenario I'd been living could be put down to the random workings of fate; the domino theory of disaster, in which one calamity triggered the next calamity which, in turn . . .

But now the realization hit: it had all been completely orchestrated, completely manipulated, *completely instigated.* To Fleck I was nothing more than a cheap-assed marionette, to be toyed with at will. He'd decided to ruin me. Like some spurious supreme being, he felt he could pull all the strings.

'Do you know what baffles me about this whole thing?' Alison said. 'It's the fact that he needed to flatten you. Like if he just wanted to buy the script with his name only on it . . . hell, I'm sure we could have come to an accommodation. Especially if the price was right. But instead, he went for your jugular, your aorta and every other major artery. Did you really make him hate you or something?'

I shrugged, thinking: *no, but his wife and I got awfully friendly.* And yet, what the hell really happened between Martha and myself? A boozy embrace, nothing more . . . and one which took place far out of view of the staff. I mean, unless there were nighttime surveillance cameras hidden in the palms . . .

Stop! That's a completely paranoid fantasy. Anyway, Fleck and Martha were virtually separated, weren't they? So why would he even care if we got a little too affectionate down by the beach.

But he obviously *did* care – because why else do this to me?

Unless . . . *unless . . .*

Remember the movie he insisted on showing you? *Salo: The 120 Days of Sodom.* Remember how you kept wondering, long afterwards, why he subjected you to this gruesome little experience. Remember as well his defence of the film:

'. . . *what Pasolini was showing was fascism in its purest pre-technological form: the belief that you have the right, the privilege to exert complete control over another being to the point of completely denying them their dignity and essential human rights; to strip them of all individuality and treat them like functional objects, to be discarded when they have out-served their capability . . .'*

Was that the point of this entire malevolent exercise? Did he want to act out his belief that he had '*the right, the privilege to exert complete control over another being*'? Did Martha factor into this equation as well – convincing him that her passing affection for me made me the obvious target for his manipulations? Or was it envy – a need to destroy someone else's career in order to assuage his own evident lack of talent? He had such deranged amounts of money, such deranged amounts of *totality*. Surely, boredom must set in after a while. The boredom of one Rothko too many; of always drinking Cristal, and always knowing that the Gulfstream or the 767 was awaiting your next move. Did he feel it was time to see if he could transcend all those billions by doing something truly original, audacious, existentially pure? By assuming a role that only a man who had more than *everything* could assume. The ultimate creative act: Playing God.

I didn't know the answer to this question. I didn't care. His motivation was his motivation. All I did know was: Fleck was behind all this. He strategized my downfall like a general laying siege to a castle: attack the basic foundation, then watch the entire edifice crumble. His hand controlled all . . . and, in turn, me.

Alison spoke, snapping me out of my reverie.

'David, are you all right?'

'Just thinking.'

'I know this is a lot to take in. It is pretty damn shocking.'

'Can I ask a favor?'

'Anything.'

'Could you get Suzy to make Xeroxes of all the documents the PI dug up?'

'What are you planning to do?'

'I just need the documents . . . and that original copy of my script.'

'This is making me nervous.'

'You have to trust me.'

'Give me a clue . . .'

'No.'

'David, if you fuck this up . . .'

'Then I'll be even more fucked than I am now. Which simply means: I have nothing to lose.'

She reached for the phone and buzzed Suzy.

'Honey, I want you to copy everything in this file, please.'

Half an hour later, I collected the file and the script. I also made a fast smoked salmon and *schmeer* sandwich, and shoved it in my jacket pocket. Then I gave Alison a peck on the cheek and thanked her for everything.

'Please don't do anything stupid,' she said.

'If I do, you'll be the first to know.'

I left the office. I got into my car, putting the bulging file on the seat next to me. Then I slapped the pockets of my jacket to make certain that I had my address book. I drove into West Hollywood, stopped by a bookshop, found the volume I was looking for, and continued on to a cyber café I knew from driving down Doheny too many times. I parked out front. I went inside. I sat down at a terminal and went online. I opened my address book and typed out Martha Fleck's e-mail address. In the space marked *From*, I typed the bookstore's address, but deliberately failed to include my own name. Then I copied out the following lines from the book I'd just bought:

> My life closed twice before its close —
> It yet remains to see
> If Immortality unveil
> A third event to me.

So huge, so hopeless to conceive
As these that twice befell.
Parting is all we know of heaven
And all we need of hell.

. . . and, by the way, it would be wonderful to hear from you.
Your friend,
Emily D.

I hit the send button, hoping that it was her own private e-mail address. If it wasn't – if Fleck was watching her every move – then I was banking on the possibility that he might consider this an innocent missive from a bookshop . . . or, at the very worst, that she'd get in touch with me before he intercepted it.

I lingered for a little while in West Hollywood, drinking a latte at an outdoor café, cruising by the apartment house where Sally and I lived, thinking how quickly I had stopped longing for her . . . if, that is, I had ever longed for her at all. Since our split, she'd never once made contact. No doubt she had put a message on our voice mail, stating: 'David Armitage doesn't live here anymore.' But passing by our building, once again that fresh scab was torn away. Once again, I silently repeated that oft-heard rumination of many a middle-aged man: *what was I thinking?*

And once again, I had no answers.

I accelerated out of West Hollywood, out of the city limits, and back up the coast. I reached Meredith by six. Les was behind the till. He seemed surprised to see me.

'Don't you like days off?' he asked me.

'I'm just expecting an e-mail. You didn't notice if . . . ?'

'Haven't checked the damn thing all day. Go on ahead.'

So I went into the little office, and powered up the Apple Mac, and held my breath, and . . .

There it was.

An Epistle for Emily D . . . .

I opened it. The message read:

To wait an hour — is long —
If Love be just beyond
To wait Eternity — is short —
If Love reward the end —

. . . and I think you know the poet. Just as I think you also know that this correspondent would be delighted to make your acquaintance again. But what's with the bookshop address? I'm most intrigued. Call me on my cellphone: (917) 555.3739. Only I answer it, which makes it the best channel of communication, if you catch my drift.

Call soon.

Bestest,

The Belle of Amherst.

I shouted out to Les: 'Mind if I use the phone?'

'Work away,' he said.

I shut the door and dialled the cellphone number. Martha answered. And curiously, my pulse jumped a beat or two at the sound of her voice.

'Hi there,' I said.

'David?'

'Where are you?'

'At Books and Company in Meredith. You know Meredith?'

'Up along the Pacific Coast Highway?'

'The very place.'

'You've bought a bookshop?'

'It's a long story.'

'I can imagine. Listen, I should have called you a couple of months ago, when all that crap was breaking around you. But let me say this now: what you did . . . what you were accused of . . . was such small beer. As I told Philip myself: if I had a dime for every script I'd read with a line borrowed from somewhere else . . .'

'. . . you'd be as rich as he is?'

'Nobody's that rich — bar five other people on the planet. Anyway, all I wanted to say was: I am so sorry for what you went through . . . especially all the vilification from that shit, McCall. But, at least, Philip was able to give you a nice cushion with the price he paid for the script.'

'Right,' I said tonelessly.

'By the way, I love the script. It's so smart, so *street*, and so truly subversive. But when we meet, I want to try to talk you out of giving Philip sole writing credit . . .'

'Well, you know how it is . . . ,' I said.

'I know. Philip explained your fear about the bad publicity that the film would attract if your name was attached to it. But I do want to convince him to leak the fact that you were the original author after the film's release . . .'

'Only as long as the reviews are terrific.'

'They will be – because, this time, Philip's starting from a fantastically strong script. And you heard about Fonda and Hopper and Nicholson.'

'It's my dream cast.'

'And it is so nice to hear from you, Mr Armitage. Especially as I wondered afterwards . . .'

'We did nothing particularly illegal.'

'Sadly,' she said. 'How's your lady friend?'

'I have no idea. It was one of the many big things that went south when . . .'

'I'm sorry. And your daughter?'

'Great,' I said, 'except that, since my photographed run-in with McCall, her mother has had me legally barred from seeing her . . . on the grounds that I am an unstable misfit.'

'Oh Jesus, David, that is horrible.'

'That it is.'

'Well, it sounds like you need a good lunch.'

'That would be nice. Anytime you're ever in the Meredith area . . .'

'Well, I'm at our place in Malibu for a week or so.'

'Where's Philip?'

'Scouting locations in Chicago. The first day of principal photography is just eight weeks away.'

'Everything okay with you guys?' I asked, trying to maintain the same casual, nonchalant tone.

'For a little while, there was a pleasant interlude. But that ended rather recently. And now . . . same as it ever was, I guess.'

'Sorry.'

'*Comme d'habitude . . .*'

'. . . as they say in Chicago.'

She laughed. 'Listen, if you happened to be free for lunch tomorrow . . . ?'

And we agreed to meet at the bookshop at one.

As soon as I got off the phone, I came out of the office and asked Les if I could find someone to cover for me for a couple of hours tomorrow afternoon.

'Hell, it's a Wednesday, and the town's dead. Take the afternoon off.'

'Thank you,' I said.

It took three Tylenol PM to knock me out that night. Before I finally succumbed to sleep, I kept hearing her say: '*I want to try to talk you out of giving Philip sole writing credit . . . Philip explained your fear about the bad publicity that the film would attract if your name was attached to it.*'

I now understood the ruthless logic Fleck applied to making his billions. When it came to war, he was a true artist. It was his one great talent.

She showed up promptly at one. And I have to say that she looked radiant. She was dressed simply in black jeans and a black tee shirt and a blue denim jacket. Yet despite the Lou Reed clothes, there was something so resolutely East Coast patrician about her. Maybe it was her long brown hair tied up in a bun – and the long slender neck and high cheekbones – that put me in mind of one of those John Singer Sargent portraits of a Boston society woman, circa 1870. Or maybe it was the traditional horn-rimmed glasses she insisted on wearing. They were an ironic counterpoint to the biker chick clothes, not to mention all the money she now represented. Especially as they were the sort of frames which probably cost less than fifty bucks, and which currently had a small piece of Scotch tape holding their left side together. I understood what that wad of Scotch tape exemplified: an insistence on her own personal autonomy, and a wily intelligence which, all these months later, I still found so deeply attractive.

As she entered the shop, she looked right through me – as if I was the Dead Head clerk whom the owner employed.

'Hi there,' she said. 'Is David Arm . . .'

Then, in mid-sentence, the penny dropped.

'David?' she said, sounding genuinely shocked.

'Hello, Martha.'

I was about to kiss her on the cheek, but I thought better of it and simply proffered my hand. She took it, staring at me with a mixture of bemusement and amusement.

'That's really you behind all that . . . ?'

'The beard has gotten a big shaggy.'

'Ditto the hair. I mean, I've heard of the "going back to nature" look. But "going back to the bookshop"?'

I laughed. 'Well, you look wonderful.'

'I'm not saying you look bad, David. Just . . . I don't know . . . you haven't simply changed; you've *transformed*. Like one of those kids' toys . . .'

'Where, with a few fast adjustments, GI Joe turns into a dinosaur?'

'Exactly.'

'That's the new *me*,' I said. 'A dinosaur.'

Now it was her turn to laugh. 'And one with a bookshop to boot,' she said, glancing around the stacks and the assorted displays, running one hand along the polished wood shelves. 'I'm impressed. It's charming. And bookish.'

'Well, the fact that it's not in a strip mall and doesn't have a Starbucks makes it something of a nineteenth-century curiosity these days.'

'How on earth did you find it?'

'That's a bit of a story.'

'Well, I'm going to expect you to tell me all over lunch.'

'Don't worry. I will.'

'I was surprised when you e-mailed me. I thought . . .'

'What?'

'Oh, I don't know . . . that you'd written me off as a fool after that night . . .'

'It was the best sort of foolishness . . .'

260

'You mean that?'

'Sure.'

'Good. Because . . .' A nervous shrug. '. . . because I felt pretty damn foolish afterwards.'

'Join the club,' I said.

'So,' she said, changing the subject quickly, 'where am I taking you for lunch?'

'I thought we'd go down to the cottage I'm staying in . . .'

'You're renting a place up here?'

'It actually belongs to one of my agent's clients. Willard Stevens.'

'The screenwriter?'

'That's right.'

She looked at me quizzically, trying to piece this little fragment together. 'So when you found this town and this bookshop, you also found a place to live that just happened to belong to Willard Stevens . . . who also just happens to be represented by your agent?'

'That's right. Well, shall we . . . ?'

I spent a few minutes closing the bookshop down, explaining to Martha that, in honor of her appearance in Meredith, I'd decided to take the afternoon off.

'I'm touched,' she said, 'but I don't want you to lose any business on my behalf.'

'Don't worry about it. Wednesday's a slow day. Anyway, Les wasn't bothered about me . . .'

'Who's Les?' she asked, interrupting.

'Les is the owner of the bookshop.'

Now she really looked confused. 'But I thought you said you were the owner?'

'I never said that. I just said . . .'

'I know. "That's a bit of a story."'

Martha's car was parked outside: a big black shiny Range Rover. 'Shall we take my monster?' she asked.

'We'll jump into mine,' I said, motioning towards my geriatric VW Golf. Once again, she did a little double-take at the *life-in-the-slow-lane* style of the vehicle, but said nothing.

We climbed inside. As always, the starter motor was acting faulty (one of the many little bugs I had discovered since buying the heap). But it finally fired on the fourth try.

'Quite a car,' she said as we pulled away from the kerb.

'It gets me from A to B,' I said.

'And I suppose it all goes with the ageing undergraduate look you're trying to foster.'

I said nothing. I simply shrugged.

We reached the cottage in five minutes. She was smitten with the ocean view. She was smitten with the cottage's designer simplicity; its white-on-white color scheme; its overstuffed armchairs and bookshelves.

'I can see why you're happy here,' she said. 'It's the ultimate writer's hideaway. Where do you work, by the way?'

'At the bookshop.'

'Very funny. I'm talking about the "real work".'

'You mean, "writing"?'

'David, don't tell me that ponytail of yours has dragged down your cognitive powers. You do happen to be a writer . . .'

'No. I *was* a writer.'

'Don't refer to your career in the past tense.'

'Why not? It's the truth.'

'But the thing is: Philip is about to film your script . . . with an amazing cast and guaranteed world-wide distribution by Columbia. Like I said on the phone yesterday . . . as soon as word gets around that it was your screenplay, you'll be flooded with offers. Because Hollywood loves nothing more than a great come-back. Before you can say "seven figures", you'll be slaving over a laptop.'

'No, I won't.'

'How can you know that?'

'I sold my laptop.'

'You did what?'

'I sold my computer. Hocked it actually – at a pawn shop in Santa Barbara.'

'David: this is a joke, right?'

'No, it's the truth. I knew I'd never be writing again for a living. And I also needed the extra bucks . . .'

'All right, *all right . . .*' she said, her voice suddenly agitated. 'What are you playing at, David?'

'I'm playing at nothing.'

'Then why all the stuff about working in a bookshop?'

'Because I do work in a bookshop – for $280 a week.'

'There you go again, talking crap. $280 a week? David, Philip paid you $2.5 million for the script.'

'No, he didn't.'

'He told me . . .'

'He lied.'

'I don't believe you . . .'

I walked over to the desk. I picked up the file containing all the xeroxed documents that Alison's PI assembled, as well as the original 1997 first draft copy of *We Three Grunts*. I handed her the lot.

'You want evidence? Here's all the evidence you need.'

And then I took her through the entire story. Her eyes grew wide as I talked. I showed her all the documentation from SATWA – and explained how the registration of all my unproduced work had vanished, only to then be suddenly listed under the name of Philip Fleck. I went through McCall's bank accounts and pointed out his large monthly retainer from Lubitsch Holdings.

'Does your husband have a thing for Ernst Lubistch's movies?'

'Well, he owns a print of all his films.'

'Bingo.'

I explained how I lost my investment portfolio, courtesy of Bobby Barra – and how I had reason to believe that my broker was acting under Fleck's instructions to hurt me financially.

'The one thing I can't figure out is this: whether he decided to do this because he somehow found out about us . . .'

'But what's to find out?' she said. 'I mean what we did was pretty Junior High. Anyway, around that time, Philip hadn't touched me for months . . .'

'Well, if it wasn't that, maybe . . . I don't know . . . maybe he was envious of my little success . . .'

'Philip's envious of anyone with real creative talent. Because he has absolutely none himself. But, knowing him as damn well as I do, he could have decided to do this for a dozen different reasons

. . . all cryptic and hard to fathom to everyone but himself. Then again, he might just have done this for the sake of doing this. Because he *can* do this.'

She stood up, pacing the cottage, shaking her head,

'I'm so . . . I can't imagine how he . . . he plays the mind-fuck games all the . . . the whole thing . . . it's so fucking, unbelievably *Philip*.'

'Well, you know him better than I do.'

'I am so sorry.'

'Me too. Which is why I need your help.'

'You've got it.'

'But what I'm going to propose might be . . . well . . . kind of risky.'

'Let me worry about that. So go on – what do you want me to do?'

'Confront your husband with hard evidence that he had stolen my scripts, and paid McCall to annihilate my career.'

'And I suppose you want me to wear a wire when I play this *J'accuse* scene?' she asked.

'One of those little pocket micro-recorders will do. I just need one single admission from him that he was behind all this. Once it's on tape, my agent – and her lawyers – will have the leverage they need. And when he realizes that we have him confessing to the script theft and the McCall set-up, I'm certain he'll want to deal with us . . . especially when he understands just what kind of publicity this will generate for him. He does have a little phobia about negative publicity, doesn't he?'

'Oh yes.'

'All I want is my reputation put back together again. I don't really care about the money . . .'

'*Care* about the money. Because money is the one language that Philip ultimately understands. There is a problem, however.'

'He'll deny everything?'

'That's right. But . . .'

'What?'

'If I provoke him enough, he just might blurt out the admission you're after.'

264

'You don't sound hopeful.'

'I know the man all too well. Still, it's worth a shot.'

'Thank you.'

She scooped up all the documents. 'I'm going to need all this evidence,' she said.

'It's yours.'

'Now would you drive me back to my car, please?'

She said nothing during the few minutes we headed back to the bookshop. I glanced at her once. She was holding the file tightly to her chest, looking completely preoccupied and silently furious. When we pulled up out front, she simply leaned over and gave me a peck on the cheek. And said, 'You'll be hearing from me.'

Then she climbed out of my car, got into her own vehicle and drove off. As I returned back to the cottage, I thought: that was exactly the reaction I was hoping for.

But days went by without even a word from her. Alison, however, was in regular contact, wondering how I had deployed that batch of xeroxed evidence. I lied and said that I was still perusing it, still trying to figure out a way that we could use it against him.

'You are such a shitty fibster,' she said.

'Think what you like, Alison.'

'I just hope you're being smart for a change.'

'I'm working on it. Meanwhile, do you or your legal eagle have any further thoughts on how we might be able to sue the asshole for Literary Theft in the First Degree?'

'We've looked at every aspect, and . . . no, nothing. The guy's got every angle covered.'

'We'll see about that.'

By the time an entire week had passed without contact from Martha, I too started to wonder if he *did* have every angle covered . . . to the point where she couldn't get a single confessional word out of him. And I found myself fighting off a wave of despondency. Because three weeks from now, an alimony payment would be due – and there was no way I'd be able to even meet half of it. Which meant that Lucy would probably retaliate by attempting to end my phone access with Caitlin. As I also wouldn't be in a position to afford Walter Dickerson's services in court (or elsewhere), she'd legally steamroller me in a nanosecond. Then there was the matter of Willard Stevens. He'd called me personally from London a few days ago for a quick *getting-to-know-you* hello, and to ask if all was fine in the cottage, and to inform me that he'd probably be returning to the States within two months, so . . .

But how would I find anything to rent in Meredith on $280 a week? Hell, the cheapest unit around town was around eight hundred a month . . . which meant that, once I dealt with the roof over my head, I'd end up with eighty bucks a week to pay for everything . . . from gas to electricity to food. In other words, Mission Preposterous.

By the time I'd played out this catastrophic scenario, I was homeless on Wiltshire Boulevard, sprawled on the sidewalk, with a hand-painted sign which read: *They Used to Return My Calls.*

And then, finally, Martha phoned. It was Friday night . . . a full ten days after I'd seen her. She called the shop around six pm. Her tone was succinct, businesslike.

'Sorry I haven't been in touch,' she said. 'I've been away.'

'Do you have any news?'

'When are your days off?'

'Monday and Tuesday.'

'Can you keep Monday completely free?'

'Sure.'

'Fine. I'll pick you up at the cottage around two.'

And she hung up before I could ask her anything.

I wanted to ring her straight back and demand to know what was going on. But I knew that, at best, that would be counter-productive. So I could do nothing except count the hours until Monday.

She showed up on time, parking her Range Rover right by my front door. Once again, she looked bewitching: a short red skirt, a tight black halter, the same jean jacket as last week, the same broken horn-rimmed glasses, and an old-style cameo around her neck. Isobel Archer meets Downtown Hip. I came out to greet her. She favored me with a big smile – a smile that made me wonder if she had good news for me. When she gave me a light kiss on the lips – squeezing my arm simultaneously – I thought: *this is promising . . . and just a little confusing.*

'Hello there,' she said.

'And hello to you. Do I detect an air of good humor?'

'You never know. Is that what you're planning to wear today?'

I was dressed in a pair of old Levis, a tee shirt, and a zip-up grey sweatshirt.

'As I didn't know what we were planning to do today . . .'

'Can I put a proposition to you?'

'I'm all ears.'

'I want you to let me take charge of everything today.'

'By which you mean . . . ?'

'By which I mean, I want you to agree that you won't question a single thing I do . . . and at the same time, you'll do everything I ask of you.'

'Everything?'

'Yes,' she said with a grin. *'Everything.* But don't worry: nothing I suggest will be illegal. Or dangerous.'

'Well, that's a relief . . .'

'So: do we have a deal?'

She proffered her hand. I took it.

'I guess so . . . as long as you don't want me to bury a body.'

'That would be far too banal,' she said. 'Come on, let's get you out of those slacker clothes.'

She walked past me into the cottage, and straight into the bedroom. Then she opened my closet and rifled through my clothes. Eventually, she pulled out a pair of black jeans, a white tee shirt, a lightweight leather jacket and a pair of black Converse hi-tops.

'That should work,' she said, handing me the lot. 'Go on, get changed.'

She walked back into the living room. I undressed and put on what she had chosen. When I came out, she was standing over the desk, looking at an old photograph of myself and Caitlin. She looked me up and down.

'A big improvement,' she said. Then she held up the photograph. 'Mind if I take this with us?

'Uh . . . no. But could I ask why?'

'What did you agree not to do?'

'Not to ask questions.'

She came over and gave me another light kiss on the lips. 'Then don't ask questions.'

She linked her arm in mine. 'Come on,' she said. 'We're out of here.'

We headed off in her Range Rover. Once we left Meredith behind us and turned north up the Pacific Coast Highway, she said, 'I'm very impressed, David.'

'With what?'

'That you haven't asked me what happened over the last ten days. That's very disciplined of you.'

'Well, you did say: no questions.'

'I will give you an answer . . . but on another proviso: that after I tell you, we don't discuss it again.'

'Because it's bad news?'

'Yes, because it is less-than-satisfactory news. And because I don't want it spoiling our day together.'

'All right.'

Looking straight ahead through the windscreen – her eyes occasionally flickering upwards towards the rear view mirror – she started to speak.

'After I saw you, I went back to LA, and arranged for the Gulfstream to fly me directly to Chicago. Before getting on the flight, I ducked into a little electronics shop at LAX and bought a tiny voice-activated micro-recorder. Then, once we were airborne, I called Philip and said that I had to see him immediately. When I got to his suite at the Four Seasons and threw the entire file at him, do you know what he did? He shrugged and said he didn't know what I was talking about. So I took him through the entire scam, piece by piece, backing everything up with all the evidence you gave me. He denied any knowledge of anything. He didn't even ask me where I got the evidence from. He ignored the whole damn thing. Even when I lost it and started screaming at him for an explanation, he clammed up and switched right into zombie introvert mode. I must have spent the better part of an hour, playing the actress, trying every trick imaginable to get him to make just one admission. But he completely ignored me. And so, eventually, I gathered up all the papers and stormed out, and took the Gulfstream right back to LA.

'I spent the next couple of days doing a little research of my own. Lubitsch Holdings is definitely one of Philip's shell companies . . . though it's so carefully "disguised" in that Cayman Island way that nobody could ever trace it back to him. And though I don't have proof, I'm pretty damn sure that, in addition to the big benevolent fund payoff, Philip also put a big bonus payment right into the pocket of James LeRoy, SATWA's executive director . . .'

'How did you find that out?' I asked.

'What's our rule today?'

'Sorry.'

'Anyway, that's about it. Everything you told me the other day turned out to be absolutely on-the-money. Philip decided to demolish you. I don't know why he did it. But he did it. He'll never admit it – he'll never explain his reasons. But I know he's guilty. And he's going pay a price for this. And the price is: I'm leaving him. Not, of course, that that will faze him in the least.'

'You've told him you're leaving him,' I asked, hoping that it didn't sound like a question.

'No, I haven't told him yet. Because I haven't spoken to him since. And yes, well done for trying to make a question sound like a statement.'

'Thank you.'

'For nothing. I only wish I'd been able to get an admission out of him. Then, at least, I might have been able to force him to put things right. Instead . . .'

She shrugged.

'It's all right,' I said.

'No. It's not.'

'For today, it's all right.'

She let go of the wheel with one hand, and intertwined her fingers with mine. And she kept them intertwined until we turned off at Santa Barbara, and she had to downshift into third gear.

We passed through the gasoline alley where I sold my Porsche and hocked my computer. We headed down the main drag of designer shops and the sort of upscale eateries where arugula and shaved parmesan were *de rigueur*. When we reached the beach, we turned and followed the coast road until we reached the gates of the Four Seasons Hotel.

'Uh . . .' I started to say, remembering my illicit week here with Sally when I was still married and oh-so-risibly arrogant. Before I had a chance to raise a question, Martha said, 'Don't even ask.'

The valet parking guy relieved us of the car. Martha led me through the main door. But instead of heading in the direction of the reception desk, she brought me down a side corridor to a pair of large oak doors, above which were the words, *The Wellness Center.*

'I decided you needed a little *Wellness*,' Martha said with a grin as she opened one of the doors and pushed me ahead of her. She took complete charge of everything, telling the receptionist that I was David Armitage, and that I had been booked in for an all-afternoon special, including 'a stint with the coiffeur'. And speaking of the coiffeur, could she have a word with him, please? The receptionist picked up the phone. After a few moments, a tall sinewy gentleman emerged from the rear doors. He spoke in a near-whisper and introduced himself as Martin.

'Well, Martin,' Martha said. 'Here's the victim.' She reached inside her shoulder bag and pulled out the photograph of Caitlin and myself, handing it to Martin. 'And here's how he looked before he moved into a cave. Do you think you can bring him back to his pre-Neanderthal state?'

A thin smile from Martin. 'No problem,' he said, handing the photo back to Martha.

'Okay, handsome,' she said to me. 'You're in for four hours of fun. See you on the verandah for drinks at seven.'

'What are you going to do?'

Another light kiss on the lips. 'No questions,' she said. Then she turned and headed out the door. Martin tapped me on the shoulder and motioned for me to follow him into his inner sanctum.

First I was relieved of all my clothes. Then two women attendants escorted me to a large marble shower stall where I was hosed down with pressurized jets of very hot water, and scrubbed with seaweed soap and a hard-bristle brush. Then I was dried off and robed and sent to Martin's chair. He used a pair of clippers to remove the vast majority of my beard. Hot towels followed, lather was applied, and a straight-edged razor appeared from a surgical sterilizer. He scraped my face clean, swathed it again in a hot towel, then removed it, and swirled the chair around and dunked my head backwards into a sink, and shampooed my long tangled hair. Then he sliced it all off, bringing it back to the short-back-and-sides style I favored until everything started going wrong.

When he was finished, he tapped me on the shoulder again, and pointed me towards another door, saying: 'I'll see you at the end.'

For the next three hours I was pounded and kneaded and mummified and covered in clay and massaged with oil and eventually sent back to Martin's chair, where he did a little blow-dry and-brush action, and then pointed to the mirror and said:

'Back to where you once were.'

I stared at myself in the mirror, and found it a little hard to adjust to this new old image. My face was thinner; my eyes deeply tired. Though I looked appropriately buffed and burnished after four hours of intensive *Wellness*, a significant part of me didn't believe this act of tonsorial and cosmetic magic. I didn't want to see this face because I didn't trust this face anymore. And I vowed to start growing my beard again tomorrow morning.

When I walked onto the verandah, I found Martha seated at a table with a perfect view of the Pacific. She had changed into a short black dress, and had her hair loose around her shoulders. She looked up at me. She graced me with a smile and said, 'Now that's better.'

I sat down beside her. 'Come here, please,' she said. I leaned forward. She put her hand against my face. She inclined her head towards mine and kissed me fully.

'In fact, that's a lot better,' she said.

'I'm glad you approve,' I said, my head swimming from the kiss.

'The fact is, Mr Armitage – there is a shortage of attractive, smart men in the world. You can find plenty of attractive/stupid, and plenty of smart/ugly . . . but attractive/smart are about as rare as sightings of the Hale–Bopp comet. And so, when an attractive/smart guy decides to turn himself into something resembling Tab Hunter in 'King of Kings' . . . well, steps have to be taken to bring the boy back to his senses. Especially as I would never sleep with anyone who looks like he's just stepped out of some Woolworth's painting of the Sermon on the Mount.'

Long, long pause. Martha took my hand, and asked, 'You did hear what I just said?'

'Oh yes.'

'And?'

Now it was my turn to lean over and kiss her.

'That was the response I was hoping for,' she said.

'Do you know how hard I fell for you that first night?' I suddenly said.

'You're asking a question again.'

'So what? I want you to know that.'

She took hold of my jacket and pulled me so close we were *tête-à-tête*.

'I do know that,' she whispered. 'Because I felt that too. But now: say no more.'

And then she gave me another kiss. And said: 'Want to try something really different?'

'Absolutely.'

'Let's keep it to a glass of wine each tonight. Two tops. Because something tells me it would be nice to be relatively sober later on.'

So we stuck to a glass each of Chablis. Then we moved on to the restaurant. We ate oysters and soft-shelled crabs, and I drank one more glass of wine, and we spent the next hour talking a lot of very amusing rubbish that made us both laugh like idiots. And then, when the final dishes were whisked away, and we turned down coffee, she took me by the hand, and led me back into the main hotel building and up an elevator, and into a large, plush suite. When she shut the door behind us, she took me in her arms and said, 'Do you know that standard-issue scene in every Cary Grant/Katherine Hepburn movie, where Cary whisks off Kate's glasses and kisses her madly? I want us to re-enact that scene right now.'

We did just that. Only the scene got carried away, as we stumbled backwards onto the bed.

And then . . .

Then it was morning. And − surprise, surprise − I woke to discover that I'd slept wonderfully. So wonderfully that, for the first minute or two of quasi-consciousness, I simply lay in bed, replaying the entire extraordinary evening over again in my head. But as I reached over for Martha, my hand touched a wooden object: the framed photo of Caitlin and myself, positioned on the adjoining pillow. I sat up and realized that I was alone in the room. I glanced at my watch. Ten-twelve am. Then I noticed a black case on the table, with an envelope on top of it. I got up. The envelope said *David* on the front. Inside:

Dearest David

I have to go. I will be in touch very soon . . . but, please, let it be me who makes contact.

The object in the case is a little gift for you. If you decide to get rid of it, I will never talk to you again. And as I do want to talk with you again . . . well, I think you can take it from here.

With love,

Martha

I unzipped the case and stared down at a brand new Toshiba laptop computer.

A few minutes later, I stood in front of the bathroom mirror, rubbing my now lightly bristled face. There was a phone to the left of the sink. I picked it up and called the Front Desk. When the guy on duty answered, I said, 'Morning. Is there any chance I might be able to get some shaving stuff sent up to me?'

'No problem, Mr Armitage. And would you like some breakfast?'

'Just some orange juice and coffee, please.'

'Coming right up, sir. And one final thing: your friend has arranged one of our drivers to take you home . . .'

'Really?'

'Yes − it's all taken care of. But check-out time is not until one, so . . .'

At five past one, I found myself in the back of a chauffeured

273

Mercedes, heading towards Meredith, the computer in its case, and on the seat beside me.

I showed up for work at Books & Company the next day. Les stopped by the shop in mid-afternoon, and spent a stunned moment or two trying to work out that it was actually me behind the counter. Then he looked at me with mock solemnity and said, 'Now in my experience, you have to be seriously in love to have cut off all that hair.'

He was right: I was seriously, *wildly* in love. Martha consumed my thoughts constantly. I kept running and re-running the tape of that night in my head. I kept hearing her voice, her laugh, her fiercely whispered articulations of love as we made love. I was desperate to speak with her. Desperate to touch her. Desperate to be with her. And desperate that she had yet to phone me.

By day four I'd reached breaking point. I decided that, if I didn't hear from her by noon tomorrow, I'd disobey her directive and call her cellphone, and tell her that we had to run off with each other immediately.

At eight the next morning, there was a loud knocking on the door. I jumped out of bed, thinking: *she's here.* But when I flung open the front door, I found a guy in a blue uniform, holding a large padded manila envelope.

'David Armitage?'

I nodded.

'Courier service. I've got a package here for you.'

'From whom?'

'Haven't a clue, sir.' He handed me a clipboard. I signed for the delivery, then thanked him.

I went back inside. I opened the package. It was a DVD. I slid it out of its cardboard box. The front of the disc was adorned with a white label, upon which was a crudely drawn heart, with an arrow bisecting it. On one side of the arrow were the initials *D.A.* On the other side, *M.F.*

I felt a deep chill run through me. But I still forced myself to feed the DVD into the player.

On the screen, there was a static camera shot of a hotel suite. Then the door opened, and Martha and I stumbled into the room.

She took me in her arms. Though the sound was harsh and tinny, I could still hear her saying:

'Do you know that standard-issue scene in every Cary Grant/Katherine Hepburn movie, where Cary whisks off Kate's glasses and kisses her madly? I want us to re-enact that scene right now.'

We began to kiss. We lurched backwards on to the bed. We were all over each other, pulling off our clothes, the hidden camera perfectly positioned to show maximum detail.

After five minutes, I hit the off button. I didn't need to see any more.

Fleck. The all-knowing, all-seeing, ever-omnipotent Philip Fleck. He'd set us up. He'd tapped her phone calls. Discovered she was arranging this liaison at the Four Seasons, Santa Barbara. Then, once again, he had his people to spread some money around, find out the number of the suite she'd reserved, and had it rigged out with the necessary covert camera and microphone.

And now . . . now he had us. Naked and in digital color. His first hard-core production . . . which would be used to destroy his wife, and to make certain that the dead zone in which I currently resided would always be my permanent address.

The phone rang. I dived for it.

'David?'

It was Martha. Her voice sounded preternaturally calm; the sort of calm that usually accompanies a deep concussion.

'Oh thank Christ, Martha . . .'

'You've seen it?'

'Yeah. I've seen it. He's just had it delivered here.'

'Quite something, isn't it?'

'I can't believe . . .'

'We need to meet,' she said.

'Now,' I said.

Five

I WAS DRESSED and on the road in five minutes. All the way south to Los Angeles, I kept the pedal flush against the floor, cranking the VW up to a thermo-dynamic seventy-eight miles per hour (its absolute top speed). It was like forcing a geriatric with emphysema to do an extended hundred-yard dash – but I didn't care. I had to see Martha immediately – before Fleck did whatever he was planning to do with that dire DVD.

She told me to meet her at a café in Santa Monica. I arrived there shortly after ten. She was already seated at a table, facing the beach. The sun was at full wattage; a light breeze wafted off the Pacific, tempering the morning heat.

'Hi there,' she said as I bounded up to the table. She was wearing dark glasses, so I couldn't properly gauge just how anxious she was. But what was immediately evident to me was her strange composure; a sang-froid which, once again, I put down to shock.

I came over and took her in my arms. But she remained seated and gave me her cheek to kiss – a gesture which immediately made me anxious.

'Easy there,' she said, gently putting her hand against my chest and pushing me towards the adjoining chair. 'You never know who's watching.'

'Of course, of course,' I said, sitting down and taking her hand under the table. 'But listen . . . I've been thinking things through all the way down here. And I now know what we have to do. We have to go together to your husband, tell him we're in love, and ask him to stay out of our . . .'

'David,' she said sharply, cutting me off. 'Before we do anything, there's an important question you need to answer.'

'Tell me.'

'Do you want an espresso, a cappuccino, or a latte?'

I looked up and saw a waitress hovering by our table, trying to control the amused expression on her face. She'd obviously heard everything I'd just said.

'A double espresso,' I said.

As soon as the waitress had gone, I took Martha's hand and kissed it.

'It has been a very long four days,' I said.

'Has it?' she said, her tone amused.

'And I can't tell you how touched I was by the gift.'

'I hope you use it.'

'I will. I will.'

'Writing is what you do well.'

'I have to tell you something . . .'

'I'm all ears.'

'From the moment I woke up alone in the hotel room, you have not left my mind once.'

She calmly disengaged her hand from mine. And asked, 'Do you always act this way after sleeping with someone for the first time?'

'I'm sorry. I know I'm sounding like a love-sick adolescent.'

'It's very sweet.'

'It's what I feel.'

'David . . . there's a larger matter to discuss right now.'

'You're right, you're right. Because I'm also just a little terrorized about what he might do with the DVD.'

'Well, that depends on how he reacts to it.'

'What do you mean?' I said, suddenly confused.

'I mean – he had nothing to do with the DVD.'

'But that doesn't make sense. If he didn't set us up, who did?'

'I did.'

I looked at her carefully, trying to discern some mischief in her eyes. But she met my stare and held it.

'I don't understand this.'

'It's all very straightforward, really. When Philip refused to acknowledge that he'd stage-managed all your problems, I decided that it was time to go drastic. That's when I hatched my little plan. And the way I figured it – if I couldn't get him on tape, then I'd have to get *us* on tape. The hotel management were only too willing to help – especially after I greased the palms of the appropriate people. And I had an audio-visual guy I knew in LA rig the whole thing up.'

'Was he there while we . . . ?'

'Do you really think I wanted anyone watching us in bed? Remember when I went to the Ladies just before we left the restaurant? I actually went back to our room and turned on the DVD recorder, which was hidden in one of the closets. Then . . . it was showtime.

'And the next morning, while you were sleeping, I took the DVD out of the machine and left. Two days later, I showed up again in Chicago – and forced Philip to sit down in his hotel suite and watch the first couple of minutes of our film.'

'How did he react?'

'In a typical Philip way: he said nothing. He just stared at the screen. But I knew the reaction he'd have to it. Though he'd never openly show it, he's fanatically jealous. I also know that his greatest fear in life is being exposed, found out, shown up. Which is why I decided on this course of action. Because I knew that a filmed record of me in bed with you would hit every panic button in his shrouded brain. But just to make certain he got the message, I told him that a copy of this DVD was with my lawyer in New York. And if he didn't put your career back together again in the next seven days, my lawyer had been instructed to release copies of the DVDs to the *Post,* the *News,* the *Enquirer, Inside Edition,* and every other purveyor of sleazy journalism imaginable. The clock is running. As of today, he's got six more days to go . . .'

'But if he calls your bluff . . . if it gets released . . .'

'Then the two of us are going to be front page news. But I don't care. If he takes it over the edge, then I'm going to give a very frank interview to Oprah or Diane Sawyer, in which I tell all about 'the joys' of living with a man worth all that money, but who still has all the sensitivity of a paper cup.

'Anyway, the only thing that matters right now is that he makes amends for what he did to you. As for me, my mind's made up: I'm leaving him.'

'You are?' I said, sounding a little too hopeful..

'That's what I told him. And according to my lawyer, if I do release the DVD to the press, it will have absolutely no effect whatsoever on my prenuptial agreement. It's a complete no-fault contract. If I walk away, if he decides he wants out – the result is still the same: I get $120 million.'

'Good God.'

'As far as Mr Fleck is concerned, it's a bargain. If we were full-time California residents, I could sue him for half of everything. Not that I'd want to. $120 million will be more than enough for me and the child . . .'

'What did you just say?'

'I'm pregnant.'

'Oh,' I said, sounding even more shell-shocked. 'That's . . . uh . . . wonderful news.'

'Thanks.'

'When did you find out?'

'Three months ago.'

And I suddenly realized why she craftily dodged all but a glass of wine the other night.

'What does Philip . . . ?'

'Well,' she said, cutting me off, 'he only found out yesterday. It was one of several little bombshells I detonated in front of him.'

'But I thought the two of you hadn't been . . .'

'There was a brief interlude a couple of months ago – shortly after I met you on the island – when Philip decided to start sharing our life again, and actually seemed to have fallen back in love with me . . . as I did with him. But that only lasted three months. Then he got all withdrawn again. And so, when I found out I was pregnant, I simply didn't tell him. Until yesterday, that is. And do you know what he said? Nothing? Complete silence.'

I took her hand again.

'Martha . . . .' Before I could speak another word, she cut me right off.

'Don't even say what you're thinking . . .'

'But didn't you . . . *don't you* . . .'

'What? Love you?'

'Yes.'

'I've known you exactly three days.'

'But you can know after five minutes.'

'True. But I'm not even going there right now.'

'I simply can't believe you've risked everything you have for me.'

'Cut the Harlequin Romance prose, please. The man treated you like dirt – primarily, I sense, because he got a full report of our night on the island. It didn't matter that we didn't do the deed. What mattered was that you were talented and I sort of fell for you. So when I found out how he pulled your career apart, I felt responsible. And when he wouldn't listen to moral arguments, I decided to play dirty pool. So that's what this is all about. Settling the score. Balancing the books. Righting the wrong. Or any other cliché you care to mention.'

'He can't just pay me off. I'm going to need some sort of professional restitution as well. A statement from him clearing up the mess. And also . . .'

'Yes?'

An idea popped into my head – an absurd, devious idea . . . but worth a gamble. Especially as I had absolutely nothing else to lose.

'I want you to insist on a joint television interview with Philip and myself. Something high profile and national. No doubt, your husband's people can set it up.'

'And what's going to happen during the interview?'

'That's my business'

'I'll see what I can do. If, that is, I can do anything.'

'You've been wonderful. More than wonderful.'

'David, stop.'

She stood up. 'And now, I've got to go.'

I got out of my chair and kissed her. This time she let it fall on her lips. There was a torrent of romantic stupidity that I wanted to blurt out, but I held myself in check.

'I'll call you as soon as I hear anything,' she said. Then she turned and walked off towards her car.

All the way back to Meredith, I kept replaying our conversation again in my head, homing in (like any lovesick jerk) on the few optimistic signals she had thrown me. She was leaving Fleck. Though she didn't admit outright love for me, she didn't deny it either. And she did confess that she sort of fell for me. And she also knew the way I felt about her before I even learned of the sum coming her way when she left Fleck. Surely, that had to count for something, didn't it?

Being the ultimate fatalist, I also envisaged a worst-case scenario: Fleck decided to play hardball. The DVDs were released. I was now publicly vilified all over again – not only for being a psychotic plagiarist, but also for wrecking a marriage . . . and sleeping with a woman who was already three months pregnant. Martha would leave Fleck, but decide to fly solo without me. And I'd be in even deeper nowheresville than before.

When I got back to Meredith, there were two urgent messages for me on the answerphone at the bookshop. The first was from my boss, asking me why I'd failed to open the damn shop this morning . . . and that he hoped this would be a one-off lapse. The second was from Alison, telling me to phone her pronto.

Which I did.

'Well,' she said after taking the call, 'the Lord works in mysterious ways.'

'Meaning?'

'Listen to this: I just received a phone call from a certain Mitchell van Parks of this big fuck-you law firm in New York. He explained he was acting on behalf of Fleck Films, and he wanted to apologize for the confusion that existed over the registration of *your* . . . yes, he actually used that pronoun . . . *your* screenplay, *We Three Grunts*. "Terrible system failure at SATWA," he said, "which, of course, Fleck Films wants to put right." To which I said: "So what are we talking about here?" And he said: "One million dollars . . . and shared writing credit." And I said: "Seven months ago, your client, Mr Fleck, offered my client, Mr Armitage, a fee of two-point-five, pay or play. Surely, given the fact that certain public questions could be raised about how Mr Fleck's name ended up on the title page . . ."

"And that's when he cut me off and said: "All right, one-point-four it is."

'But I said: "No dice."'

'You didn't . . .'

'Of course I did. Because I naturally countered, saying that, given the "intriguing" circumstances surrounding the authorship of this script, surely Fleck Films would like to make a further gesture to settle the matter once and for all . . . and to ensure that the unfortunate confusion which arose remained a private matter between my client and Mr Fleck.'

'To which the lawyer said?'

'Three.'

'To which you said?'

'Sold.'

I put down the phone for a moment. I put my face in my hands. I didn't feel triumphant. Or vindicated. Or exonerated. I didn't know what to feel . . . except an acute, strange sense of loss. And an overwhelming desire to take Martha in my arms. Her crazy wager had paid off. And now – if she was willing to roll the dice with me again – our life together could . . .

'David?' Alison shouted into the phone. 'You still there?'

I picked up the receiver. 'Sorry about that. I got a little . . .'

'No need to explain. It's been a long six months.'

'Bless you, Alison. Bless you.'

'Now don't start going religious on me, Armitage. We're going to have to do a lot of non-Christian dirty work on the subject of shared or sole credit. I've asked van Parks to Fedex me the shooting script. I'll get it up to you tomorrow. We can take it all from there. Meantime, I'm going to go buy myself a bottle of French fizz . . . and I suggest you do the same. Because, hey . . . I just made four hundred and fifty thousand big ones this afternoon.'

'Congratulations.'

'Ditto, ditto. And some day, you're going to tell me how you managed this reversal of fortune.'

'I'm saying nothing. Except: it's good to be back in business with you.'

'We were never out of business, David.'

As soon as Alison ended the call, I dialled Martha's cellphone. But I was connected with her voice mail. So I left the following message:

'Martha, darling, it's me. And it's worked, your amazing gamble's worked. Please call me. Anytime. Day or Night. Just do call. I love you . . .'

But she didn't call that night. Or the next day. Or the day after. Instead, Alison rang me with more intriguing news.

'Can you get hold of a copy of today's *New York Times*?' she asked.

'We actually sell it in the shop.'

'Go to the Arts and Leisure section. There's an exclusive inter-view with our favorite *auteur*, Philip Fleck. You should read what he says about you. According to him, you're the most persecuted writer since Voltaire, and your alleged crimes were nothing but trumped-up charges by a journalistic Joe McCarthy. But what's really beautiful – what really appeals to my low opinion of all human nature – is the fact that, according to Fleck, you had been so systematically vilified by McCall and ruthlessly abandoned by the entire industry, that both you and Fleck felt it was in the best interest of the film if you remained off the credits . . .'

By this time I had grabbed a copy of the paper from the shelf in front of the register, and was reading along.

'Listen to what comes next,' Alison said: *'But according to Fleck, the idea of a writer's name being kept off the credits reminded him so much of the dreadful days of the 1950s blacklist that he felt compelled to break his silence on this issue – not to mention his long-standing antipathy for any sort of interviews with the press – and come to the defence of his writer.'*

'"Without question," Fleck said, "David Armitage is one of the most original voices in American film and television. And it is shameful that his career has been virtually ruined by an individual who – due to his own lack of professional success – decided to lead a vendetta against him. If anything, David's brilliant script for We Three Grunts *will vindicate him completely, and remind Hollywood what they've lost."'*

'Fucking hell,' I said.

'Too bad they're not doing a remake of *The Life of Emile Zola*. After that performance, Fleck would be a shoo-in for the part. Nice to see that he's calling you by your first name as well. So, are you now going to finally tell me what happened on that island of his all those months ago?'

'My lips are sealed.'

'You're no fun at all. But, at least, you're lucrative again. And, I tell you, this article's going to re-open a lot of doors for you in this town.'

Certainly, the phone at the cottage kept ringing that night – as I gave quotes to *Daily Variety,* the *Hollywood Reporter,* the *LA Times,* and the *San Francisco Chronicle.* And what did I tell them? What was my official line on Philip Fleck's spirited defence of me? I played the game, of course. And said, 'Every writer needs a director like Philip Fleck . . . for his generosity of spirit, his loyalty, and his rare and wondrous faith in the written word.' (This last comment was, of course, a message to Fleck and his creative team: don't think you're going to be rewriting this one.)

And when the journalists asked me if I had any ill-will towards Theo McCall, I simply replied: 'I'm just glad I'm not his conscience.'

That evening, I tried to ring Martha again. But again I was connected straight to her voice mail. I left a simple message, saying how thrilled I was with the *Times* piece, how I was still hoping that Fleck would consent to the joint television interview, and how I needed to speak with her.

She didn't ring back. And I resisted the temptation to e-mail or drive down to Malibu and knock on her door. Because, of course, I realized what Fleck was doing: beside ensuring that that video would never see the light of day, he was also telling his wife that he didn't want to lose her.

The following day, the entire Fleck interview was reprinted in the *LA Times.* And early that same morning, I received a call from a producer on NBC's *Today* program, informing me that a reservation had been made for me on the 2pm flight that afternoon for New York. A limo would pick me up at Kennedy. A room was arranged for the night at the Pierre. And I'd be interviewed with Mr Fleck sometime during the final hour of the program tomorrow morning

I glanced at my watch. It was nine-fifteen. To make it to LAX in time, I'd have to leave within the hour. So, after confirming that I could collect my ticket at the airport, I hung up and called Les at home.

'I know this is very last-minute,' I said, 'but I really need two days off.'

'Yeah, I saw the piece in the *LA Times* this morning. I guess you're not going to be working with us much longer, David.'

'I guess not.'

'Well, it's fine by me about the next two days. But would you mind if you worked out a two-week notice, until I find someone new?'

'No problem, Les.'

Then I packed a suit bag, made heavy by the four scripts I threw in with my change of clothes. It took just over two hours to get to the airport and six hours to be flushed across the continent. I was in my hotel room at midnight. But I couldn't sleep. So I got dressed and wandered the streets of Manhattan until dawn cleaved the night sky. Then I walked back to the hotel, and got into my suit, and awaited the arrival of the NBC limousine. It arrived just after seven. Fifteen minutes later, I was having pancake base and flesh-toned powder applied to my face. The door opened, and Philip Fleck came in, accompanied by two large gentlemen in stiff black suits. Bodyguards. Fleck sat down in the chair next to mine. I glanced over at him, and noticed the big puffy bags beneath his eyes – a hint that I wasn't just the only person who'd slept badly last night. His disquiet was manifest. So too his refusal to look at me. The make-up woman tried to put him at ease by chatting incessantly as she daubed pancake on his fleshy face – but he just shut his eyes and blanked her out. Then the door swung open again, and a hyper-efficient woman in her late twenties walked in. She informed us that her name was Melissa ('Your assistant producer this morning'), and then briefed us on our five minutes of screen time. Fleck said nothing while she ran through a list of potential questions that the co-host – Matt Lauder – might toss our way.

'Anything else you need to know, gentlemen?' she asked. We both shook our heads. Then she wished us luck and left the room. I turned to Fleck and said, 'I wanted to thank you for such fulsome praise in that *Times* interview. I was very touched.'

He said nothing. He just stared straight ahead, his face tense with unease.

And then, suddenly, we were being escorted across a backstage area and on to the *Today* set. Matt Lauder was already there, sitting cross-legged in an armchair. He rose to pump our hands, but didn't have a chance to say anything more than a basic greeting as a pair of sound technicians swooped down on us to pin microphones to our lapels, while two make-up women dabbed touch-up pancake on our foreheads. I placed a pile of scripts on the coffee table in front of us. Fleck glanced down at them, but continued to say nothing. I looked over at him. His forehead was mottled with sweat, and his stage-fright was now seriously evident. I'd read so much about his pathological hatred of interviews. Now I was seeing – in extreme close-up – just what a trial it was for him to face the cameras like this. And again I realized: he's only putting himself through this because he's desperate to keep Martha.

'You okay, Philip?' Matt Lauder asked his sweating guest.

'I'll be fine.'

The stage manager announced: 'Fifteen seconds.' We all tensed in readiness. Then the stage manager gave the five-second count-down, and pointed to Lauder, who was immediately off-and-running.

'Welcome back . . . and for those of you who love a good Hollywood scandal, well here's one that's been making the papers for the past few days. Only unlike most scandals, this one has had a happy ending for David Armitage . . . the Emmy-award-winning creator of the hit series, *Selling You*, who was fired off his own show after accusations of plagiarism. But now, his reputation has been completely rehabilitated, thanks to the intervention of one of America's most prominent entrepreneurs, Philip Fleck.'

And then he gave a quick précis of the charges against me, the smear campaign waged by Theo McCall, and the way that Fleck stepped in to restore my good name.

'Now I know that you generally shun publicity, Philip,' Matt Lauder said, 'so why did you decide to go public and help David Armitage?'

Fleck began to speak in a hesitant voice, his head slightly lowered, unable to meet Matt Lauder's gaze.

'Well . . . uh . . . David Armitage is, without question, one of the

286

most important screenwriters around right now. He also happens to be writing my next movie . . . and when his career was pulled apart by a vindictive journalist – a man who is nothing more than a paid assassin – well . . . uh . . . I just felt like I had to intervene.'

'And his intervention must have the great turning point for you, David . . . especially after having been so vilified over the past few months, to the point where you were essentially shut out of Hollywood.'

I smiled broadly and said, 'You're absolutely right, Matt. I owe my professional resurrection to one man – the gentleman sitting on your left, my great friend Philip Fleck. And I want to show you just what a remarkable friend he's been to me . . .'

I reached over to the coffee table and picked up one of the four scripts I'd left there, opening it to the title page.

'When my reputation was in tatters – and no one would hire me – do you know what Philip did? He acted as a front for me – putting his name on four of my old scripts. Because he knew that, if my name was on them, no studio would be interested. See – here's one of my first scripts, *We Three Grunts* . . . but as you'll notice, Matt, the writer's name on the title page is Philip Fleck.'

The camera moved in on a close-up of the title page. Over this, Lauder asked Fleck:

'So you actually acted as David Armitage's front, Philip?'

For the first time ever, Fleck met my gaze – and his eyes radiated chilly incredulity. He knew I had him now, and there was nothing he could do about it but play along. So when the camera switched back to him, he reluctantly said:

'What, uh, David said is right. His name had been dragged through such mud that he was considered an untouchable by all the Hollywood studios. And, uh, as I wanted to have the films I'm making from his scripts distributed by a major motion picture company, I had, uh, no choice but, uh, to put my own name to the scripts . . . with David's consent, of course.'

'So, besides *We Three Grunts*,' Matt Lauder said, 'which is going into production next month with Peter Fonda, Dennis Hopper and Jack Nicholson, you're also planning to film three other David Armitage scripts?'

Fleck looked like he wanted to crawl under the chair. But he still said, 'That's the plan, Matt.'

I quickly came in here: 'And Matt, I know Philip's going to be embarrassed about what I'm going to say next – because he's someone who really doesn't like to have a big deal made about his generosity – but when I was completely out of work, not only did he buy these four scripts, but he also insisted on paying me $3 million per script.'

Even Matt Lauder seemed dazzled by this sum of money.

'Is that true, Mr Fleck?'

He pursued his lips, as if he was about to contradict my statement. But then he nodded slowly.

'Now that's what I call a real act of professional faith,' Matt Lauder said.

'You can say that again,' I said, all smiles. 'And what was even more remarkable about this deal was the fact that Philip insisted that the $12 million package for the four scripts would be on a *pay-or-play* basis . . . which is a legalistic way of saying that, whether or not they get made, that $12 million is still paid to me. I kept telling him he was being way too generous. But he was so emphatic about helping me out – and, more to the point, putting his faith in me – that I had to say "Yes". Not, of course, that it took much convincing.'

That last comment elicited a laugh from Matt Lauder. Then he turned to Fleck and said, 'Sounds like you're a screenwriter's dream come true, Mr Fleck.'

Fleck fixed me in his sights.

'David's worth every penny.'

I met Fleck's stare.

'Thank you, Philip.'

Thirty seconds later, the interview was over. Fleck immediately left the set. I shook Matt Lauder's hand, and was escorted back into the make-up room. I'd left my cellphone on one of the counter tops. It started ringing as I reached to retrieve it.

'You crazy, dangerous sonofabitch,' Alison said, her voice downright giddy. 'I've never seen a sting like it.'

'Glad you approve.'

'*Approve?* You've just made me one-and-a-half million bucks. So, of course, I fucking approve. Congratulations.'

'And congratulations to you. You're actually worth the fifteen per cent.'

A hoarse tobacco-cured laugh from Alison. 'Get your ass back here. Because, after this, the phone's going to start jumping – and you're about to become The Man in Demand.'

'Fine by me – but I can't do anything for the next two weeks.'

'Why's that?'

'I'm working out my notice at the bookshop.'

'David, stop talking like a goof.'

'Hey, I promised the guy . . .'

Suddenly the door opened and Philip Fleck walked in.

'Got to go, Alison,' I said. 'Catch you later.' And I hung up.

Fleck sat down in the chair next to mine. A make-up woman approached him, jar of cold cream at the ready, but Fleck stopped her by saying, 'Could you give us a moment, please?'

She left the room, closing the door behind her. We were alone now. Fleck said nothing for several moments. Then:

'You know, I'm never making any of those scripts of yours. *Never.*'

'That's your prerogative.'

'I'm even pulling the plug on *We Three Grunts.*'

'That's your prerogative too . . . though you might end up pissing off Mr Fonda, Mr Hopper, and Mr Nicholson.'

'As long as they get their money, they won't give a damn. It's the movie business, after all. No one cares about anything as long as the contract is honored, and the check ends up in the bank. So, fear not, you will get your $12 million. It is a *pay-or-play* deal, after all. And $12 million . . . to me it's pocket money.'

'I don't care if you pay me or not.'

'Yes, you do. You care very much. Because, thanks to this $12 million deal, you're back to Hollywood Golden Boy status. So you have much to thank me for. Just as, in the process, you've done wonders for my public image. Made me seem like a great humanitarian . . . not to mention a writer's best friend. In other words, this has been a mutually beneficial experience.'

'You really need to control everything, don't you?'

'I don't follow your line of thought here . . .'

'Yes, you do. Because it was you who set out to shatter everything in my life, to demolish . . .'

He cut me off.

'I *what?*' he said.

'You decided to stage manage my downfall . . .'

'Really?' he said, sounding amused. 'You actually think that?'

'I know it.'

'How very flattering. But let me ask you this, David. Did I tell you to leave your wife and child? Did I force you to come to my island? Did I put a gun to your head to sell me your script . . . even though you hated every idea I had about it? And when that odious McCall fellow pointed out that you had inadvertently lifted a few lines from some old play, did I tell you to go on the offensive against him?'

'That's not the point here. You put the whole plot against me in motion . . .'

'No, David . . . you did that yourself. You ran off with Ms Birmingham. You accepted my hospitality. You were willing to pocket the $2.5 million I offered you for the movie. You came out swinging against that ghastly journalist. And you also fell in love with my wife. I didn't have a hand in any of that, David. You made all those decisions yourself. I played no games with you, David. You simply became a victim of your own choices. Life's like that, you know. We make choices, and our circumstances alter because of those choices. It's called *cause-and-effect*. And when bad things happen in the wake of the bad decisions we make, we like to blame outside forces, and the malevolent hand of others. Whereas, ultimately, we have no one but ourselves to blame.'

'I admire your amorality, Mr Fleck. It is truly breathtaking.'

'Just as I admire your refusal to acknowledge the truth of the situation.'

'Which is *what?*'

'You set yourself up. You walked right into . . .'

'The trap you laid?'

'No, David . . . the trap you laid for yourself. Which, of course, makes you most human. Because we're always laying traps for

290

ourselves. I think it's called *doubt*. And the thing we most doubt in life is the person we are.'

'What do you know about doubt?'

'Oh, you'd be surprised. Money doesn't end doubt. In fact, it often heightens it.'

He stood up. 'And now, I must . . .'

I interrupted him.

'I love your wife.'

'Congratulations. I love her too.'

Then he turned and walked towards the door. As he opened it, he turned back to me and said, 'See you at the movies, David.'

And he was gone.

On my way to JFK that afternoon, I left two messages on Martha's cellphone, asking her to call me. When I reached Los Angeles seven hours later, there were a dozen or so messages from assorted one-time colleagues and friends, congratulating me on my television appearance. But the one message I craved – *her* message – wasn't there.

I picked up my car and drove up the coast. The next morning, I opened the *LA Times* and discovered an extended piece in their Arts section, entitled: *Theo McCall and the Art of Vendetta Journalism*. The story was very well researched, very well sourced . . . and essentially amounted to a complete exposé of McCall's Stalinist methods; his love affair with character assassination; his need to destroy careers. There were also some interesting personal details: like the fact that he went around telling everyone that he was a graduate of Trinity College Dublin, whereas he barely finished high school. Or the way he walked out on two different women after getting both of them pregnant – and then refusing to pay a penny of child support. All the stuff about him being fired from his one proper writing job at NBC got dredged up again – as did a little known fact: a year or so before *Selling You* hit the screens, he actually pitched an idea (which went nowhere) about a sit-com set in an advertising agency. The conclusion: no wonder he had a thing against David Armitage and his wildly successful show.

Within a day of this story appearing, Theo McCall went to ground. *Hollywood Legit* announced that his column would no longer appear – and though many a fellow journalist tried to unearth him (in an attempt to get his response to the *LA Times* story), he was nowhere to be found.

'Rumor has it that the guy has vanished back to England,' Alison told me on the phone. 'Or, at least, that's what my PI tells me. You know what else he told me? According to McCall's bank statements, he got paid a cool million last week from Lubitsch Holdings. And you can guess exactly what kind of deal Fleck cut with him: you take the fall, you get your reputation trashed, you leave town in a hurry and don't show up again, you collect one million dollars.'

'How does your guy find all this stuff out?'

'I don't ask. And he's not my guy any more. As of today, he's off the case. Because the case is closed. Oh, and by the way, the contracts for all four scripts arrived today from Fleck Films. $12 mil. Pay-or-play . . .'

'Even though he'll never make any of them.'

'With the exception of *We Three Grunts*.'

'But he told me he was killing it.'

'Yeah, but he said that right after you trumped him on *Today*. I think his wife has convinced him otherwise.'

'By which you mean . . . ?'

'There's a story on page three of this morning's *Daily Variety*, announcing that *We Three Grunts* will start shooting in six weeks' time, and that Fleck's wife Martha is now the movie's producer. So obviously, you've got a real fan in Martha Fleck.'

'I don't know about that.'

'Hey, who cares if the dame likes you or not? They're making the movie. It's good news.'

And the good news kept rolling in. A week later, I got a call from Brad Bruce.

'I hope you're still willing to talk with me?' he asked.

'I don't blame you for anything, Brad.'

'That's more generous than I'd be under the circumstances. But thank you. How's it going, David?'

'Compared to the last six months, somewhat better.'

'And you're still up the coast in that little place Alison said you were living?'

'Yep. Working out my notice in the local bookshop.'

'You've been working in a bookshop?'

'Hey, I had to eat.'

'I hear you. But now that you've scored that $12 million deal with Phil Fleck . . .'

'I'm still working in the bookshop for the next five days.'

'Fine, fine. Very admirable, in fact . . . but you *are* planning to come back to LA, aren't you?'

'It's where the money is, right?'

He laughed.

'How's the new series shaping up?' I asked.

'Well . . . that's what I'm calling you about. After you left, we put Dick LaTouche in charge as overall script editor. And we've got six of next season's episodes in. But I have to tell you: the powers-that-be are less-than-pleased. They lack all the sharpness, the edge, the manic wit that you brought to the series.'

I said nothing.

'And so, we were wondering . . .'

A week later, I signed a deal with FRT to return to *Selling You*. I would write four of the last eight episodes. I was back in charge of overall script supervision (and agreed that my first order of business was to sharpen up the first six scripts for the new season). And the debt I allegedly owed for the disputed episode in the previous season was instantly cancelled. I was given back my 'Created By . . .' bonus, not to mention my office, my parking space, my medical insurance, and – most of all – my street cred. Because as soon as the new FRT deal – worth just over $2 million – was announced in the trades, everyone really wanted to be my friend again. Warners rang Alison to say that they planned to get *Breaking and Entering* back on the development track (and – *naturally* – that silly business about the first half of the first draft fee . . . please tell Mr Armitage to keep the change). Old business acquaintances phoned me up. A couple of industry pals asked me out to lunch. And no, I didn't think to myself: *where were they when I needed them?* Because that's not how it works out here. You're in, you're out. You're up, you're down. You're hot, you're not. In this sense, Hollywood was a purely Darwinian construct. Unlike other towns

– which veiled the same merciless streak under elaborate layers of politesse and intellectual affectation – this place operated on a simple premise: *I'm interested as long as you can do something for me.* To a lot of people, that was LA superficiality writ large. But I admired the ruthless practicality of this world-view. You understood exactly what you were dealing with. You knew the rules of the game.

The same week I signed the FRT contract, I moved back into town. Though I could have easily started house hunting, a new elemental caution kicked in. No snap decisions. No grabbing the first glossy thing on offer. No more belief in the red-hot incandescence of success. So – instead of the big minimalist loft or some hyper-nouveau-riche Brentwood pile – I rented a pleasant, modern town house in a pleasant, modern development in Santa Monica. $3000 a month. Two bedrooms. Nice and airy. Well within my means. Sensible.

And when it came time to choose that essential LA symbol – a car – I decided to keep my battered VW Golf. The first day I showed up back at FRT for work, I arrived just behind Brad Bruce in his Mercedes SR convertible. He eyed my jalopy with amusement.

'Let me guess,' he said. 'It's a retro college thing . . . and you've got a glove compartment full of Crosby, Stills and Nash tapes.'

'Hey, it got me from A to B up in Meredith. So I figure it can get me from A to B around here for a while.'

Brad Bruce smiled knowingly, as if to say: 'Okay, do the sackcloth and ashes routine for a while . . . but you'll upgrade soon enough. Because that's what will be expected of you.'

I knew he was right. I would get rid of the jalopy eventually. But only when it didn't start one morning.

'Ready for the big welcome back?' Brad asked me.

'Yeah, right,' I said. But when I entered the *Selling You* production office, the entire staff stood up and applauded me. I gulped and felt my eyes sting. But when this little ovation died down, I did what was anticipated of me. I made a quip:

'I should get fired more often. Thank you for that extraordinarily nice greeting. None of you belong in this business, you know. You're all too damn decent.'

Then I retreated to my old office. My desk was still there. So too my Herman Miller chair. I pulled it out. I sat down. I adjusted the height. I leaned back. I thought: this is a place I never expected to see again.

After a moment, my old assistant Jennifer knocked on the door.

'Well, hello there,' I said pleasantly.

'May I come in?' she said, all anxiety.

'You work here. Of course, you can come in.'

'David . . . Mr Armitage . . . ?'

'Stick with David. And I'm glad to see they didn't fire you, after all.'

'I got a last minute reprieve when one of the other assistants decided to leave. But David, will you ever forgive me for the way I . . . ?'

'That was then. This is now. And I'd love a double espresso, please.'

'No problem,' she said, the relief showing. 'And I'll also be back with your call sheet in a moment.'

Same as it ever was. Prominent on that call sheet were two names: Sally Birmingham and Bobby Barra. Sally had called once late last week. Bobby, on the other hand, had phoned twice every day for the past four days. According to Jennifer, he'd all but pleaded for my home number. And he kept giving her the same message: 'Tell him I've got good news.'

And when she told me that, I knew that Fleck's hand was behind whatever good news Bobby was going to give me.

But I still refused to take his calls for a week – just to let it be known that I wasn't going to be won over that easily.

Finally I capitulated. 'All right,' I said to Jennifer when she told me that Bobby was on line one for the third time that day. 'Put him through.'

As soon as I said hello, Bobby was off-and-running.

'You really know how to make a guy suffer,' he said.

'That's rich, coming from you.'

'Hey, you were the putz who went ballistic . . .'

'And you told me you never wanted to deal with me again. So why don't we simply tell each other to fuck off and leave it at that?'

'Ooh, listen to the cool customer. Back on top of the world, and back treating the little people like *ca-ca*.'

'I am not at all *size-ist*, Bobby. Even though you are a nasty, duplicitous, short little shit.'

'And here I was, about to give you some great news.'

'Go on,' I said, sounding bored.

'Remember that ten grand you left on account with me . . . ?'

'I never left any money with you, Bobby. When I closed the account . . .'

'You forgot about ten thousand dollars.'

'Bullshit.'

'David, I'm going to say it again: *you forgot about ten thousand dollars*. Got that?

'Uh-huh. And what, pray tell, happened to this 'forgotten' ten grand?'

'I bought you a small, but significant position in a Venezuelan dot.com IPO, and hey presto – the stock increased fifty-fold, and . . .'

'Why are you telling me this absurd story?'

'It's not absurd. You've now got $500,000 back on account with Barra & Company. In fact, I was about to get my people to send you and your account guy a statement today.'

'Do you really expect me to believe this?'

'The fucking money is there, David. In your name.'

'That I believe. But this Venezuelan IPO yarn? Couldn't you do better than that?'

A pause. Then:

'Does it matter how the money found its way into your account?'

'I just want you to admit . . .'

'What?'

'That he told you to set me up.'

'Who's *he*?'

'You know exactly who I'm talking about.'

'I don't talk about other clients.'

'He's not a client. He's fucking God . . .'

'And sometimes God is good. So stop with the sanctimonious shit . . . especially when God's also paid you $12 mil for four old scripts that were picking up Athlete's Foot in your sock drawer. And while you're at it, congratulate me on leaving you $250k better off than where you were when it all went down.'

I sighed. 'What can I say? You're a genius, Bobby.'

'I'll take that as a compliment. So: what do you want me to do with the dough?'

'As in: how do I think you should invest it for me?'

'That's what I'm asking.'

'What makes you think I still want you as my broker?'

'Because you know I've always made you money.'

I considered this for a moment.

'You know, after Alison's commission and the IRS, I'm also going to have about $6 million of the Fleck deal to play with.'

'I had done the math, yes.'

'Say I wanted to take that $6 million – along with the half-million you just made for me – and put it all in a trust fund . . . ?'

'We certainly do trusts. They're not the sexiest kind of investment . . .'

'But the funds can't somehow get switched into an Indonesian IPO, can they?'

Now it was his turn to sigh loudly. Instead of making a retort, however, he said: 'If you want safe, blue-chip investments – with iron-clad permanence – that's easily do-able.'

'That's exactly what I want. Ultra-safe. Rock solid. And to be put in the name of Caitlin Armitage.'

'Nice one,' Bobby said. 'I approve.'

'Why, thank you. And while you're at it, thank Fleck for me too.'

'I didn't hear that.'

'Don't tell me you're going deaf?'

'Hadn't you noticed? We're all falling apart. I think it's called *life*. Which is why, my friend, it's best to maintain an amused attitude at all times – especially during the bad ones.'

'And you're a philosopher to boot. How I've missed you, Bobby.'

'Ditto, David . . . with bells on. Lunch next week?'

'I suppose there's no avoiding it.'

But I did keep avoiding Sally's phone calls. Not that she was as persistent as Bobby. But her name kept appearing on my call sheet once a week for my first three weeks back on the job. Eventually, a letter arrived me for me on Fox stationery:

Dear David

I simply wanted to write and say how pleased I am to see you back in business after that dreadful campaign of vilification by Theo McCall. You are one of this industry's major talents – and what happened to you was nothing short of appalling. On behalf of everyone at Fox Television, congratulations on overcoming the worst possible adversity and triumphing again. Sometimes the good guys do win.

I also wanted to let you know that Fox Television is extremely interested in moving forward with the comedy series idea, *Talk It Over*, which we discussed some time ago. Your schedule permitting, it would be nice to meet up for lunch and chat things over.

Hope to hear from you soon.

Best,
Sally

PS You were brilliant on *Today*.

I didn't know if this was Sally's way of sending me an apology. Or if this was some carefully veiled hint that (as I was now bankable again) she'd like to *chat things over*. Or if she was simply playing the canny television executive and chasing the so-called 'talent'. I didn't care to find out. But I wasn't going to be rude or triumphalist either . . . because, quite frankly, there was nothing to be triumphalist about. So I sat down and – using official FRT stationery – wrote the following businesslike reply:

Dear Sally

Many thanks for your letter. Pressing work on the new series of *Selling You* means that I won't be available for lunch. And my writing commitments are such that I am not interested in pursuing any work with you for the foreseeable future.

Sincerely

And I signed my entire name.

Later that week, there was one final piece of good news. Delivered to me by Walter Dickerson, who after months of negotiating with the other side, finally got what I'd been longing for.

'Okay,' he said when he called me at the office. 'Here it is: you've got your physical access back.'

'Lucy actually relented?'

'Yes – she finally decided that Caitlin needed to see her father. I'm just sorry it took so damn long. But the good news is: not only can you have your regular access back, she's not insisting that it be supervised . . . which is often the case in a situation where access has been suspended for a while.'

'Did her lawyer give any reason why she changed her mind?'

'Put it this way: I'm certain Caitlin played her role in changing her mother's mind.'

But there was another reason – and one which I only discovered when I flew north for my first weekend in eight months with my daughter.

I drove a rental car from the airport to Lucy's house in Sausalito. And rang the bell. Within a nanosecond, the door flew open and Caitlin fell into my arms. I held her for a very long time. Then she nudged me with her elbow and said, 'Did you bring a present?'

I laughed – both at the splendid impertinence of the comment and at her extraordinary resilience. Eight freakish months had gone by – yet here we were again, father and daughter. As far as she was concerned, nothing had changed.

'The present's in the car. I'll give it to you later.'

'At the hotel?'

'Yes – at the hotel.'

'The same hotel we stayed in once – up in the sky?'

'No – not that hotel, Caitlin.'

'Doesn't your friend like you anymore?'

I stared at her, bedazzled. She remembered everything. Every detail of every weekend we spent together.

'It's a very long story, Caitlin.'

'Will you tell it to me?'

But before I could find a way of answering that little question, I heard Lucy's voice.

'Hello, David.'

I stood up, still holding Caitlin's hand. 'Hi.'

An awkward silence. How can you exchange pleasantries after all that enmity, all that horrible legal stupidity, all that useless damage?

But I decided I should make an effort, so I said, 'You look well.'

'So do you.'

Another awkward silence.

A man emerged from the rear of the house and came into the doorframe where Lucy was standing. He was tall, lanky, in his early forties, dressed conservatively in that standard issue WASP weekend uniform: a button down blue shirt, tan Shetland sweater, khakis, boat shoes. He put his arm around Lucy's shoulder. I tried not to flinch.

'David, this is my friend, Peter Harrington.'

'Nice to finally meet you, David,' he said, extending his hand. I took it, thinking: at least he didn't say, '. . . *and I've heard so much about you.*'

'Nice to meet you too,' I said.

'Can we go, Daddy?' Caitlin asked.

'Fine by me.' I turned back to Lucy. 'Six o'clock on Sunday.'

She nodded, and we left.

On the drive back into San Francisco, Caitlin said:

'Mummy's going to marry Peter.'

'Ah,' I said. 'And what do you think about that?'

'I want to be the bridesmaid.'

'I'm sure that can be arranged. Do you know what Peter does?'

'He runs a church.'

'Really?' I said, mildly alarmed. 'What kind of church?'

'A nice church.'

'Do you remember the name of it?'

'Uni . . . uni . . .'

'Unitarian, maybe?'

'That's it. Unitarian. Funny word.'

Well, at least, as religions go, it was civilized.

'Peter's very nice,' Caitlin added.

'I'm glad.'

'And he told Mommy that you should be allowed to see me again.'

'And how did you know that?'

'Because I was in the next room, playing, when he said it. Did Mommy stop you from seeing me?'

I stared out at the lights of the bay.

'No,' I said.

'That's the truth?'

Caitlin, you don't need to hear the truth.

'Yes, sweetheart. That's the absolute truth. I was away, working.'

'But you'll never be away that long again, will you?'

'Never.'

She extended her tiny hand. 'Deal?' she asked.

I grinned. 'Since when did you start working in Hollywood?'

She ignored the wisecrack and extended the hand further.

'Deal, Daddy?'

I took her hand and shook it.

'Deal.'

The weekend passed in a delightful blur. And then we were back in front of Lucy's house at six pm, Sunday. When the door opened, Caitlin ran to hug her mother, then turned back to me and gave me a big wet kiss on the cheek and said, 'See you in two weeks, Daddy.' Then she charged inside, clutching the assorted Barbies and other useless plastic objects I'd bought her over the weekend. Lucy and I suddenly found ourselves alone on the doorstep, facing into another awkward silence.

'Good time?' Lucy asked me.

'Wonderful'
'I'm glad.'
Silence.
'Well then . . . ,' I said, backing off.
'Okay,' Lucy said. 'Bye, now.'
'See you in two weeks.'
'Fine.'
Then I nodded and turned to leave.
'David,' she said, making me turn around.
'Yeah?'
'I just wanted to say . . . I'm glad things seem to have worked out for you, professionally speaking.'
'Thank you.'
'It must have been awful.'
'It was.'
Silence. Then she said, 'I also want you to know something. My lawyer told me that, when everything went wrong, you lost all your money . . .'
'That's true. I kind of got wiped out for a while.'
'But you still managed to meet our maintenance every month.'
'Had to be done.'
'But you were broke.'
'Had to be done.'
Silence.
'I was impressed, David.'
'Thanks,' I said. Then, once again, we fell into constrained silence. So I said goodnight, and walked back to my car and drove to the airport, and took the flight back to Los Angeles, and got up the next morning, and went to work, and made lots of 'creative decisions,' and took lots of phone calls, and had lunch with Brad, and found three hours in the afternoon to stare into a computer screen, and manipulated my characters into something approaching life, and actually ended up working on until eight, and closed up the empty office myself, and picked up some take-out sushi on the way home, and ate the sushi and drank a beer while watching the last two quarters of a Lakers game, and got into bed with the new Walter Mosley novel, and slept a

reasonably sound seven hours, and got up, and began the entire process all over again.

Somewhere in the middle of all that routine, the reflection did dawn: everything you wanted restored has been restored. But with that knowledge came another realization:

You're alone now.

Yes, there were the collegial pleasures of work. And yes, there were the two weekends a month that I was granted access to my daughter. But beyond that . . .

What? There was no family expecting me at home come night. Another man was already playing day-to-day Daddy for my daughter. And though my professional standing had been resurrected, I now knew that success only carried you as far as the next success. Which, in turn, only transported you to . . .

Where exactly? What was the ultimate destination? That was the most puzzling thing about all this. You could spend years struggling to get *somewhere*. But when you finally did – when everything fell into your lap and you procured what you'd so craved – you were suddenly confronted with a strange truth: had you really arrived anywhere? Or were you simply at a way-station, en route to an illusory destination? A place which vanished from view the moment you were no longer considered touched by success.

How can you ever reach a terminus that doesn't exist?

And if there was a scrap of insight I had picked up along the way, it was this: what we're all pursuing is some sort of desperate self-validation. But that's only found through those who've been dumb enough to love you . . . or whom you've managed to love.

Like Martha.

For the first month, I left her a phone message every other day. I tried a daily e-mail. Eventually I took the hint, and dropped all further attempts at contact. Even though I thought about her constantly – like a dull, but persistent ache that simply wouldn't go away.

Until, one Friday, around two months after our last meeting, a small package arrived in the mail. When I opened it, I found a rectangular object, wrapped in gift paper. There was also a letter-sized envelope. I opened it. I read:

Dearest David

Of course I should have answered all your calls, and all your e-mails. But . . . I'm here, in Chicago, with Philip. I'm here with him because, in the first instance, he did as I asked – and, from what I've read in the papers, your career seems more than somewhat back together again. And I'm here because, as I think you know, I'm now producing the movie you wrote. But I'm also here because, quite simply, he begged me to stay. I'm certain that sounds absurd: Philip Fleck – Mr $20 Billion – begging anyone for anything. But it's true. He pleaded with me to give him another chance. He said he couldn't bear the idea of losing me and his child. And he uttered that time-honored entreaty: 'I'll change.'

Why did he do this? I'm not sure. Has he changed? Well, at least we're talking again and sharing a bed . . . which is an improvement. And he seems reasonably excited about the prospect of fatherhood . . . though the movie is naturally in the forefront of his mind right now. Anyway, for the moment, we're in a relatively decent place. I can't predict if this will last or if he'll revert to his introverted ways, and I'll finally reach the point of no return.

What I do know is this: you have taken up residence inside my head and won't go away. Which is wonderful and sad . . . but there you go. Then again, I am a desperate romantic . . . married to a desperate unromantic. But say I had run off with you? A desperate romantic involved with an even more desperate romantic? No way. Especially since desperate romantics always pine for what they don't have. But once they have it . . . ?

And maybe that's why I couldn't call you back, couldn't answer your letters. Because it would have been such high drama. But when the high drama ended . . . then what? Would we have stared at each other (as you said you sometimes stared at Sally) and wondered: what was the point? Or, perhaps, we would have lived happily ever after. That's the gamble – and we're always itching to take it . . . because we need the crisis, the drama, the sense of danger. Just as we always fear the crisis, the drama, the sense of danger. I think it's called: never knowing what we want.

So there's a part of me that wants you. Just as there's a part of me that fears you. And meanwhile, I've made my decision: I'm staying put with Mr Fleck, and hoping for the best. Because the bump in my belly is now quite a significant one, and I don't want to be on my own in the world when he-or-she arrives, and because I did/maybe still do love his-or-her very strange father, and I wish this was your child, but it isn't, and life is all about timing, and ours didn't work out, and . . .

Well, you get my rambling point.

Here's a little ditty by our favorite poet, on the same topic (only in a far more succinct style than yours truly):

> *This is the Hour of Lead*
> *Remembered, if outlived,*
> *As freezing persons, recollect the snow*
> *First – Chill – then Stupor – then the letting go –*

I hope you're letting go, David.

And as soon as you've finished reading this letter, do me a favor. Don't brood about it. Don't imagine what could have been. Just go back to work.

With love
Martha

I didn't immediately follow her last directive. Because first I opened the wrapped present – and found myself staring down at an 1891 First Edition of *Poems of Emily Dickinson*, published by the Robert Brothers of Boston. I held the book in my hands, marvelling at its compact elegance, its venerable heft, its aura of permanence – even though, like everything, it too would eventually crumble. Then I glanced upwards and caught sight of myself in the flat black screen of my laptop: a middle aged man who, unlike the book he was now holding, would definitely not be here in one hundred and eleven years' time.

And then something else crossed my mind – a request made to me by Caitlin when I was visiting her last week. As I tucked her into bed in our hotel room, she asked me for a bedtime story. Specifically, The Three Little Pigs. But with a proviso:

'Daddy,' she asked, 'can you tell the story without the Big Bad Wolf?'

I considered this for a moment, wondering how I could make it work:

'Let's see now . . . there's a house made of straw. There's a house made of sticks. There's a house made of bricks. What happens next? Do they form a residents' association? Sorry, sweetheart, the story doesn't really work without the Big Bad Wolf.'

Why doesn't it work? Because all stories are about crisis. Yours. Mine. The guy sitting opposite you on the train as you read this. Everything's narrative, after all. And all narrative – all storytelling – confronts a basic truth. We need crisis: the anguish, the longing, the sense of possibility, the fear of failure, the pining for the life we imagine ourselves wanting, the despair for the life we have. Crisis somehow lets us believe that we are important; that everything isn't just of the moment; that, somehow, we can transcend insignificance. More than that, crisis makes us realize that, like it or not, we are always shadowed by the Big Bad Wolf. The danger that lurks behind everything. The danger we do to ourselves.

But who, ultimately, is the mastermind of our crisis? Who is the controlling hand? To some, it's God. To others, the state. Then again, it might be the person you want to blame for all your griefs: your husband, your mother, your boss. Or maybe – just maybe – it's yourself.

That's what I still couldn't figure out about everything that had recently happened to me. Yes, there was a bad guy in the story – someone who set me up, smashed me down, and then put me all back together again. And yes, I knew the name of this man. But . . . and it's a big *but* . . . might he have been me?

I glanced again at the blackened screen. Within it, the outline of my face was framed against the inky darkness. What a phantom-like silhouette. What a spectral portrait. And it struck me that, from the moment man could see his own reflected image, he was wracked with all the usual cavernous ruminations that creep up on us daily: *who am I in all this . . . and does it even matter?*

And then, as now, he could find no answers. Except perhaps, the one I was currently telling myself:

Forget about pondering all such impossible questions. Forget about the futility of everything. And don't imagine what might have been. Just get on with it. Because what else can you do? There is only one remedy. Go back to work.